It Happened at the Ball

It Happened at the Ball

Edited by Sherwood Smith

IT HAPPENED AT THE BALL
Copyright © 2018 by Sherwood Smith

Published by Book View Café Publishing Cooperative
P.O. Box 1624
Cedar Crest, NM 87008-1624

ISBN: 978-1-61138-753-7

Cover design by Augusta Scarlett
Interior design by Marissa Doyle

Contents

Foreword

*L*ast summer after yet another wave of bad news, I found myself longing for escapist feel-good wish-fulfillment, and what is more indicative of escapist wish fulfillment than a ballroom filled with grand costumes, beguiling music, intrigue and romance?

I asked around, does anybody else feel the same? It seems I was not alone. While the following authors followed their inspiration, I did some delving, to make sure that my idea hadn't been thought of by a host of others already. There was one delightful anthology with a similar idea, featuring stories set in underwater ballrooms, Stephanie Burgis's and Tiffany Trent's *Underwater Ballroom Society*, which came out in spring.

Other than that, there were surprisingly few, considering how long this sort of idea has been around — beginning with the silver fork novels of the early nineteenth century. That subgenre was kicked off with Edward Bulwer-Lytton's insouciant *Pelham* (which started the fashion that put men in black suits for the next couple of centuries), culminating in Catherine Grace Gore's witty *Pin Money*. This subgenre became so popular that William Makepeace Thackeray felt obliged to skewer it in *Vanity Fair*. But he didn't kill it. The silver fork novel took a turn during the middle of the twentieth century with Georgette Heyer's Regency and Georgian romances.

Silver fork novels always included balls. Otherwise, stories about balls were few, outside of variations on "Cinderella." There was one exception. Patrick Leigh Fermor, whose brilliant memoir The Time of Gifts is one of my favorite pieces of writing of all time, penned a single novel, inspired by a true story of the night of a splendid ball held in Martinique 1902. Midway through the night the volcano behind the city erupted, wiping everybody out but two witnesses. He fictionalized this story in a baroque, even mannerist short novel called The Violins of Saint-Jacques, after being invited by James Laver, a fashion historian and archivist, to contribute to an anthology called Memorable Balls. It's a vivid, gripping story, but escapist wish-fulfillment? Not so much.

Patrick Leigh Fermor's piece was not included in that anthology, probably because it was too long. I can't tell if the rest of this anthology was based on real balls or fictional ones—it's too costly for my mingy book buying budget—but I suspect it has to be a stinker as it sank without a trace. I wonder if the balls he wrote about were all disasters. History is full of plenty of those, from the infamous ball given by the Duchess of Richmond, hastily thrown together and then interrupted by the call to arms as Napoleon advanced on Waterloo. There are plenty of Renaissance balls at which stabbings and poisonings abounded, and of course there's the Duc d'Argent's ball in Paris, at which a bunch of rich young nothing-will-happen-to-me-because-I'm-a-duc's-son nit-wits got the, ah, hot idea of wearing costumes with real fire, and nearly burned the palace down.

I did not want disasters, dystopia, or downers. The news provides plenty of all three. I wanted stories that readers could enjoy right before turning out the light, or on the commute, or as a substitute for the endless yammer of the media.

Not all the following stories are romantic, though I think it's safe to say that they are romances in the sense that the OED defines: *since vernacular texts were usually narratives and often featured the adventures of heroes of chivalry, the terms* **romanz, romans,** *etc. came to denote such works in particular.*" As the modern novel blossomed, "romance" came to be connected with fantasy, wonder, and the imagination, until the nineteenth century when "romance" earned its now-familiar association with love and passion.

Not surprisingly, given that the authors read and write in English, in this anthology you'll find three London balls set during periods when palaces were fabulous and so were the clothes. Almack's makes an appearance, a salute to the long shadow cast by Georgette Heyer—a subject that gets dealt with in another story, along with the liminality of fan fiction.

But not everything here is homage to the venerable Regency romance. You'll read about a masquerade that changed three governments, another that changed two lives; fae and fashion find a diplomatic solution at a dazzling ball, and a heist at another.

One story's ball is implied, another story, taking place in medieval times, is not a ball, but illustrates the importance of dance. One story takes place in a science fictional setting, and another in American history—Galveston on the eve of the Civil War—demonstrating that even under the shadow of political and military strife, there are good people trying to do good things.

Welcome to the virtual ballroom!

Sherwood Smith
September 2018

The Şiret Mask

Marie Brennan

*D*angling from a rope two hundred feet above the rooftops of Râu Tare, I find myself questioning the decisions that have led me to this point.

It is abundantly clear to me — far too late to be of any use — that the whole affair is a joke. What makes the Şiret Mask so valuable? Not the gems and precious metals that decorate it; lovely as they are, they pale in comparison to the Ceresc Mask of Lezaur, much less the Zeiţă Mask of the queen, and would not be worth a tenth so much outside of their setting. Not the craftsmanship, either — the mask has been repaired several times, where inferior joins have given way. No one recalls the name of the artisan who made it, so little was she famed; and even the design is unremarkable, being very similar to that used in a hundred other festival masks.

No, what makes the Şiret Mask so valuable is this: that fools like me have dangled two hundred feet above their possible deaths, just for the glory of saying we once had it in our possession.

I'm sure the joke will be very funny later. If I survive the final line.

The chain of decisions that culminated in my acquaintance with that rope is so long that it would be foolish to attempt to recount it all from the beginning. Let us choose as our point of departure a certain afternoon in the parlor of my dear friend Oana, shortly before her brother Codruț stormed in to interrupt our conversation.

Oana had been an acquaintance of mine in our school days, and I had renewed the connection when I came to Râu Tare the year before. She had helped me find my place in Taral society, and in exchange, I served as her confidante in the matter of her secret lover, the dashing Conte Vântul.

Of course the conte was not her lover in a physical sense. Oana was not so foolish as to throw her future away on a man of such mysterious origins, no matter how much he charmed her. But she assured me that they had pledged their love to one another countless times in the six weeks she had known him, and that he was unquestionably the finest of gentlemen. "You simply must meet him yourself," Oana said earnestly one day in her salon, clasping my hands and gazing into my eyes. "During the Festival of Changes. I trust your judgment, Viorica. If you think well of him, then I will introduce him to Codruț, and persuade my brother we simply must be wed."

I did not share her optimism. Codruț was an arrogant and grasping man; he did not let go of his possessions easily, and he counted his sister among that inventory. Had their father still lived, by now Oana would have been married to her sweetheart Nicu, who had adored her since they were children. But Nicu lacked enough money to satisfy Codruț, and while undoubtedly Oana's conte had the wealth to please him, a mysterious nobleman would threaten Codruț's sense of control.

On that particular afternoon, however, I had no chance to try and convince Oana of this. Before I had done more than draw breath to speak, the door banged open hard enough to strike the wall. Codruț stormed through the gap. "It is an outrage!" he announced to the room at large.

Oana and I shot to our feet. "Dear brother, calm down," Oana stammered.

"What is an outrage?" I asked.

In response, Codruț flung a sheet of paper on the floor in front of me, badly crumpled from being clutched in his fist. I retrieved it, smoothed it out, and held it where Oana and I could both read.

Before the Festival of Changes is over, the Şiret Mask will be mine.

No signature identified this terse message. Only a stamp in vermilion ink: the swirling winds of that infamous master criminal, Laperi.

"He's going to steal the mask?" Oana gasped.

"Over my dead body," Codruț snarled.

I passed my hand over my face to ward off ill luck. "Of course it will not come to that. Were you not intending to wear the Iavol Mask this year? Your vault is impregnable; with the Şiret Mask safely inside, Laperi's plans will come to nothing."

Codruț stopped dead in the middle of his pacing. "Leave it in the vault? Absurd!"

"But you cannot possibly risk it!" Oana said. "You spent so much money acquiring the mask—"

He cut her off with a swift chop of his hand. "I would make myself the laughingstock of Râu Tare if I cowered in fear of this criminal Laperi. No, dear sister—I will wear the mask. With a score of my finest guards around me. Let him try for it; I will leave him bleeding in the street."

"You do recall he has an airship full of minions," I reminded Codruț. Everyone knew of it: the *Vulpea Cerului*, with its black-painted balloon, like a piece of the night sky itself. "He will swoop down on you from above, and his minions will overpower your guards."

"Then I will hire a wizard, too!" Codruț had the bit in his teeth. "I went to great lengths to acquire the mask, and I will no more hide it away than I will let that bastard take it from me."

This is a sample of the behavior the mask engenders in those who come within its orbit. People have whispered from time to time that the mask itself is enchanted—or perhaps cursed—because they can think of no rational reason why people would go to such lengths to acquire it. They fail to understand that the reason is *not* rational. Men and women of a certain character are bound to crave prestige. The Șiret Mask is a prestigious item; therefore they desire it, and will not let anyone else have it. Human nature, not magic, is the explanation.

Rationality does assert itself in other places, though. Codruț could not hope to hire a wizard, not for such a venial purpose as guarding his trinket. He was determined to try, though, and soon stormed off to do precisely that. In his wake, Oana sank back into her chair. "Gods of the change! It will serve Codruț right if he loses that mask. Such a silly thing—he only wanted it because he didn't have it."

I remained where I was, looking at the door Codruț had slammed behind him. "Oana—darling—"

"Yes, Viorica?"

I bit my lip, then turned and crouched at her feet. "About your Conte Vântul. I . . . have a terrible suspicion."

She blinked down at me. "Whatever do you mean?"

"Don't you think it's just a little too convenient? He shows up in Râu Tare, and not long after, we have Laperi announcing his plans to steal the mask. The mask your brother is so proud of owning. And you yourself have become so very dear to him in such a short time."

One infinitesimal movement at a time, Oana's look of confusion transformed into disbelief. "You—you cannot be suggesting that he works for Laperi." Another moment passed. "That he *is* Laperi?"

"I am not certain," I hastened to reassure her. "Only . . . cautious. The Conte Vântul was in Malspre last year, was he not? And so was Laperi, when he filched the Star Sapphire of Avere. Tell me—has your conte ever been to Riazănoapte?"

Her silence was answer enough. And in Riazănoapte, of course, Laperi had stolen the famed Book of Ceannanas.

I took her hands and squeezed them. "It could be coincidence. Or your conte might be hunting Laperi, trying to bring him to justice! But . . . be careful."

"How can I be careful?" Oana whispered. "You—please, Viorica, you *must* see him for yourself. You will know he cannot possibly be such a man. Or if he is, you will be able to tell, I'm sure of it. And then I will wash my hands of him forever."

Myself and the Conte Vântul, both at the Festival of Changes. Laughing, I said, "It will be a very interesting night."

⁕

Word got out, of course. Laperi had announced his plan to steal the mask, and Codruț made no secret of his refusal to keep it hidden away for safety; there was no better fodder for gossip. Half the street plays I passed in the following days were hastily written pieces about the history of the Şiret Mask: how it was buried in a field to protect it when the Keleti invaded and found years later by a farmer with his plow; how a priest had pronounced the mask cursed, as a way of tricking Domn Avutins into surrendering it to his care; how the infamous thief Răsuşa had stolen the mask just to prevent her rival from acquiring it; how Doamnă Paniu took a drunken bet to place it on her horse and lost it when the horse bolted. The puppeteers for the horse were quite impressive.

The other half of the street plays were tales of the thief Laperi, and those did not have to be written in haste, for they had been scripted over the years of his infamous career. Singers and actors on every other corner told of his exploits, the treasures he'd stolen and the traps he'd outwitted. In the right parts of the city, I was sure, one could place bets on the outcome of this duel. I wondered how many were betting on Codruț, and doubted the odds favored him . . . especially after the *Vulpea Cerului* was indeed sighted in the mountains outside the city.

All of this simply added to the chaos that accompanied any Festival of Changes. The celebrations were each person's chance to shed their bad luck, donning a mask so that the gods would lose sight of them. For the city it marked the start of the new year; for the citizens, it was the chance of a new life, even if only for a few hours. Nobles could cast off their responsibilities and commoners speak their minds. The brave and the desperate could even go to a wizard and ask to be changed — to wake up tomorrow a different person entirely.

My own plans were not so ambitious. "Here," I said to Nicu, under the shadow of the Skewed Arch near the river. I pressed a lover's token into his hand. They were a common symbol of the festival; exchanging them was a sign that the two parties had exchanged hearts. "She'll be at the foot of the Estic Bridge at midnight. Don't be late."

Nicu curled his fingers around the token, an intricate knot of thread. "Are you sure?" he said anxiously. "This Conte Vântul —"

"Will be out of the running long before then," I assured him. "But Oana will need you tonight, Nicu. Don't fail her."

"I won't," he said fervently.

The river was on fire with the light of the setting sun, the Gagiu Bridge stretching its shadow along the water. The Festival would officially begin at sundown, but revelers already crowded the river walk and the bridge itself, and when a figure appeared atop the bridge's central market, one might have thought it simply a drunken fool out to impress his lady-love.

Except that the figure was garbed all in black, his flowing cloak and wide-brimmed hat instantly recognizable. We had seen a dozen actors impersonating him on the streets of Râu Tare.

"Laperi!" Nicu gasped.

The master thief's laugh carried across the sudden hush that fell. "I have thrown down a gauntlet, and Codruț Deleanu has taken it up! Let him hide behind his guards in the Plaza of Gems; it makes no difference. The Şiret Mask will be mine!"

City guards were already scrambling after Laperi, but they

made only slow progress through the crowd. Too many people were shouting and clapping, rather than stepping aside. What did the common Taral citizen care for Codruț and his mask? They wanted only to be entertained—and Laperi was nothing if not skilled at entertaining his audience. With a swirl of his cloak, he leapt down into the market. I had no doubt that he would be long gone by the time the guards arrived.

"Maybe if I help Codruț—" Nicu began.

"Help him?" I said with a sniff. "If he loses the mask, it will be no more than he deserves. Help Oana, Nicu. The Estic Bridge at midnight—don't forget."

He touched his fist to his heart. With a pat on his shoulder, I left him and went to find Oana.

⁂

Had I not seen Oana's costume before the Festival, I might never have found her in the mass of people that thronged the Plaza of Gold. She was resplendent in costume as a lady of ancient Sarazdat, with a mask in the filigree style that was more a nod in the direction of concealment than an effective shield. There are advantages to being a tall lady looking for another lady of considerable height; I was able to spot her and wend my way to her side.

"Did you see Laperi?" I asked.

Oana fluttered her fan nervously. "I did. But I have not seen the conte."

Her tone made her suspicions more than clear. "I am sure he will be here at any moment," I soothed her. "Shall I fetch you some iced pomegranate wine while we wait? I think I see a vendor over there, and I am parched."

She nodded, distracted, and I slipped away into the crowd.

On an ordinary night, fetching two cups of wine would have been the work of a moment. In the teeming masses of the Festival, one might as well try to fetch the Şiret Mask itself. I returned to

Oana's side a good deal later with my hands empty. "I am so sorry," I told her. "I think I chased him halfway across the city, but by the time I caught him, his barrel was empty."

"It does not matter," she said. "The conte was here, and full of apologies for his tardiness. I do not know whether to believe him or not. He could not possibly have been atop the bridge, could he? I cannot imagine that he could have switched from that dreadful black outfit into his costume so rapidly."

"Where is the conte?" I asked, craning my neck. Dancers filled the center of the plaza, close-packed enough that it was a wonder more of them didn't step on trailing hems or snag their jeweled embroidery against someone else's cloak.

Oana scowled. "That shrew Cosmina claimed him for a dance. I haven't seen him since."

"I am sure he has better taste than to favor Cosmina over you," I said, laughing. "But I will go remove her claws from him, if you like."

"Would you?" Oana said. "I told the conte you would be back soon, but I fear he thinks I've made you up."

"Then I shall teach him otherwise," I said, folding my fan with a decisive snap. "Wish me luck. And if you see the conte before I return, then both of you stay right here, or I may never find you again." With that, I dove once more into the crowd.

⋘ ❧ ⋙

What transpired next was less than ideal.

While Oana waited for me to return, hopefully with the Conte Vântul in tow, she kept an eye on the crowd, hoping to see him swirling by in the dance — or better yet, returning to her side of his own free will. And indeed she saw him . . . but neither dancing with Cosmina or some other lady, nor on his way back to her. Instead he was at the nearby edge of the plaza, slipping into a narrow alley.

I had, of course, told her to stay put. But when her back is up,

Oana is no more tractable than Codruț. And so she followed him.

Two men stood a little way down, their backs to her. One was the conte, in the costume she had seen before: the knee-length cloak of the Cuvântat age on one shoulder, with the curving, crescent-moon horns of his mask rising above his head. The other was a man much more plainly dressed, with a simple cloth domino mask. As Oana crept closer, she heard the conte's familiar tenor — but cold and brisk as she had never heard it before.

"In the Stradă Martescu," the conte said. "Your men are in position and ready?"

"We outnumber him two to one," the man in the domino mask said. "He won't stand a chance. The mask will be yours before midnight."

"Good man," the conte said, and coins winked in the scattered lamplight as they changed hands.

Now, a sensible girl would have crept away and gone to warn her brother. But Oana's passions were up, and she had drunk a little wine; furthermore, she was built like the statue of a Sarazdat goddess, and had often gotten into trouble for brawling when we were in school.

"You *cur!*" she shrieked. The man in the domino mask fled; the conte turned to look. He was just in time to receive Oana's fist to his jaw.

It was an exceedingly stupid way to hit him. His mask protected his entire face; had she struck it any harder, she would have broken her own hand. But she followed this up with a much more effective punch to his gut that sent him staggering back a step, before her inflamed sentiments got the better of her tactics for good. The remainder of her attacks were more flailing than fighting, and he easily caught her wrists to immobilize them.

"I hate you!" she screamed in his face. "You have been manipulating me from the start. I'm done with it! You'll never have the mask. And you'll never have me!" With a swift raise of her knee that tore her skirt, she delivered her final blow, then fled back out into the plaza.

⌒⊙⌒⊙⌒

This was the point at which my evening began to spin off its intended path and into the wilds of chance. All I can say is that the gods of the change have their own peculiar senses of humor, and I should have known better than to bait them thus.

I found an archway shadowed enough to shelter me and took off my mask. Oana's blow had cracked it; I would have a bruise underneath, and my other mask covered only the upper part of my face.

The mannerisms of Vântul drained away from me like water, for I had no need of him any longer. Rubbing my jaw and cursing under my breath, I set to work transforming myself once more.

First I yanked off my long cloak and held it temporarily between my knees while I unlaced my other half-mask from my shoulder, where the cloak had concealed it. Then I shrugged out of my jacket and turned it inside out before slipping it back on. The flamboyant cuffs of the conte's outfit went into one concealed pocket designed to enhance the profile of my otherwise flattened bosom; the other I filled with the cloth undermask that had protected my face against the pressure of the conte's formal festival mask. With those in place, I settled the crescent horns around my hips, then let the mask itself hang down as substitute for the bustle I was not wearing. Finally I spun the cloak so its former lining faced outward and tied it around my waist, transmuting it into a skirt covering the horns, the mask, and the boots of the Conte Vântul.

That left me with the light half-mask of Oana's good friend Viorica, and a mark on my jaw it would not cover. I donned it anyway and went back out into the crowd. There were plenty of women out there in the fluttering silk veils of piandel dancers; with a small knife concealed in my hand, it was trivial to snip a suitably colored veil off one of them and drape it from the edges of my mask. Not ideal, but it was the best I could do on short notice, and I could not spare the time for more.

When I was done with this, I saw Oana.

She shouldn't have been there. She should have gone straight to her brother at the Plaza of Gems and told him about the ambush. Instead she was standing alone, a scrap of fabric wrapped about her injured hand, staring into the distance.

When you must hide something, give the observer something else to think about. I rushed up to Oana, veil fluttering. "You have to hide me!"

It jarred her from her thoughts. "What?"

"I heard that Dănuț Vidraru is going to offer me a lover's token. I've put on this veil so he won't recognize me, but I must get out of — why, Oana, whatever is the matter?"

Sniffling, she told me of the conte's perfidy. "That's dreadful!" I exclaimed. "You must go and tell your brother at once!"

"No," Oana said, flaring up. "He will only mock me for being so silly. I hate them both — and that stupid mask! I wish Codruț had never bought it!"

If Oana did not warn him, then Codruț would have no provocation to go to the Stradă Martescu and get into a fight. If he did not get into a fight, then the rest of my plan would swiftly come apart.

I thought rapidly. Could I invite him to dance? No, Codruț never danced. An ambush elsewhere — but anywhere else would be too public.

I would simply have to improvise.

"Oh, my darling, I am so sorry," I said, hugging her close. My right hand slipped a folded piece of paper into one of the deep pleats around her shoulders. She was forever straightening them; she would find the paper soon enough. "Come with me. I think you need something stronger than pomegranate wine."

Beneath those comforting words, my mind was whirling. I would need a pipe. Some *ngimri* leaves. A new costume.

And I needed Laperi to keep on distracting everyone.

৽৹৹ ৹৹৹

The order of ceremonies in the Festival of Changes was well-known.

From sundown until shortly before midnight, everyone was free to dance and carouse, to enjoy the liberties of the night. In that final hour, the members of the Consiliu — of which Codruţ was one — would visit a fortune-teller in the small hut constructed at the base of the steps that led to the Temple of Transformation. Everyone visited fortune-tellers during the Festival, but this woman was specially chosen to perform this duty; the fates of such important men could not be left to chance. Codruţ, being the most junior member of the Consiliu, would have his fortune told last.

It was the one point during the festival when he would be alone.

And no one in their right mind would attempt to steal the mask from him during that time. There could be no escape: his guards would ring the hut, and if Codruţ did not emerge with the mask, they would descend with blades drawn. If the *Vulpea Cerului* tried to swoop in, a city airship would catch it before it could rise again. Codruţ was perfectly safe. After that he would be in the temple, and then he would return home, to lock the mask into his vault.

Laperi and his men burst out of a dragon puppet when Codruţ was nearly to the Temple Plaza. There was never any chance of success; there were too many witnesses, too many people who saw a chance to curry favor by capturing so notorious a criminal. It was only by the narrowest of margins that the would-be thieves eluded their hunters and vanished into the night. Codruţ never even had to raise a hand to defend himself. He shouted obscenities at Laperi's fleeing back, and likely would have pursued him were it not for the pressing matter of his duties. His companions recalled him to his task, and they continued onward.

Robed and hooded, I sat in the little hut and did my best for the other members of the Consiliu, as if the real fortune-teller were not in a drugged sleep under the table. I've been a fortune-teller in my time, as need arose, and can be quite good at it when I have cause.

But when Codruț entered the hut, I was determined not to divine his fate . . . but to change it.

The sinuous curve of the Șiret Mask gleamed in the candlelight, gold and darkness intertwined. Up close, though, it was less impressive. I could see where the upper part of the curve had been welded back onto the base, and someone had tried to restore the paint on the cheek, but hadn't quite matched the precise shade of midnight blue. It was an ordinary mask, really.

Yet it was also one of the most coveted objects in the world — and tonight it would be *mine*.

Codruț's step weaved back and forth as he approached my table. I had gone to a great deal of trouble the night before to break into his household shrine and get access to the cloth undermasks stored there. Had Codruț and his men brawled in the Stradă Martescu as I intended, their sweat and the increased heat of their skin would have activated the chemical mixture soaked into the fabric. After breathing in the result, they would have collapsed in delirium, making them easy to rob. But the night was only warm enough for Codruț to work up a mild sheen of sweat — not enough to do more than put him off-balance.

So I drew a mouthful of ngimri smoke from my borrowed pipe and breathed it into his face.

It worked on him just as it had on the fortune-teller. I caught him before he could fall over and lowered him gently to the floor. Off came my stolen robe, which covered the reversible costume of Viorica Mareșoiu and Conte Vântul. Shed of the skirt and masks, I stripped Codruț of his own garb and put it on. His jacket was much too big for me, even with my own jacket inside; wincing at the waste of fine embroidery, I cut apart my own skirt-cloak and used it to stuff the gaps. I was nearly tall enough; with his cloak over me and the Șiret Mask proclaiming my identity, I should be able to pass muster. The deception only needed to last a short time.

I made sure to wipe down the inside of the mask before I donned it, with Vântul's clean undermask to protect me. The last thing I needed was to lose my own balance along the way.

Then I squared my padded shoulders and went out to join the Consiliu.

ഛ൯ ൯ഛ

There was never any chance that I could make it through the entire ceremony that marked the Festival of Changes. Only members of the Consiliu, a few select clergy, and the temple guards ever attended; I did not know where to stand, what to say, or anything else that might preserve my masquerade. Had I planned this moment well in advance, I might have been able to gather the necessary information . . . but this was all a last-minute gamble, thrown together when the Stradă Martescu ambush failed. Entering the main chamber, I devoted only a little attention to following the Consiliu members. The rest was on the archway that led to the temple spire.

I had to choose my moment with care. Not too late; if they discovered my ruse, I would find myself with a great many new problems and no solution up my borrowed sleeve. But not too soon, either, or—

Shouting came from behind us.

The question of timing suddenly became very simple. As Codruț burst into the temple sanctuary, wild-eyed and stripped to his smallclothes, I bolted for the archway.

In a night full of abysmal luck, I could at least thank the gods that everyone was looking toward Codruț, which gave me a head start. I tore off my stolen cloak as I went and hurled it in the faces of the first guards to follow me up the stairs. The heavy fabric tangled them, and they went down in a painful-sounding heap. I did not stay to watch. Instead I flung myself up the spiraling stairs two or three at a time, cursing the insufficient efficacy of *ngimri* smoke on men of Codruţ's size.

The bells of the city tolled midnight as I burst out into the open air of the lower gallery. The heavy door would hold off a hundred pursuers, but only if I could find something to block it with, and the walkway around the spire's base was bare stone. With footsteps approaching at speed, I had no choice but to continue fleeing, up the second staircase to the top of the spire itself.

Behind me I heard Codruţ bellow, "You're running out of places to run, bitch!"

He was right. The stairs were so narrow that the padded shoulders of his jacket scraped as I forced myself through the last door, and the lintel nearly knocked the Şiret Mask from my head. Here at least I had no need of anything to wedge it shut; the top gallery was so narrow I could brace my back against the door, planting my feet at the base of the railing that kept me from plummeting to my death.

A moment later something thudded against the panels at my back. It did not trouble me. Codruţ, or whoever was trying to bash the door down, was at a disadvantage: the narrow passage afforded him no good angle of approach or way to build up speed.

He knew it, too. The thudding stopped after a moment, and a voice began speaking. I couldn't make the words out clearly — they were too muffled by the wood and drowned out by the wind — but I could guess. He thought he had only to wait there until I tired of holding him out, or a city airship came to pluck me from my perch. I could hear a whistle in the plaza below, calling for such an airship even now; that gleam off to my left was one approaching. It would be here soon.

But not soon enough.

The bells of the city began to strike the midnight hour. If *anything* tonight had gone according to plan, then Oana and Nicu were at the Estic Bridge, exchanging lover's tokens. If the gods of the change had any sense of charity, she at least should come out of this happy.

I took a deep breath. A second. A third.

Then I unbraced myself from the door, climbed up onto the railing, and—just as Codruţ threw the door open and lunged to grab my ankle—leapt into the air.

⁊ℰ ℰ⁊

If I die because Codruţ's gloves are too big for me, I will be very, very upset.

My grip is slipping. I'm clutching the rope with everything I've got, but I'm sliding out of the gloves, and I don't dare trust my weight to a single hand for long enough to shake the other one free. Especially not when I'm barely three handspans from the rope's bottom end—I almost missed it entirely. There isn't enough of a tail left for me to catch it between my knees.

I wonder if they'll be able to repair the Şiret Mask after I fall to my death. I suppose it depends on whether I land facedown. The thought shouldn't make me want to giggle, but it does.

The rope starts moving upward. My right hand skins out of the glove, and only a desperate flail renews my acquaintance with the rope before the same thing happens to the left. Now there's only one handspan between me and a swift introduction to the city rooftops passing far underneath my feet. The gloves tumble away into the patchwork of darkness and light below.

But at least my grip is more secure now. I begin climbing as the rope itself drags me upward. Soon I reach the railing, and climb over it onto the deck of the *Vulpea Cerului.*

The Şiret Mask has slipped askew. I untie it from my head, letting the cloth undermask fall to the deck and blow overboard. It can go join the gloves.

My first mate and lover Cserjén claps me on the shoulder. "You made it! Lykos laid a wager that you wouldn't, what with all the last-minute changes to the plan."

"I hope you threw him overboard," I say, catching my breath.

"He should know better than to wager against Laperi."

Cserjén tugs off the black cloak and swirls it around my shoulders, where it settles into place like an old friend. More softly, he says, "We almost didn't make it in time. It was a hell of a scramble, getting from the Temple Plaza to the ship, and then up to that spire."

"I knew I could trust you." I lean into his warmth. Being Laperi has gotten easier since Cserjén joined me. He's good at taking people's eyes off me, so I can do things like drug innocent fortune-tellers and take their place.

As Râu Tare recedes in the wake of my airship, I study my prize. Welded and repainted and battered by the years, the Şiret Mask gazes up at me with blank eyes.

Cserjén says quietly, "Was it worth it?"

My layers of masquerade, months of preparation, my final, desperate gamble: all for this. An unremarkable mask, whose only true value lies in the stories told about it.

Stories to which I have just added my own chapter.

I smile at Cserjén. "Absolutely."

Just Another Quiet Evening at Almack's

Marissa Doyle

April 1810
Almack's Assembly Rooms
London

"That one, *there*."

"Which one?" Annabel Fellbridge tried to descry the young lady in the line of dancers in Almack's elegant ballroom to which her dear friend and fellow Lady Patroness, Emily Cowper, was trying to draw her attention. "And don't say, 'the one in the white dress.' They're all wearing white."

"I know. And only about three of them manage to look anything other than horrid in it. I mean *that* one—the dumpy one with spots."

Annabel didn't reply that such a description still applied to at least half the girls in the line—all likely in their first London season—but did her best to follow Emily's subtly pointing chin. "The one with yellow ribbon rosettes on her slippers?"

It was Emily's turn to squint shortsightedly at the dancers. "Yes, that one. There's something not quite right there. You may need to follow her."

Annabel didn't ask how Emily knew such a thing about a girl they'd never seen before; reading others' thoughts was her ability, just as being able to hide in shadows and turn more or less invisible was Annabel's. All of the Lady Patronesses of Almack's had some secret, magical skill or attribute; it was why they'd been chosen in the first place by Mr. Almack himself, who hadn't let a little thing like being dead for thirty years keep him from continuing to manage the inner workings of the assembly rooms that bore his name.

The first Lady Patronesses with unusual powers had used them to quietly keep the *beau monde,* who came to Almack's to gossip and gamble, from cheating at cards. Mr. Almack had noticed, and had slowly recruited more such ladies—and helped them expand their scope until they had become *de facto* guardians of law and order amongst the upper classes. Irrepressible Emily had suggested they should call themselves the King Street Runners, to the annoyance of a few of their more decorous members.

Annabel thought it an apt comparison.

"What's not quite right with that particular girl?" she asked.

"I happened to be near her in the ladies' withdrawing room. She was practically shouting her thoughts—I didn't even have to listen especially to her. She was wondering if *it* would work, because she didn't have a hope otherwise."

"If *what* would work?"

"I don't know. That's what we have to find out."

Annabel sighed. "And here I was hoping it would be just another quiet evening at Almack's."

"It's *never* a quiet evening at Almack's. You should know that by now."

Annabel kept a careful eye on the girl with the regrettable complexion and yellow rosettes on her slippers making her way through the dance. She seemed innocent enough, peeking up at her partner through her eyelashes just as any young girl might—when she wasn't darting anxious looks about her, presumably to make sure she was not about to collide with another dancer. What had Emily seen that made her worth watching?

At last, with a flourish of violin and oboe, the dance came to an end. The couples made their reverences, bowing and curtsying to their partners. The girl curtsied too; as she completed the movement, her face crumpled into an odd expression, and she burst forth with a vociferous—and very wet—sneeze.

Annabel winced on her behalf and looked quickly to the girl's partner, a dandified young man with purple heart's-ease embroidered on his pink satin waistcoat. What a time to succumb to an attack of catarrh! She hoped he would have the grace not to snub the poor thing.

Rather to her surprise, he did. In fact, he nearly fell over his own feet lunging forward to offer his handkerchief, utterly ignoring the spots of moisture on his exquisite waistcoat. "Oh, Miss Yardley—pray let me offer—"

But he was too late. Three other men, from a green youth probably in his own first season to an elderly man Annabel knew as a hardened roué had leapt in ahead of him, proffering *their* handkerchiefs.

"Miss Yardley, allow me—!"

"You must permit me, ma'am—"

"My poor, *dear* child—if I may—" The roué won by sheer strength of address. He tenderly dabbed at the girl's nose with his lace-edged handkerchief while cleverly cutting out the others with one lifted shoulder and a ruthless elbow as he hurried her away. They hurried after them nonetheless, waving their handkerchiefs in protest. A few other men in the line followed, their eyes fixed on the unfortunate Miss Yardley. The young man in the pink satin waistcoat trailed behind, looking bewildered.

"That was . . .singular," Annabel said after a moment. Another explosive sneeze resounded from Miss Yardley's general direction.

Emily watched the little cavalcade, brow furrowed. "It was *suspicious*, if you ask me. That chit wasn't a particle upset—she was practically crowing with glee inside. Whatever *it* was, it worked." She paused, thinking. "I think we need reinforcements."

Annabel did, too. "Who else is here tonight?" She looked around the room. Not all the Lady Patronesses came to every ball—one did have social commitments outside of Almack's, after all. But at least three or four of them were usually in attendance.

She didn't have to look far to spot one. Sally Jersey, the presiding officer of the Lady Patronesses in their less public role, was moving purposefully through the crowd, which parted before her seemingly without being aware that it did. Annabel knew better; a puff of air from Sally's lips could have blasted them aside like feathers in a tempest. But she often used a subtler breath to move obstacles from path—as she was doing at present.

"There's something most irregular going on," she announced on reaching them.

"So we've noticed," Emily said.

"That Ennis girl—if she hadn't been the Duchess of Bristol's grand-daughter I can't imagine why we would have given such an unprepossessing thing a voucher. But the child has at least six men following her—" She frowned. "You've noticed?"

"We just saw it happen, but with a different girl." Annabel said. "A Miss Yardley."

"Who was quite pleased by the ruckus she'd kicked up," Emily added.

"A different girl?" Sally sighed—carefully. "I should have expected it. Someone tries it every year. We've had nullification wards set up around the building against them since forever, but someone invariably finds a new one that gets through."

"A new *what* that gets through?" Annabel asked.

"An attraction charm, of course."

"Good heavens." Annabel could not help smiling. "I though they were nonsense. You mean they actually work?"

"Oh, come now, Annabel." Emily nudged her. "Didn't anyone

you know try one when you came out?"

"Not that I noticed. But I was betrothed to Freddy by June and stopped going to quite so many parties."

Sally harrumphed. "They're quite real. That's what the wards are here for. This one does seem unusually powerful, though. We shall have to ask Lady Lansell to recast the protections to take care of this one, too. *If* we can contain it."

Emily raised an eyebrow. "Surely it won't be that difficult a matter."

Sally laughed mirthlessly. "Wait and see. That's two girls we've seen so far, yes?"

"Are there likely to be more?"

"Have you forgotten what it's like to be seventeen? Of course there will be more. As soon as one girl finds something new — a shop selling silk stockings cheaply or a milliner no one else has discovered — she has to tell at least two of her closest friends about it, who in turn each tell their closest friends — "

"Nonsense," Emily interrupted her. "If I were seventeen and had found someone selling attraction charms, I would not have told anyone. Well, except for my brothers, maybe."

"Your family feeling is commendable," Sally said drily.

"Look!" Annabel grasped both their arms.

A girl — in a white dress, of course — was tripping past, exuding an almost palpable air of smugness. She bore a strong resemblance to a mother duck with her line of ducklings trailing behind her, only these ducklings wore knee breeches and elegant topcoats. The girl paused and sneezed loudly — and just as they had for Miss Yardley, the men following her leapt forward to offer their handkerchiefs. "Miss Twye, take mine!" one beseeched her.

"No, mine." Another man pushed the first aside. "It's much finer linen for your delicate nose."

"Linen?" a third man sniffed. "Mine is silk — please, my dear girl — "

"To hell with a handkerchief — take me!" A fourth man surged forward and seized her in a stifling embrace. "We shall be married tomorrow — a special license — "

"Good Lord!" Emily gasped. "Why, that's Lord Bigham. Isn't he already married?"

"Blackguard, she's mine!" Another man took double handfuls of Lord Bigham's coattails and yanked.

Lord Bigham fell backward, but another man quickly took his place, dropping to his knees and clasping the girl, who had lost her smug air and was now red-faced and near tears, around her legs. "My darling!"

"That's Admiral Haye, and he's married and a grandfather," Sally declared in tones of outrage, and drew herself up. "That will be quite enough of *that*, gentlemen," she said, putting the force of her breath behind the word.

Annabel had seen a sigh of Sally's stop traffic on Pall Mall; it had much the same effect here. Heads swiveled, and the clump of men besieging the tearful Miss Twye froze. Sally strode into their midst, took the girl by the arm, and extracted her from her knot of admirers. "I think it's time we found your mama and asked her to take you home," she said firmly.

Cries of "No!" and "Don't go!" rose from the group. One went so far as to clutch at Miss Twye's skirt, muttering, "You shan't be taken from me!"

"For shame, sir!" Sally shot him a look that would have halted a cavalry charge, and he subsided. "That goes for the rest of you. I hope you're all feeling quite ashamed of yourselves." She put a protective arm around Miss Twye's drooping shoulders and began to lead her away. "Go look for any others, and send them home before we have any further disgraceful displays," she added in a low voice to Annabel and Emily.

"I'll go down to do the supper room," Emily said. "You finish up here in the ballroom and check the tea room."

Annabel found a girl cowering in the far corner of the ballroom, using one of the chairs provided for chaperones to fend off a cluster of eager swains, and took her downstairs to hide in the ladies' withdrawing room. "Don't you even think about leaving this room," she exhorted the sniffling girl. "I'll find your mama and send her to you."

"You mean my aunt." The girl rubbed at her eyes. "Mama wasn't feeling quite the thing tonight, so my aunt brought me with my cousin. We decided we'd try *it* together and I wish we hadn't, because it's *horrid*. I didn't expect them to behave like this!"

"'It?' What do you mean?"

The girl gulped back a sob. "The decoction my cousin Primrose said would make every man we meet fall in love with us. Oh, I wish I hadn't gone along with her to that shop! If Aunt Yardley finds out, she'll be cross—"

Annabel stopped her. "Aunt *whom?*" Wasn't that the name of the girl she and Emily had seen?

"My Aunt Yardley—and she'll tell Mama-a-a-a—" Her sobs gave way to a wail, and she buried her face in her hands.

"Pfft. These gals today—they're a prodigious sad parcel of watering-pots!" a voice like a creaky gate—a familiar creaky gate—commented. "No one in my day with any gumption would be hiding with the cloaks and shoebags when there was dancing going on!"

Annabel turned. "Great-Aunt Philippa! What are you doing here?"

Her great-aunt, dowager Viscountess Mompesson, had been the reigning belle of her day—which had occurred back during the reign of George II. But she continued to attend every social event she could—even ones she hadn't been invited to. As far as Annabel knew, she hadn't applied to the Lady Patronesses for a voucher to Almack's, because it never would have occurred to her that she had to.

"What am I doing here? What does one usually do in the ladies' withdrawing room?" Great-Aunt Philippa turned. "Is my skirt down in back? It got caught when I went to the privy at Lady Murchison's rout the other night, and I ended up showing the whole room my backside when I went back out to her salon."

"Oh, aunt!"

"Didn't even get me any indecent offers." She sighed. "I s'pose I am getting old. Now, what's the to-do with this chit here?"

"She, er—she had a run-in with some not-very-mannerly young men."

"And she's crying about *that*?" Great-Aunt Philippa snorted. "That Johnson man with the dictionary had it right—youth is wasted on the young. You gals don't know when you've got it good!"

The girl's sobs redoubled. Annabel patted her shoulder, took her great-aunt's arm, and led her to the door. "I could use your help right now, dear aunt. There's another girl we have to find—"

"Is she as weepy as this one?"

"I don't know," Annabel said. "But we'll find out."

They found out rather sooner than Annabel expected. On the way back to the stairs, she caught sight of a familiar satin slipper adorned with a yellow ribbon rosette lying next to one of the support pillars in the front entrance hall. She picked it up, then peeked around the pillar.

Miss Yardley was there, vigorously attempting to remove the man clinging to her, his head buried in her ample bosom. It was the elderly roué who had so solicitously led her from the dance and given her his handkerchief.

"Stop it!" Miss Yardley cried, resorting to ineffectual kicks. "Oh, you dreadful man—you're worse than my brother's dog! Someone help me!"

The roué may have said something, but with his face buried in Miss Yardley's chest, it was hard to make out the words.

Great-Aunt Philippa cackled. "Oh ho! Is that you, Crowston? I always knew you were a breast man but this is monstrous, even for you!" She grabbed his old-fashioned powdered queue, neatly tied with a ribbon, and gave it a hard yank. "You're going to get your maquillage all over this poor chit's dress if you keep that up!"

"Ow!" The man withdrew his face from Miss Yardley and

scowled up at them through a cloud of powder. "Philippa Mompesson! I'll thank you to trouble yourself with your own affairs, your la'ship!" He reburied his face.

"And I'll thank you to leave this child be, sir." Annabel said sternly as she stepped toward them.

"Oh, thank y—Lady Fellbridge!" Miss Yardley seemed torn between relief at her rescue and dismay at the identity of her rescuer.

Annabel ignored her dismay and pulled her away from her assaulter as Great-Aunt Philippa held doggedly onto his queue.

"She's mine!" he panted, grabbing ineffectually at Miss Yardley and squirming like a fish on the hook. "I must—have—her—"

"Might I be of assistance?"

Annabel could have groaned aloud. Why, of all people, had the Marquis of Quinceton been the one to happen upon them in this extraordinary—and embarrassing—tableau? He had been in her late husband's circle of friends, but certainly not in hers; something about the intensity of his gaze whenever they chanced to meet had always disconcerted her. "Thank you, sir, but we are in no need of your help."

Great-Aunt Philippa obviously felt differently. "We certainly are! If you want to make yourself useful, young man, help me keep this old goat off this child. As I live, you would not be blamed for mistaking this for a farmyard."

"I am quite certain that we can manage on our own," Annabel said quickly. The last thing she needed was the Marquis being affected by Miss Yardley's attraction charm and himself turning into a slavering goat. With his size and strength, they would have a far worse time keeping him from the girl than they were having with the elderly Lord Crowston.

"Oh, pish-tosh, Annabel! Remove this scarecrow, won't you?" Great-Aunt Philippa handed him Lord Crowston's queue.

Lord Quinceton leaned forward—perilously close to Miss Yardley—and grasped the older man under the arms. Annabel tensed—but he pulled Lord Crowston away and set him back on his feet. The man tried to lunge once more for her, but Lord Quinceton dropped a heavy hand on his shoulder. "I am under the impression that the young lady would rather you kept your distance, sir," he said.

Lord Crowston tried a few more feints to evade Lord Quinceton, who did not relax his iron grip. Great-Aunt Philippa watched them, head to one side. "Annabel, there's something monstrous odd going on here, and I think you know something about it."

"I can't help suspecting you're right, ma'am," Lord Quinceton said, stepping to the side to keep the old man from twisting out of his grip.

Miss Yardley's face puckered. "It was the bees! It worked on them, and I thought it might—"

Oh, bother the girl for practically confessing in front of everyone! "I'm sure I don't know what you're talking about, Aunt. Please excuse us; I promised Miss Yardley's mother that I would return her daughter to her." She gently tugged on Miss Yardley's hand.

"Oh, no!" Miss Yardley's eyes grew large and she almost seemed inclined to bolt, but Annabel held fast.

Great-Aunt Philippa narrowed her eyes. "Hmmph. Come along, Crowston, and tell me what you are doing chasing girls young enough to be your grand-daughter whom you haven't actually hired for the night." She seized the old man's arm.

"Bees?" Lord Quinceton looked amused.

Annabel practically dragged Miss Yardley back around the pillar and toward the ladies' withdrawing room. Once safely inside, she drew the girl into a corner. "Would you care to explain what is going on here and what your role in it has been?" she asked in the same tone she might have used with her young—and very mischievous—sons.

Miss Yardley's lower lip trembled. "You'll be angry with me."

"I'll be more upset if you don't explain. There are several frightened girls here tonight who've evidently done something very silly and thoughtless, and I think you know something about it."

"Several? But I only told my favorite cousin Lucinda —" Miss Yardley's expression went from woebegone to indignant. "Oh! She swore to keep it a secret. I can't believe she told anyone!"

"Who seems to have told someone else, who may have confided in *her* favorite cousin," Annabel added.

Miss Yardley was now righteously aflame. "But I told her not to! I wasn't sure it would even work properly — tonight was supposed to be our practice —" She closed her mouth and averted her eyes. "You're going to take away our vouchers, aren't you?" she asked in a small voice.

"It's not solely my decision to make, but the Lady Patronesses are less likely to do so if you tell us the truth now so that we can tidy up this mess."

Miss Yardley hesitated, then sighed in defeat. "It wasn't — we didn't mean any harm," she began, and Annabel didn't need Emily's thought-reading abilities to know she was sincere. "It was just that — oh, I was so afraid of having to come out! You know how it is — one week you're in the schoolroom doing your lessons and wearing your hair tumbling down your back, and the next you're expected to put it up and go to dinner parties and balls and be charming and clever so that some man will want to marry you. Well, look at me — who's going to want to marry me?" She gestured at herself, lips curled in distaste. "I'm not beautiful or witty, or rich enough to make up for it. Only —" She looked down at her hands. "My papa thinks I am, and has been talking all spring about how I will take London by storm and have all the men falling at my feet. Just like Cinderella, only without the cruel stepmother part."

Oh, the poor child. That would drive to desperation any girl sensitive about her appearance. "And so?"

"So I cried a lot in bed at night," she said simply. "But then I had an idea. My mama is devoted to her gardens, and I'm not supposed to know this, but she gets a special decoction to spray on her flowers to make them more attractive to bees. I've seen her do it – the bees get quite excited and are all over the flowers." She leaned forward and lowered her voice. "Mama gets it from an apothecary in London who's supposed to be a *witch*. And I thought, well, it works on the flowers and the bees. I wondered if it would work on me and the gentlemen at the balls in London."

"The . . .bees. I see." It was a near thing, but Annabel just managed not to laugh. Magical charms and potions for gardeners had been around forever; her own father probably used them on his beloved roses back home at Belsever Magna, though he would never admit to it. But she'd never heard of their being employed for non-gardening purposes, much less this one. The other Lady Patronesses would find this very interesting – once they stopped giggling.

"It makes sense, doesn't it?" Miss Yardley said defensively. "Bees and men do the same thing, when you think about it. Well, almost," she added after a moment's thought. "I think bees might be a little cleverer than some of the men I've met in London."

"Quite so." Annabel couldn't help thinking of her late husband. "Pray go on."

Miss Yardley seemed to find her gloved hands of great interest. "I told my cousin Lucinda about my idea, and we went to the apothecary's shop – I looked up the direction from a letter in mama's desk. We told him that my mama had sent us for more of the decoction, and he gave it to us just like that, a whole jar of it. Lucinda and I divided it in half since she helped pay for it. I wouldn't let the shop bill my mama for it because then she'd wonder where it was. We decided we'd try it tonight, so I soaked a sponge in it and brought it in my vinaigrette and we dabbed it on after we arrived and went up to the ballroom to see what would happen." She frowned. "It's been making me sneeze dreadfully ever since I put it on. Mama usually mixes it with diluted spirits of brandy before she sprays it. Perhaps we ought to have thinned it with something, too, before we used it." She looked up at Annabel. "And that's all, really. We didn't know it would make them act like *that*. It was horrid!"

Annabel believed her. The poor girl would probably return home and become a lifelong spinster as a result of what had happened this night, but one couldn't blame her for wanting to try *something* to keep from disappointing a loving papa. She would ask the other Lady Patronesses not to judge her too harshly.

But in the meanwhile, there were still an unknown number of girls causing the men around them to behave like bees driven mad by a garden in full bloom. She and Emily and Sally could find the rest of the girls—thank heavens the decoction was making them sneeze—and hide or hurry them away. But how were they going to deal with the men buzzing about like drunken bees—

"That's it!" she said.

Miss Yardley sneezed. "What is?"

"How we tidy matters up. Promise me you won't stir from this room until I or one of the other Lady Patronesses give you leave."

"I promise, Lady Fellbridge."

"And the instant you get home, wash thoroughly—and don't ever think about doing this again." She smiled at the girl. "It may not be as hard as you think to prove your papa at least partly right. I was very much like you when I first came out . . . and was engaged to be married by June. You need to give yourself a chance."

Miss Yardley looked up, eyes wide. "Do—do you think so?"

"Yes, I do," Annabel said firmly, and left her to go in search of Emily and Sally. There was one thing that might counteract the effects of Miss Yardley's decoction—assuming that Sally would agree to help, and that she could find what she needed.

Instead she found Lord Quinceton lingering in the front hall, leaning against the pillar behind which Miss Yardley had been lured. "Ah, Fellbridge." He straightened. "I have been looking for you."

When would he stop addressing her as "Fellbridge," as if she were the earl and not the earl's widow? It was most improper, not to mention disconcerting—as was the smile that lurked in his eyes when he did. "I can't imagine why. I am very busy just now, so please excuse me, my lo—"

He ignored her attempt to ignore him. "I was wanting to offer my assistance, should it be required again."

"Your assistance was not required the first time."

He bowed slightly. "I stand corrected. Perhaps not 'required.' Shall we say, 'found temporarily convenient in a trifling way?'"

There he went, smiling at her in that devilish fashion once again. "Well, it's not convenient just now—*oh.*" She stopped speaking as a thought struck her. The last thing she wanted to do was to enlist his help, but this *was* an emergency—

"Go on," he encouraged. "I hold myself ready to spring to your command."

"Don't be nonsensical. Have you a cigar I might...er... borrow?"

"A cigar?" Surprise and amusement vied in his countenance. "You astonish me, Fellbridge—I had no idea you cared to blow a cloud."

She flushed. "I don't! But I need one at once."

Amusement won; the corners of his mouth twitched upward as he replied, "Alas, I don't. Tobacco is one of the few sins I am not inclined to indulge in. But I can certainly do my best to obtain you one, given a few moments. Shall we meet here in ten minutes' time?"

"Th-thank you!"

He bowed again and, still smiling, ascended the stairs. Annabel watched him go, not at all convinced of the wisdom of having accepted his aid, then gave herself a little shake and followed after him in search of Emily and Sally.

She found them in the vestibule at the top of the stairs, standing grim-faced near the entrance to the tea room. "We were about to go look for you," Emily said as she joined them.

"Did you find more girls?"

"We certainly did." Sally grimaced. "Two in the tea room and at least six in the ballroom, all besieged by men. I don't know what we can do, aside from making them leave as soon as possible. Were there more downstairs?"

Annabel told them about her encounter with Miss Yardley and what she had learned. "So it's not an attraction charm at all," she concluded. "Not in the usual sense, anyway."

"I'm delighted to hear our wards have held," Sally said, a little impatiently. "But they aren't helping us with the hordes of males making amorous spectacles of themselves. Emily and I had to step in to prevent two duels in the ballroom already." She nodded toward it. "And Lord Bigham has proposed to three more girls."

"I think I might have a plan," Annabel said. "We just need to—er, excuse me a moment."

Lord Quinceton had emerged from the card room across the vestibule from them. As he always seemed to, he caught sight of her at once. She hurried over to him. "Were you successful?" she demanded.

"I am always successful at getting what I want, Fellbridge—a point of information you might want to keep in mind." He held out a large cigar.

Annabel wasn't sure why a flood of color should have warmed her cheeks just then. "Thank you, sir," she said, and braced herself to meet his eyes. Now he would be sure to ask why she'd needed a cigar so desperately, and for some reason she felt too flustered to compose a convincing reason on the spot.

But to her surprise, he didn't. "Always at your service, Fellbridge," he said with a bow, and then turned and went back into the card room.

Annabel snatched a small shadow from a fold of her gown to conceal the cigar and returned to Emily and Sally. Trying to decipher any meaning from Lord Quinceton's cryptic words would have to wait.

"And?" Sally demanded.

Annabel brushed the shadow from the cigar. "You know how devoted my father is to his roses, yes?" Lord Shellingham's floral obsession was well known—and a source of gentle teasing—

among his acquaintances. "He also has bees at Belsever Magna, and when he and the beekeeper need to do anything with the beehives, they kindle a pan of smouldering muck from the stables and let the smoke fill the hives. It calms the bees, evidently. I thought we could do something similar." She held the cigar out to Sally. "So if you wouldn't mind . . ."

"What!" Sally's voice rose two octaves. "You want *me* to—to use that disgusting thing to blow smoke at people?"

Emily's voice shook only a little bit. "Annabel, that's brilliant. Of course you must be the one, Sally. You can circulate the smoke more efficiently through the rooms than either of us can."

"I can't wander around Almack's smoking a cigar! Not even gentlemen are permitted to smoke here!"

"Did you have another idea?"

Sally glowered at them. "Very well!" she snapped. "But I'm not doing this on my own. Annabel must hide me in a shadow."

Emily glanced at Annabel. Annabel winked back at her. "Well, I *suppose* I might be convinced to do that," she said.

"You're absolutely right you're going to!" Sally looked at them, then broke into an unwilling smile. "Oh, blast the pair of you. Very well, how does one light one of these horrid things?" She took the cigar between forefinger and thumb and regarded it dubiously.

Emily fetched a candle, and they retreated into a corner for Sally to light the cigar. She inhaled half-heartedly, then began to cough. "Ugh! How can men enjoy these things? I may be sick."

"You most certainly may not be sick until you've calmed the bees. Lord Bigham has probably proposed to two more girls by now," Emily said.

Annabel reached for a length of deeper shadow from the corner behind them, shaking it out and fluffing it into fullness. Sally, holding the cigar at arm's length, watched her anxiously. "Make certain it covers all of us. Are you *sure* we'll both be concealed?" she demanded as Annabel draped it over them.

"So long as you keep close, we will."

Sally clutched at her arm. "And I'll be able to blow this dreadful smoke through it?"

"It's a shadow, not an oilcloth," Annabel replied patiently. "Of course you will."

"Good luck," Emily murmured. "I'll watch from the doorway in case you need help."

"There's not much help she could give us from there," Sally grumbled as they moved into the ballroom.

"Better she stay there than risk bumping into us — oh, dear." Annabel halted as she looked around the room. "At least we don't have to wait for girls to sneeze to find out who's using Miss Yardley's decoction."

Scattered about the capacious ballroom were half a dozen knots of humanity. From a distance each resembled an exotic, dark-petaled flower with a pale center — men in their evening clothes clustering around a girl in a white gown.

"Remind me to give the enterprising Miss Yardley a good scold when we're through here," Sally muttered. "I hope one cigar will be sufficient. Let's start with them." She nodded toward the nearest group.

They inched carefully around the milling men, all of whom were vying for the attention of a very nervous-looking girl. Sally drew deeply on the cigar — and broke into a coughing fit. Fortunately no one noticed, so intent were they on the goddess in their midst, but some of the smoke that Sally coughed out wafted to the outer bands of admirers. First one, then more of them paused, looking about them in puzzlement. One consulted his pocket watch with a concerned air.

"I think it's working!" Annabel whispered. "Try it again."

"If I don't perish from suffocation first," Sally whispered back. She took a smaller puff this time and sent it directly over the crowd.

The results nearly made Annabel cheer aloud. More of the men stopped importuning the girl in their midst, blinking owlishly. Several concealed enormous yawns. And then, with another waft of smoke from Sally, they began to melt away, eyelids drooping, murmuring about the lateness of the hour. In a few moments the girl was left standing by herself. Emily glided over and said a few words to her; she nodded and, looking dazed, also departed the ballroom.

The other clusters dissipated almost as simply. A couple of the girls looked disappointed as their coteries melted away; a couple of swains more affected than their fellows required extra smoke blown practically in their faces before they too broke into yawns and stumbled away.

"Did you *smell* that?" A be-turbaned older woman, seated not far away in the chairs set against the wall for mamas and other chaperones, hissed to her neighbor. "I do believe someone is smoking tobacco! In Almack's!"

Her neighbor, possessed of an even more terrifying turban, raised an eyebrow. "Indeed? I would not know the scent of tobacco, of course, as I do not permit its use anywhere near me."

"Insufferable female," Sally whispered savagely as they moved on to their next group. "I'll show her what tobacco smells like. I will require two baths and a gallon of tea with peppermint to remove any vestiges of it."

"We're nearly done," Annabel whispered back. "As my boys would say, you're a trusty Trojan, Sally."

"Hmmph." But Sally moved a little more briskly to the next group and made short work of it before they proceeded to the tea room. Within a few minutes, that room was cleared as well.

"I," Sally announced after they had moved to a quiet corner and shaken off the shadow, "am going home. And if anyone ever dares to partake of a cigar in my presence, I shall blow him to kingdom come. Literally." Her face grew serious. "That was well done, Annabel—even if you did make me smoke that beastly thing." She swept to the door to ask the footman there to call for her carriage.

Glowing with Sally's praise, Annabel went upstairs to the ladies' withdrawing room to release any girls who might have taken shelter there. She found Miss Yardley and her cousin Lucinda just preparing to depart with Lady Yardley.

"You should be able to go downstairs without trouble now, but don't linger," Annabel said quietly to Miss Yardley after greeting her mother.

"Are you certain?" Miss Yardley still seemed fearful. "That horrid Lord Crowston . . ."

"I'm certain my great-aunt has him well in hand," Annabel reassured her. "But I will walk you to the door, on one condition."

"Y-yes, Lady Fellbridge?"

"No more bee decoction at Almack's, if you please!"

She was glad to see the girl smile, albeit sheepishly. "No, ma'am. I've learned my lesson. Though it was . . . please don't be cross with me, but it was a little thrilling to see what it would be like to be Cinderella, if only for a little while."

They had not quite reached the entrance when a voice called out, "Miss Yardley!"

"Oh, no!" Miss Yardley gasped.

Annabel moved protectively toward her as the young man in the pink satin waistcoat with whom she had danced at the start of the evening hurried up to them. He sketched bows to Annabel and Lady Yardley then turned to Miss Yardley. "Your servant, ma'am!"

"Mr. R-Rilling," she stammered.

"Miss Yardley, I—er, I found this, and thought it looked familiar." He held out a satin slipper adorned with a yellow ribbon rosette. "I—I admired them greatly, when we danced."

"Oh!" Miss Yardley blushed crimson and reached out a tentative hand to receive her slipper. "Yes, that's—I mean—thank you!"

"I—well, I'd thought about keeping it till tomorrow so that I would have an excuse to call on you. But it didn't seem fair to make you go home with one bare foot. And . . . and I decided that I could use the excuse of inviting you to go driving for my call," he finished. "If you're not otherwise occupied, I mean."

Miss Yardley opened her mouth—and then her eyes twinkled. "Mr. Rilling, you may certainly call tomorrow to ask me to go driving with you."

Annabel slipped away after that, smiling to herself. Miss Yardley had had her Cinderella moment after all.

Interesting, though, that the young man had paused to greet her and Lady Yardley before addressing Miss Yardley, and that his address had been all that was polite and mannerly— completely unlike the behavior of all the other men under the sway of bee decoction. Why was that? Could it be because his attraction to Miss Yardley had been a true one and not dictated by artificial means? Hmm.

She recalled his astonished face at the end of the dance earlier that evening as Lord Crowston and the others had fallen upon Miss Yardley like lions upon a particularly plump antelope. Of course, it might be that Mr. Rilling was naturally resistant to the effects of bee decoction. Or did the decoction have no effect on someone whose affections were already engaged?

It was all very mysterious. She would have to discuss it with Emily and Sally sometime soon—

"Was the cigar to your liking, Fellbridge?"

Annabel jumped. "Lord Quinceton! You startled me!"

He bowed his head. "My apologies."

"You don't look very sorry," Annabel said severely. What was it about this man that removed the gatekeeper from her tongue? "And as I did not touch the cigar, I have no opinion as to its quality."

He stepped closer to her, his nostrils flaring. "But you were near to the one who did."

"Perhaps." Oh dear—evidently she needed a bath, too.

"Mysteries, Fellbridge? I can never resist a good mystery."

He couldn't, could he? Very well, then—here was her chance. "Tell me, sir—did you notice anything...*amiss* here this evening?"

She could swear she heard him chuckle, but when she shot

42

him a glance, his face was solemn. "Amiss in what way? I will grant that Lord Crowston usually restricts his attentions to nubile young women to more private settings, so there was that."

Hmm. "Did you notice anything interesting about Miss Yardley?"

"The chit Crowston was pawing? No, not particularly. Should I have?"

"Er . . ." There it was, just like Mr. Rilling: was he, too, naturally resistant to the bee decoction, or were his affections already engaged? No, that was ridiculous—Lord Quinceton had been pursued by marriage-minded girls and their mamas for years, but had evaded all lures cast his way. It must be a natural immunity, then.

"Unlike old Crow, the infantry hold no allure for me, Fellbridge. I find women much more interesting, and —"

"Annabel!" Emily had emerged from the supper room. "There you are! I think they've all been accounted for, except—oh, good evening, Quin. May I please borrow Annabel for a moment? It's a Lady Patroness matter."

"Heaven forbid I should stand in the way of the rapid resolution of a Lady Patroness matter. I bid you good night." He bowed, gave Annabel one of his enigmatic smiles, and walked away.

Annabel frowned after him. Emily's call had made it difficult to hear the last part of Lord Quinceton's statement, but surely he had not said what she'd thought she'd heard him say — or had he?

Emily waited until he was out of earshot. "There. As I started to say, all of the girls who used the decoction seem to have left."

"Oh, good. So has Sally." She thought about asking Emily's opinion on why Mr. Rilling and Lord Quinceton had not been affected by the decoction. But going home seemed like a much more attractive prospect just now. Plenty of time to discuss the evening at the next meeting of the Lady Patronesses. "I think I'll follow their example —"

Emily shook her head. "Not yet. You have to do something

about your aunt."

"My—you mean Great-Aunt Philippa? Why, what has she done?"

"I don't know that she's done anything—yet. But I did find her doing her best to bully Miss Yardley's cousin into telling her what they'd done to get all the men so riled up this evening. I don't know if the girl told her, but we can't have her showing up at Almack's next week drenched in bee decoction."

It was too much; they both burst into giggles. "I'll see what I can do," Annabel finally said. "But there's no stopping Great-Aunt Philippa when she gets a bee in her bonnet."

Emily groaned. "On that note, I'll say good night. See you tomorrow at the Downshires' rout party?"

"I'll be there," Annabel promised.

Only a little while later, ensconced in her carriage and on her own way home, did she think again about what she thought she'd heard Lord Quinceton say, looking down at her with his customary glint: *The infantry hold no allure for me, Fellbridge. I find women much more interesting, and young widows most fascinating of all.*

Singular man!

Homeworld Stranger

Sara Stamey

An excerpt from the novel Wild Card Run. *Ruth Kurtis, a gamer living on the high-tech planet Casino, has been forced to return to her low-tech, polyandrous home planet as a spy for the ruling Cyber entities. She's investigating unsanctioned changes to the WorldPlan.*

✺

*E*xpectancy glowed up from the dark yard and its ring of colored paper lanterns. The guests would soon arrive for the party to celebrate the day's earlier marriage Solemnities. Even now they were pulling the festooned groom cart through the restless wheat, carrying their own paper lanterns and singing as they came.

I drew back through the window into the dark bedroom and felt for flint and lantern on the dressing table. The immaculate white curtains snapped and fluttered ghostlike into the room. The wick caught and chased shadows to the corners. I looked at myself in the mirror.

A stranger stared back at me, hand to her hair. Somehow Marda had tamed it into smooth, intertwined curves to frame my face in a sort of halo that swept back into a thick coil behind my head. The full strands of braiding gleamed dark red in the light, glinting with the scented oil she had combed through it. The scar on my cheek was barely visible in the shadowy depth of the mirror.

The woman in there was a Poindran, her slender curves embraced by the soft folds of a dark green satin dress, her pale hand dropping from her hair with unconscious grace as she leaned forward in the mirror. I saw with a little shock how bright green her eyes looked, wider under the arch of brow echoed by the gleaming sweep of hair, the curve of cheek running down to slightly parted lips, a spot of color high at each temple, delicate ears partially hidden by the heavy ropes of braiding. I wondered if Marda realized what she had done, how she had made this young woman look so . . .

So much like Helen. I could almost be looking at Mother.

I jerked in ridiculous panic away from the mirror and yanked up my skirts, striding from the room. I didn't want to look in that mirror again. I was afraid I'd see Helen's mysterious serenity smiling back at me.

"Jeez Louise!" David jumped, thrusting something hastily behind his back when I appeared on the shadowed porch. He peered up at me, grinned sheepishly, and plopped himself down on a step, chomping into an iced tart he'd filched. I settled beside him.

"You sure as hell don't look like a spacer, Aunt Ruth! But I guess that's okay. You still have to tell me more about the weird places you've been."

I settled my skirts carefully onto the step. "Okay, I'll tell you about a really strange place. The women are so kind and lovely they leave fine threads of light floating behind them. Pretty soon, the threads get woven into a beautiful web, with an intricate pattern that you can hardly see unless the sun hits it just right, and then you see it's got a Plan. It's so light and airy the men and children want to be lifted up by it and feel how soft and gently they're held. And they're all balanced so carefully, each in the right spot designed to hold his weight, so they won't tear the web or knock against anyone else, and they're all smiling . . . And it is lovely, and there's no reason why anyone should come along and get the urge to shake that web . . ."

David munched and swallowed. "Sounds funny to me. What is it, some sort of force field? But then if they had that, they could probably have some kind of flight thrust, right? Tell me about the flying ships!"

I shook my head, chuckling as he pulled his thin legs up, knees by his ears, hunching on the step with his round spectacles gleaming in the shadow, looking exactly like the brooding night-owl of Targuar. "How about birds? Did you know there are birds kind of like our trotters, only they have real wings and fly?"

"You mean like the transports do? Or more like a mechanical drive? I saw some pictures on the console once, drawings like of flying machines, but they must not of worked, otherwise the console wouldn't have cleared them that first time, even with—"

"What do you mean, cleared them?"

He licked his lips nervously. "Oh, nothing, I just mean they don't show us Taboo stuff, you know. Machines and stuff we can't have in the Plan." He cleared his throat. "But since Mother and the elders told me it was wrong, I don't mess around with the console anymore." He shrugged unconvincingly.

"David!" I lowered my voice. "What are you up to? It sounds like you're climbing on a thin line. If Marda—"

He shot me another worried look, lenses flashing a colored streak of light. "You're not gonna—"

"No. I won't tell. But watch it with the cybers, David. It's harder to fool them than you think. You break too many Rules, you're in trouble. I know . . ." I swallowed. "Look, it's like tower climbing, you know. You have to watch out for the backlash and whip on the fast gusts, or you might get spinning out of control."

He gave me a puzzled look. "It's true? You really worked on the towers with Joshua and them when you were a kid?" He shrugged. "But beats me what you're talking about. I don't climb those things."

"What? Here you're talking about flying machines, can't wait to get on a transport, and you don't even use your own wings?"

He gave me an indignant look. "Big deal! So I don't climb the towers! What's that got to do with star ships?"

My voice picked up his scornful tone. "You can have it, and you don't even want it! Listen, you've got some big ideas about star ships, and flying to the planets, but it's not what you think. Here, on the wind sails, you can feel it. It's real when you get up into the air and you're part of it. You'd better find out what that's all about before you start dreaming about the stars. Believe me, they've only got more worlds around them, about as ordinary as here."

"You sound like Mother!" he hissed. "You think I'm gonna swallow all that stuff about how great it is here?"

"But I was a girl, David. I had no choices here." I sighed, remembering the day I became a woman, denied the freedoms enjoyed by men. "Well, I guess it takes all kinds."

"You ask me, you've gotta be really crazy to get up there. All I do is get dizzy, all upside-down and sideways. So they just let me help with the tower electronics. I'm really good," he added proudly, "way better than even the older guys in repair-shop class. But that's just kid stuff, anyway. What I really want to know about is the high-tech stuff the console's not supposed to show me . . . I mean, like the transports and all. I figure they must use some kind of energy-flux modification, right? But I can't work out how they'd do that. I gotta go somewhere I can find out all that stuff, Aunt Ruth! Why don't you take me back to space with you? Please?"

I looked down at his eager face, at the ridiculous, freckled nose, the outlandish glasses, and the absurdly wiry hair, but I didn't feel like laughing. I touched his shoulder and made my voice as gentle as I could. "David, you don't understand. It's not just Poindros. It's everywhere. The cybers don't tell us those kinds of things. They're Taboo on the other worlds, too. And it's dangerous to try to find out."

"But ... dangerous, what do you mean? You're crazy!" He jerked away from me. "You're lying, like the rest of them. You just don't want me to go! But you'll see. I'll find out. I'm gonna be a spacer!" He flung himself off the steps and ran away into the night.

A bright chain of colored lights winked out of the darkness from the direction he'd gone, following the route of the monorail. They curved and snaked toward me, a submerged glow flowing through the dark field, but all I could hear was the restless breeze.

"Just about time. Give me a hand with this rope, Ruth?" It was my brother Joshua leaning over the porch rail.

"Oh. Sure." I straightened and stepped down into the light from the bobbing lantern, turning to look up at him.

"Marda wants this — Ruth?" He broke off, his mouth hanging open. "Blazes! For a second there, I thought ..." He shook his head and grinned. "Hit me with a heat wind if you don't look like a real gal tonight, Ruthie! Come on."

I helped him spread the plaited straw rope Marda had interwoven with papery blue wildflowers into a loose circle around the largest fan tree. He stepped back to admire it. "There! Looks real pretty. Just like she did for our binding party."

"That was only four years ago, wasn't it?"

"Yep. Glad Peter's binding in, I missed him." Peter was one of Joshua's childhood friends. "And we can sure use the help in the fields."

I picked up the traditional copper lantern to hand him. "Then you don't mind having a little less of Marda already?" I spoke without thinking.

He paused in the act of hanging the unlit lantern from the lowest bough, giving me the old look of incomprehension. "You always did say the darnedest things, Ruth."

He grinned and waved as Marda and Thomas appeared with the children. There was a faint murmur of voices beneath the wind as the lights flowed toward us through the field. David came pelting out of the dark, taking his place with us in the family circle and proclaiming breathlessly, "They're coming!"

Then in a swirl of wind and bobbing lanterns and music they burst out of the night. The singers went before, the players on instruments followed after. Amongst them were the maidens playing with timbrels.

The Book of Words came alive in a riot of voices, ringing bells, and swirling skirts as the women, singing and playing their instruments, scattered into the yard. Horns and flutes took up the tune of the binding song, and the rich voices of the matrons followed them. Children swarmed into the yard and formed a circle, hands clasped as they turned and joined the song in a merry round. Deep bass tones filled in as the children spun faster in their bright colors, and the men broke out of the night, bellowing their song and pulling the flower-and-bell-laden wagon to a stop at the edge of the lights.

The dark-haired young man sitting on top grinned sheepishly and stood. A cry of welcome rose from the throng.

Bells and horns and tambourines tumbled into the racket, and the dancing circle exploded into a rush of bodies to surround the wagon. A cheer went up as the men hoisted the groom onto their shoulders and carried him once around the yard, trailing the excited crowd of children. They set him on his feet before the family circle, and everyone fell back in an expectant hush.

Peter, the white groom sash tied in its complicated knot around his waist, touched his hands to his heart and then held them out to Marda. He remained silently standing, his eyes sparking as they fixed on her.

She smiled, and I understood his ardent look. She was the perfection of Poindran womanhood as she stood poised in her pale-blue gown among the excited crowd, small and delicate and rounded, smooth porcelain tinted with soft hues beneath a dark crown of hair interwoven with a blue ribbon.

"Welcome, Peter." Her low voice fell into the hush. Thomas

and Joshua echoed her.

Two small boys came forward from the crowd, walking with nervous care as if afraid they might drop the thin sheaf of grain and the lighted lamp they gave into Peter's hands. He walked slowly toward us.

As Marda reached out her hand to guide him over the plaited rope, Joshua took the sheaf and Thomas reached up to light the copper lantern from the flame of Peter's lamp. The underside of the rustling leaves lit up in a bright green canopy overhead.

Marda and Peter turned outward to the guests, raising their clasped hands, and a roar of approval met them.

A young man burst from the throng in a series of handsprings across the dirt yard. A tumbling knot of his friends followed, tossing and catching each other as their strong bodies flashed in arcs above the ground, honed by their work high in the windtowers. I caught an eager breath as I watched their play, the springing forms launched by quick arms and caught by others, the exuberant leaps through windy air. Around the lithe figures a great spinning wheel seemed to take shape, tower arms rising into the wind and sun, catching a gleam of holding lines as Joshua and I counted out the rhythm of the cycle and launched ourselves from the arm into a flying leap for the next rising spoke.

Freedom in the high air . . . I sighed as the young men took their last springs backward and the crowd rushed in to engulf us.

෧෨෧ ෨෧෨

The night was a blur of laughing faces, music, bobbing lights and shadow, and skirts swirling in the dust of the rowdy festival dances. I took my proper place behind the refreshment table, cutting cakes and pouring juice for the matrons who came in curious flocks. I pretended not to notice their shifting glances, the whispered conferences, the slight hesitations before they accepted food from the hands of a spacer.

I tried to imitate Marda's gracious smile and not see the young bachelors gathered by the mead barrel, laughing and throwing looks my way and daring each other to talk to me.

"Go on, Luke, you—" A brown-haired young man was pushed away from the laughing group.

"Hey! Blast you!" He whirled in a cloud of dust to grapple the arms that had pushed him. Amid shouts and jeering, a wrestling, struggling knot of sun-browned bachelors writhed across the dirt and knocked over the mead barrel, sending it rolling toward the dancers and leaving a moist, pungent trail behind it.

"By the Founder—!"

"Merciful cybers, what's gotten into them?"

The matrons fluttered back in shock and the music rattled to a stop, the dancers turning in bewilderment. As the dust settled, Joshua and Thomas strode through the silence to disentangle the contentious young men.

"Here, now, you young pups!" Thomas took two by the back of their unembroidered bachelor vests. "What's got into you?"

Joshua separated two more who were rolling and thrashing through the dust. "If'n you can't handle your mead, then don't drink with the men!"

A pale flutter of blue drifted through the milling crowd, and behind it the music rose again into the night. The dancers resumed their circular patterns. Marda moved gracefully from matron to matron, drawing them away to help her unwrap and display the gifts brought by the guests. But I still stood isolated by a circle as plain as the family's flowered rope. The matrons shook their heads as they moved off, and even above the wind and music I caught snatches of words. "Whatever are they thinking?"

"Inviting a spacer to bring more trouble! As if we haven't had enough! You know what they say about them."

"It's not fitting. Why, just look at her face, and you can see what sort she is! Probably one of those . . ."

I busied myself tidying the table and helping Joshua and Thomas put the cups to rights near the rescued barrel.

"You're not going to get away with it, you know."

Startled, I looked up, and then up the husky height of the stranger into the snap of very blue eyes. "What?" Had they found me out as a spy already?

He winked, and a humorous smile animated his pleasantly homely face. "Prettiest gal here, and not dancing! Would you do me the honor, Mistress?" He held out his arm.

"Oh!" I hesitated, seeing the faces still staring at me across the yard. I raised my chin. "Thank you, I will." The stares followed as he walked me across the yard and the music announced a festival dance. I held my back straight, my lips in a careful smile.

But my partner grinned and winked as the music swelled, and I couldn't help joining his laughter as his large hands caught me around the waist and swung me into the opening twirl. His exuberance was irresistible, and all the dancers smiled, jumping with one will into the flowing circular patterns. I dove recklessly into the passing line, weaving and brushing the twisting bodies, laughing and peering through the gold-lighted haze of rising dust, slapping the palm of my returning partner, spinning, then away again, gasping into the quickening beat of drums. Then he was back, that great grin, and up! My head swept the night air and my skirts flared in a gleaming circle around and around in a bright blur of light and laughter.

His big hands guided me gently through the settling dust, and he smiled. "I thank you, Mistress." He glanced up at the night sky and back to me, winking again. "Give my regards to the stars next time you're out that way."

I stood watching after the broad back of his embroidered vest, then slowly smiled. I nodded and threaded my way through the noisy flock to the deserted house. And the cyber console that might be hiding threats to these—my—people and their peaceful WorldPlan.

Kerygma in Waltz Time

Charlotte Gumanaam

"Book," my roommate says, her perfectly groomed fingernail tapping a printout from Craigslist.

"Go away," I mutter. "It's barely the butt-crack of . . ."

"Eight a.m." Megan states it with the inexorable moral superiority of She Who Rises Early.

I try to pull my pillow over my head.

It's said that the most irritating phrase in the English language is *I told you so.*

Don't get an English degree. There are no jobs, there's nothing you can do with a BA in English, headhunters will look at you as if your eyelashes crawled with pinworms as they ask, "Is there anything *else* you can do?" As if the study of one of the most spoken languages in the world, and its river of literature reflecting centuries of cultural evolution, is . . . well, like air, invisible.

I did try studying theory of mind and behavioral and social sciences to find out why the world of books is so intrinsic to my existence, but they all seemed to be spinning conclusions from the reflections on the cave wall, only in terms more modern than Plato.

Besides, all I ever wanted to do is sink into the world of story.

After scrimping pennies all through college and a couple years beyond, I'd come to New York City, believing it the center of the literary world. In these digital days, surely there is a place for the English major?

Yeah, *I told you so.*

"Noooo," I moan.

Yesterday I went to a job fair, which meant standing for hours among hundreds of people just like me breathing their anxiety and unhappiness into the stuffy air, the elbow-jabs and hip knocks of covert competition making it extra fun. I'd promised myself to stick it out until the doors closed, and what did that prove? That I looked more pathetic than anyone else.

Megan yanks the pillow away. "This one is really you."

I close my eyes, like the cat that thinks it's hidden.

"If you don't land this one, I will never, ever, try to find you a job again. I won't have to," she adds in a brisker tone, "because you won't be around to nag. Five days from now, you'll owe us rent for three months. Remember your promise on moving in."

Three months no rent, and you are out. No ifs, ands, or buts.

My savings had run out at warp speed. I'd been cleaning the apartment for my roommates—I'd even cooked—and they were grateful, but Megan makes minimum wage at her "part time" job in the finance district (the rest of her eighty hours a week are "volunteer," in hopes she'll get hired for real) and Parker ekes an existence as a backstage grunt as she tries to make it in the theater.

The daily-more-palpable moral weight of their silence was my real reason for holing up to sleep through the day.

I am totally, thoroughly, unequivocally up shit c. without a p.

I sit up and take the printout from her hand. There, circled in pink highlighter, are the words:

Virtual game test subjects. Knowledge of literature a must.

I look up at Megan's merciless black eyes.

"I know, right?" she says. "It's so you, it's ridiculous."

"What do you mean? Computer games? I've never played one in my life. CGI blood and guts creep me right out."

"'Knowledge of literature a must.' Says nothing about guns and blood. And did you take in that last line?"

Salary and benefits, both expected and unexpected.

"What's that supposed to mean?"

"I don't know, but I already emailed them on your behalf," Megan says. "You're scheduled for your interview at nine. I've got the hot water running in the shower, and Parker ironed your interview outfit before she left for the theater. So get your butt out of that bed."

The subway is slow. My cell was turned off last month, so I keep nervously checking the time in every store window and over the shoulder of everybody on their cell while I hustle down Fifth Avenue, afraid to be late.

The address turns out to be a mansion just off Central Park, a beautiful building in *fin de siecle* grandiosity. The front door doesn't open to a public hall, so that means whoever owns it still owns the entire house.

Promptly at nine I rap the knocker, which is a shiny brass arabesque in the mouth of an art-deco lion, pocked and weather-worn as if it has scowled down at that street since the 1890s.

A round-faced white woman opens the door. "Come inside, please."

On straight-backed chairs in a grand tiled hallway sit what has to be the rest of the candidates, save for one who has her own seat in a wheelchair.

I head for the single empty seat, but scarcely does my poly-and-linen-clad butt touch the finely sanded wood than the door opener—I think of her as our host, so much better than gatekeeper and easier than judge—walks past me to a pair of carved walnut double doors at the other end of the hall. These she opens, and with an inviting gesture. "If you will?"

She stands aside as the candidates file past, everybody avoiding one another's eyes in the way people do when they suspect they're in competition, but sidling glances to check out the others.

Who am I up against? As last arrival I'm the caboose to the shuffling train, so I scope them all out from the back. We seem to be mostly female and mostly white, from barely college age (first couple) to a stooped gray-haired guy with glasses putting out a heavy English Professor vibe, probably from some college that downsized their English department to make room for more business adjuncts.

An Asian guy wears a suit and tie, and the white man with the shaved head and tats shuffles in sagging jeans and a faded T with a picture of a nineties band, leaving sinus-scorching nicotine toxins in his wake. The large woman in the wheelchair behind him, breathing into a handkerchief, might be ten years older than me, the skinny woman with the briefcase and beaded dreads the same.

I enter last, expecting to see an office with a bank of computers. To my total surprise, I step into a vast ballroom. The patterned hardwood floors gleam under what looks like thousands of books heaped up in piles.

The walls between cartouches and long, beautiful mullioned windows have bookshelves built in. It looks like moving day. The shelves are completely bare, all the books stacked in piles on the floor.

Morning light filters through the tree-lined terrace outside, mostly blocking the view of the building next door. The massive chandeliers overhead, unlit, look like cold ice without giving off light or heat.

The host—round of face in a vaguely familiar way—says, "You'll find clipboards and pens on this table here."

She opens her palm toward a claw-footed side table beside the door, on which is stacked clipboards with paper, a box of pens and pencils beside the stack. "The first test is to demonstrate on the clipboard how you would organize this library. You do not have to touch the books," she adds, her gaze lingering on English

Professor Man and Wheelchair Woman. "This is not a race, or a physical contest. Before we progress further, I want you to comprehend that we are interested in not only your knowledge of literature, but how you categorize it. How would you shelve these books?"

"Alphabetical, of course," states the youngest, a nervy-looking person with eyebrow, nose, and lip piercings, her buzz-cut hair dyed platinum. She casts the rest of us a scornful look and adds, "Me and Xander here can have these shelved before lunch, if everybody else stays out of our way."

Xander nods. He looks pretty much like his partner, except his skin is pale and freckled, his very short hair dyed black.

The host says, "The only reason you need to touch the books is to move one if it blocks your view of another title. Write down your list in categories."

There is no sound except the rustle of clothes, the shuffle of feet, and the muted clatter of pens against clipboards as the rest of us get our equipment.

The host says, "Over to you, then."

Wheelchair Woman raises a hand, as if we are in school. "There's a specific organization that we're supposed to suss out, is that it?"

"Any way you see fit."

I say, "Are we competing against each other for one spot?"

"Not at all. We're looking for a certain, ah, perspective. We've found that people will say anything in interviews. This experiment is better at selecting what we seek."

"But you won't tell us what you seek," Wheelchair Woman says.

The host shakes her head slowly, smiling. "I know it seems arbitrary. We have our reasons."

Bosses always have their reasons. They also have the power of the purse, so either ones puts up or shuts up.

I turn to face the ballroom.

Xander and Buzz-Cut whisper, then separate, each to opposite sides of the room. They bend and started scribbling madly, their strategy clearly to be the first to list every single book.

The only other noise is the muted whir of the wheelchair as its operator slowly moves between the stacks. She bends to study the piles, as do the others.

A ballroom filled with books! Short of an actual ball — hypothetically, as I've never been to one — what could be better? So much to read, in a gorgeous setting. There is nothing like the feel of a book in hand, and the smell of ink, paper, and binding, especially in a room that breathes of good wood, marble, polish. My throat tightens as I survey the scattered library, the morning light slanting through the tall windows illuminating a microcosm of history. Imagination. A life among the benefits of civilization.

Whatever this job is, I have to get it.

I look around, wondering what to do first; as I do, the ballroom door opens, and I turn in time to see the smoker slope out — with the clipboard. The door shuts behind him.

Okay, looks like one down.

I turn back to the books, resisting the urge to wipe my free hand down my pants. My toes are already pinching unmercifully in my thrift-store heels. I bend carefully to look at the closest piles. The books have been stacked neatly. The dust film is negligible. The books are cared for.

O-o-o-okay. Clutching my clipboard, I start to reconnoiter.

Smollett, Swift, Mrs. Inchbald, and Eliza Haywood draw my eye first: fragile, ancient books with gilt lettering on the binding. I pivot and begin scanning the top titles of all the piles. Everything is mixed, modern and new.

I straighten up, and begin walking. As far as I can tell, these books are mostly literature written in, or translated into, English, though here and there I spot an autobiography (Trollope, Agatha Christie) and many, many collections of letters.

The fiction includes mash-ups and sequels. I find enormous stacks of Jane Austen continuations, beginning with *Shades of Pemberley*, going right up to the contemporary ones with magic or detectives stitched in, stacked next to the "diaries" about the characters' bedroom sports.

Curious, I glance about, and yes, there's *The Wide Sargasso Sea*, sitting haphazardly on a pile of Bulwer-Lytton's novels; I find the Brontes under a statue alcove. Baroness Orczy's entire collection lies under a window. All the Waverley novels teeter nearby, behind the works of Dorothy Dunnett and Dorothy Sayers, stacked side by side.

In the middle of the room lie Sayers continuations, and before the alcove on the opposite wall I spot a lot of the historical Scots romances and even the science fiction that Dunnett had inspired, such as *The Sparrow*, and the time-travel historical romance *Outlander*. I glance past that to see if I can find more Dunnett-driven id-vortex fic — and sure enough, C.S. Pacat lies nearby.

As far as I can tell, autobiography and letters are less represented. Should I go Dewey-Decimal, or just include those with each author's fiction? No answer, of course. The books sit there, dust motes lazily circling in the windows' slants of light.

So I get to work, noting down books in loose categories, roughly according to author last name. When I begin categorizing the D's, I discover scattered through the room an enormous mass of Sherlock Holmes pastiche. Laurie King — Lloyd Biggle — Manly W. and Wade Wellman — and there's a fragile copy of Mark Twain's "A Double-Barreled Detective Story" lying next to a novelization of the film made from Mary Norton's *The Borrowers*. Should the first one go with Twain, or should it be classed with Doyle's own writings, fictional and non? And what to do about the second one — the novelization of a film of a novel — with Norton's actual work?

I look around for clues, and see everyone else either reading or counting or cruising the stacks, except Buzz-Cut and Xander, who grimly work at scribbling down titles.

Then what? I wonder.

Convinced that there has to be some pattern here besides the alphabet, I turn the novelization over. It looks well thumbed, as if some little kid, or maybe a score of them, had read it over and over. Then I set it aside in expectation of finding Mary Norton's books somewhere. And there they are, over by the claw-footed table.

Behind me lies an old copy of Polidori's novel, which means there has to be a slew of vampire stuff in the piles. I decide to leave all that for later, and concentrate on hunting all the Holmes spinoffs, to see if I'm finding a vector.

What about that book-mountain over there? Further spelunking turns up strata of Arthuriana from across the centuries. Wolfram von Eschenbach—Chrétien de Troyes—the entire medieval bandwagon, right up to Malory, and in another massive stack, the Victorian Arthuriana. That was a fraction of the twentieth-century piles. Looks like all of it is there, the good, the bad, the nearly forgotten.

I straighten up. Maybe it isn't fair to judge people by their books, but I do that. *Humans* do that. We judge by books, by clothes, by cars, by speech. We're creatures of judgment and of hierarchy, though the social contract requires us to decently mask it if we can't rein it in.

Would it be better to attempt not to pass judgment, but to alphabetize books with direct influence, and leave indirect influences—in conversation with—to the reader as well as the volatile subject of worth? If so, *Pride and Prejudice and Zombies* could be included in mass of spinoffs after Jane Austen's fiction, letters, biographies, and litcrit, but *The Sparrow* (science fiction that seems to have Dorothy Dunnett's much-tortured handsome hero in the *Lymond Chronicles* as its inspiration) would be alphabetized according to its author's name. That way, the mass of fantasy that had Tolkienian roots would also be filed under their respective authors' names.

Pending further instructions, I'm thinking as I look around and knuckle my lower back, I'll keep on as I've begun.

Sorting, writing. Sorting, writing. When I hit a stack of Thackeray, I stand there blinking wearily down at *Vanity Fair*.

Was that the ur-text for Margaret Mitchell's *Gone With The Wind* for anyone but me? Not really an ur-text, it was the character Becky Sharp who inspired Scarlett O'Hara, in the same way that Percy Blakeney was the inspiration for Zorro and for Lord Peter Wimsey.

"When in doubt, stick to the alphabet," I mutter as I bend to pick up a handful of Thackerays.

"Doubt?"

I jump, not realizing until then that I had spoken out loud.

Behind me is Wheelchair Woman. "You said you were in doubt?"

"Um," I respond intelligently. "Alphabet when I'm unsure how books interrelate."

"Interrelate?" she repeats.

I flop a hand. "They have a lot of sequels."

"I categorized them as spinoffs," she says.

"Some are, some aren't," I mutter as Professor Guy casts us a frowning look from two stacks over—as if this were a public library, and we were breaking the No Speaking rule. Then he transfers his glance to a pile of Holmes spinoffs, his upper lip crimping the way of someone who has just discovered a dead cockroach in their half-eaten slice of pie.

I lower my voice to a whisper. "Those are easy, and I'm thinking, put them in with the ur-author, I guess you could say. But some, like Angela Thirkell, are sort-of sequels. I mean, they take place in Barsetshire, but a different time, and I don't think the two sets have much to do with one another besides names. But she was definitely, oh, in literary conversation with Trollope."

"Literary conversation," she says. "I always thought of her as applied literature."

"Applied literature?" It's my turn to echo a question.

She mops her face wearily with her handkerchief. "Most characters in books aren't aware of literature. Like no one on TV watches TV. But Thirkell's characters reflect lifetimes of reading."

"True," I say, thinking about this for the first time. Thirkell to me has always seemed nothing more than pleasant between-wars escapism—endless country teatimes, the war a rumble in the distance, like a remote thunderstorm. Then, as my toes throb in my shoes, I remember why I'm here, and wrench myself back on topic. "But it doesn't tell us how she—or whoever owns this library—wants things done. I can put the pastiches and mashups with their ur-author or their own author." As I look around, I can't help laughing, though I manage to smother it. "At least these are print books, finite in number. So glad I don't have to deal with fan fiction on the Net."

Her lips part, and I think, *She knows what I'm talking about!*

She whispers in an apologetic tone, "I don't mean to be picking your brain. I believed her when she said they aren't pitting us against each other for one slot. But then I don't need this job, though I'd like to trade in soul-destroying content writing for anything that has to do with literature." She cocks her head at the young and pierced, who don't seem to have slowed, but the way Buzz-Cut rattles a page on her clipboard and scribbles madly indicates grim determination of another sort.

"I'm Jen." She smiles.

"Nice to meet you, Jen," I say, and turn to survey the vast ballroom. "Books, and a job. A job with books?" My toes are throbbing. "Too good to be real. Has to be a catch, and looks like we're in it. Somehow."

"I would have hated to tell her what she could do with her competition if it really was for one slot," Jen says. "No, actually, I'd've thoroughly enjoyed it. But I've had a lifetime of people expecting me to keep myself decently invisible." She glances away, her face tightening as if she feels she's said too much.

"It seems so strange," I say, trying to bridge the awkward moment. Did I cause it? I've always been the invisible one. "We have the morning to figure out how to organize this mess, but they won't give us a hint about how. I've racked up some weird job interviews among the many degrading ones, but this one is the weirdest. At least it's fun."

"I think they want to see if we're on the same wavelength."

"Which is?"

"Well, that's what we figure out. My first thought was, they want us to know the difference between fiction and non-fiction, maybe a general knowledge of Dewey D., enough for field triage after," Jen offers.

"But?" I ask. "I hear a but."

"There are all those pastiches. A lot of them in stacks of type, rather than author."

"Right! So if those are important to categorize, how? Do we want all fifty billion Jane Austen-related works under the A's?"

"*I* don't want any of them," Jen says with a dismissive wave. "I can't read anything that gets me arguing on the first page. Take magic. If they had it in Jane Austen's time, the industrial revolution would never have happened, Napoleon would have been turned into a statue crowned in birdshit around the time he decided to go imperial, and Keats would have lived to be a hundred—as well as Jane Austen—or else what *use* is it?"

I sneeze like a gunshot. Everybody in the room gives me a dirty look. "Sorry, sorry," I say, shrinking behind a pile of Dickens, and in a lower voice to Jen, "The magic ones mix wish-fulfillment with Georgette Heyer's Regency, you know, minus the grinding misery of early industrialization. A feature for many readers."

"Look, I'm not against crossovers, or even continuations," Jen whispers as the others turn away. "I fell in love with *Pride and Prejudice* after mainlining the Colin Firth production. But there are only the six Austens. So I went on to Regency romances, just like a billion other women more or less our age."

"Count me in," I admit. "I remember how happy I was when the public library where I was living at the time had all the books Georgette Heyer had written. It was worth the two bus rides to get there."

Jen's mouth quirks. "My point is, I like them if I there's a sense of what drew me to Austen in the first place. It's not just the issue of consistent worldbuilding. Many say, and rightly, that there's little sign of Napoleon's war in Austen's novels, and as for clothes, we only read that Fanny Prince wears a gown with white spots, and that the Thorpe sisters dress smart."

"There are also the authentic attitudes of the day," I say.

She gives her head a shake. "But you can get those in any writer of the period, including Sir Walter Scott, who invented the historical novel. Jane Austen wrote metaliterary romance. Not the narrow definition used in marketing genre today, she wrote the romance that is the mythos of which comedy, tragedy, and irony-satire make up such a bewitching combo. Metaliterary not just in literature being self-aware. But . . . higher, the world as it should be."

"'Higher.'" Is that a pun? "How do you rate Georgette Heyer, who was certainly meticulous about the details of the Regency world?"

"Exhaustively so," Jen says. "And the comedy and wit in her good ones are almost as good as Austen's, though I think Austen would have hated her prose. Too much figurative triteness, exactly what Austen edited out of her manuscripts, according to Arthur Axelrad over there. Heyer's also writing what she thinks the world should be, but without Austen's moral center."

She pronounces the name *Hay-urr*, instead of *High-urr*. "In the Heyer world, noble blood will always prove true, whereas in Austen, did you notice that not a single noble is admirable? There's nothing about slender white hands. Elizabeth is brown, and Darcy thinks nothing of it." She looks around at the stacks and stacks of continuations. "As for Heyer, she loathed the writers who obviously used her research and situations, yet just about all these spinoffs are copies of her details, situations, and above all her idiosyncratic language. Especially the ones written in the last thirty years. It's kind of funny in an ironic way."

I say, pronouncing the name the way she does, "Georgette Heyer's world might not be like Austen's, but it's complete in itself. You can sink into it to reread, knowing what you're getting."

A corner of Jen's mouth turns up. "Though eventually you begin to wonder how a tiny island could support all those handsome and wealthy earls, and you have to blink hard past the smugly casual anti-Semitism, which I think extra chilling considering when she was writing those books. But for unbelievable, well, did you ever try Barbara Cartland?"

"The elipses! The untrammeled hearts, and the big eyes! And the heroines with last names that all sounded like Waif!"

Jen shakes all over as she chuckles. "And all the dukes seem to be named Blayse Ravensomething, who manage to get on a first name basis with the winsome young governess within a day. Cartland's stuff is like a paper that's been recopied so many times it becomes a distorted blur. The reader has to do all the work. All the author provided was bog-standard tropes, glued together by ellipses. And nothing, really, of what makes Austen so readable."

"But somebody in this house must like all these spinoffs, or they wouldn't have them in their library, while I notice a distinct lack of the sort of literary award winners you only read once. Or mean to read, but never get past page twelve. Wow. When you think of it, how many writers hoped their books would inspire others, whether or not they won awards?"

"And how little control they had, or have, over what inspires people, and where they will take the ideas. Heyer would no doubt be hurling tons of lawyers across the decades if she knew about all these copycats, but at least that's harmless. As well as fun to read."

"Human beings are absurd animals, with all kinds of design flaws, but we do at least have imagination," I say. "Maybe our one saving grace."

Now it's Jen's turn to look about her as if she's found that cockroach, and is remembering the dire *There is never just one.* "What's graceful about imagination? Unless you find fire graceful."

"You're against grace?"

"I want there to be grace," Jen retorts as she scoots her chair along another aisle. "I would give anything to know there is grace." Then her lip curls, and her voice sharpens to its usual mordant tone. "But for us to recognize grace we seem to first need the opposite. We imagine torture instruments. Nuclear bombs. Ways to cheat others. There it is, I thought I saw Bulwer-Lytton's *The Coming Race*."

I shrug, wondering at the connection. "He's pretty much unreadable, but I remember some prof saying that novel inspired Madame Blavatsky and the Theosophist writings. Pretty harmless."

"Though it was not his intent—the futuristic supermen in his novel are all brown, looking like Native Americans—he also inspired the Aryan cultists that glommed onto Hitler, did you know that?"

"I didn't." Now it's my turn to feel the unseen cockroaches skittering. "I don't see any Hitler spinoffs here, at least. Not that I've ever heard of any."

"Maybe not in here, but it's out there, all right. Those uniforms, the whole *Triumph of the Will* atmosphere—the entire Nazi brand was designed to appeal to the imagination. A look at the number of books and films and shows about it since 1945 makes it clear that humans, mostly male humans, in my experience, are fascinated by it, even though the actual Nazi leaders went down in flames."

I crouch down to ease my toes, and try to crack my neck. One minute break, then back to it, I think, as I say, "You're right about the films and shows and books. What's the draw, anyway? Do you think it's the prurient fascination for evil, or for unlimited power?"

"I tend to think of it as the cancerous extreme of testosterone-poisoning."

When I smother a laugh, she holds up her palm, then lowers her voice. "Not joking! Think about it. Taken as individuals, Hitler and Himmler were a couple of boring, weak-chinned couch potatoes. It's doubtful Hitler was even able to *have* sex—and we can be grateful for that, as his genes aren't clogging the gene pool even worse than it is already. But put that pair of ass-clowns in those uniforms, up on monstrous platforms with hundred foot tall flags behind them, overlooking hordes of jackbooted uniforms precision-marching with arms stuck out at an up-prick angle, and the scene metastasizes into the ultimate in violence porn."

"Sure. For skinheads and neo-Nazis and other crazies."

"Not just them. The actual Nazis burned themselves and their world out seventy-odd years ago, taking a huge portion of the European population with them, but like I said, ever since, guys can't shut up about them, books, movies, you name it."

"Right." I force myself to my feet. "At least we don't have to deal with that here. Back to what we've got."

"I suggest clumping together the sequels and spinoffs and such sideways ones."

"Sideways?"

"Like these obvious Harry Potter next-gens with the serial numbers filed off. And the variations mentioning Austen's name, or her characters' names, or place names, but aren't retellings, or sequels—sort of in conversation with, as you said. Margaret Drabble's 'The Dower House at Kellynch.' *Bridget Jones's Diary*."

"I'd categorize those as adaptations." I try to ignore my still-throbbing toes. "Okay, so how about nonfiction. Stuff like the Martin biography of Jennie Churchill. Did you see that over near Wharton's *The Buccaneers*? Which I remember hearing is a *roman a clef*, one of the characters being based on Jennie. So how to deal with fiction based on real life?"

"To start with, biographies with their subject," Jen says. "Autobiographical novels with them."

"And the same with Austen's letters?" I ask, nodding. "I saw they had Deirdre Le Faye's latest edition, and also Axelrad's *Jane Austen: Caught in the Act of Greatness*. Would that go in a third sect-ion, for litcrit? If it was my own library, I'd keep all the Austen stuff together—letters, biographies, litcrit. But what if I'm wrong?"

"We don't know what's wrong." Jen is firm. "Since we don't know what they're really looking for, outside of the fact that this entire collection here seems to be confined to inspired-bys of one kind or another."

"Then every form goes with its ur-author," I say, noting Briefcase Woman passing by, crouched over the stacks. She looks like OCD incarnate—colored pens clipped to one sleeve. Her clipboard, which I glance at as she passes, is neatly written, in color codes. I wonder what she makes of spinoffs.

And what it means to this mysterious job.

Suddenly it's noon, and the host reappears.

Buzz-Cut stalks up to her. "We listed every book, alphabetized by author. We finished half an hour ago," she adds, with a scary look in our direction, as if we are all going to howl *We finished first!*

The host says, "Let's see what you have."

Pierced-Nose yanks Xander over. "We used a lot of abbreviations—this would have been faster on a tablet," she states. "But we have every single book. Xander started at that side and I at this, and we met in the middle."

"So you mixed nonfiction with fiction?" our host asks.

Buzz-Cut flushes. "Well, how were we supposed to know what was in them? You didn't say we had to read any of it!"

"Thank you," the host says, taking the clipboards. "Good luck in your future endeavors."

"You mean we're not hired?"

"If I'd wanted an alphabetical listing," the host says gently, "I would have asked for it."

"Douchecanoe," Buzz-Cut mutters and marches out, her chains jingling.

"I wondered if we were supposed to separate them," Xander mumbles.

Buzz-Cut yells, "Get your ass in gear, Xander," and he follows her out the door and into the real world.

Suit Man had already vanished. Professor Guy sets down his

empty clipboard on the stable and says, "Four hours amidst a mix of trash and treasures. What is the point here?"

"You tell me," the host offers, smiling.

Professor Guy shakes his head. "Not my area of interest." And he is gone.

Briefcase Woman is next.

"Ah, the nonfiction organized by Dewey Decimal," the host says. "Very nicely done."

A tick of silence, then Briefcase Woman says, "But not what you were looking for?"

"I would have asked for it," the host replies, sounding apologetic. "But I happen to know someone looking for a person with organizational skills like yours." She writes something on a sheet of paper ripped from an unused clipboard, hands it off, and Briefcase Woman takes it with a word of thanks, and is gone.

The host turns to us. Jen extends her hand for me to go first, so I hand over my list, saying, "I'm not even half done, but as far as I got, I grouped everything together under original author. Original work, biographies, letters, memoirs. Then other people's sequels, alphabetized under a sub-header. If it didn't come under that heading, over here I alphabetized fiction, and nonfiction by type."

"I did pretty much the same," Jen says. "Except I began breaking down the spinoffs and sequels, and I started to separate the keepers from the schlock, except the schlock pile way outnumbered the keepers."

The host's brows lift. "You're familiar with them all?"

"Most." Jen reddens. "I have spinal issues. I read a lot."

"You both chose to organize the books connecting to specific authors," she observes. "Let us talk about that further."

Jen goes first, leaning forward a little as if she wants to get there a bit sooner. The host leads us through the back door of the ballroom/library into a hall, where a dark-skinned young man is waiting. Wainscoting with old-fashioned paper above it mark either side of the hall, punctuated by carved wooden doors. The hall smells of old-fashioned beeswax polish and clove-spiced mulled wine.

"This is Thomas," the host says, and the young man holds the door to one room wide so Jen can scoot inside. I notice that the door has an old-fashioned latch with a stylized wheel of the zodiac around a Greek face. Kronos?

"Come this way, please," the host says to me.

Up close, our host is one of those fair-skinned, fair-haired people who could be anywhere from twenty-five to forty-five. She really does seem familiar.

I follow her into a room containing the expected desk and chair, but with packed bookcases along the wall. I try to see the titles without being obvious, but all I catch is gilt lettering in nineteenth century styles, and leather binding. Old-looking.

She sits down behind the desk, glances at my clipboard, then sets it aside and folds her hands. "Tell me about why you divided the books the way you did."

As an interview strategy, it works like gangbusters as an instant B.S. bypass.

If you have a marketable skill, I imagine it's easy: *We need a software engineer who can write in Dart for cloud computing.*

Yep, I have three years of experience in Dart, transferring data to the cloud.

Good. Here's an enormous check to get you started, and by the way we roll out in four months, so here's your hammock to sling in your office, because you won't have time to spend any of the megabucks we pay you.

But when your only trained skill is research papers for college profs, which is a skill nobody else wants, you try to be whatever the interviewer is looking for.

But my clipboard had gotten me past the first gate, so something had to be right. I launch into pretty much what Jen and I had talked about that morning.

She listens all the way through, then asks, "Tell me about your engagement with fan fiction."

My jaw nearly clanks onto the polished desk top. "Everybody

seems to consider it noble literature's bastard child," I say slowly, looking for the verbal trap. *Aha! You waste your valuable time reading claptrap, clearly you are unfit for a Proper Job.* "And you could say that there are a lot of bastards."

"And yet," she counters, "it has mirrored literature at least since Virgil pulled the minor character Aeneas out of *The Iliad*."

In a classroom setting I would launch into how even defining fiction is a slippery slope, especially when talking about the centuries in which originality was more of a bug than a feature. But in a job interview, the power is all on one side. So I try to look intelligent, but all she says is, "The next stage is to test a sample."

She gets up, and lays a tablet before me. "Just touch the screen."

Expecting I don't know what, I tap the screen, which flashes words in a pretty Copperplate font: *The World of Jane Austen*.

Austen! What little fan fiction I'd written was all in Jane Austen's world.

Then:

Would you go back to the early nineteenth century if you could? A) Yes B) No C) Yes or no with conditions D) I do not understand this question.

"Huh." I always land between the offered answers on tests like these. Conditions? What if one's conditions were different for yes or no?

Wary but intrigued, I tap C, barely aware of the door closing behind me.

You are invited to the Netherfield Ball. You may attend as: A) Elizabeth Bennet B) Fitzwilliam Darcy C) Jane Bennet D) Charles Bingley E) Another character

I suppose everyone who makes it this far chooses Elizabeth. But that's the obvious choice, the point of view the narrator of the novel already gave you. And I'm wary of some modern romance distortion of Darcy.

So I hit E, and a new set of choices scrolls up:

You may attend as A) Mary Bennet B) Caroline Bingley C)

Lydia Bennet D) Charlotte Lucas

Charlotte Lucas?

The most interesting character in the entire book—a complete anomaly for the time! No, she was not romantic, but she got exactly what she wanted, without paying for it with her life for her temerity. I've always thought of her as the nerd's heroine, or the heroine for those, like me, who aren't smart enough to aspire to nerd status.

She's always been my favorite.

I hit D.

The tablet then scrolls the words: *Lay your palm on the screen.*

I do.

The screen gives in a way that reminds me of mercury with its weird surface tension. I stare down as my fingers appear to sink through the screen, then jerk my hand away.

Then I feel stupid. I'm here for a job, and this tablet is projecting some sort of holographic image or high-tech VR thing that is a part of said job. What's more, they're offering me my favorite story ever.

I put my palm down more firmly, prepared for that sense of my hand sinking, then forget it as colors flicker, resolving into the entry hall of a Georgian house, evoking scents buried in memory: candle wax, pomade, wine punch, and the faintly sweet aroma of dried rose petals that Lady Lucas insists the girls lay their good clothes in when putting them into the clothes press.

It's not only a virtual world, but I'm inside Charlotte Lucas, thinking with quiet pleasure about how Father called out the old berlin so that they would not have to carry their dancing shoes in a bag, which nicety Mother also appreciates.

Maria walks ahead on her toes, her careful curls—still smelling slightly singed—bouncing on her shoulders, and alas, coming looser with each step.

Charlotte puts out a hand to still her, and when Maria turns her way, says, "I see Kitty Bennet over there behind Mrs. Bennet, and Lydia is not by."

Maria—frightened by Lydia's careless cruelties—brightens, then begins to scamper up the stairs, not wanting to miss a moment of the evening's felicities.

"Maria," Mother whispers.

Maria stops so abruptly her flounce flares over her slippers. She touches her curls tentatively, then minces the rest of the way up to the drawing room's double doors, and past Mr. Bingley and his sisters lined up inside to greet their guests. She bobs a curtsey (which is barely acknowledged) and then speeds inside to find Kitty Bennet.

"Lydia is no doubt searching about for officers," Mother says under her breath as we hand our wraps to the servant to put in the cloak room.

Father murmurs into his carefully starched cravat, "Wherever there are officers and silly girls, it might be said that they will find one another."

"That's all very well for Lydia Bennet," Mother states. "As long as *my* girls do no such thing." She takes Father's arm, and they mount the stairs to be greeted enthusiastically by Mr. Bingley and in languid drawls by his sisters.

Charlotte follows behind, expecting to be ignored, as she is by the two women. Mr. Bingley smiles on her and bobs his head in a short bow, but Charlotte senses that he doesn't see her, either. At least he is polite about it.

I-inside-Charlotte am thinking that none of that dialogue is in the book, then my awareness sinks again as Elizabeth Bennet rushes up, eyes wide enough to reflect the candle flames overhead, cheeks a ruddy color that owe nothing to powder. "There you are," she exclaims, and lowers her voice confidentially. "Mr. Wickham is not come. Mr. Denny hinted that he might not be invited."

"Oh?" Charlotte says, and pretends an interest in a gentleman she has no interest in at all, as Elizabeth goes on in a rush of words to extol the absent Mr. Wickham and almost in the same breath to excoriate the tall, proud Mr. Darcy, the enemy of perfection.

Charlotte has heard it all before, which grants her the freedom to look about her while Elizabeth vents her passion. Mr. Darcy, quite the tallest man in the room as well as the least known (and the best dressed), dominates the company merely by his presence.

When Elizabeth runs out of words on this topic, hearing no encouragement to expatiate, she catches sight of her cousin bowing to someone on the other side of the chamber, and whispers with a speaking glance, "There is Mr. Collins." She draws Charlotte to the opposite side of the room.

Charlotte was introduced to him at church, and even exchanged a few words about the sermon, but Mrs. Bennet has not chosen to invite anyone to meet him socially—or at least, anyone with marriageable daughters, Mother pointed out when they walked home after divine service.

Charlotte listens to Elizabeth's description of a prodigiously troublesome week with a mixture of sympathy and guilt, aware of her own mother's increasing disappointment every birthday that Charlotte passes as a single woman. But Charlotte cannot help sympathizing with Mrs. Bennet, too, vapid as she is. She has five daughters to marry off, in a community with relatively few suitable young gentleman, as so many are either gone off to the navy, the army, or to London.

Mr. Collins moves ponderously about the room, bowing as he introduces himself. Charlotte suspects that he is closer to her own age than to Elizabeth's. He has very formal manners, so formal they appear awkward among people who have known one another all their lives. As Elizabeth disparages him, Charlotte thinks that there could scarcely be two people more ill-matched.

"Ah, the musicians are in preparation," Charlotte points out when Elizabeth pauses to draw a breath.

And here is Mr. Collins himself, bowing with punctilio to Elizabeth as if they have just met, and to Charlotte as well. Charlotte curtseys back, then watches Elizabeth's reluctant steps as they take their place in the forming line.

The musicians strike up a lively German air, and the floor

reverberates under the dancers' footfalls.

Nimble Elizabeth seems a sylph in contrast to her heavy cousin, who appears to be unable to keep time, or place, without his elbow banging his partner or the couples around them. Both partners are cross, Charlotte sees: Elizabeth is irked by her partner, but Mr. Collins seemed to be provoked entirely by the necessity to mind his steps and his place in an exercise he is clearly unused to.

Mr. Collins is performing his duty, just as clearly as Charlotte is in standing against the wall of yet another ball; if she were to dance, she would be minding her own steps. A ballroom, under such circumstances, clearly gives him as little pleasure as it does Elizabeth, though for profoundly different reasons. Charlotte sees the high flush of mortification in her friend's face, then looks past her to the tall gentleman whose attention follows Elizabeth's movements as she does her best to keep her slippers from being smashed beneath her cousin's stamping feet. Mr. Darcy is not the only one watching, though his gaze is the steadiest. There could not be a greater contrast between the lady, so sprightly and graceful, and her blundering partner, highly entertaining to those who look for such absurdities.

Charlotte watches them all. It is very clear what is going to happen, even if Elizabeth — usually so observant — cannot see it. And so it is: no sooner has the dance ended, and Elizabeth makes her way to Charlotte's side, fanning her heated face as she whispers imprecations, than the tall, London-tailored Mr. Darcy moves unsmiling through the deferring crowd and gravely asks Elizabeth to dance.

She looks up, lips parted in an expression of surprise, and Charlotte suppresses the urge to pinch her. Here is that rarity in their neighborhood, a very eligible man — and four sisters at home to be provided for.

"I dare say you may find him very agreeable," she whispers once he has moved away again.

Elizabeth does not take the hint. And as the musicians prepare to play Sir Roger de Coverley, she moves away, her shoulders rigid and her chin lifted in challenge.

Charlotte finds a better place from which to watch the dancers. Ten years ago her invisibility had dismayed her, for she knew her duty, but how is a proper young lady to catch the eye of a potential husband while behaving with proper delicacy? A ball is supposed to produce a husband, but what if the gentlemen never look one's way? Perhaps Lydia, in chasing after the young men, had it right after all, in spite of the whispers always trailing after her. Time would tell.

Charlotte moves along the perimeter, the hem of her flounce brushing the spindle legs of the many empty chairs awaiting flushed and overheated dancers. It is sometimes a secret relief to be effectively invisible, for Charlotte can entertain herself by examining how the room—rooms, two formal drawing rooms opening into one another—are furnished. Everything is new, evidence of much money but little thought. How delightful it would be to furnish a house to one's own taste! How enjoyable to oversee all the details of such a gathering, without the worry and fatigue of catching the roving, restless eye of some young man!

A large figure approaches, and to Charlotte's surprise, Mr. Collins bows to her. "I trust," he says, "you enjoy tripping with the nymph Terpsichore?"

"Thank you, Mr. Collins," Charlotte replies—having learned as a child that men will hear pretty much what they wish to hear. She wonders if he wishes to be congratulated for his reference to Mr. Dibden's *Ode*, but she has never made any pretense to wit.

So she says nothing more, and as expected, he turns his gaze outward, taking her assent for granted. "Mine is an entirely charitable intent," he states. "One might say a happy one, which is to honor my cousin exclusively with my attention, having gained the permission, and perhaps I may add the encouragement, from her excellent mother, Mrs. Bennet."

Charlotte curtseys slightly in acknowledgement of his words, as at one end of the long chamber, Mrs. Bennet's shrill tones rise above the general hubbub. At the other end, Lydia's equally shrill giggle rings as she and Mr. Denny romp down the line, his epaulets dancing on his shoulders.

"My excellent patroness, Lady Catherine de Bourgh, recommended specifically that I apply myself in this manner, as young ladies are all partial to such exercise," Mr. Collins states instructively. "Or, all who enjoy excellent health, which I cannot, alas, attest to in the case of Lady Catherine's daughter, the Honorable Miss de Bourgh."

Charlotte had never heard anyone actually speak the designation 'Honorable' before; she recollected when her mother looked out the etiquette of honorifics, after Father was awarded his knighthood, and discovered to prodigious disappointment that none of her children were entitled to it even in writing. Unless Mr. Collins means honorable as an adjective?

"Pray, what is Miss de Bourgh's ailment?" Charlotte asks, as the gentleman seems to want to talk about this family unknown to anyone in Meryton. "I hope it is nothing serious."

The flash of white muslin catches Charlotte's attention. Here is Elizabeth dancing down the line, her back straight and her neck arched. Charlotte knows that look: something has put Elizabeth in a pelter. Useless to remind her, whose wits are customarily so quick, what she owes her family. So odd. Elizabeth is not usually a quarrelsome girl—a miracle in that family—and yet it seems she must seek reasons to dislike the most eligible single man to come into the neighborhood in either of their lives.

"Miss de Bourgh is delicate in constitution, quite delicate," Mr. Collins states with evident pleasure in confiding these details. "The case quite confounds the faculty, I may say. Lady Catherine, I hasten to assure you, serves as an example to all as the epitome of a cautious, careful parent. Nothing is too small to be noticed, no detail too trifling. A physician drives out at least once a week to call upon them both, and Lady Catherine sees to it that Miss de Bourgh takes all prescribed medicines, keeps her out of dangerous airs, and is known to send meals back twice, even thrice, if everything is not prepared to her satisfaction . . ."

As Mr. Collins goes on to illustrate, with apparent satisfaction, a life that sounds, as Elizabeth would say, confoundedly crib'd and confin'd, Charlotte listens in mounting pity for this unknown young lady. Does she have no true friend?

"But I digress," Mr. Collins says, when he has finished describing each dish and remove at the dinner his patroness had invited him to the evening before his departure for Longbourn. "My mind is currently preoccupied with Hymen's saffron robe, as the excellent Milton put it so well, for Lady Catherine was good enough to advise me that what a gentleman in my station in life requires is a wife who is a thrifty manager as well as an example to the parish."

Charlotte suppresses a sigh. That does not describe Elizabeth. She is an excellent friend, lively and witty, but alas no thrifty manager. As for an example to the parish, while there is absolutely nothing to be said against Elizabeth's morals or manners (as there might be said about Lydia, for example), Charlotte could think of fewer young ladies within her admittedly circumscribed acquaintance who would wish less the position of clergyman's wife. *Whereas I am an excellent manager*, she reflects as Mr. Collins goes on to describe, in detail, the mythical wife this Lady Catherine has extolled.

No, the sort of man Elizabeth ought to be matched with is giving her hands across at this moment, as Lizzy turns her gaze the other way.

How could Elizabeth dance in this room full of officers and not reflect that the sword and rifle are confined to their hands, as is the law to their solicitor brothers, and even Holy Word interpreted through their cousins in the clergy? The ordering of the world truly lies in male hands. Unless a woman is to dwindle to what amounts to a well-dressed servant to her brother's wife, she must needs secure the means to preside over a household of her own, even if she cannot own it.

The music begins drawing to a close. Mr. Collins bows, saying,

"I must discover who that gentleman is, and whether he is married."

He marches away as Elizabeth crosses the room from the opposite direction. She goes to Miss Bennet's side, no doubt seeking the sympathy she is certain to get. Miss Jane Bennet can be trusted for that. She can also be trusted to make a good marriage whenever she chooses to bestir herself. Whenever men see her, they seldom notice anyone else in the room — and so it is with their host, Mr. Bingley.

He appears at Jane's other side, causing Elizabeth to excuse herself and look around. When it comes to a sister, Charlotte thinks as she sets out to meet her, Elizabeth knows well what to do.

Charlotte prefaces the sensible remarks she has been considering by saying, "Was your partner pleasant after all?"

Elizabeth's expressive brows meet, but before she can speak, a heavy tread and an equally heavy scent of pomade presages the reappearance of Mr. Collins.

He exclaims warmly, "I have this moment made a most important discovery!"

As he speaks, Elizabeth's eyes widen in horror, and she earnestly, then passionately, attempts to talk Mr. Collins out of introducing himself to Mr. Darcy on behalf of Lady Catherine de Bourgh. The more determined the lady is to carry her point, the more stubborn the gentleman becomes. Charlotte tries to get a suggestion in, but in hearing how determined Mr. Collins is to gainsay Elizabeth, gives it up.

It's a shame. Charlotte suspects that Mr. Collins might very well give in if Elizabeth took a little extra care to word her response so that he would believe it was all his own idea — exactly as Mother does with Father. But instead, each vies to carry their point, until Mr. Collins goes off to address Mr. Darcy, Elizabeth gazing after, and coloring when Mr. Darcy's lip curls with contempt.

Mr. Collins is soon back, complacent with what he imagines as success. As he describes that success, it strikes Charlotte that such an unobservant gentleman would be very easy to manage —

"Are you finished?" someone asks behind me, then the door closes again.

Somewhere a grandfather clock bongs. I don't count them, except to note that there are more than one. But it feels as if I've been or watching — or living — that virtual Netherfield Ball for five minutes.

I gasp, finding myself sitting before the now dark tablet as I blink against the garish light of the real world. I have to know more.

I open the interview room door and go into the hallway, where I find the the vaguely familiar woman I first interviewed with — but she looks different. More distinct, somehow: round face, prim lips, shorter than I, round of form. I notice her clothes for the first time, a long empire-waisted summery dress, and she wears a lace cap on her head. I didn't remember noticing that. It makes me wonder if she's doing some theater gig, or going to a theme party.

"I have *a lot* of questions," I say in my best professional interview voice. "Beginning with, what about those benefits mentioned in the advertisement."

"Benefits," she repeats, and gives me a thin smile, her light brown brows slightly raised. She extends a hand. "Pray step this way." I notice then that her accent is English.

She goes before me. I notice that her gown is laced up the back, and it looks as if it's made out of muslin. Also, there are lines under the gown across her shoulder blades, as if she wears stays.

I'm sufficiently distracted by her clothes to not pay much attention when she opens a door and steps through into what appears to be a tiled garden. I follow her, watching warily in all directions. I kept arm's distance behind her as the door swings shut behind me.

We walk around the ivy-colored side of the house to . . .

A street of shops, picturesque as all get-out. The gold stenciled lettering in the glass window of a shop states: *Meryton Apothecary*.

Meryton?

How could there possibly be a *Pride and Prejudice* film being shot in the middle of New York City, and I hadn't known about it?

She turns my way. "Here is an example of the promised benefits. Enjoy yourself. Until you are written in, no one can see you," she adds as a couple of guys in tight pale-colored pants and even tighter blue coats curving over their hips to tails saunter by. They ignore us, but lift curly-brimmed hats to girls in high-waisted gowns, bonnets, and shawls, who trip on the other side of the street, holding their muslin hems expertly above the cobblestoned street.

I snap my gaze back to my guide. Now I recognize her. She's a 3-D, color version of the drawing of Jane Austen that's been reproduced on the fronts and backs of a zillion books, and even more sites all over the Net.

I gawk at her, thinking:

1. I have gone insane.

2. Jane Austen could not possibly be a) alive, and b) tootling about in a town she had made entirely up.

As usual, my brain snags onto what it could deal with. "Meryton doesn't exist."

"As you see," she says, "it does. Here. Built by a vast number of minds over all the years since Miss Cassandra Austen argued for how the streets must lie."

My mind reels into paradigm shift. "You're talking mass hallucination . . . collective memory creation?"

"Define it however it pleases you," she says, and flicks her fan open, taking in the entire street with an expert gesture. "Here it is."

I turn in a slow circle, taking in the ivy twining up weather-worn brick walls, iron railings, resin-covered torch sconces on buildings cornering the crossroads, chickens cackling in a tiny pen between the bookseller and the apothecary.

It's as real as the woman standing next to me, her lips pressed together thinly, maybe to hide her teeth, or maybe because it wasn't polite back then to flash your pearlies constantly the way Americans do. I don't bother asking her if she's Jane Austen. I've been to too many Renaissance Faires and reenactments wherein characters insist on staying in period character no matter what questions you ask. Somebody who could wear stays under an obviously hand-made gown (I can see the slightly uneven stitching at the top of her near shoulder) is being Jane Austen with all her might. However one defines "being."

"Who is doing this?" I ask.

"Everyone."

But it's far too . . . real. Surely "everyone" in my time would create a Hollywood backdrop sort of Meryton: there certainly wouldn't be that church steeple, for example, and those young ladies at the other end of the street would be sashaying about with no hats or gloves, calling each other by their first names and bamming each other and making cakes of themselves in a mix of Americanese and Heyer-speak.

Unless she means everyone from as far back as Austen's time —

"When you wish to return, open any door, think of the library, and step inside," she says.

She suits action to the words, opens a slatted door in the side of a fence, and is gone, leaving me behind.

I could follow, but I hesitate. Whoever she is, one thing for sure: she's crap at answering questions.

So I'd answer a few myself. Like how big this place is, and if it's really some kind of dream version of P&P, where in the story I might find myself.

Therefore? First thing to do, set out for Longbourn. I recollected reading somewhere that someone used to triangulating spies from radio transmissions had for fun worked out that Longbourn lay to the south of Meryton. So I glance up at the sun to orient myself, then think: what day is this, really? What year?

A team and curricle clop and jingle by, the horses' ears

forward as if I were invisible, and the red-faced driver oblivious to me standing there in my wrinkled interview outfit. I wonder if there are watchers watching me, then I remember I'm not written in yet, whatever that means.

So am I not real while I'm standing here? I don't know what's real anymore.

When I open my eyes, my gaze catches on five female figures some distance down the south path. I run a little, hearing my footfalls crunching on the ground. I pause to look down, and see my footprints, but my toes no longer hurt though the road is rutted and uneven with tufts of cat's ear and yarrow, which leads me to think of thousands, millions of readers envisioning that mile and the five sisters walking along it.

I bend down and stare at clover, pebbles, seed husks, and a tiny trail of ants wending slowly into a patch of ground elder. Perhaps English minds of Austen's time, familiar with the Shropshire countryside, imagined the details. But that argues for imagination lasting beyond their lifetimes . . .

I look ahead at the five females, of course the Bennet sisters. Though I only see that distinctive high-waisted line with the shoulders pulled way in, the edge of their spencer jackets absurdly high, and the backs of bonnets, they could be no one else. The round-shouldered one walking sedately in the middle has to be Mary, the two on the right chattering, one kicking at rocks, Lydia and Kitty.

So the ones on the left must be Jane and Elizabeth, and I wonder what style of beauty the cumulative hallucination would assign Jane. But then maybe it all translates out into my head in terms familiar to me, in which case, is it possible I might see a face on her like Amanda Seyfried, whereas Japanese fans might envision Erika Sawajiri, and the patterns on the fabric of their gowns in plum blossoms?

A few words float back on the balmy, garden-scented air: assembly, shoe ornaments. Partners, dancing. I realize I'm more interested in the larger questions than in seeing the faces of a story

I know well, and the temptation is strong, nearly overwhelming, to abandon this road and seek Lucas Lodge, but what could I do there if I am invisible? *Not written in*, whatever that means?

The lure is so strong that I scan more slowly, and spot what I had nearly missed behind a tangle of flowering blackthorn and elm: a tumbledown thatch-roof cottage around the curve of a prettily overgrown lane. I tread that way, skirt a copse of trees, and spy a small barn next to the cottage.

Open a door, the Jane Austen reenactor said. Even though this is the weird zone, and I can't be seen, the notion of opening a door into someone's home makes me queasy, so I opt for testing the dilapidated barn first.

I put my hand to the door, thinking about that ballroom library, open it—and there, *Adjustment Bureau* style, is the ballroom with the books. The door snicks shut behind me and I lay my hands on the old, carved wood with acanthus leaves around the brass latch. I am beyond question. And yet there are so many questions.

My toes throb in time with the pang in my head as I make my way to the hall with the interview rooms, where I find Jen waiting.

There you are! What scenario did you get?"

"Jane Austen. *Pride and Prejudice*, Netherfield Ball. You?" I ask, still too overwhelmed to articulate my experience.

"I got Lord Grenville's ball," she says, and at my uncertain glance, she adds in an ambiguous tone, "*The Scarlet Pimpernel*."

I'm still trying to force myself back behind the bars of reality. "You don't sound as if you liked it."

"Oh, I liked it. It was . . . perfect." She breathes the word again, "Perfect." She closes her eyes for a long moment, then opens them, her voice wary and full of question as she says, "I take it you have some kind of connection with *Pride and Prejudice*?"

"Me and fifty billion other people, judging by all those spin-offs out in that ballroom," I say, sidestepping, but she doesn't smile.

She continues to study me. "You don't seem to want to

answer. Same reason you didn't tell me your name?"

"I didn't tell you my name because for a little while I can be anybody," I say recklessly, for I'm light-headed on top of the headache, partly from not having eaten all day, and my feet are throbbing worse than ever. "I don't have to be a randomly named Jane Doe found in a crack house before being funneled into the system. And yes, I'm grateful to be alive."

"I wasn't going to say that."

"It's a defensive response, trained over a lifetime. And I *am* grateful for what social security net we have, but you cannot force people into families. Especially if you take them out again after a year—" Far too bitter.

I force a shrug.

Why not answer your real question?

"Okay, I used to write fanfic, for an audience of maybe two. About the Lucas family. I've always gone for books about families. Made families, when the people choose one another, not assigned families, such as my string of foster homes. I know it's trite and sentimental, my point is, I got this sense that the virtual thing might go in the direction my stories did." I stop there—nobody has ever expressed any interest before, except of course to deliver a scornful opinion about fan fiction, and anyone who reads it.

"What direction is that?" you prompt.

"Charlotte makes friends with Anne de Bourgh, and rescues her from Lady Catherine's clutches," I admit. "She rescues Kitty Bennet, too, and . . . well, I know it's stupid, and definitely not canon—"

And you—yes, I'm writing this for you, Jen, who else would ever care? You say in a low, intense voice, "I've written fan fiction all my life. Reams of it. If you read 24/7 for long enough, some of it seems to start spilling out of you, and what else do I have to do?"

Then you whir your machine to jink sideways, and close the door to the interview room as you say, "There's always watching the tube, of course. And I did a lot of that when I was young, especially when recovering from surgery, and the pain meds made it difficult to read. I was maybe ten when I went through a box of my parents' old VCR tapes, and found the 1982 Scarlet Pimpernel production with Anthony Andrews and Jane Seymour. I binged it until the tape broke. By then I'd been allowed to check out library books from the adult side. One of my first selections was the Baroness's original tale, which I'd reread so many times by my thirteenth birthday that I pretty much had it memorized; when we were offered a foreign language in middle school, I chose French, and I devoured other fiction, and even nonfiction, if it was about personalities instead of politics, about the French Revolution in order to feed my brain about the principal figures in Paris at that time."

You see, I remember every word.

Then you sigh. "That's when I discovered Charlotte Corday. Another Charlotte! Have you ever noticed that the Charlottes are never the heroines, at most maybe sidekicks? Or victims?"

Of course I notice the invisible people of fiction, being nearly invisible myself.

"So little was written about Charlotte Corday, though she caused a major change in the politics of the Terror, that I had the freedom to write what I wanted about her. Gradually Charlotte replaced Marguerite as my first person heroine, the Pimpernel having saved her from the guillotine in the nick of time by substituting one of Fouché's dedicated mass murderers from the slaughter in the South of France. Marguerite and Charlotte became BFFs, and the Pimpernel saves them, and they him, as they go out to rescue people rich and poor alike from the mob."

You pause to check to see if I'm listening, and say, "By then I'd read enough to discover that the poor were just as targeted as the rich, maybe even more so, as there was no trial. If you sneezed and accidentally crossed yourself, as Catholics had been taught to do before the Revolution, and the wrong person saw it, you could be hanged from the nearest lamppost by the mob, and nobody would blink. It happened a lot, especially if you were wearing or carrying something that someone else wanted. I liked writing rescues of those people, and the defeat of Robespierre's bloody-minded Jacobins, one by one. In my stories, the League always met at Lord Grenville's ballroom, where the Terror would not be let past the door, after the single time Chauvelin got in. My longest novel was about Charlotte helping to bring down Fouché."

Did I get that right?

"My Revolutionary France was shaped by the BBC production, but by the time I'd been writing for years, it and the characters had evolved into their own selves. I didn't reread the book again until I was winding up the Fouché storyline, and for some reason I felt this urge to go back to the source, which I hadn't revisited since I was fourteen or so."

"Wait, was all this secret, or were you posting it?"

"Posting. And I'll get to that. First, the book. Whoa. As I said, I reread it after a bunch of years. The Suck Fairy had not just waved her wand over it, she had landed her army and set up camp. When you're fourteen, there is no such thing as bad writing. It never occurred to me just how terrible a writer Baroness Orczy was. Not only her up-your-nose bigotry and snobbery—the aristocrats all have innate grace, slender white limbs, and the phrase *noblesse oblige* is taken absolutely seriously—but the metric butt-ton of unexamined trite expressions, like 'the proverbial wet blanket,' merely call attention to an overused, uninteresting simile by forcing the reader to break the fourth wall long enough to reflect on how there are no actual proverbs about blankets, wet or dry. Suzanne looks at Sir Antony with 'unuttered hope' moments after she was uttering a whole lot of preposterous dialogue, some of which sounded hopeful as well as woeful and doleful and wimpy."

I nod. "I only read it once. It also has a really boring plot, as I recollect. The films do it better."

"Yes. It's clear that that novel began its life as a play, for it opens at an inn, where most of the main characters sit around telling each other long histories that you'd think they already know, and the clever," here she makes air quotes, "young bucks leading the League of the Scarlet Pimpernel manage not to see a spy climb directly under their table while they stand around gassing about their secret exploits in order to impress the gawking, admiring peasantry."

"That's what I remembered," I say, rolling my eyes.

"You laugh now. Well, I do, too. But at the time, I was angry — no, betrayed. All my rich inner images, the sense of high honor and heroism, the loyalty and tightly bonded friendship as well as romance that had pulled me through the sordid years of operations and tests and *we'll wait and see* while enduring the warehouse of public education where looks are everything. There wasn't much 'there' there in the book, just the kernel of an idea."

I say, "Yet that kernel has inspired a bunch of films."

"Yes! Films in nearly every decade of the twentieth century — in spite of the wars. That basic idea, badly written as it is, motivated others to transform it into a better story, a place your heart could inhabit though war was ripping apart the rest of the world. Leslie Howard's brilliant *Pimpernel Smith* not only raised hope during the darkness of World War II, but it inspired a Swedish diplomat to go out and save lives."

"I didn't know that," I say. You see, I remember everything, as this has become the most important conversation in my life.

"Because that story wasn't your passion, as it was, is, mine. Passion is the key. Fanfiction doesn't earn a penny. What I learned after tearing myself away from that incredibly detailed, I hate to say it, but *real*-seeming Lord Grenville's ball, was just how transformative that passion can be."

I open my mouth to tell you about my journey through the door to Meryton, but you have that thousand mile stare. "Okay, backtrack a little. Talk about stupid, I'll show you stupid."

"Nothing you've said so far sounds stupid to me," I say, but I don't think you even hear me. That's okay. I'm used to it.

You say, "I got better at writing, and kept posting, which grew me a larger and larger audience. At school and in the real world I was a social reject, or a pity target, but in the world of online fiction, I had a following. I floated in the clouds of creative success until the day I ego-searched not on my name, as usual, looking for reviews, but on my characters. And guess what. I discovered that there were a ton of fics out there using *my* characters, *my* situations, even some of the banter I'd worked so hard on, but making errors in fact and language. In other words, people were writing fics on my fic! I felt pretty much like Georgette Heyer did about her copycats, as if slugs had crawled over me. So I took my marbles and went home."

"I don't understand what's so bad about people writing fic based on your fan fiction. Isn't that the ultimate compliment?"

"Not when you've convinced yourself you own the characters, and your vision is the only one, and that those others are full of the sort of errors you really hate reading in other stuff."

"Oh," I say.

"What I saw in that virtual ballroom today was not a slavish reproduction of my vision, but a vision that transcended mine, and the Baroness's, and the Beeb's, and the films. And so I went out to look for Thomas, the guy who interviewed me. He told me all about what's going on here, which is basically that they're setting up a virtual world that maps what's stored in readers' memories. Kind of like a brain cloud."

Your tone goes from sardonic to tentative. As if you don't quite trust it, and I remember what you said about grace. "This is just a part of a larger project, for instance, science fiction. I know, right? Who could ever have guessed that a third-rate three seasons of solid cheese, called *Star Trek*, could inspire IDIC, infinite diversity, infinite combinations, another face of grace? But there's worlds of *Trek* fic out there, forty years of it, that does exactly that. They find the stories that inspire the most—eh, you have to have heard it all too, right? Where were you just now? Getting a tour upstairs?"

"Not quite." At last I tell you, and watch you go from surprise to wonder, and then comes the narrowed eyelid of question.

"Really." You breathe the word when I finish. "Really? Are you sure you aren't hallucinating? When did you eat last?"

And that's when I say, "I'm going back."

Until I said it, I hadn't meant to, but once the words were out, I know. "I'm going back through that door."

You don't argue. You stare at the door as you say, "Northrop Frye wrote that once the potential is perceived, the kerygmatic can be discerned in all literature everywhere."

"What does that mean?"

"I don't know," you say, "so I have to think around it. There's a quote from T.S. Eliot about listening to music so deeply that you become the music while it lasts. While it lasts, that's the main point. Writers have been debating for centuries about that moment when fiction so moves us that it sets up a card in our mental catalogue alongside actual experience. Liminality — equipoise — verisimilitude — truth — those terms crash around like crash test dummies in the critical debate. The French have their favorite theories, and Nabokov, excellent in a bunch of languages, found Russian to be the best for certain kinds of truth."

"Kind of what Tolkien talks about in 'On Fairy Stories'?"

"Yes. Truth written in the interstices of fiction. History and fiction, fact and faith are mirrors reflecting back and forth, and because of our limitations, we can only, oh," (you wave at the tablet lying there on the table) "dance the cotillion a step at a time. And yet, if enough of us are doing it, are we creating another world?"

I am suddenly reminded of my roommates, who are probably writing the Craigslist ad right now. We never became friends, but you spend three months around people and notice things, like how Parker tries to live through the twilight world of the theater, and even ferociously focused Megan has a single indulgence: reading XianXia and XuanHuan novels as often as she can get them, the longer the better.

It strikes me then that you haven't argued with me.

"If," I say, "people have been creating this world by two

centuries of love and passion and thousands of pages, then we can do anything. *Be* anything."

You nod very slowly. Tentatively. I take a breath, and ask the true question. "Are you coming?"

"No." You look away, and study that century-old wainscoting.

Then you say, "I've been disappointed too often to be anything but a skeptic. If what you say is real, and you're not schizo or lucid dreaming, what happens if the power goes out in this building? Does whatever lies behind that door vanish?"

"Not if we're in a brain cloud," I say, though my heart hammering against my ribs seems to beat out a rhythm to the words *don't know, don't know, don't know.* "But five minutes there felt more real to me than all these years here." I jerk my thumb outward, toward the street.

Somewhere that grandfather clock ticks, and I finally see the truth: of course you wouldn't go, even if you believed me. You're a maker, whereas at my best I was a dreamer.

You sigh and reach for the door. "There has to be a restroom here. Be right back."

You go out.

I look down at the tablet, thumb it to life, and there is an icon for dictation.

I tell you my story, starting with Megan waking me to the most important day of my life. As I try to make every word true, I wonder if you are deliberately dawdling because you don't want to see me go through the door and vanish—or if you suspect that if you try the door all you will see is coats and umbrellas.

Or you'll open the door to nothing but darkness.

But I believe you will come back to this room to see if I am here. I can even imagine what you're planning to say as a way of talking sense into me. But what you will find is this tablet, because I will be gone, leaving you this, the beginning of my story, in the hope you will write me into the world as it should be, and bring that world to life for others like me.

Call me Charlotte.

Dancing Bangles

Irene Radford

"*I* have the perfect solution, Trude!" Madame Magdala proclaimed, clapping her hands and bouncing up and down. Her fashionable blonde curls jostled, threatening to defy her orderly hairpins. "You shall go to the ball in my stead."

Trude suspected her sister's enthusiasm. As children, Elise—now the fashionable patroness of a salon on the edge of polite society and mistress of an international spy network—always led her younger sister and brothers into mischief, usually escaping without blame while the rest of them went without supper or had to sit for hours in the cold dairy barn, in winter on Lake Geneva, as punishment.

Now she billed herself as the bastard daughter of a Gypsy King—despite being fair of skin and hair—who conjured visions of the future in tea leaves or coffee grounds or somesuch.

Elise threw open the doors of her wardrobe and started hunting through the dozens of frothy gowns.

"No," Trude said as firmly as she could. "I am a pirate. I captain a dirigible. I don't know how to dance. I'm too tall to be fashionable, my skin is sunburnt, and I refuse to wear dainty slippers." She gestured toward her thigh-high boots of heavy leather that hid numerous weapons tucked inside or built into the toes and heels. "I wear breeches and boots for a reason."

"You don't need to dance, there are paints for your complexion, and as for boots—nonsense. You clank with every step. I assure you there are plenty of hiding places for weapons in all of my gowns." She pulled forth a bright red contraption that promised to droop too low at the neckline and trip her at the hemline. "You are slighter than I, and a bit taller, so we won't have to lace your corset quite so tightly."

"Did you not hear me? I said no."

Elise studied her through narrowed eyes. "If not red. Perhaps blue." She continued digging through wafts of fabric hanging from hooks in her wardrobe. "As for your height—aren't the tribes from northern India quite tall? And your lack of girth..." She looked down at her comfortable plumpness. "It's surprising what can be accomplished with proper lacing of a corset."

"I do not own a corset and will not wear one." Trude braced herself for another argument. Puffed-up subordinate officers quailed when she took that stance. Chinese warlords and powerful Madames from Singapore were known to compromise when Trude Vollans, Captain of the *White Swan*, Queen of the Pirates, and therefore virtual monarch of the China seas, took that stance.

But not her older sister.

"I came to London to deal with my bankers and visit my sister, not attend balls and steal jewelry like any common cutpurse. I'm a pirate, and my dirigible needs a new boiler. I don't dance, I don't flirt, and I don't run your errands." She took her glower to a deeper, more piratical level.

"Nonsense. It's the only way to get that encoded piece of jewelry away from *his* current mistress. The Ottoman ambassador gave it to *him*, thinking he was still my lover, and he'd deliver it as directed. The ambassador and I cannot be seen together without suspicion. The bangles contain pertinent information about our foreign affairs. I don't know if *that man* is truly stupid, or playing a long game I haven't fathomed yet."

"Wait, are you saying that you are no longer Sir Andrew's mistress? I thought you two were one of the epic love stories of all time."

Elise's expression smoothed into a blank mask, betraying no emotion. How she schooled the fine lines around her eyes and mouth to flatten, Trude could not fathom.

"I was never Drew's mistress. We were lovers, yes. But I insisted upon supporting myself, owning and running my coffee shop and lending library on my own, and living in a suite above. He never supported me, though he asked many times. Now he has found a more pliable woman who curtsies to his demands."

Elise turned her back on Trude and fussed inside the wardrobe. Her back rippled with a convulsive sob, then she stiffened, set her shoulders and head proudly again before turning back with a pair of slippers that matched the ruby red gown. "You need the red. It will set off your dark hair and weathered complexion. It also has a matching gauze shawl, and the neckline is higher than the blue to disguise your lack of cleavage."

"Is *he* the reason you cannot accept the invitation to the ball? He will be there with his new woman?" Trude's voice softened in sympathy. She'd been betrayed by men as well. Elise was more emotional than herself and might not have the courage to follow through with her plan if she met Sir Drew again.

"I cannot go because I am a demimondaine, and Queen Victoria is scheduled to attend with Prince Albert of Saxe-Coburg. They are rumored to be close to a betrothal. Though I have a slight acquaintance with Her Majesty, society demands that we not attend the same social functions. Besides, if Drew's woman loses a piece of jewelry while I am in attendance, I will be the first suspect."

"If you cannot go because you will offend polite society, I can't go either. There are more than a few warrants out for my arrest, most of them stemming from Hudson's Bay Company Directors. Some of those men will be in attendance."

"But Captain Trude Vollans will not attend. Maharani Rudée

will. If we use the red shawl as a veil, you can hide in plain sight. I hope you have not lost your pickpocket skills. The clasp on the bracelet might prove tricky to unlatch."

Trude looked at her callus-hardened hands and shook her head in doubt. As a child she had stolen sweet buns from the baker with ease. Now she stole beaver and otter pelts with loaded steam cannons.

"I think you should attend the ball, Elise, as the Maharani Rudée. You can spill some wine on milady's gown and steer her into a cloak room to sponge it off. I'll await you there and spirit away the bracelet you have removed with your more nimble fingers. I'll dress as your maid so I don't have to wear the corset . . ."

"These shoes should come close to fitting you."

৩৫৩৫৩

Trude squirmed beneath the restrictions of the corset. She couldn't draw a breath or twist without turning her entire body. To distract herself from the discomfort, she looked askance at the brilliant gas lamps lighting the exterior of Trevalyne Place, a palace known for backroom political maneuvering. So much for sneaking into the ball. Not a single portal or hatch sank into shadows. This was how she would arrange for a private ball to remain private and free of thieves and scoundrels and lesser folk who just wanted to see what a real ball was like.

"Here's the printed invitation. Make certain you hold it so your fingers cover my name. And don't take your gloves off. You must wear them the entire time you are in view. High society folk don't touch one another's skin unless they are related."

Trude grumbled curses in an obscure Indonesian dialect she was certain her sister had not learned. Yet. "You look like a governess in your high-necked black bombazine. Surely you can stay by my side as a proper chaperone."

"Nonsense. I'll go around to the servants' entrance and be

ready to receive the bracelet. You'll do fine. Just keep your English proper with a refined accent and don't let your veil slip. The diamond necklace as a form of tiara to keep the gauze in place was an inspired idea. The pendant centered on your forehead hides the lack of a caste mark and draws attention away from the shape of your face and the length of your nose, both remarkable and memorable."

"If I didn't know you better, I'd accuse you of taking up my profession."

Trude still didn't like the notion of invading this party just to steal a bauble. No, a bangle. The bracelet had been described as a four-strand plait of silver wires with a dozen tiny charms dangling from it. The placement of the bangles and the jewels that decorated them was supposed to be the code. Elise needed the bracelet open and stretched out flat to determine the proper order of the words.

With a deep breath for courage—as if ready to fire the first volley in battle—Trude exited the carriage without waiting for the footman to offer her assistance or even to lower the steps. Of course, the delicate red slippers that sparkled with iridescent beading came close to landing in a puddle. She neatly avoided the mud as she would a tricky course through the lesser islands of Indonesia.

Then she set her chin and firmly walked forward, imagining a plank beneath her feet and shark-infested waters beneath.

Ahead of and behind the hired carriage drawn by real horses, not the unreliable steam-powered beasts, petulant ladies whined and demanded to be carried across the puddles by men wearing real footwear—boots.

Damnation! She wanted her boots and the sixteen weapons she could secrete in them.

The elite of London society couldn't be any worse than the Chinese Warlord who had controlled the biggest network of white slavers in Asia, until she'd shot him, cowering in his bed with a ten-year-old girl from Madras.

With that image firmly in mind, she paraded up the entry stairs and presented her invitation to the liveried footman. Automata could not read, so this man had to be human. Then she whisked it out of his hands before he had time to see more than the engraved letterhead.

At the top of the interior staircase, Lord Richard and Lady Trevalyne greeted a thinning line of arriving guests. Most of the invitees were already in the ballroom. From the sound of shuffling feet and vibrant strains of music, Trude guessed she'd arrived fashionably late. She dipped her head at the host and hostess. A Maharani outranked a baron, so she needn't curtsey. Not that she thought she could perform one with anything resembling grace.

"I am the Maharani Rudée, a guest of Sir Barclay, Baron of Barclay Hall," she explained. "The *banker*." She named her own financial advisor, as much a pirate as she, knowing he controlled enough other people's wealth to break every lord and lady attending the ball.

They passed her on to a footman with some haste, as if uncertain of how to deal with her, but unwilling to upset her sponsor.

The footman, in a more elaborate red and gold livery than the first one, directed her toward the ballroom entrance several steps down the corridor.

Trude paused at the top of the three steps leading down to the massive ballroom, surveying the crowd.

"Interesting disguise, Elise," a gentle, male voice whispered into Trude's ear. "The veil is a stroke of genius, and the black wig. Better than your usual effort of grime and tawdry beggar clothes."

"I am not . . ." Trude started to protest, then assumed a posture of indignation. She'd learn more about her quarry, and her sister, by maintaining silence than pridefully protesting.

"Last time I saw that gown, I was removing it from your lush body. I must say it does become you, but I'm surprised you can breathe. You appear three stone smaller. You must miss me terribly if you can't eat your own marvelous sticky buns."

She raked him with her gaze from fashionably arranged dark blond hair, square chin, and height equal to her own. Ah, so this must be the infamous Sir Drew.

"Miss you? Hardly. I have been too busy straightening out the messes you helped make." She didn't know what adventure had led to his dismissal. But knowing her sister and suspecting this man incapable of cleaning up his own messes—like any man— there had to be a scandal brewing. "If you do not wish a broadsheet published *detailing* your messes, I suggest you do not speak of a previous acquaintance with me. Madame Magdala knows all." She dropped her voice an octave to give it a darker, and more menacing tone.

He turned abruptly away from her. Then swung back, a sneer marring his handsome face. "Your Highness, Maharani Rudée, may I present Lady Michael Greyfalls." He bowed to a simpering teenager in a pale lilac gown with a cloud of lace as fine as cobwebs.

Lady *Michael*. So, she took her title from her husband and therefore had none of her own. Judging from her youth, she must have been married off to a much older man, either trading her dowry for his second son's title, or him rescuing her bankrupt family. Then she'd taken a virile lover shortly thereafter because Lord Michael was a countrified bore, or impotent and in need of an heir. Even second sons needed heirs, especially if the first son had no children.

Trude preferred to make her own money—and she had made lots of it over the years of raiding furs, and later grain, from the Hudson's Bay Company. She'd never be dependent upon any man. None of them could be trusted to keep a bargain. She'd learned that the hard way.

"It is an honor, Your Highness." Lady Michael dipped a hasty curtsy, her attention already wandering to the ballroom. "They are playing a waltz, Sir Andrew," she hissed at the baronet, tugging his sleeve. She draped her arm on him possessively, displaying a bracelet full of bright bangles: Turkish worked silver with charms depicting splendid mosques, lockets, and semi-precious stones caged within more silver wire.

"Like it?" Lady Michael asked, shaking her wrist so that the bangles rang prettily. "I hear Queen Victoria has developed a fascination with bangles. And she may arrive later." The girl tossed her head in imagined triumph.

"My dear, I believe this waltz is the latest music from Vienna. Will you do me the honor?" Sir Andrew held out his arm. "Excuse us, Your Highness." He dipped his head to Trude. "Love the gown." His lazy smile suggested fond memories of the last time he'd seen it.

Trude nodded her head as regally as she could manage without dislodging everything.

"Next time, remember that Indian women are rarely taller than a mouse and never allowed out on their own." Sir Drew retreated with his new lover to the safety of a waltz.

"You haven't met some of the bloodthirsty warlord princesses that I have," Trude muttered to herself, trying to find an epithet vile enough to describe him.

A crystal champagne flute slid forward from the wall on a platter, pushed by a mechanical arm. When it was exactly in place, another mechanical arm, holding the wine bottle, poured a precise amount of champagne into the glass and retreated into the wall. "Smart." She admired the engineering of the device. "But how many men did it put out of work?"

She took the glass from the platform and raised it to her mouth. Then she had to figure out how to drink the sparkling wine without removing the damned veil.

In the end, she sipped the champagne through the gauzy fabric rather than chance being seen and recognized. She'd seen enough shipping magnates in the company of Sir Barclay to know that at least a few of them had suffered losses at the hands of Trude Vollans, Captain of the *White Swan*.

She should communicate with Sir Barclay at least. That would allow her to keep Lady Michael in view.

Her prey flitted from partner to partner on the dance floor, laughing gaily and flashing her unique bracelet as often as possible. An easy target. Lady Michael announced quite loudly to a bevy of twittering girls waiting to dance, "I saw it in the drawer of Sir Andrew's desk, in his private study, and just knew he'd bought it for me. I had to have it right then and there, and not wait for him to present it to me."

How crass. And what was she doing rummaging through his desk in his *private* study?

That would explain why he had diverted the direction of vital information. Or had he merely taken advantage of the situation to spite Elise? Maybe she would get the bracelet eventually. Maybe she wouldn't.

Trude knew how to stalk her prey until they presented a vulnerable broadside. The trick was to stay below, behind, and to starboard, the blind spot of most Hudson's Bay sky barges being towed by clumsy, underpowered dirigibles.

She waved her fan at her banker. He broke off a conversation with three men who appeared to have more money than sense.

"So kind of you to sponsor me tonight, Sir Barclay," Trude said as he approached her from an oblique angle, in her peripheral vision but more casual than a formal introduction.

"Your Highness." He bowed, eyes peering upward so that he never lost sight of her expression or posture. Then he smiled with recognition. "Or is it Captain?"

She acknowledged his assumption and proceeded toward a potted tree next to the French doors leading to a balcony. The doors stood comfortably ajar to admit a breath of cool evening air as well as to invite private assignations.

"A pleasure to have the company of a client with investments as extensive as yours." He bowed slightly. "Though I would appreciate it, Captain, if you did not steal from my friends tonight," Sir Barclay whispered.

"I have no intention to *steal* anything tonight. But I will borrow something from a foreign spy for a bit." She turned a falsely pleasant smile on him. "I do not wish the agent to know that I have perused essential information."

"Foreign intrigue? How delicious. If the agent knows that you, or your sister, has intercepted the information, he might change his plans. May I help?"

"There will be no glory in this night's work. If it is to succeed, no one will know it ever happened."

"As it should be, my dear Captain. I fought Napoleon in my youth. It is my duty to continue the battle if I must."

"Very well. Do you know the lady currently dancing with Sir Andrew Fitz-Andrew?" She nodded toward the swath of lilac fabric and tipsy giggles. Those mechanical wine dispensers were proving dangerous. Good human servants knew when to pretend not to see requests for more wine from those who had already partaken of too much.

"Unfortunately, I have had to manage her father's overdraft for many years. Her marriage to Lord Michael, which brought a very large marriage portion, was a desperate effort to get an heir on her when he'd rather spend his time with young men. The plot is doomed to failure."

"Unless she produces that heir with the aid of a different man?" Trude added. "Does Sir Andrew at least resemble the husband in height and coloring?"

"No." He frowned in thought, then his face brightened, and his charming smile spread. "But I do. I believe we must aid Lady Michael in her quest to get an heir for her husband, and thus save her family from bankruptcy and his from losing title and honors for lack of a successor."

Bartered Bride, Trude thought. *Bought and sold on the open market. Call it what it is.*

"I need the code embedded in her bracelet," Trude confided.

"The loss of such an unusual gift might drive a wedge between her and her current inamorato." His grin grew.

"The bracelet was intended for another and then diverted out of spite."

"I believe the music is ending. It is time I claimed a dance with the daughter of an old acquaintance. Be ready when I steer her in this direction." The banker strode off, twisting the ends of his distinguished mustache.

"It takes a pirate to aide a pirate," she muttered to herself.

Trude watched Sir Barclay bow with a sophisticated grace that made Sir Drew look like a countrified oaf.

Lady Michael giggled behind her fan and accepted his proffered arm for a lively polka, a very new offering from Vienna. Sir Drew shot Trude a suspicious glance then stalked to the sidelines to flirt with one of the dowager chaperones.

Sir Barclay bounced around the ballroom like a man half his age. As he led his partner in a wide circuit, Trude edged toward the half open door and gathered the ends of the veil. Her sister had wisely had the hem weighted with tiny glass beads to give it a consistent drape — turn it into an unexpected weapon.

Sir Barclay pranced closer. Lady Michael flushed and panted, working too hard to keep up with a man as old as her father. Champagne tended to creep up on those unused to the effects.

Trude opened the French doors another inch, offering a cool respite.

Lady Michael broke her hold, gasping.

Trude turned sharply, letting the veil fly outward.

The red gauze snagged the bracelet. Lady Michael didn't seem to notice as she gazed up into Sir Barclay's entrancing eyes.

Then Lady Michael broke the intimate moment by looking away and fanning herself vigorously. Sir Barclay smiled and whisked her away again, before she could notice her bracelet dangling from the veil.

Trude faded behind the potted tree and thence into a back corridor. At the third door on the left, a shapely, long-fingered white hand snaked out from behind the open door and drew her inward.

Elise unsnagged the bracelet from the veil, taking care not to pull any threads. "I want to wear that gown and shawl again," she answered her sister's unasked question.

"What does the message say?" Trude asked from a post by the door where she kept an eye on the corridor for signs of pursuit.

"Give me a minute," Elise protested.

First, she retrieved a tiny scroll of paper from her substantial cleavage and laid it flat on the desk beneath a bright gas lamp. The bracelet came next, stretched out at the base of the paper. She shifted both scroll and jewelry until the silverwork lined up with a series of strange markings on the document.

A moment of close study, and Elise attacked the charms. She unscrewed the body of a miniature mosque and retrieved another tiny square of paper from it. Then she reassembled the charm. The silver cage of a green agate flattened into the shape of some Arabic lettering when separated from the stone. The bracelet coughed up six more clues before Madame Magdala, the spymistress, nodded and smiled.

"What does it say?" Trude asked anxiously. She heard a fuss erupting in the ballroom, punctuated by a high-pitched squeal. "Lady Michael is staging a fit of hysteria."

"I believe the phrases in three different languages say: THE FRENCH MUST WITHOLD THEIR DEMANDS TO CHANGE CUSTODY OF HOLY PILGRIM SITES FROM GREEK OTHORDOX TO CATHOLIC."

Trude knew more about Asian politics than European, but this sounded ominous. "What does that mean?" Trude asked upon a whisper.

"It means that Russia will use such a change as an excuse to invade the Ottomans and eliminate their influence in the Holy Land as well as the Balkans. The Russian Tsar sees himself as the *only* monarch with a God-given right to rule that area. The Ottoman Emperor is a stinging fly in his backside," Elise said. "Such fools these men are, all for the sake of empire."

"That's what they want you to think." Trude bit back a Mandarin curse. "Russia *needs* a year-round sea port. That means the Balkans have to fall to them. Through the Ottomans if necessary. They'll spout a Holy Crusade to rally the people and the Orthodox Patriarchs, but it is all truly to secure a port in the Crimea. They'll go to war eventually."

"But England needs time before they can commit to her allies—both France and the Ottomans," Elise mused. "Victoria is too new as a monarch. Her Prime Minister and his government need to stabilize, as well as secure resources before going to war."

She tucked three tiny pieces of paper liberated from the charms into a secret pocket in the side seam of her bodice.

"A few whispers in the right ears will delay this war. That is the best I can hope for. I can create delay, but I doubt I can stop a war of this magnitude."

"Does Sir Andrew want a war?" Trude asked, trying to follow the threads of this plot and finding many of them missing, or knotted.

Elise bit the insides of her cheeks. Tears glistened in her eyes. "Quite possibly he does. I know he speculates in arms development. He could make three fortunes in a short period of time." She firmed her back and her chin, handing the bracelet back to her sister.

"I know some of those developers and dealers in arms. They will listen to rumors that one speculator is unreliable. Or perhaps owes his banker more than he is worth."

"Truth?" Elise gaped at her sister.

"I know whom to make it true."

"You make as excellent a spymistress as myself."

Trude frowned at her sister and shook her head, negating the statement. She also dislodged the diadem atop the veil and had to right them.

"Lady Michael is becoming anxious. I must return the bracelet to her before Lady Tevalyne dispatches a dozen footmen to find the lost trinket and arrest the thief."

"Return it. And wish her well of her new benefactor." Elise curled her upper lip in contempt. "I dismissed him because I could not trust him."

Trude lifted an eyebrow as she made certain both the veil and her gown were straight.

"He knew. If he is close enough to the Ottoman ambassador to be trusted as courier, then he had to know that those bangles carried an important message, and Drew diverted it. I was right to dismiss him."

Trude hid her smile behind another veil adjustment and resetting the diadem.

Back in the ballroom, she spotted the panicking lady amongst a circle of gentlemen, eager to soothe her while her protector hung on the edge of the crowd chewing his lip. If looks could kill, Sir Barclay was in serious danger.

"My lady." Trude elbowed aside three gentlemen, including Sir Barclay, to reach her objective. "I saw you wearing this earlier. It was on the floor over by the French doors." She draped the bracelet over the girl's arm and retreated, making sure she stood between Sir Drew and the banker, a tiny stiletto she'd retrieved from her bodice pressed against Sir Drew's ribs.

"Elise? You wouldn't," he hissed.

"I'm not Elise. Nor am I Madame Magdala. I'm a pirate, and I have no qualms about spilling your blood. Speak of my presence now, and you lose a vital organ. Speak of it tomorrow, and you will find your scandals spreading through London faster than the Great Fire." She didn't mention her plans about giving him the appearance of bankruptcy.

Sir Barclay fastened the bracelet clasp for the lady. He, not Sir Drew, escorted her to the nearest champagne dispenser.

Trude smiled and withdrew the stiletto. A flick of her wrist sent a footman scurrying for her carriage.

"A job well done, sister," Elise said as Trude settled into the conveyance.

"A job I will never do again." She removed the ill-fitting slippers and dumped them in her sister's lap, followed by the veil. The diamond necklace she kept. Then she set about loosening the corset. "Where are my boots? I will be aloft and halfway to China by dawn."

She searched beneath the seat of the carriage and came up with boots, trousers, and a loose linen shirt. Ah, comfort and protection.

"I will need you to take a message to some agents in Byzantium and Jerusalem," Elise said. "You'll know which banker to draw into our plot. You have time to write a letter before you depart."

"No. I am not one of your agents, or your messenger service."

"Of course you aren't," Elise said, handing her two envelopes.

A Plague of Dancers

Gillian Polack

"Stop jostling," Robert grumbled. "She'll be here soon enough."

"I can't see past your big country shoulders," Margery complained. "How can I see the train if you're in my way?"

The fact that Margery had washing-strengthened muscle and ate the good food of both castle and farm was irrelevant at that moment. Robert was certainly bigger, and he was the only one of the young people standing in her line of sight. Adam would have been in her line of sight intentionally, and she would have followed her usual custom of standing on his toes as hard as she could, but Adam was flirting with every young lady he could find. It had been a scarce winter and spring, and this summer he was ready for romance.

Besides, Margery wanted an excuse to nudge Robert, which she would not normally do in church. She didn't have the excuse that most of the others had, of making sure he knew they wanted to negotiate for his woodwork skills, but she was still bent on catching Robert's eye and bumping into him "by mistake." The two knew they'd get married in the usual way, when she was pregnant or both of them had enough money, but the church pretended not to know this, and so within those walls they both behaved as if they were innocent youth.

One effect from the many tragedies of the last year, they'd be married soon. Robert commanded extra wages and Margery was not only paid more, but was permitted to work almost anywhere. So many of their friends and neighbours had been lost that their lives were opening up sooner and more richly than they had expected. Good came from ill, sometimes.

She'd heard from travellers that not everyone was so fortunate. This made her very grateful for God's gifts and very determined to work hard for them. If there was a time in her life when Margery's true self showed, this was that moment.

Margery felt guilty at her relief at avoiding having children for a little while longer. She loved children and wanted a family and had been willing to force the new priest to marry them, as was customary, but to have time to set up a household was such a great and unexpected blessing. Margery looked around, guiltily, hoping no one had seen that she was happy. With all the loss, she should not be. From shore to shore people had died, said the first pedlar to appear after the crisis. No one knew how many were dead, but everyone who still lived had the blessing of God. It wasn't real happiness, she convinced herself. It was accepting small joys in a difficult year. With the blessing of God.

Father Matthew hadn't made an appearance yet, and Mass was probably going to be late. Margery knew that the fault for this was almost certainly Isabella. "Ma Dame" to Margery when she was at the castle. "Isabella" when something went wrong and one of them sought help from the other. Margery didn't mind working there, but calling Isabella "Ma Dame" was . . . odd. They'd hardly talked privately for years. Isabella was married and ran the castle and was very much "Ma Dame," no longer able to join most village pursuits. It still felt wrong to Margery. They had played together when Isabella had escaped her staff and sought a friend. It was always Margery she sought.

Everyone from home to the next market town knew Isabella

was going to wear the dress with the long train today. That meant full service of the best possible kind. The first in so very long. The priest knew it as well as the villagers. The church was bursting at the seams with visitors from any number of villages, and Margery would have laid a bet on Father Matthew peeking out from his room and waiting until the optimal moment.

Before that thought had completely left her mind, the lady herself appeared, walking past them all, three of her people holding the beautiful green train just off the ground until she reached her adult friends near the altar. Her adult friends were all tightly bound to the family and most were kin. "Near the altar," everyone called it, but it wasn't that close.

This was the signal for service to begin. Margery was certain that the lady intended walking in at that precise moment to make it seem as if she controlled church time. She surely didn't wear that dress just to provoke *that* sermon? The sermon that was delivered without fail whenever she wore a dress with a train. Adam might have intentionally provoked the priest. Isabella was more likely to set life up to revolve around her. Adam's provocation had targeted the previous priest, now Margery stopped to think about it. Isabella enjoyed setting herself against the new priest. He was old and wise, everyone said, and his sermons often told her how to do her duty. Isabella would provoke him whenever she could, for she held the land for God. Not for the priest.

Mass was everything it usually was. Always was. Margery didn't pay much attention. She was there for the sermon. It was the single big advantage their new priest presented, in her mind.

"A year ago," Father Matthew began, "the head of the northern church, our very own Archbishop Zouche, told us to beware the mortalities, pestilences and more. We have survived. On this feast of St John, we celebrate the Baptist and the ending of a quarter of the religious year. This year we celebrate something more: we celebrate God having granted us life."

Margery wanted to feel happy at this, but she couldn't. She

looked around the uncomfortably-full room. Margery could see almost everyone she knew from miles around. They should not be able to fit. Not even close. She had a future, but too many of her friends had gone on ahead.

"The Feast of St. John the Baptist, the very feast we celebrate today, is the day last year when the Great Mortality reached our shores, or so I am told. It is a time for quiet contemplation concerning the soul, of preparing ourselves for whatever comes next to inflict us, not for the wearing of . . . of . . ." The priest lost his words, trying to find a way of describing the horror that stood in front of him. He resorted to old thoughts, things he had said uncountable times. "The reason her ladyship needed three bearers to carry her train was because of the tiny devils cavorting on that train. Invisible to you, those devils are dancing as if their position in Hell depends on it. Holding onto her pride and rejoicing in it. Pride is a sin. Pride is one of the worst of the sins, and . . ." He lost it again. When he found more words, he finished quickly.

"Not as good as usual," said Robert, thoughtfully, when the service was over and they were outside, in the graveyard. "Although it's pleasant to know he knows we're dressing up again and celebrating being alive. Isabella did us all a great favour by wearing that dress today."

"He hates it," added Margery. "The dress and the happiness. He's a walking misery, that priest."

"Father Bob was kinder," agreed her love. Father Bob had died almost a year ago, of course, so it was safe to remember his kindness and very easy to dispose of the memory of his rages.

"Where's the dance?" asked Henry, who lived so far outside the village that he was often said to belong to the next one. With him was his sister, Catherine, almost jumping out of her skin with excitement.

"Here," said Robert, his arms taking in the whole of the churchyard, with its graves and its trees and its space. "To make it easier for the visitors."

"I'll spread the word." And Henry walked straight into the

crowd as if his soul were gone forever.

"Do we have enough musicians?" asked Margery.

"One to lead each trail of dancers. If most people stay, we might have long trails. I wish we could ask the musicians to play together or add a drummer to the rear of each group of dancers, but there are so many of us . . ."

"First dance since all the deaths. We need each other," commented Margery. "It's not going to be easy."

"It's not, but . . ." Robert put on his stalwart voice, "It's going to bring us all back into our world, and we'll be able to live again."

"Robert," interrupted William-the-Baker, "would you help me set up the crowd so that we look sociable and so that the priest and his people don't know what we're doing?"

William was very young to be a baker, but he was the only one of his family who had survived. He'd married, and his first child was on the way. This night was to be a charmed moment when he could be with his friends and pretend the world was not on his shoulders. His big shoulders. William was one of the shortest men in the village and one of the strongest. Not even Robert with his height and muscles could carry what William carried. Margery looked at William's flustered brown hair and thought of the burdens of St. Christopher. Christopher was a saint she never wanted to become, and it hurt her to see William with all his burdens.

"Weren't we going to wait until they were asleep?" Robert looked puzzled.

Margery lost patience with her stupid friends. "Don't they know anyway?" she asked sharply. Too much dwelling on what had changed for them, and each bit of dwelling hurt. She was determined to put it behind her. Be Adam, not Margery.

"Oh," said William.

"I'm not sure he can stop us tonight, even if we start earlier," Robert said, comfortably. "All the young people from all the parishes—we want to be here. And how many of us do what he says outside the church?"

The conversation moved on to something more important. "The drink?" asked Henry whose land was so close that he always looked harried when he came to church. Today was no exception.

"Hidden on the other side of the church. Not near your land, so you won't be blamed for it," Robert said. "Guarded. Leave it there. Ale and graves and merriment do not belong together, remember? Last time we brought ale into the churchyard, we all had to do penance."

All was ready. Everyone had brought bread and cheese and other portable food, and they sat in the churchyard, eating and drinking and pretending decorousness so that no one would throw them out too soon. It was a bonding time. The first time that so many of them had come together since all the deaths.

They didn't talk about the past, but they relished the company.

Adam spent this whole quiet time either mimicking the priest or mimicking Lady Isabella. As Isabella, he waddled with his shoulders pulled back. You could almost see the demons sitting on her train, trying to drag her backwards, head-first into Hell. None of them could actually see the demons, even on Isabella's actual train. Margery put her hand over her mouth, afraid to laugh. Imaginary demons waddling exactly like Adam waddled.

It was dusk, or thereabouts. No one checked on the priest or asked about the hour. The dance began when a musician was ready for it to begin. The crowd quietened to listen to the strings playing a carol. One at a time, two at a time, young people joined behind the musician, following where she led and tracing the rhythm of her strings with their feet. When the trail of dancers was so long that the music couldn't be heard, another musician sprang up and started playing the same tune, attracting his own line of dancers.

"It'll be slow dances all night," Margery commented to her companions. One of her hands was in Robert's and the other held Adam's. The dance was so gentle that conversation was simple. All she had to do was have her palm upwards and fingers gently curled for Adam and the other hand resting in Robert's.

"The price we pay for numbers and carols," Robert said.

Adam laughed. "We can always make it more interesting." He gambolled and frivolled and pretended the dance was one of those that were full of leaps, all the while keeping his hand in Margery's on one side and holding Catherine's hand on the other.

Robert was in that line, along with Henry and William. Isabella joined them quietly, just as soon as she'd come back from changing into a dress she could dance in.

"I thought you'd wear that dress and dance with the train in one hand or hooked into your girdle," said Margery, as they snaked past each other in a carol.

"Not tonight," Isabella answered. "Metal and my most expensive garment would have led to disaster, and honestly, that train is too heavy to hold in one hand. Besides, I wanted to show off that I have more dresses and I wanted to be able to enjoy the dance and I wanted . . ."

"To be able to play with your old friends as if the castle didn't exist," said Robert.

"It always existed," said Isabella, "but I'm to be married again soon and then all of this will be gone." Her arms spread to encompass not only the castle, but the village and her friends. Her land, her duties, her people.

"They found you a replacement?" Adam was looking for ways to tease the most important woman in the crowd, as if he had no interest and as if he had a chance. "What do you do to them all?"

"Just stop it, Adam," said Robert. What was funny over a year ago was no longer a joke.

"I can't hear the music above your chatter, you know," said Margery, and the lines continued to ambulate through the green grass more quietly, step after step of walking into a bright future.

After a few dances, Margery needed a break. The dancing was slow, but the paths were sometimes narrow. She'd kicked her right foot against a tombstone three times. Each time she'd muttered a "sorry" to the tombstone and kept dancing, but right now she needed a break. Her excuse (should anyone ask) was that her right shoe was rubbing against her little toe.

Margery wasn't the only one to stand watching. She found herself next to the priest.

"Father," she said politely and nodded her head.

"This will lead to woe," said Father Matthew, gloomily. He always said that. He'd come to them after all the deaths. For his sake as much as theirs, the archdeacon had explained. The young priest they were expecting had been sent to York, for the larger congregations had to be filled first and there weren't enough priests. The rumor from the castle was that they had a priest where others missed out because this priest was incapable of the pastoral side of his job. This was when Margery had discovered that the deaths weren't local. The whole of the north had suffered. Maybe even the whole of England. Margery joined in the laughter over the jokes played on him, but she also treated him as a lost soul.

"Don't stop it," said Margery, urgently. "We need it so."

"You need to dance your way to Hell?" The good father was perturbed. "I couldn't stop it last time. I wish I knew a way of stopping it this. I do not want to see another of my congregations doomed."

"Another?"

"Last year, on St John's Eve." That was all he said, as if she knew all. And she did.

"The coming of the illness. We are so few compared with then. It's . . . I'm glad we're through it." It was easy enough to dwell on in her mind, but Margery found words very difficult when the death of so many people she knew was the subject.

"Nothing," said the priest. "Pestilence is nothing. If I had to handle that, there would be time to give proper rites to most people, to send them to heaven. Dancing leads men and women straight to the Devil. I saw it. I was there. When I came here, that was all I could think of. Everything I do here is to prevent it happening again." He sounded so angry. She wondered if he even thought that God was listening. All he did was talk. Why was dancing such a problem?

"I cannot see it," said Margery, politely. She hoped her face didn't show that she thought he was a madman. Inside, however, she felt a despair. Ma Dame's train was one thing—this attack on their pleasures was something far more worrying. A priest who didn't allow his people to be human and to enjoy life would be a priest who led to despair, and despair now, when finally they were all pulling through, was inconceivably awful. At least he didn't pretend he could order them around. Something had cured him of that.

She saw that Father Matthew was watching her, not the dancers. The skin around his eyes crinkled sympathetically. She frowned, just a little, and this prompted him to speak.

"What happened to my congregation is not what you're thinking."

"I'm sorry," Margery said, and spread her hands to show she meant her apology. "There must be something I don't know."

"There was a dance," he said. "It began like this. Quiet. Refined, almost. I stayed indoors and rested, because I was called on at all hours. So many people. So much illness. So very many deaths. I will say, when I'm upset, that I gave everyone due time, but at the height of the trouble it wasn't possible to spend enough time with them to help them in their final steps. We dug big graves and lined up the bodies, with respect, and we prayed for them, and I prayed with as many as I could prior to their death. I was the last priest left in the town. Everyone received last rites. Everyone. So I slept when I could. I ate . . . sometimes."

"The night of the dance," he continued, his voice so solemn it invested the word "dance" with a feeling of death, "I had said farewell to three of my best congregants. Holy. Devout. Comforting. They all died in a single afternoon. I was alone."

"When the dance started, I was exhausted. I rested and, eventually, I fell asleep. I don't know how long I slept. Maybe hours. Maybe days. When I woke up, I didn't know how many services I had missed or how many people died alone."

The dance line Margery had left looped around on itself, and Adam tripped William. William fell and so did Isabella and Henry and Catherine. Adam bowed in charming un-apology, and Robert sent him to the back of the line, where he could cavort all he liked but was reduced to following.

"Right now," the priest said, quietly, "this is different. Or maybe it was the same at the beginning."

"At the beginning?"

"The beginning of the dance. When I woke up it was full night and St. John's Eve. I went outside to see why the music lingered. Half the town was still there, dancing as if there were no tomorrow. They had been taken by evil."

"Taken by evil?"

"Friends and family called their names, and the dancers did not hear them. Some were forced to drink water, but most danced and danced and danced without food or drink or rest. I called on them, on St. John, then on the Lord himself. No one listened.

"The musicians played and did not stop even though their fingers bled. The lines danced after them.

"When I pulled the musicians out, the dancers kept dancing. No music. Dancing. And dancing. And dancing. A line of unholiness that started on St. John's Eve. Three days they danced. Then some danced more. So many died. So many were injured." He drifted off.

Margery found her eyes telling history for him, replacing the people in front of them with the memory of the dead. Her deaths were not from dance, but her friends and family were still gone. Ghosts dancing on their own decaying bodies.

Margery's body froze. It felt as if the priest was sending the evil forth by watching the dance. Whether it could happen here or not, she had to do something. She kept her voice light, even as her hands clenched into fists.

"I wish my voice were louder," she said, ruefully. "We must make sure your dance of death doesn't happen here." She couldn't bear to see how much he hurt. And she had to prove to him and to herself that her people were not possessed. But the pestilence had changed her, and she no longer raced into crises or lost her calm over them.

She walked briskly up to Robert and moved her feet to the music to stand next to him. She told him what the priest had said, and he kept dancing. She told him what he should do. "Father Matthew needs it," she said. "He's hurt beyond anything I've seen. And we need it. To prove to ourselves that we're not possessed."

"Not for me to instruct the village, my love," he said, and kept dancing. "I know my place."

Margery stopped, and the dancers slowly swirled past. Her lips pressed together, bottling all the emotions that wanted to explode from her. Her feet were frozen with fear. She thought, "St. John's then and St. John's now. Maybe they will all die." Then she thought, *Too many are already dead. These are my friends and the rest of my life. I can prevent death and I can cure the priest.*

Margery shouted, "Quiet, everyone. Stop dancing. We need to talk. There's ale! You can dance afterwards. Quiet!" she shouted, "Stop dancing!" She heard her small voice fade against the night. She needed someone louder.

She asked Father Matthew if he would call out and stop everyone. "Just for a prayer," she suggested. "We need a prayer of thanks for being alive after this awful year."

The priest looked at her, his eyes bleak and his posture despairing. "I can't do anything," he said. "I tried last time and no one listened. It was just like you, shouting to the night. It won't work."

Isabella had taught Margery the perfect word for moments like this. "Damnedeus!" she said, as if she were swearing. Of course she wasn't. Calling on the Lord God was hardly offensive. It felt good. Very good. It emboldened her. She said it again, "Damnedeus!"

She tried talking to Adam the way she had with Robert.

"Get lost," he said, cheerfully.

There was a stick by one of the graves. She picked up it up and whacked Adam's knees with it.

Adam stopped dead in his tracks, pulling Robert out of place and stalling the line behind him. Margery grabbed his forearm and pulled him out. The dance continued without him, and Adam stomped heavily on the ground, letting his annoyance travel deep into the earth.

"You're treading on a grave," said Margery, amused at the place he chose to stomp.

"Well don't do that," he said, irritated. "Don't whack me when I'm dancing. I didn't hurt anyone when I tripped William, you know. You don't need to revenge yourself. Besides, Robert wasn't affected —"

"I know," she said, "But I need you. And Isabella. How do I get Isabella? You can do something wicked, you know, just as long as the priest doesn't see it."

"Easy," said Adam. "And I shall fulfil a dear, dear dream."

He went up to Isabella in the dance, just as Margery had with Robert. Instead of talking, he edged closer and closer until he was touching her. He kissed her, then danced away, out of reach. Isabella dropped her dance companions and chased him, furious.

When Isabella had calmed down, Margery explained the problem. Isabella only half believed her. "I shall talk to the priest," she said. She came back to them quite quickly, and very melancholic. "What do you want us to do?"

"I want you, as Ma Dame, to lead a small prayer of thankfulness when there's even a hint of what Father Matthew is scared of. That will stop everyone and give them time to catch their breath or to have a drink or go home. And it will remind us why we're here. This is a celebration."

"And me?" Adam looked plaintive.

"Do you think that shouting is going to stop anyone, at all?"

He looked across and shook his head. "Not tonight."

"You're essential, then. Whether Father Matthew allows you

or not, you're going to ring the bell. Over and over. No one can hear music above the bell, and they'll all have to stop until Isabella has the attention to lead her prayer."

"How long do I ring the bell? I can't see what's happening out here from in there."

"It's like measuring time to cook, except that you're measuring time to lead a prayer."

"I don't know how to cook," retorted Adam.

Margery sighed. "You choose a song that's the right length, and you sing it in your head."

"I know the exact song," crowed Adam. "You know the one I sing in church. It's perfect for bellringing. Religious and everything."

"A prayer?" asked Isabella. "Which one?"

Margery laughed. "I know the one. Isabella, you avoid being near him on that day, every year."

"That's not a prayer," Isabella said, firmly. "No song is a prayer when the chorus goes 'Hee haw, Mr. Donkey.'"

"It's better than that," said Adam, reproachfully. "Much funnier. And holy. Oh, so holy."

"I'd rather the good father led the prayer," said Isabella, mildly, changing the subject.

"He's a mess," said Margery. "I asked him if he'd lead a prayer, and he refused. This is up to us." The other two, looking at the way he stood like a thundercloud, arms crossed and face dark, had to agree. "Besides, if we can make this work, it will change how the Church talks to us. Whenever he wants to rant about devils on trains or . . . almost anything, in fact . . . all one of us will have to do is start whatever prayer you lead us through tonight. Not the donkey one. And dance a step or two. We're good Christians, and we know it."

"And if we lead the prayer, then it's our village, not his." Margery could see Adam planning dance steps to use when the priest needed reminding.

"I wouldn't go that far," said Margery. "I was thinking about the blessing of the field he did when he first arrived. How he tells us that Rome is more important than everything we know and how the fields remain unblessed. How he said Mass without using a bit of the field to be blessed and the way he kept the procession inside and didn't take it around the field."

"You want less talk of devils and more of the old stuff?" Isabella was thinking it through as she spoke.

"The entertaining stuff," said Adam. "Processions to keep storms away and stories from the Bible and alcohol. Lots of alcohol."

"They have the Easter plays in town," Isabella said, wistfully.

"We've always had our own ways. Special prayers. Special ceremonies," said Margery. "We've lost too many people, and this new priest comes from somewhere folks don't do anything interesting. If we ring the bell all night, we'll cure his melancholy and we'll earn ourselves all the good things."

And so it was. Every time Adam rang the bells for the length of time that it took him to sing the most indecent religious tune he knew, all the dancers stopped, and Isabella led them in a quiet prayer. At first the priest was bewildered, but as the evening passed he left the dancers to their own devices. Late at night he joined them when the bell rang, and followed Isabella's quiet prayer. He didn't try to lead. Not once. He didn't even join in. Margery asked him about it.

"I made my decision earlier," was all he said. Margery wanted to know what that meant, but didn't dare ask more. The priest looked as if he'd built a wall around himself, and she was too tired. She'd done enough. The wall would have to wait. Or it would have to be dealt with by the clergy. She gave a small smile when she realised that in his self-imposed solitude, the priest had missed entirely the group of young men who, instead of praying, went to the back and drank ale.

And this is how Adam became the bellringer and Isabella became a force to reckon with when anyone tried to obliterate custom and why Margery was treated with more respect by the priest than anyone else in his parish.

Years later, Robert told their children, "Bell, ale, and carol is more effective than bell, book, and candle at getting rid of demons." He never told them that his part was the ale.

They eradicated the invisible demons quietly and without fanfare. Just like a carol, in fact, a dance of grace and gentleness and many twists and turns.

Author's Afterword

St. John's Dance, St. Vitus's Dance, dancing pilgrims, choreomania, dancing mania, all these names described the dancing plague. The year it danced alongside the Black Death was one of the worst years in European history. Some districts never recovered. No one bothered to describe on parchment or paper the specific event that began in Yorkshire on St. John's Day, a year after the Black Death. Chroniclers, annalists, even the keepers of the small local records—none of them were interested. This means that it may have happened . . . or this story may be a complete fabrication.

A Borrowed Heart

Deborah J. Ross

18 April

*U*nder ordinary circumstances, Lenore Hasland would not have accepted an engagement with a patron she herself had not approved. A succession of wealthy men and more than a few ladies had left her financially secure. However, Lord Robert had become a friend as well as benefactor, so she could not easily refuse his plea.

"My son pines away," he told her. "He languishes. These past weeks, he's become a spineless wreck. I know none so capable as you, dearest siren, in rousing a man to cheerfulness."

Because of rumors of a vampire in the district, Lenore arrived at the young lord's townhouse wearing a silver cross on a ribbon that matched her gown. She carried a vial of holy water along with her usual dagger.

She paused at the entrance and assembled her sweetest expression. Here was she, a good two hours late and already regretting her promise. What had she been thinking? And why did so many fathers insist that an evening with a beautiful lady would "make a man" out of their sons, when so clearly an evening with a beautiful gentleman was preferred? She should be packing for her visit home, a visit too long impossible. At least she'd be able to sleep during the journey, for the use of Lord Robert's carriage had been part of her fee.

The steward, no doubt forewarned, escorted her upstairs, indicated the appropriate door, and then discreetly withdrew. The door swung open on its oiled hinges and Lenore stepped into a gentleman's parlor, the dark, heavy furniture quite masculine in taste. Sounds — the creak of weight shifting on furniture, the rustle of linens — issued from the interior room.

The bedroom door was slightly ajar and through it drifted the scent of perfume. She frowned, for she prided herself on her knowledge of fragrances. This one she did not know, powerful and subtle, but not one a man would choose.

If the son had already found a companion, so much the better. It would not be the first time an anxious parent had intervened without need.

"No . . . Please, no more, I beg you . . ." The voice was young, raw. Male. And in earnest, not love-play.

"Ahhh . . ." A woman's voice responded, resonant with hunger.

"For the love of God!"

Lenore slid through the open door. Ranges of candles, an extravagance of half-melted beeswax, flooded the chamber with honey-soft light. A huge, elaborately carved bed dominated the chamber. The satin coverlet tangled with articles of clothing.

Even in the yellow-toned light, the bare body of the young man was as devoid of color as marble. His hair clung to his shoulders like seaweed on a drowned corpse. His head was turned to the wall so that she could not discern his features, but his limbs were long and shapely.

A woman sat astride his hips, her skin as luminescent as pearl, her unbound hair cascading past her waist. Her body pulsated with desire on the brink of culmination. The man arched his body to meet her rhythm, even as he continued to struggle. His fingers twisted in the sheets. He threw his head from side to side, and Lenore saw his face —

Doubt vanished.

Lenore darted across the room and grabbed a handful of the other woman's silky mane. As she had been taught, she set her stance and used the strength of her torso to drag her adversary to the floor. The woman spun away, loosening Lenore's hold, and rolled to her feet.

Unashamed of her nakedness, the woman faced Lenore — no, surely this could not be a mortal woman. She was not flesh but rose and pearl and shimmering gold. A scent rose up from her skin like every desire unspoken in the dark.

Not human, then. Lilith-kind?

The succubus hissed, "Get out, she-creature! This is none of your affair!"

"Indeed?" Lenore slipped one hand between the folds of her skirt and drew her dagger from its sheath. "This boy's father has placed him in my care. He is mine."

"Take him if you want him," the creature said in a careless tone. "He's almost drained. I'll find more delectable hunting elsewhere."

Lenore did not relax her guard. "Young sir! If you value your life, leave this room instantly!"

With a rustling of bedclothes, the youth stumbled through the outer door. Lenore dared not take her gaze off the succubus to see if he had taken any article of clothing with him. From the expression of the demon, he had not.

For a long moment, neither spoke. Each held her position, Lenore on guard, dagger poised, the succubus increasingly impatient.

"Are you going to keep me here all night? If you know what I am, and I see that you do, then you also must be aware that I pose no threat to you. I cannot feed on your kind."

"By *my kind*, you mean women."

The succubus shrugged.

Lenore wondered why the unearthly creature made no move to rush past her. As an experiment, she advanced a pace, keeping the dagger before her. The succubus flinched.

Ah. The blade was steel, and steel consisted primarily of iron. And iron meant death to some supernatural creatures.

"Sit." Lenore indicated the bed with the dagger's point. "We are going to have a conversation, you and I, on the subject of *feeding.*"

The succubus obeyed with supernal grace. Lenore felt no trace of physical attraction, but her spirit responded to such sublime beauty. She reminded herself that this creature was a murderess many times over and utterly beyond redemption. *Beyond redemption* had been her father's parting words.

She lowered herself to the opposite corner of the bed. "Is this—" she indicated the sheets soaked with sweat and lust— "your entire existence?"

"It's yours, isn't it?"

Lenore permitted herself a bemused smile. "If you mean I am a whore like yourself and therefore in no position to pass judgment, then you are right. But there are many other things from which one may draw sustenance."

The expression of the succubus altered. "For your kind, perhaps. Never for mine."

"Why not?"

"What would be the point?"

That, Lenore thought acidly, was the problem with jumping from one bed to the next with no heed for anything beyond physical satisfaction.

"Do you never—?" She broke off the half-formed question. "What happens if you do not . . . feed? If you are celibate?"

"You mean, would I wither like a vampire deprived of blood?" The succubus shook her head. "Lady, you know nothing. I am vastly older than you, older than these cities or the walled fortresses before them. I remember when the heavens were the color of blood and the moon covered half the sky. Your *never* is a long time. But, no. I was formed for one purpose only."

"To seduce men and drain them."

"To ravish them with pleasure and drink it down like wine."

"Until they perish."

"All mortals perish. Is such ecstasy not worth the inconvenience of doing it a little sooner?"

Lenore did not answer straightaway. She thought of the men she had bedded, and the women as well, of how so many had sobbed on her breast as they whispered their secrets, and then slept in the first peace they had known in years. She wanted to cry out that need or loneliness or simple shame did not warrant death.

The succubus waited as one condemned, in imminent expectation of the executioner's axe.

Lenore laid the dagger on the rumpled sheets. "And you, if you were free to choose . . . if you were not compelled to lie with men . . . what would bring you joy?"

Bewilderment frosted the smoky eyes. The succubus had no idea what she was talking about, no notion of poetry or music or the intricate joys of science, but she knew — Lenore saw that she knew — she was missing something.

"Lie down," Lenore said gently.

The succubus obeyed, in a movement so elegant and so sensual, it took Lenore's breath away. "You may torture me for as long as it pleases you."

"I have no thought to bring you pain."

The succubus closed her eyes. Her chest lifted, accentuating the curve of her breasts.

She is shaped like a woman. Should she then not have a woman's capacity for pleasure?

Lenore took one rose-pearl hand between hers and began to stroke the long fingers, the delicate wrist. As she moved up the arm, she experimented, caressing lightly or massaging more deeply, always searching the other's face for any hint of discomfort. She did not touch the rounded breasts, for that was what a man would do, a man thinking only of his own desires.

Instead, she traced the sternum, circled the muscle of the shoulders and the curve of the ribs.

The succubus was breathing more slowly now. Tremors shivered across her belly. Lenore wondered if she had made a mistake, if what she attempted were impossible. Then she glimpsed a gleam of wetness at the corner of one eye. The next instant, the tear was gone. Lenore kissed the sweetly arching cheekbone and tasted salt.

The succubus lay very still.

She was not made for this. It may be the first time in all her existence that anyone has touched her with kindness.

Kindness. Not lust or violence or the need to possess.

Lenore placed her hands on the belly, fingers curved to follow the contours. The skin was cool and taut, the muscles braced as if in anticipation of a blow. She made her touch as soft as possible, tried to imagine soothing a frightened kitten. The skin warmed under her palms.

The succubus drew in a shuddering breath. Her scent changed, no longer alluring but tinged with metallic overtones. She curled on her side away from Lenore, and her hair fell across her face like a pall.

Lenore wrapped her arms around the succubus, not as a courtesan might embrace a lover or one woman might hold another, but as she might cradle a child. Some men might condemn her, for surely the succubus had taken many lives over the millennia of her existence. Lenore did not give such men the right to judge her, any more than she had once allowed them to brand her evil. She had long since made her peace with a life outside her father's rigid morality.

She woke to find that the candles had burned into puddles of wax. Pale light sifted through the curtains. Her arms were empty.

The succubus stood beside the bed, a shadow among shadows, a tracery of silver against the dying night. Innumerable metallic threads circled her neck. From each one hung a pinpoint of ruby brightness.

To the faint chiming of chains, the succubus moved closer. This close to dawn, she was already dissolving like dew. She lifted her hands, colorless and nearly transparent, drew one of the chains over her head, and offered it to Lenore.

Fine as spider silk, the chain nestled in Lenore's palm. The single ruby winked once, twice, in a double-timed rhythm.

The succubus said, "It is the heart of a man. I don't know whose."

"You steal hearts?"

A ghostly smile answered her. "I steal nothing. I collect what is offered to me by those for whom it no longer has any value. You may find a better use for it. I—I will not remember you in any other way, other than the absence of a heart I once possessed. You understand this? The oppression of so many hearts?"

How could anyone endure such a thing?

Lenore closed her fingers around the heart. She was not aware of closing her eyes, but when she opened them, she was alone.

21 April

The morning deteriorated under the weight of too many tasks, the return to her own quarters, the remainder of the packing, the note from Lord Robert expressing his profuse thanks, and finally the departure for the country. Lenore slept as much as the motion of the carriage would allow, which was considerably more rest than she would have found in a hired coach. She'd selected a traveling dress cut in unimpeachably conservative style and slightly too large, both for comfort and because it was less likely than most of her wardrobe to provoke an argument with her father.

Lenore woke when the coachman stopped to water the horses, and took the opportunity to walk about. She had spent so much of her adult life cultivating the interior landscape that the outdoors— even stables, battered water troughs, road mud, and horse droppings—interested her. Lord Robert's men behaved with impeccable politeness, but she knew how they saw her, a woman of flexible morals and powerful friends.

She returned to her seat after another such stop and took out the packet of letters. Her father's was short and notable as much for what he did not say as for what he did. The older letters, though, the ones from her younger sister, sent without their father's knowledge or leave . . .

The pages were cross-written and full of high spirits, for Elisabeth, the pampered baby of the family, had amused herself by falling in and out of love. At first, this latest infatuation had begun like the others in playful flirtation. Then Elisabeth's descriptions shifted from fashionably extravagant to unadorned and poignant. In between her sister's increasingly desperate belief in her lover's fidelity, Lenore read the sad end to the adventure. He had tired of her. The dalliance was over. Poor Elisabeth, to be snared like this.

No one dies of a broken heart. However, despair could weaken an already compromised constitution. The family was not consumptive—Lenore herself had always enjoyed robust health—but other ailments could be just as deadly.

"She calls for you," Sir Elward Hasland had written, and Lenore read in the crabbed script how much it had cost him to pen the next words: *"Come home."*

She folded the letters, blinking at the gray-brown fields, and tried not to remember how he had thrown her out.

❧

They traveled through the twilight and into the early hours of the evening, for the roads were good enough to navigate by lantern light. By the time they arrived at Hasland Hall, the horses were tired and hungry, as was Lenore herself.

The carriage clattered along the gravel-paved drive. There was the usual bustle of unloading and seeing to horses and men and tack. The household steward thawed enough to bid Lenore welcome.

"Your old room is ready for you, Miss. The master asks would you join him for sherry before dinner."

"Thank you, Barrun. Please convey my respects to my father and tell him I will wait on his pleasure directly I have seen my sister."

Lenore made her way up the stairs to the family quarters. The house dated from a more expansive time, when spacious chambers and the labor to keep them habitable had still been within the family's means. Now she saw the traces of shabby gentility in the threadbare carpet, the empty sconces, and the pitting on the brass latch.

The door cracked open a few moments after she knocked. An elderly woman wearing the cap and gray serge dress of a nurse peered out. She carried a lit taper, its glow soft on the pleated skin of her face. Her eyes brightened.

"Miss Lenore! We did not look for you so soon!" Here at least was one member of the household who was happy to see her. The next moment, they were standing in the hallway, hugging each other as if nothing else mattered.

"My dearest Mrs. Talbot." Lenore pulled away before she broke into tears. "My sister—?"

"Sleeping at last, poor lamb. The apothecary was here this afternoon and says she is very bad, very low indeed. He advised against bleeding her again—but it is not my place to say even that much. I plead an old woman's errant tongue."

"You have nothing with which to reproach yourself," Lenore said. "I would a thousand times rather hear a harsh truth from you than a soothing falsehood from anyone else."

"Ah, miss! You always were one for facing a problem squarely."

"Indeed. Had I been born a son, I would have made a great career in the army. Now I'd like to see for myself how my sister fares."

"Do not wake her," Mrs. Talbot said as she handed the candle to Lenore. "She has been feverish these last three days."

"I promise." Lenore kissed the old woman's cheek and then pushed the door open.

As a child, Elisabeth had exhibited a romantic predilection. Time had not tempered her taste. Every detail of furnishing, from the bed curtains to the dressing table with its mirror and blown-glass perfume bottles to the little writing desk, suggested a time long gone and a world that had never existed. Lenore felt as if she had strayed between the pages of her sister's favorite novel. At any instant, an armored knight, handsome and chivalric, might come striding in, or a tousle-haired poet emerge, rose in hand, from behind the draperies.

The young woman propped up on those lace-trimmed pillows belonged to quite a different tale. At first glance, Lenore might not have recognized her sister, so thin and haggard was the sleeping girl.

No one dies of a broken heart.

Lifting the candle for the best angle of light, Lenore studied the sleeping form. The parched lips and hollows around the eyes could reasonably result from restless sleep and lack of appetite. The extreme pallor, on the other hand . . .

Elisabeth roused, whimpering, before falling back into fitful sleep. The nightgown had been laced so high, Lenore could not examine her sister's neck without disturbing her. She circled the room, testing the latches on the windows. They were so stiff, she did not think she could open them. Then there was nothing to do but change for dinner.

One of the servants had unpacked Lenore's trunk. Lenore selected a gown of soft, dark green wool with a high neckline. It had been made in Paris to her design so that she needed no help in putting it on.

She found her father in the drawing room, looking as if he had not left it since their last interview. He stood before the fireplace, jabbing the logs with a poker. The flames rushed up, bathing his face in a hectic glow. He whirled around, poker still in hand. The clock on the mantle ticked remorselessly. She curtseyed and waited for him to speak.

"So you've come home at last," he said, and she wondered what he meant, for Mrs. Talbot had said they did not expect her so soon. *At last . . . after all these years?*

"Good evening, sir."

"Well, then." He held out his hand and she took it. She could not remember the last time they had touched.

She had thought him unchanged, but that had been an illusion. He looked more careworn than angry, as if he had sought to hold back the sorrows of the world with the force of his will, and had failed.

With a gesture, he indicated for her to precede him to the dining room. He had been waiting for her, then. The courtesy surprised her even more than had the offer of his hand. When they were seated and the soup course had been served, blessedly still hot, he inquired after her journey.

"It was well enough," she answered. "The roads were dry and I am a hardy traveler."

"Very little troubled you as a child." He looked up, spoon half raised. "You've seen your sister, then?"

Lenore set down her own spoon. "Father, what ails her? You gave no details in your letter, but I did not expect to find her so very ill."

"My own physician was at a loss to explain it. Oh, he babbled on about humours and fluxes. Nonsense, all of it! The apothecary, who has more sense than any ten doctors, bled her twice and, when that didn't help, dosed her with laudanum. At least, my poor girl can now sleep. But what she will do, how she will fare, when it wears off . . ." He broke off as the servant removed the soup dishes and brought in the next course.

Lenore picked at her turbot, shoving the parsley garnish around her plate. "Is there any possibility her malady might be supernatural in origin?"

"What do you know about such things?"

At least he hadn't raged at her for being gullible and

superstitious. "I live in town. She wrote me of a—" *lover*, but Lenore would not use the word in front of her father " —an admirer. What do you know about him?"

He pushed away his fish plate. "Name's Henri d'Ombrossa. Calls himself *comte*. She met him at a party at Lady Ellsworth's, all frippery and dancing. You know your sister's enthusiasm for such things. At the time, I thought it a harmless enough pastime."

"Dancing is healthful exercise," Lenore agreed. "D'Ombrossa ... that's an unusual surname." By her tone, she implied it could be not his real name.

Her father paused in his chewing to consider. Clearly *Comte* Henri would not have been a suitable son-in-law under any circumstances, so his ancestry had until now been of no significance. Lenore found herself liking her father a great deal better. She said, "I gather that he has given her up, so it does not matter."

The discussion ranged over a variety of topics but never Lenore's profession. If this visit accomplished nothing else, the infinitesimal movement toward reconciliation would be worth it. She waited, therefore, until the cheese course had been served in the Continental manner and then taken away.

"You indicated that *Comte* Henri is a member of Lady Ellsworth's set. I would like an introduction." At her father's sharp look, she added, "On my sister's behalf. Perhaps nothing can be done, but I must ascertain that for myself."

"He's as worthless a piece of overbred foreign trumpery as ever walked beneath the sun, but I suppose you'll not be content until you've seen him for yourself. As it happens, the lady has just sent over yet another of her invitations. It's for tomorrow evening, although that's likely insufficient time for you to finish your fripping or frilling or whatever ladies do to prepare for such things."

"Tomorrow will suit me very well."

"What does Lady Ellsworth think a man my age would do at such a gathering?" her father continued. "Prance about like a popinjay?"

"Perhaps she sees you as a suitor. I believe she remains a widow."

He sighed, the faintest breath. "No one will ever take your mother's place."

22–23 *April*

Candlelight touched the ballroom at Ellsworth Manor with a creamy golden radiance, glinting on silk gowns, jewel-set rings glimpsed through lace cuffs, headdresses of peacock's feathers, and brooches set low on porcelain bosoms. Music, sweet and temperate, summoned dancers to their places. Lenore watched them assemble, ladies on one side of the glittering hall, gentlemen on the other. A gesture and a nod divided them, ranks of soldiers on a battlefield.

And I, what am I? Spy . . . or assassin?

She resisted the impulse to touch the neckline of her gown, moiré silk that fell in chocolate folds until movement burnished it to gold. The chain was all but invisible, the ruby nestling between her breasts under the copper-thread embroidery. She lifted her chin, shifting her posture to display her figure to advantage, and studied the room. By some miscalculation on the part of Lady Ellsworth—herself leading the set on the arm of a youth so beautiful he must be a fay in human disguise—the number of ladies present exceeded that of the gentlemen, and more than one went without a partner.

"My dear Miss Elisabeth—"

The voice was smooth, quintessentially masculine, and so close that Lenore felt a whisper of breath on her neck. She recovered, turning to face him.

He was not tall, only a hand's-breadth more than her own height, but something in his air, his carriage, the way the moon-pale velvet set off his shoulders and tapered waist, made him seem taller. He wore his hair a bit long for the current fashion, sweeping back from a widow's peak in a torrent of ebony. By far his best feature was his eyes, so dark they seemed to be all pupil.

Her mouth went dry. He was too beautiful, too pale and deathly to be mortal. She dared not breathe for fear of what she might inhale, the lingering taint of the grave.

For the moment, she was in no danger. He would not dare an overt assault in this public gathering.

"I beg your pardon!" he exclaimed. "How impudent you must think me, when we have not been properly introduced! I mistook you for someone else."

Lenore reached for words as a swordsman might draw his blade. *Engage:* "You are perhaps acquainted with my sister."

My sister who is so ill, she barely recognized me this morning.

"You are remarkably alike, that same sweetness of countenance."

Feint: "You have the advantage of me, sir."

"Henri d'Ombrossa, *comte*, at your service." Was there a hint of mockery in his bow? Had he already marked her for his next victim?

She responded with a precise courtesy. "You are French, then? You have almost no accent." *Riposte.*

A flicker of light, perhaps a stray reflection of the candles, touched those dark eyes. "My name may be, but I am not. My family is an old one, and I am far from my native soil."

Invite: "Far from home? Do you then find England a trifle cold?"

His smile intensified the beauty of his pale features. "You are kind to ask. But no, I am never cold."

No, you would not be. His tone implied that mere physical discomfort paled to insignificance in the presence of a lady such as herself. She wanted to slap him. Instead, she flicked her fan open as if she, too, found the room unpleasantly warm.

Redoublement: "That is fortunate, indeed, for the county abounds in large, drafty houses. One might hazard to say that any estate worth the price is so afflicted."

"If by that, you mean to inquire if I have taken up residence in the neighborhood," he said dryly, "and under what terms, then I must disoblige the lady's curiosity." He offered her his arm. "I detect the opening measures of My Lord Byron's Maggot. May I have the honor?"

She allowed herself to be escorted to the floor. Now to lure him with a bit more flirtation, perhaps a stroll on the veranda or a tête-à-tête in a secluded corner . . .

The knot of matrons seated beyond the punch bowl were agog at her partner's choice — she knew perfectly well what they must be saying about her. Out of the corner of her vision, she caught d'Ombrossa's brief, conspiratorial wink.

Point!

Lenore was not often discomposed, but the audacity of his gesture confounded her momentarily. As a consequence, she missed a beat of the opening figure, one she knew by heart.

"Is aught amiss?" her dancing partner inquired. "Did I mistake your wish to dance as well as your identity?"

Disengage. The steps of the dance drew them apart, temporarily prohibiting further conversation, and when they came together again, there was no point in answering.

The closing bars of the dance, along with the requisite honors, granted her a moment in which to collect herself. D'Ombrossa moved to her side, perfect in his attendance upon her. His fingers enclosed hers, his skin as cool as silk. She allowed herself a half-smile and a murmured reference to the heat of the room and her own fatigue. This had the desired effect of a solicitous offer of wine punch. She allowed him to guide her to a sofa in the quietest corner of the salon. In his absence, she drew out the vial of holy water and loosened the stopper, then rearranged the folds of her skirt to cover it. Her hands trembled.

He might not be human — she was reasonably confident now that her initial suspicions were correct — but he was male, and she was not inexperienced. She found him attractive, but she had long ceased to be governed by every vaporish longing. Elisabeth would have found him irresistible.

He returned in a gratifyingly short time with a glass of punch and a plate of nut-studded pastries.

"You do not take refreshment?" She watched him over the gold-edged rim of her cup. The punch was overly sweet for her taste. "Or perhaps you do not care for wine?"

He brushed aside her question as if his only concern were her pleasure and not his own. Lenore set down the cup, still almost full. Her fingers curled around the vial. The glass was warm.

"Perhaps you are not yet sufficiently acquainted with the local custom," she said, "or you would be sensible of the impropriety of paying court to a woman whose sister lies dangerously ill from your own cruelty."

"I?" Although he did not smile, he sounded more amused than concerned. He did not, she noticed, deny that he was *paying court* to her. "I am sorry she is unwell, but that is not my fault."

"No? I find it impossible to believe that you are not responsible for how you have treated her. Is it your nature to be heartless?"

D'Ombrossa's expression hardened, the muscles of his jaw stark against the paleness of his cheek. "If I am heartless, I have good reason," he replied in a voice so bleak that if Lenore had not been so outraged, she would have pitied him.

Pity . . .

Greater harms than his had been healed, and hearts more grievously wounded had once regained their capacity for love. In the beds of her patrons, in their choked sobs, in the flood of their confessions, she had witnessed such transformation. She knew the pulse and rhythm of this dance. She was good at it, very good. Had she not wrung tears from a soulless succubus? If she could draw the poison of d'Ombrossa's despair, could she not turn even one such as he from cruelty to compassion? Temptation swept through her, shaking her beyond the power of mere physical lust. She would not have him take up his courtship of her sister, but a word of kindness might do much to speed Elisabeth's recovery.

What was she thinking? This was no man, but a monster every

bit as evil as the succubus. More so, because he lacked any awareness of the suffering of his victims. His callousness had brought
Elisabeth near to death.

It ends now!

Lenore dislodged the stopper and hurled the contents of the
vial across his face.

He stared at her as the water dribbled over his expensive silk
shirt and waistcoat. His mouth dropped open and his eyes blinked
very fast. His chest rose and fell. The moon-pale velvet of his coat
soaked up the liquid, turning dark.

Voices buzzed nearby. "Did you see—?"

"The Hasland girl—you know, *that one*—"

"Only to be expected—"

Sputtering, d'Ombrossa leapt to his feet. He looked as if he
would strike her.

Not a suggestion of smoke curled from his drenched skin.

Lenore gaped at him, unable to understand why he had not
burst into flames. He should be dust, ashes!

A manservant rushed up with an armful of towels. By the
exclamations throughout the salon, Lady Ellsworth was even now
being informed of the barbaric actions of one of her guests.
D'Ombrossa snatched the topmost towel.

He was not a vampire. Yet how could he be anything else?

Sweet heaven, what have I done?

Before he could withdraw, Lenore scrambled to her feet. The
glass vial clattered to the floor. She laid one hand on his arm. He
startled, but her touch produced the desired effect. He whirled to
face her.

"I'm so sorry! I didn't mean—I had no idea—" She drew
herself up with what dignity she could muster. "I have made a
terrible mistake and treated you abominably. Although I have no
hope of your accepting it, I offer you my apology."

He rubbed the towel over his eyes, leaving them reddened as
if with long-unshed tears. How could she have been so stupid, so
unfeeling? He had spoken the truth when he said he had good

reason for behaving in a heartless manner. His own had been stolen.

Her hand fluttered to the neckline of her gown where the ruby heart lay. The gem had once been the heart of a man like him. Perhaps this very one—no, that was unlikely. The succubus was millennia old.

What if she offered it to him? Would it magically fuse with his flesh, with his very soul? Would he then regain a human heart, one capable of human feeling?

"Madam, I take my leave of you." He bowed to her, back straight and toes precisely turned out.

"Sir, if you will come this way." The manservant with the towels gestured toward a door at the back of the salon, likely to a chamber where he might dry himself and change into fresh garments, whatever could be provided by the hostess. As Lenore stood, dazed and immobile, the two men departed.

The air turned thick and the voices fell into silence. In the ballroom, the dance had ended and the dancers were dispersing. The musicians put up their instruments for a recess.

She must not let him get away. In a few minutes, if she knew anything about men, he would have forgotten the cause of the incident and his barbaric treatment of a gentle young lady. He would remember only the ill-mannered behavior of a woman of low repute. If she were to wrest any good from the confrontation, she must act now. She bolted after him.

Beyond the tastefully muted colors of the salon, the servants' corridor closed around her like a mining tunnel, dark and airless. Her heart felt as if it were flinging itself against her ribs. There were no lights, only the flicker of a hand-held candle as it disappeared through the doorway at the far end. The door swung closed, but not before Lenore had marked its direction and distance. She fumbled for the latch, jerked it free, and pulled the door open. Beyond lay a staircase and a second, shorter hall, lit dimly from a doorway at the end. She headed for it.

A few moments later, Lenore burst in on a pair of maid-servants, sitting a rough table and taking their ease over a late supper. A single candle, tallow rather than beeswax, sat beside a second, unlit. The younger of the two maids scrambled to her feet, chair legs scraping over the bare floor.

"Oh, madam!" Even in the poor light, the girl's pock-marked face darkened in surprise.

"I am sorry to intrude," Lenore murmured. "Have you seen a rather wet and extremely vexed gentleman pass this way?"

"Oh, madam!"

Lenore rushed back the way she had come, to the sound of smothered laughter. Of course! D'Ombrossa would not be taken to a servant's room, he'd be given the best guest quarters where he could repair his attire and recover his composure.

The stairs were steeper and narrower than she was accustomed to. She stepped on her hem a couple of times before bunching up her skirts in both hands. What an idiot she'd been, first delaying and then taking the wrong way, the easy way!

The top of the stairs came into view. She pushed through the door and stumbled out into another hallway. By its lit candles, richly patterned carpet runner and faint smell of wood polish, this one was clearly part of the family living areas. All the doors leading from it were closed.

Lenore muttered some extremely indecorous words under her breath. If she had to check each one, so be it. She ran her hands over her gown to restore it to some semblance of order, strode to the nearest door, and placed her ear against it.

Nothing.

What if he were inside but alone? Would she be able to hear his breathing, the soft rustle of garments, perhaps the splash of bathing water? With her luck, he might be sitting utterly still, silently plotting his revenge.

Her fingers closed around the latch. What did she have to lose if it were the wrong room? She'd already destroyed her small pretense to polite society.

The door cracked open, oiled hinges moving soundlessly. She

peered at the darkened interior for a moment before withdrawing.

Lenore startled as the third door on the opposite side opened and the manservant came out, no longer carrying his armful of towels. Without any sign he'd noticed her, he turned in the opposite direction. When he disappeared around a corner, she was able to breathe again.

This time, she did not bother to knock. She had seen enough unclothed men, many of them nowhere as comely, to be beyond prudery.

Light from a bank of candelabra filled the room. The furnishings followed the style of a decade ago, so this room must have seen little use. D'Ombrossa stood before a clothes frame, his jacket and waistcoat laid over its bars, his shirt a sodden heap at his feet. His bare skin gleamed like ivory. He held a dry small-shirt, scowling as if uncertain how to put it on by himself.

When he saw her, the scowl increased. "You again! What are you, a harpy bent on tormenting me? Are you not content with half-drowning me, but must dog my very footsteps?"

"You said you had good reason to be heartless. Someone, some woman, stole your heart."

"If so, what business is it of yours?" He shifted, subtly accentuating the width of his shoulders, the muscled contours of his chest. Here was a man sure of his sexual appeal, of his masculine power. His scent tinged the air, daring her to desire him.

Under her fingertips, the thread of gold tingled. The chain lifted easily over her head. In the brilliance of the candles, the ruby heart pulsed so fast it glittered.

One corner of his mouth twisted, marring the beauty of his features. "What is this? A love-offering?"

"It is a heart." She took a step toward him as she might approach a frightened horse. "It can be yours. I offer it to you as a gift. Take it and be whole again. Love as you once did."

He lashed out with the small-shirt, snapping it like a whip. The edge caught the ruby and ripped the chain from Lenore's hands.

"You sentimental cow! Why would I—or any man of sense—ever want to *feel* again? Should I *seek* to wallow in agony and degradation? I'll have nothing to do with it or you! Get out!" When Lenore hesitated, he added, "And take your bauble with you!"

The ruby gleamed, nestled in the rumpled linen. She snatched it up and fled, too numb to feel defeat.

I've failed, she thought, rocking with the motion of the carriage on her way home. How could she tell Elisabeth what had happened? It would be unspeakably unkind to relate d'Ombrossa's reaction. Yet how could she say nothing, or worse yet, lie? Elisabeth would expect a report. She would cling to every word as a morsel of hope.

May he rot in hell!

Lenore touched the tiny jewel where it hung once again around her own neck. It came to her, a thought quite unexpected, that d'Ombrossa had no need for hell, for he would carry it within him wherever he went. The thought pleased her in a sad way.

They had almost reached the modest gate of Hasland House. A light shone from Elisabeth's window, as Lenore knew it would. There was no help for it. She must go up to her sister. At least she had a sister, and Elisabeth had her, and that was no small cause for gratitude. She might even have a portion of a father's love as well.

Poor d'Ombrossa.

Elisabeth was sitting up, wrapped in a thick knitted shawl and reading by the light of the fire. Poetry, Lenore assumed as Elisabeth set the book aside. Elisabeth looked up with a half-smile. Her skin, when Lenore kissed her cheek, felt cool.

"As you see, I am much better," Elisabeth said. "I am heartily ashamed at having put my family to so much trouble. You came home! Father told me—he's actually speaking your name again!"

Lenore settled herself on the footstool, basking in the unexpected barrage of words.

Elisabeth lowered her gaze. "I always did chatter on, didn't I?"

"Yes, love, you did."

"Then *you* must talk. How was your journey? And how did you pass this evening?"

"Well enough." They were dancing around the unspoken question like fencers unwilling to commit. Lenore's nerves still rankled from the encounter on the dance floor. "I've come from Lady Ellsworth's."

Elisabeth folded her hands in her lap. Lenore saw the book was not poetry but a history of the lives of the saints.

Poor Elisabeth.

The moment stretched on, overlong. Elisabeth said in a small voice, "He will not see me. You could not change his mind."

"I could not change his heart."

"He has none, or he would not have behaved as he did. And even if — even if he came back to me, if he became everything I thought I wanted, how could I trust him not to leave me again?"

Lenore slipped the ruby heart over her head, searching for the right words. "Do you — " she began, but Elisabeth cut her off with uncharacteristic force.

"Do not rebuke me with his unworthiness! I do not want to know! It doesn't matter! My own behavior has been no better, wailing after a lover who existed only in my own fevered imagination! I simpered and sighed and gave every indication of perishing for love, just like the lady in the poem. But we don't die from broken hearts, do we?"

"I have never seen it so," Lenore said. Elisabeth swayed and put a trembling hand to her cheek. The book slid to the floor. "Come, you have sat up long enough. You must rest."

Elisabeth allowed herself to be helped back to bed. Lenore plumped the pillows and smoothed the coverlet the way their nurse had done when they were children. Elisabeth grasped her hand. "Stay with me a while longer. Just a little while."

Lenore kicked off her slippers and settled herself on the bed. Elisabeth nestled against her side. In the fireplace, embers tumbled into ashes with a hush. The room fell quiet except for the breathing of the two sisters.

"Do you want to know what changed my mind? Why I decided to live?" Elisabeth whispered, as if they were children again, sharing secrets.

"Since your—since d'Ombrossa—had no part in it, I admit to being curious. I doubt such a resolve was inspired by the lives of the saints."

Elisabeth giggled. "No. That was only to put me to sleep. *You* had something to do with it."

"I? You were asleep when I arrived, and too ill to speak with me earlier today."

"After you left, Father raged for a six-month. With each new report, his temper worsened. I didn't think he'd ever let you in the door again."

"Neither did I."

"Or that you would come if he asked."

Until now, I would not have. I would have let the old tyrant stew in his own venom.

"But he did ask," Elisabeth went on, her voice now soft and sweet as a child's. "And you came."

She looked up into Lenore's face. The fire had fallen away, leaving only the glow of the embers. "Don't you understand? He *asked*, he swallowed his anger and his pride—and you *came*, you set aside all the terrible things he'd said—out of love for me."

Oh.

"I know it isn't the same as the love of a man for a woman," Elisabeth said in that quiet, sure voice. "You can cover it with bitterness and quarreling, but it never goes away. Someday, I'll be able to love someone else and not care if he loves me back. Until then . . ." Her body softened and her head sank into the pillow. ". . . this is enough."

The dying fire was suddenly too bright. Lenore closed her

eyes. The warmth of her sister's body seeped into her own. Around her, the familiar old house settled into the night. She could almost hear the breathing of the other sleepers, Barrun, Mrs. Talbot, the horses in the stables, the owls in the trees, the badgers in their dens. Her father, who had given it all back to her in the only way he could.

She wondered if she would ever leave this place again, or ever want to.

The Gown of Harmonies

Francesca Forrest

The dresses as golden as the sun, silvery as the moon, and as sparkling as the stars had been a tremendous success, but they had set a dangerous precedent. For the past two seasons, balls had been an eye-piercing affair as young ladies of quality strove to outdo one another with dresses as dazzling as lightning in the night sky, as searing as lava in the earth's deep furnaces, and as glittering as sunset in the northern ice fields.

"Tastes have to change," sighed Mistress Meran, Atelier Aurora's master seamstress, "or guests at a ball will end up as blind as you, my dear." This to her assistant in attendance, Grazia.

Grazia had been born with an impenetrable veil over her eyes, but Mistress Meran valued the girl's sensitive fingers. When Grazia sewed a seam, those fingers kept track of every tiny stitch, ensuring each followed on each, the same size, in a straight line, exactly the right distance from the edge of the fabric.

Mistress Meran's fashionable and flattering dresses had won

her many clients, but this season the most illustrious was Princess Allegra. Winning the princess's patronage had earned Mistress Meran both the envy and the pity of her peers — envy, because Princess Allegra was not only the season's most eligible young lady, but also one of the most beautiful, which meant the public would take note of her gowns and remember her seamstress; pity, because despite her beauty, Princess Allegra had what everyone discreetly agreed was a naive sense of style and did not take direction, or even suggestion, well. Mistress Meran had shown the princess fabric for a gown like the breath of dawn on forest ferns and another as lambent and gauzy as sunbeams in the waters of coral reefs, and Princess Allegra had admired them — of course she had; no one could help but admire fairy silks and gauzes — but had come back to her perpetual theme.

"They're lovely, but my dress for the Midsummer Ball has to be staggering. Don't you have something that — I don't know — scintillates? Otherwise how will I stand out? I want everyone to see me and forget the ball entirely!"

What a grandiose request, Grazia thought, to wish for admirers to forget the very occasion for which they all were gathering! But the truth was that although Princess Allegra was beautiful, she was at best — if one were speaking kindly — a lackluster dancer. The love of dance had gone entirely to her younger sister, Princess Marguerite. Marguerite was as plain of face as Allegra was beautiful, and as light of foot and graceful of movement as Allegra was awkward. Evidently Allegra knew her own weakness in this regard. She seemed determined to make her impression during the opening promenade and perhaps hoped her partners would be too besotted to notice if she fell out of rhythm or stepped on toes. If only she could be made to understand that in a room of full of sparkling, glittering gowns, scintillations would make her just another member of the flock!

Grazia could hear the tension threading through Mistress Meran's faultlessly polite suggestions and replies, and wondered if now might be a good moment to try a suggestion of her own.

She had never spoken up to any of the mistress's clients, but she knew that eventually an assistant should. You had to choose the occasion wisely, however—too soon, and you were being presumptuous; too late, and you were likely to be thought lacking in confidence, your ideas unjustly dismissed as timid or unworthwhile.

"Your Highness, if I may be so bold," Grazia began, taking just one step toward the princess. That step put her within the aura of the princess's signature scent—orange blossoms, with undertones of thyme and honey. "There are other ways to stand out—other senses to appeal to. May I?"

The princess murmured an assent, and Grazia draped a fabric over her shoulders. She felt the princess's shiver and smiled inwardly at the princess's little exclamation of delight. The cloth was woven to be as soft as velvet and as light as milkweed floss.

"Now lift your arms," Grazia directed, hastily adding, "if it please Your Highness." She knew when the princess had complied by the sound of wind in autumn leaves—one of the aural threads Grazia had commissioned the weavers to add to this fabric. Grazia's cheeks flushed with pleasure at the princess's gasp.

"And perhaps you could also take a few waltz steps?" suggested Grazia. Reluctantly the princess assayed a few one-two-threes. A tinkling, as of small bells or wind chimes, rose from the fabric, deepening into the tones of distant church bells pealing as she whirled about. The sounds faded away when she stopped moving.

"My goodness, that's clever!" the princess exclaimed. "Just imagine my sister in a gown of this stuff—the ballroom would become a carillon."

Grazia smiled.

"But of course that wouldn't do, would it," the princess continued. "It would make conversation most difficult—and think of the poor chamber orchestra, struggling to make itself heard!"

Grazia's smile melted away. She'd been so entranced with the sounds the fabric made that she hadn't even considered the practical implications.

"Very true, Your Highness, very wise," Mistress Meran said. A further rustle of leaves and tinkle of chimes told Grazia that her mistress had lifted the fabric from the princess's shoulders. "But thank you for indulging my assistant. It was most gracious of you."

"The idea's not entirely bad," the princess said. "Indeed, I think—yes: I would like you to add bells—tiny ones, mind—to the lace at my gown's wrists. You'll recall I did say I want a positive explosion of lace? My wrists are delicate, and lace shows them to advantage. And don't forget about scintillations. I must have scintillations."

"Of course, Your Highness," Mistress Meran said, and only Grazia heard the resignation in her voice.

Which was worse, the princess's casual dismissal of the aural fabric, or the fact that her reasons were so sensible? A hot brick of disappointment and shame lodged in Grazia's stomach.

"I apologize for the presumption, mistress," Grazia murmured after the princess had left.

"Not at all, not at all. My patience was wearing thin, and it was a clever idea. You heard Her Highness request bells for the sleeves. Count it as a victory and learn from the criticism. But" — and here the mistress's voice took on an admonishing tone— "until the Midsummer Ball is past, I need your attention entirely on the tasks I assign you, yes? No side projects, no distractions!"

"Yes, mistress," said Grazia, but Mistress Meran's words failed to have a proper chastening effect, for the seed of a new idea was germinating within her. Learn from the criticism. It's true you couldn't have dancers' gowns obscuring the rhythms and melodies of the musicians. But what if—somehow—a gown could be made to harmonize?

The rest of the afternoon was punishing: stitching only relieved by snipping and cutting, cutting only relieved by pressing, and then back to stitching. By the evening, Grazia's fingers were stiff and her neck was sore, but she excused herself early from supper with the other assistants. She wrapped her shawl around her and headed through the town center and down the muddy path to the willow sheds where the fairy looms were clacking, even at this hour, creating the cloth out of which Mistress Meran and her peers would create the rarest, finest raiment—cloth with all the delicacy, wonder, and magic of the Fair Vale, but also the tangibility and permanence that could be gained only in the human realm. Fairy strands lay side by side with fibers of silk, cotton, flax, or wool, the where and how of it dictated by the vision of Master Grayling, the fairy master weaver who had foreseen how precious such fabrics would be to fairies and humans alike.

The girl who went to fetch Master Grayling for Grazia was a mere child—Grazia could tell by the high-pitched voice that issued from no higher than Grazia's own shoulders—and she was surely human, not fairy. Fairies enjoyed design and supervision, but disdained mere labor. Grazia shivered. Not for the first time, she was glad that the holy sisters at the foundlings' home had taught her to sew—otherwise she too might be working in the willow sheds.

"Here she is, Master. Miss, here's Master Grayling come," the girl announced, then her footsteps disappeared back into the din of the manufactory.

There was a tingling in Grazia's fingers and along the back of her neck that she'd learned meant a fairy was present.

Master Grayling spoke: "How did the princess like the fabric of chimes and bells?"

"Oh, very much," Grazia said—technically not a lie.

"Of course, of course. How pleasing. My workers are always whining about their fingers getting singed by the incandescent threads in such demand these days. Worse, their eyes become dim, and then they bumble about most clumsily and require reprimands—so tiresome! It was refreshing to be working with sound for a change. Have you come to request more of the same?"

"No, I need something a bit different." Grazia described what she was imagining: a fabric that could pick up a melody and offer counterpoint or descant, a cello or flute to complement violins, perhaps a flash of brass, with tempo and dynamics matching that of the chamber players. When she finished, the fairy was silent. Grazia waited. When at last Master Grayling spoke, his voice was thoughtful.

"That's not an easy thing you're asking. Threads of water bouncing over rocks, or a dawn chorus of birds—just warp the loom properly and the resulting cloth must sing. In the ballroom or the bed chamber, wherever the young lady goes, the sounds will be the same. But that's not what you're asking for. You're asking for a fabric that will respond to the sounds it encounters. It wouldn't be enough to weave in violin or harpsichord or oboe. It's not their voice you're wanting, or not that alone, but their *response.*" He drifted into silence, and when he spoke again his voice was harsh and eager.

"I could weave you a fabric that listens—yes: I could do that. But you would have to teach it the principles of harmony. You would have to command, with your needle, which instruments you wish to have respond. You know the art of dressmaking, but are you also a musician?"

"No sir," she confessed, "but I would find a way."

"Ah, no, no, no. Not good enough. Do you understand what I have accomplished, here in your little human town? The fabric I create is that rare treasure, something prized equally by human and fairy nobility alike. My reputation is flawless—I assure you, princes are not more admired than I. But success has its enemies. There are those in the Fair Vale who can't abide a fairy creation adulterated by the materiality of the human realm. One spectacular failure on my part could destroy all I have achieved. So you see, I am not eager to take on a project whose success depends in large part on the skill of someone such as you."

Grazia's mouth went dry, but she licked her lips, swallowed, and said, "But if I—if we—succeed, think of your reputation then.

Think of the glory of creating something never before heard or" — because it was so important to the sighted— "seen."

"And then there's the dancer," Mr. Grayling went on, as if Grazia hadn't spoken. "She would have to be spectacular as well—no false moves, no hesitations. Your mistress's royal client, Princess Allegra, now. She's pretty, for a human, but as a dancer . . . Well, let us just say that if someone like her were to wear the dress, my fate would be sealed."

"I know Princess Allegra isn't much of a dancer. I-I have someone else in mind: her sister, the Princess Marguerite."

Master Grayling erupted in laughter, and Grazia froze, but the fairy's next words were warm.

"Brilliant—yes, even someone such as you recognizes Princess Marguerite's gift. Truly, she moves as if she had fairy blood. If she were to take to the floor wearing such a dress—her skill, my fabric . . ."

But then his voice chilled. "That still leaves you, the weakest element in this scheme. An assistant seamstress with no knowledge of music. If I'm to take this risk, I'll need some surety from you—something of yours that becomes mine if you fail."

"Sir, I—" What did she have that could possibly be of value to the master weaver?

"How about your mind, so quick with ideas?"

For a moment it felt to Grazia as if the fairy had stolen her bones and replaced them with icewater, but somehow she kept herself standing and her voice calm. "No," she said, "that's too great a thing to ask for. You might as well ask for my life."

"Then—the skill in your fingers. If I ruin my reputation because of your mad scheme, I'll be finished as a weaver. It would be only fair that having cost me my livelihood, you compensate me with yours, no? And you know, I might fancy life as a tailor."

And if you take the skill in my fingers, what's left for me? Grazia wanted to ask, imagining herself without means of support, cold and hungry on the streets.

"Well?" the fairy pressed.

Everything he suggests will be too much, Grazia realized. *But only if I fail. And I won't fail. I'll succeed. I have to.*

"That seems reasonable," said Grazia at last, struggling to sound unconcerned.

"Wonderful — then it's settled! You must excuse me. I want to get right to work on this — you'll need it as soon as possible if you're to train it successfully in the ways of music. I shall have it for you in two days' time!" Did he follow this bold declaration with a flourish and a bow? Grazia couldn't know, but she inclined her own head in acknowledgement all the same.

"Thank you," she said.

"He's gone, miss, winked out the way he does when he's crossing to the Fair Vale." It was the high, bright voice of the girl who'd brought him.

"Oh! Well I —"

"Miss. We'll be making more sound cloth, won't we." Eager, conspiratorial tone.

"Yes, but you mustn't tell anyone. Can you keep a secret?"

"Of course!" Mildly offended. "I'm the best secret keeper in my family. But miss . . ."

"Yes?"

"The other cloth we made for you. It won't be used for the princess's dress, will it." A statement, not a question.

"No, I'm afraid not," Grazia replied. "But a different princess's gown will be made from the new cloth you'll weave."

"Flea buttocks, miss, I don't care about that. But I was wondering. We was all wondering . . . If you won't be needing the old cloth, could we buy it from you, me and the other girls? We pooled our wages." A hot, callused hand caught Grazia's wrist and thrust Grazia's hand into a small sack, where her fingers encountered a collection of small copper coins.

"Is it enough?"

It was nowhere near enough — months of Grazia's stipend had gone into that fabric, all for nothing. Could she part with it for this pittance? Grazia recalled the careless way Master Grayling had spoken of his workers' fingers and eyes and made a decision.

"Yes," she declared. "Yes . . . I think this will cover it."

"Oh, miss! Thank you! Wait till I tell the others!"

Suddenly there were small, strong arms squeezing Grazia tight, a warm cheek pressed against Grazia's chest, and an odor of unwashed hair, sweat, and burnt tallow, along with the living, tingling scent of magic. Just as suddenly, Grazia was released from this embrace.

"Come by tomorrow—but not early. After you finish work," Grazia said. The girl thanked Grazia again and then ran off, hollering out the names of her mates to tell them the good news.

✎❦ ❦✎

The dampness in the air as Grazia walked back toward Atelier Aurora spoke of clouds thickening and lowering. Grazia pulled her shawl over her head as the first raindrops came pattering down. A scent of starch and rosewater as she approached the door of the atelier told her that the mistress was waiting on the threshold.

"Mistress Meran!" With the mistress standing in the doorway as she was, Grazia couldn't enter. The rain was coming quickly now, soaking through Grazia's shawl.

"Grazia. It's nearly curfew. The other girls said you left supper early." Mistress Meran's tone was cool. Though she hadn't asked a question, she seemed to be waiting for an explanation.

"I . . . felt I needed a little fresh air. I thought I'd take a stroll."

"A lengthy stroll."

Grazia cast about for how best to respond, but Mistress Meran spoke first.

"Grazia, were you meeting an admirer?"

Grazia's astonishment at the question was surpassed only by her relief that the mistress hadn't hit upon the actual reason for the excursion.

"No, mistress! I know the rules; I would never go out walking with someone without seeking your approval first."

"Very good. But Grazia . . ."

"Yes, mistress?"

"I was serious when I said I need your attention entirely on your work here. You know this is our busiest time. I don't want to have to worry about your commitment."

"Of course not, mistress! You have my commitment," Grazia assured her. It was true, she told herself. The mistress did have her commitment. *But not your entire attention,* whispered another internal voice, and Grazia felt the pricks of conscience.

Mistress Meran seemed satisfied, however. She stood aside, and Grazia entered.

The next morning was busy with several consultations and measurings. Grazia's hands did their work as her mind tackled the problem of how to approach Princess Marguerite, but even her imagination's best inventions could not overcome the chasm between the princess's station and her own. *It's impossible,* she thought dispiritedly. *I will have to pick a different young lady, maybe one of these here today.* She ran her measuring tape (notched, so she could feel each finger-width, half-finger-width, and quarter-finger-width) from the neck to the waist of Lady Stella.

But no other could dance like Princess Marguerite, and no other would be introducing the ecstasie, the dance that was sweeping the continent. Princess Marguerite would take the floor with a partner (who would it be? Many names were whispered, but gossip hadn't settled on one yet), commanding the attention of all assembled. Grazia sighed. On anyone less than Princess Marguerite, the dress she was planning would be wasted.

" . . . is offering another tutorial this afternoon at Golden House, and I said I would go, but I don't want to, Nini; I'm so tired of the ecstasie. How can a dance be both so exhausting and so complicated?"

What had been background chatter to Grazia's ears now registered with sharp force. "Nini" was Lady Stella's pet name for her older sister, Lady Serena, whom other hands were measuring.

"You don't want to make a fool of yourself at the Midsummer Ball," Lady Serena replied. "The princess is gracious to offer these tutorials—just go, as you promised!"

Grazia's hands froze on the notepaper where she was marking down measurements for the sighted to read and translate to cloth. It had to be Princess Marguerite offering this tutorial.

"No, I tell you, Nini, I'm not in the mood today," Lady Stella replied, fretful. "Maybe another day. The princess is so mad for this dance, I'm sure I'll have another chance. Lila, when we're finished here, you must convey my regrets to Golden House." That last directed at the maidservant who had accompanied them.

"Stella, you can't send Lila on that errand!" the older sister admonished. "You know I need her to—"

Grazia saw her opportunity and seized it.

"My ladies, let us aid you in this matter. Mistress, did you not mean to request Princess Allegra's presence for the gusset adjustment? I can bear that message to Golden House and also let Princess Marguerite know that Lady Stella will not be attending the tutorial."

"Why yes; yes, that's right," said Mistress Meran, surprised. "Good thinking, Grazia."

And so Grazia contrived to meet Princess Marguerite after all—even had a request for a private audience granted.

⚬⊙℘ ℘⊙⚬

"My sister mentioned you," the princess remarked as Grazia rose from her curtsey. "The blind seamstress's assistant with the noisy cloth."

Grazia felt the blood rush to her cheeks. Would the princess even deign to consider Grazia's proposal? She took a deep breath. "Your royal sister was very wise—that fabric was ill conceived. The dress my mistress is working on now will be much more suitable." Mindful of her ostensible errand, Grazia mentioned the gusset adjustment next, and then turned to her true topic. "Your

Highness, I wish to speak to you about something different. There is a fabric being woven as we speak that will make a gown only a dancer such Your Highness should wear – a very special dress."

"I'm not interested in a special dress." Dismissive. "Your atelier is going to adjust one of my sister's gowns for me, taking it in and letting out where necessary. I'll have fabric added at the sides so it will swirl nicely when I turn. That's all I need. That's all I want." Rustling followed those words as the princess turned to go. Grazia's opportunity was slipping away.

"Your Highness." The words caught in Grazia's throat. She tried again. "Your Highness, this will be a gown unlike any other. This will be a gown that weds the wearer more closely to the music. Indeed, as the wearer dances, she becomes the music."

There was a swish – the princess turning round? Then stillness and silence for a long moment, and then more rustling as the princess drew nearer. She must have come close indeed, for Grazia could feel the warmth of her.

"This dress you propose – how would it accomplish that?"

"Your dancing will turn it into an instrument, which as you move, you play," Grazia said. "Music, dancer, and dance, united in one person."

"To dance clothed in music," breathed the princess. She was silent again for a moment. When she spoke, her voice was sharp. "And you can really accomplish this? With no noisy bells?"

"No bells at all, Your Highness." Grazia felt sweat beading along her hairline and at the back of her neck.

"My partner . . ." the princess began.

Grazia tensed. The mysterious partner whose identity no one was sure of.

"He is an enchanting dancer, but how can I say it. He thinks very highly of himself. If you can create a gown that does all you say – well, I should very much like to wear it, not just for the delight of it, nor for the delight it will bestow on others, but for the pleasure of seeing the wonder in my partner's eyes. So bring me this dress, when you have finished it, and I will try it on. If it does all you promise, I'll wear it. But I still expect to have my sister's gown adjusted for my use—just in case."

"Of course; I understand. Thank you, Your Highness!" Grazia tried to maintain her composure, but a rush of joy made her voice tremble. Then, remembering, "Oh! And one other thing. Lady Stella will be unable to join your tutorial this afternoon."

Princess Marguerite emitted an unprincesslike snort. "Of course. Stella is almost as bad as my sister about mastering anything more complicated than a waltz. No matter. The tutorial will go more quickly without her."

And with that, the audience was over. Grazia practically floated back to the atelier.

The next day Grazia bent her mind entirely to the tasks Mistress Meran set before her, so that she was surprised when, at supper, Mistress Meran's maid Betty announced to the table at large that someone from Master Grayling's manufactory had come round to the back door, hoping to see Grazia.

"The weaver girl!" Grazia exclaimed, remembering her promise. She excused herself and hurried up the stairs to the assistants' sleeping quarters to fetch the cloth that Princess Allegra had rejected. "Noisy cloth," she murmured as she picked it up. "So unfair. If I had to describe you, I'd call you bell cloth. Much nicer." She sighed. "You're not suitable for a ball, though; the princess was right about that."

She brought it down to the waiting weaver girl, who wrapped herself in it right then and there and twirled round—creating a rustling of leaves and wind-chime tinkles.

"And if you do a few dance steps, bells will start to ring," Grazia told her.

The girl gave Grazia a quick, tight embrace like she had the previous day, then kissed Grazia's cheek and squeezed Grazia's hands between her own, pumping them up and down and repeating her delight and thanks. Grazia laughed, embarrassed and pleased. Betty closed the door after the girl as she left, and only then did Grazia become aware of Mistress Meran's starch-

and-rose presence beside her.

"You gave your special fabric to that child? That was very generous of you." The mistress's disapproving tone belied her words.

"N-not really," Grazia stammered. "The princess was right; no lady would want a dress of it. And I can't clothe myself in it; I rely on my hearing too much to be surrounded by bells and chimes."

"Mmm. How did the child happen to ask you for it?"

Grazia was momentarily confused by the question, then realized what the mistress was hinting at. A little flame of panic leapt up within her. The girl couldn't possibly have asked Grazia for the cloth—would have had no opportunity to do so—had Grazia not been at Master Grayling's manufactory. She cast about for a clever story, a chance encounter, but came up with nothing. At last she blurted out, "I went to the Master Grayling's workshop. I-I wanted to have some cloth made. For myself—for later! I'm focused on my work, mistress, I promise."

"I see," said Mistress Meran, but Grazia heard suspicion in her voice.

The following night, when the girl from the manufactory returned, this time bearing the precious parcel of fairy cloth, Grazia was not surprised to hear the mistress's footfalls draw up alongside her.

"May I see this fabric you've commissioned?" Mistress Meran asked.

Reluctantly, Grazia opened the parcel.

"Raw silk—a little luxurious for you, isn't it, Grazia? But undyed and unfigured—too understated for today's young ladies." The mistress was musing out loud. Grazia bit her lip and said nothing.

"And this is truly not part of some outside project? You're not letting some will-o'-the-wisp idea distract you?"

"I'm focused on my work, mistress," Grazia replied carefully. She held her breath as Mistress Meran took the cloth from her. It whispered in the ordinary way of fabric as the mistress shook it out and examined it. Nothing about it revealed Grazia's plans for it.

"High-quality material of the sort Master Grayling always produces," Mistress Meran remarked. "Here it is, then. Make sure you put it away for now."

"Yes, mistress."

The mistress's footsteps receded down the corridor, and Grazia was left fumbling with the fabric.

"Let me help you, miss—I'll take one end and you the other, and we'll meet, like folding bedsheets."

The weight lessened in Grazia's hands, and between her and the weaver girl, the fabric was soon a tidy bundle once again.

"Thank you, ah . . ."

"I'm called Wisp, miss, on account of Papa says I'm just a wisp of a thing."

"Thank you, Wisp."

"It's nothing. I'm happy to see you again, miss! The master had a message for you, too, about the cloth, but I didn't want to mention while that other lady was here."

"I appreciate that!" Grazia said, silently blessing Wisp for her discretion.

"Master says, you have to teach it. Talk to it and let it hear music, so it learns."

"Thank you very much, Wisp. I'll do that!"

The two parted, and Grazia bore her precious package up the stairs to the sleeping quarters.

᎐᎐᎑ ᎑᎐᎐

Grazia had two tasks now: infuse the fairy fabric with knowledge of music, and sew from it a gown for Princess Marguerite. The latter could not be done until Golden House sent over the gown of Princess Allegra's that Atelier Aurora would refit for Princess Marguerite, and each day came and went without its arriving, even as the date of the Midsummer Ball drew nearer.

But there was no reason, Grazia reasoned, why the fabric couldn't be educated in music before it was turned into a gown, so every other evening she'd been skipping supper and heading to Cygnus Conservatory, where all the aspiring musicians trained. Each night she'd pick a different window to stand beneath. One night it would be violins and cellos, the next, flutes, the next, the harpsichord.

"Do you hear how mellow the horns can be?" she'd whisper to the cloth in her arms, as trumpets played, and when oboes joined in, she'd say, "Do you hear how they support one another, like brothers?" And her fingers would tingle as the magical fibers in the cloth vibrated.

It was the oboe she liked best—both winsome and throaty, odd enough to catch the attention and yet as well-behaved as any of the instruments when played by someone accomplished, like the musician who tutored in the room with the third window on the south wall. He was a good teacher, too, patient even with the most tone-deaf pupils. His pleasant voice had a touch of the southern coast to it, and that very voice addressed her one evening, when, as the hour of curfew drew near, she pulled her shawl around her and headed down from her listening post.

"You must love music very much to listen to the efforts of beginners—Oh! . . . Oh."

Grazia recognized from experience the reaction of dismay and regret that her sightless eyes could provoke in strangers.

"No need, sir, for that tone," she said with asperity. "My ears' pleasure in music isn't diminished by the condition of my eyes."

"I beg your pardon." Sounding rueful, sincere.

"No matter," said Grazia with a sigh. "I listen to beginners because I—because I am trying to learn, for myself, the mysteries of harmony and how the instruments speak to one another."

"Do you not wish to play an instrument, yourself?"

"No—no, I-I just want to hear and understand." Beneath her shawl, she squeezed the fairy fabric to her chest.

"In that case, may I invite you to listen from inside the

classroom? It will do the students good to know they have an audience. My name is Junio Fenwood—I'm an oboist."

Grazia's cheeks warmed at the invitation.

"Thank you. I know you're an oboist." Flustered by her own admission, she quickly added, "I'm Grazia Goodchild, one of Mistress Meran's assistant seamstresses at Atelier Aurora."

"Ah! The blind seamstress! Is it true you made a dress that chimes when the wearer moves?"

"No, not a dress," Grazia murmured, shame rising. "It was just fabric, fabric that I commissioned from the fairy weaver. It was a foolish idea."

"Why foolish? Imagine how pleasant a gazebo would be, decorated with chiming streamers. And even as attire . . . well, I think it has potential."

Just like that, Grazia's shame disappeared. She smiled.

"About your invitation. If you're sure it's no intrusion, then I'll come the day after tomorrow to your classroom," she said.

On Grazia's first visit to the classroom, Junio noticed and inquired about the cloth she was carrying, but she put him off. He asked again after her second visit, and Grazia was so won over by his friendly manner that after some hesitation—and the departure of his pupil—she explained what it was and why she brought it with her.

"Fascinating!" he said. "May I see it?"

She let him take it, heard him unfold it ("oh . . . lovely stuff," he said), heard him turn on his heel, heard the fabric shift and slide.

"But . . . there's no music," he said.

"Because there's no one playing," Grazia replied. "This isn't like the bell fabric. This fabric will only respond when music's playing, and when its wearer is moving."

"I see. Then I'll play, and you dance." He draped the cloth over her shoulders.

"I—"

But Junio was walking to the far end of the room, and soon the oboe's reedy, sonorous tones came floating over, a sedate little melody.

I don't dance, Grazia had been going to say, because she had never been tutored in dancing. And yet as a child she'd whirled and spun about the way all children do in play. She remembered the explosive joy she had felt when the holy sisters let her and the other foundlings into the courtyard to play, remembered pulling off shoes and stockings and twirling round and round on the sun-warmed gravel until she could stop and the world would keep spinning around her. Now, so many years later, she extended her arms and turned and turned on the tips of her toes.

As she did, two oboes could be heard: Junio's, playing the melody, and Grazia's cloth, dancing in and out of the melody in a spritely fashion. Junio brought the tune to a close.

"Brilliant, just brilliant!" he said. "Can it do other instruments as well?"

"For now, it can only echo the instrument it hears. If I want others to join in, I must embroider their names—but to play them, it must know them."

"Ah. Then we must contrive to have it hear the fairy pipes." His voice grave, thoughtful.

"Fairy pipes? Why is that? Fairy pipes are not part of a chamber orchestra."

"No, but the dance your princess is going to premier, the ecstasie—it's a fairy dance. Did you not know? That's why it's so devilishly hard for all the young ladies and gentlemen to master. The orchestra has been promised that a musician from the Fair Vale will come to play with us, but so far no one has joined a rehearsal."

Cold dread settled in Grazia's stomach. Here was a new obstacle. She felt a breath at the back of her neck and imagined it was Master Grayling, laughing—but it was just the air from the hallway as Junio opened the door of the classroom.

"I promise I'll send word to you when I know the fairy piper will be joining us," he said, giving Grazia's hand a reassuring squeeze. "And perhaps—but no: you must keep your mind on your work."

Grazia's spirits rose at Junio's *perhaps,* though she couldn't have said why.

"Perhaps what?" she asked.

"Perhaps I'll mention it next time you come," he replied, teasing.

Grazia returned to the atelier with a spring in her step and a smile on her face, in spite of the news about the piper.

But at the atelier Mistress Meran was waiting in the doorway for her once again.

"I see you haven't given up your evening strolls," she observed. Grazia was at a loss for how to reply.

"I am not happy with this habit of yours," the mistress continued.

Grazia's momentary pleasure evaporated.

"Mistress, it's not every night. And the quality of my work hasn't suffered, has it?" Grazia was aware that fatigue sat more heavily on her shoulders than it used to. Sometimes she'd find herself pausing, needle in hand, for a long moment, head in a fog, but had the mistress noticed?

"It hasn't suffered, no," the mistress admitted. "But I still don't like your absences."

Grazia gathered her courage. "It's after hours, mistress. I'm not meeting an admirer—" (but here Grazia's heart beat a little faster) "—and I'm returning by curfew. Are you forbidding me to go out?" She held her breath.

"In the past I wouldn't have needed to even consider such a thing," Mistress Meran said. "And yet now? I don't know, Grazia! I don't like the notion of you wandering about the town of an evening! It seems . . . disreputable."

"Mistress, I would never do anything to shame myself or you."

"I suppose not." Mistress Meran sighed. "And it would be wrong to punish you prospectively. So no. I am not forbidding you to go out."

Grazia curtseyed silently and headed to the sleeping quarters.

⁕⁕⁕

"Can you please lie down? I can't fall asleep with you sitting there doing . . . whatever it is you're doing." From the bed facing Grazia's came the whiny voice of Grazia's least-favorite fellow assistant, Marigold. Lights-out had passed some while ago, and Grazia had believed the other five assistants to be sound asleep. Taking advantage of the fact that she didn't need light to work, she'd been embroidering the names of instruments just above the selvage of her cloth. At Marigold's complaint, however, she cut the silk floss, folded the fabric, and slid it under her mattress.

"What *were* you doing?" Marigold asked suspiciously, lowering her voice as Beatrice and Delphine stirred in their beds.

"Practicing embroidering," Grazia said — an almost-truth.

Marigold snorted. "You should stick to seams and assembly. Who's going to want a dress embroidered by a blind person? Suppose you pick up the wrong-colored floss one day? You'll be merrily embroidering a dove, only it'll be orange or violet or who knows what color. What a disaster!"

In fact, Grazia had a method for keeping track of what color each of her cards of floss were — as with her tape measure, it involved patterns of notches — but she knew better than to bother trying to explain it.

The bed next to Grazia creaked noisily and Dephine said irritably, "Would you two mind saving the conversation for morning? Some of us are trying to sleep." Whump! Delphine must have pushed herself up on an elbow to deliver this request, and now she fell back emphatically onto her pillow.

"I'm sorry," Grazia said. "I'm lying down now." Across the way, Marigold sniffed, but said no more. Delphine's bed creaked again as the girl brought her head closer to Grazia's.

"Don't mind Marigold," Delphine whispered. "She's anxious

and cross because Mistress Meran gave her the Princess Marguerite job and is already criticizing her work—and with not many days until the ball!"

"What? The dress for Princess Marguerite is here?" Grazia kept her voice to a whisper, but it still came out ragged and harsh.

"It was delivered this evening . . . you were out . . ." Delphine's words melted into mumbles and then silence. Grazia was left alone with her racing heart and thoughts in the thick stillness of the night.

Nor did morning bring any relief. Bright and early Betty came into the workroom to announce (with a giggle) that there was a gentleman with a message for Grazia. Burning with mortification, Grazia went swiftly to the front door, thankful that Mistress Meran had not been in the room to hear.

It was Junio.

"You can't come here like this and call on me," Grazia said, aware of Betty hovering nearby. "We can't have callers without the mistress's approval."

"Yes, all right—I will have to obtain that—but listen: the fairy piper is coming today to practice with us. He'll arrive around noon and stay through evening. You must come!"

"I can't—I went out yesterday. The mistress—" Grazia couldn't finish the sentence. Invisible hands were wringing her insides like a dishrag. What would the mistress say if Grazia went out two nights in a row? What would she say if she learned that a young man had come calling here? And how could the piper be at the conservatory today, when she needed to concentrate on getting her hands on the dress for Princess Marguerite?

"You must. He may not come again before the Midsummer Ball. For your project to succeed . . ." It was Junio's turn to leave a sentence hanging.

"Thank you for the message," Grazia said. "I'll . . . see what I can do."

She closed the door. Only then did the realization hit her: Junio had said he would have to get the mistress's approval to call on her! It was as if a flock of sparrows inhabited her insides and had chosen this moment to suddenly rise in flight. But no time for such fancies now. *The princess's dress. The piper. The princess's dress. The piper.*

In the workroom, Marigold was complaining loudly that the mistress had required her to redo several seams on the altered gown. Beatrice was offering perfunctory sympathy. Two other assistants, Magda and Helena, were working silently.

"The mistress has retired to her quarters—headache," Delphine confided as Grazia took her place.

Not surprising, thought Grazia as Marigold continued listing the many ways the mistress was unfair. Usually, Grazia would just ignore the other girl, but not today. She took a deep breath and turned toward the stream of complaints.

"Marigold, would you like some help with the seams on Princess Marguerite's gown? I'd be happy to work on them."

"Oh, sure. It's not enough that you were the lead assembler on Princess Allegra's dress, now you want credit for Princess Marguerite's too? No, thank you; I'll manage it."

"I—No, no . . . That's not it at all. I-I just . . ." Grazia felt a dangerous confusion. She had no intention of stealing credit for Marigold's gown alteration, but wouldn't her plan, if successful, eclipse Marigold even more completely? Marigold was always irksome and sometimes downright unpleasant, but Grazia had no desire to hurt her. But what was she to do now? Not make the dress? And forfeit the talent in her fingers to Master Grayling? She grimaced.

"No need to look so offended," Marigold said. "If you really want to help, you could go to Master Grayling's manufactory for me and fetch some more of the noonday sunlight thread. I'm going to add some sunbeam flashes to the gathers the princess asked to have added in."

"Marigold!" exclaimed Delphine. "Grazia's not your servant! Go yourself if you want more thread, or send Betty!"

"You know Betty won't go—she's got a fear of the fairies, and I don't blame her. Everybody knows fairies are dangerous, and Master Grayling gives me nightmares. Those spindly legs and those awful long fingers, ugh. If Grazia really wants to help me, she'll go." Petulant, sulky voice.

"I will go!" Grazia declared. *And on my way, I'll stop at the conservatory and let my fabric hear the fairy piper,* she thought, shoving away her moral qualms about stealing Marigold's glory. "But it may take me a while," she added. "Master Grayling has a way of keeping people waiting."

"You can stay away all afternoon, as far as I'm concerned — just bring back the thread," said Marigold, and when Delphine protested she shot back, "What? The goody two-shoes always manages to catch up if she falls behind, and I'll be glad for an afternoon without having to look at her prissy face." As Grazia departed, she could just hear Marigold saying, "I'm sure she has some scheme up her sleeve, anyway. You saw how she jumped at the chance to leave."

The halls of the conservatory were much more crowded when Grazia arrived than they had ever been during her evening visits. Competing, expensive perfumes, powders, and scented pomades reached her nose, along with undercurrents of sweat and fresh flowers. She wove her way through the silk- and brocade-clad crowd until she reached the door of Junio's practice room. All around her people were talking in excited whispers, and then, "That's him! He's here."

The inaudible hum of magic was in the air, the scent of it, almost like pepper, as people jostled and moved aside to let the fairy piper through. From within the practice room, Grazia heard Junio say that they'd be practicing the music for the ecstasie — and then the music started.

Chills swept through Grazia. It was all she could do to keep her feet and body still — she could feel others around her struggling against the same urge — and the cloth practically came alive in her arms, its fairy weft snapping with energy. And then Grazia was no longer aware of the cloth or the crowd or even herself. There was only the music, the irresistible, enchanting music.

Sometime later, Grazia realized that people were talking again and moving away from the doorway, and that the music had stopped. She pushed against the flow of the departing crowd, hoping to catch Junio, when an unexpected voice reached her ear.

"Ah, it's the seamstress with the secret project. Are you still working on that for me? The Midsummer Ball is just three days away." Princess Marguerite.

Grazia's heart drummed. So little time! But the magical skirl of the piper's playing was still within her, and anything seemed possible. "Of course, Your Highness," she replied lightly. "I shall bring it to you in two days' time."

This drew an indulgent laugh from the princess. "Very good," she said. "I look forward to it." And she swept by.

In the princess's wake, Grazia shivered. The influence of the fairy melody was fading. Could she truly cut and sew the dress in time? She would have to get hold of Marigold's work this very night. *Marigold. The sunlight thread!* She had to hurry.

"Wait! Miss Goodchild! You made it! And now you're leaving without saying hello? We'll still be practicing for hours more—can you not stay longer?" It was Junio, breathless, but full of questions. "How did you like the music of the fairy pipes? How did you like the ecstasie?" His warm hands clasped one of hers, which she reluctantly slipped free.

"Mr. Fenwood, hello! I am sorry to make my visit so brief—I would like to stay—but I've already been absent from my work too long, and there's still an errand I must run."

"Then when am I going to have a chance to dance with you?" he burst out, and the question startled Grazia to a standstill.

"Oh, Mr. Fenwood," she replied, regret and chagrin almost bringing tears to her eyes. "I don't dance—how could someone like me dance? I am a working woman, a—a professional, not a lady, and—"

He interrupted her with an incredulous laugh. "You think

only ladies and gentlemen dance? All people dance. My father's a bricklayer, and he dances."

"But not this kind of dancing." With a wave of her hand she indicated the conservatory, the orchestra, and by extension ballrooms and balls. "I know nothing of it—except the gowns the ladies wear."

"Then let me teach you!"

What delicious temptation! But the danger if Grazia didn't complete the dress for Princess Marguerite was too great for her to give in.

"Another time," she whispered, and hurried away.

ఎంల ఆ

"Ugh, don't come so close; you stink of magic," Marigold said, snatching the card of sunlight thread from Grazia's hand. "I think I'm going to sneeze!"

"Only Marigold could dislike the smell of magic," whispered Helena to Magda.

Grazia returned to her seat and pulled out her work. She thought she might jump out of her skin with impatience for the day to end and everyone to go to sleep. After a supper that seemed to pass twice as slowly as usual, though the chiming clock said otherwise, Mistress Meran made a brief appearance to dismiss her assistants for bed. Lights out followed, and sometime later, general stillness and long, slow breathing from the beds around her told Grazia that the house was hers.

Carefully and quietly she got up, took her fabric from beneath her mattress, and made her way downstairs. She shivered; the night air was cold when all one was wearing was a sleeping shift. She went to Marigold's seat and took out the gown that Marigold was altering for Princess Marguerite.

With a tiny pair of scissors in her right hand, Grazia felt for the seams of the gown with her left. She would have to take this dress apart to use the pieces as models for her own. Her mouth felt unaccountably dry. She wished she dared get some water, but the less moving around she did, the less likely it was that anyone would wake up. Quietly, she began snipping the threads of the seam.

Next she cut pieces from the fairy cloth, basting certain ones together rapidly and marking others with diamonds, squares, and triangles to remind herself which ones should go with which. Then, with silent footsteps, she climbed the stairs to the sleeping quarters and slipped the work-in-progress into its hiding place. Back in the workroom, she worked with concentration and diligence to return Marigold's dress to its original state. The bodice—always a fussy potion of a gown—done. The sleeves— done. The extra gathers—done.

At some point, it became hard to keep her mind on the work. She wanted to put her head down—and did, just for a moment. She found herself half imagining, half dreaming that she was back in the conservatory, with Junio's voice in her ear and his hand on her back.

"Come dance with me," he was saying.

"Just let me finish this," she begged, holding up Marigold's work.

"But all you've got left are the long seams," he pointed out. "Long and straight—easy. You can finish them in no time. Let's dance."

Soon Grazia was deeply asleep. Until—

"Miss, what are you doing down here? Sun's not up yet—how come you're not in bed? And where's your clothes? And ain't that Miss Marigold's seat?"

Grazia woke with a start, banging her knees against the work table. It was Betty, who always rose first to open curtains and help Cook prepare breakfast. A knife of fear went through her heart. The long seams! Her fingers found her needle and she quickly began sewing.

"I-I'm just . . . I'm helping Marigold with the seams," she stuttered.

"But Miss Grazia . . . You're still in your shift. And you was sleeping."

Heat burned in Grazia's cheeks. She opened her mouth, but no words came out.

"Maybe you was sleepwalking or something," Betty suggested. "Let me fetch the mistress."

"No, no, there's no need!" Grazia jumped to her feet and succeeded in knocking Marigold's chair into Helena's. "I'm fine," she insisted, straightening the chair. "I'll—I'll go back to bed. I just—"

"What's going on here? Grazia, what are you doing down here at this hour, dressed like that?"

Mistress Meran. In the background Grazia could hear the thud of footfalls and other voices—the other assistants, awakened by the commotion.

"Princess Marguerite's dress—that's my project! Mistress, Grazia is ruining my work! She's taking it apart!" Marigold's voice, rising in pitch and volume with each word.

"No, I'm not!"

"Then why is this seam undone?" Marigold was next to Grazia now, her sour morning breath full in Grazia's face. "I had this seam done, mistress! And look at it!" Marigold was practically in tears now.

"I'm putting it back together! I'll finish it in no time," Grazia said.

"How came it to be undone?" asked the mistress coldly.

"It's because she went to Master Grayling's," whispered Magda to Helena. "He bewitched her." Delphine shushed her.

Grazia had no answer. She couldn't tell Mistress Meran about the dress she'd been working on—the mistress had said no side projects, and Grazia's last initiative was the subject of ridicule. She couldn't claim she was helping Marigold—Marigold would deny it loud and long.

"You're an ambitious girl and a secretive one, but I don't believe you're malicious," the mistress said. "Tell me the truth:

what were you doing?"

"She was trying to ruin my dress!" Marigold cried.

"I wasn't!"

"Did you take out this seam?" Mistress Meran again, stern.

Grazia bit her lip.

"Answer me!"

"Yes, I did."

The other assistants' gasps faded into a resounding silence.

"You'll ask her to leave now, won't you mistress?" Marigold said triumphantly. "You can't let someone who'd do such a thing stay on!"

"Peace, Marigold," Mistress Meran said sharply, and then to Grazia, "Explain yourself. Whatever possessed you — what possible reason could you have to — to. . ." The question hung unfinished in the air.

Grazia had a sudden urge to confess, to throw herself on the mercy of the mistress. Maybe, after all, Mistress Meran would forgive everything; maybe — just maybe — she would embrace Grazia's project.

And if she doesn't? If she somehow prevents you from finishing? Will you gamble the skill in your fingers on her forbearance?

Grazia's eyes filled with tears.

"I-I can't explain," she croaked.

Mistress Meran exhaled deeply. "Then Marigold is right. I'm sorry, Grazia, but I must ask you to leave."

"Mistress, I-I assure you —"

"You assure me nothing! You tell me nothing! Now, when I need you most, you bring things to this!"

Grazia's heart constricted, but her tongue remained a lump of lead in her mouth.

"Go pack your things," the mistress said.

Dumbly, Grazia went upstairs one last time. She got dressed and packed her few personal items, including the secret gown, into the valise she had brought with her from the foundlings' home four years ago. The mistress was waiting for her in the hall by the front door.

"You may not claim any association with Atelier Aurora, and you should expect no reference from me," the mistress said, cold and formal. "Here is the payment owed you." She placed a soft velvet bag, not that heavy, in Grazia's hand. Then, much more quietly: "I'm sorry things came to this, Grazia. But I need to be able to trust my assistants."

"I understand, mistress," Grazia said, voice quavering. And she took her leave.

ഇരുള ളിരു

The last place Grazia had any intention of going was Master Grayling's manufactory, and yet somehow she found herself by the willow sheds, with the clacking of the shuttle bar and the thumping lift-and-fall of heddles filling her ears. When she leaned against the nearest wall, the vibrations went right through her, and the scents of magic, oil, and human labor seeped out from within.

I should have gone to the conservatory, she thought. *Junio –*

Junio what? another part of her demanded. *You have a gown to sew. Were you planning to sit yourself down beneath his window – or in his classroom – and take out your needle and thread?*

The thought filled her with shame. Here, at least, not many would see her—few ladies or gentleman came down to the manufactory, and the workers were surely too busy within to notice her. She straightened up and stood far enough away from the wall that her fingers only just reached it when she stretched out her arm. Then she let those fingers guide her along the wall's length. When she felt a bush brush against her waist on the other side, she sank down. Here she'd be hidden from sight. The damp seeped up through her dress, but she paid it no mind. She opened her valise, took out her pin cushion and scissors, and lifted the gown into her lap. Time to sew.

At some point her stomach complained about the lack of

lunch, but Grazia ignored it. She ignored it again when it begged for supper. Could it be that late already? But yes, the sun must have traveled the full arc of the sky, for when Grazia had sat down to sew, her left cheek and shoulder had felt its warm touch, and now it was her right cheek and shoulder that did, though only weakly. The sun must be very low, almost set. Grazia shifted her legs and winced as the blood flowed back into them. Carefully she folded up the gown and put it back in her valise. It was almost done, but she couldn't take it to the princess almost done. She'd promised it for tomorrow, and there could be no delaying—the Midsummer Ball was the day after.

Fine; she could keep working—she was even less likely to be noticed after the sun set—but first she must stretch, find some place to answer the call of nature, and possibly buy a bite to eat.

She got to her feet, but her head felt strange. The world seemed to be tipping and spinning, and she lost her balance and landed on her knees. She tried again, slowly this time. Success. She brushed at the wet patches on her dress, hoping it was not too badly stained.

A sound like wind chimes and distant bells met her ears, something with a hint of magic to it, raising the hairs on her arms and the back of her neck. It was regular, rhythmical, like a river over rocks. Another wave of dizziness assaulted Grazia, and she clung to the wall of the willow shed for support. The bells and chimes faded away.

"Miss, what are you doing here?"

It was Wisp, the young girl from the manufactory. "Are you all right?" Wisp asked. "You look quite poorly, if you don't mind my saying. Are you going to faint? Here, let me give you a hand."

Leaves rustled and the wind chimes tinkled again as Wisp's hand found Grazia's arm.

"The chimes," Grazia murmured as she let Wisp lead her away from her hiding spot. "Is it—are you wearing something made from the cloth I gave you?"

"Oh, yes! I got two kerchiefs made of it, with fringe—all the girls do. My team's off early tonight and tomorrow because of the midsummer festival, and we're dancing. Boys'll be watching—not that I care about that, but the older girls been talking for days about who they might give a kerchief to." A pause. "Do you want to come? But you ain't well. Maybe you need to rest a spell first. You can lie down on my bed. You can stay with me as long as you like!"

At Grazia's request, they stopped first at the latrine, then entered the dormitory for the manufactory's pickers and frame spinners.

"It's my sister come for a visit, but she's feeling poorly, so I'm just going to have her rest up," Wisp announced, hustling Grazia past the matron. "Lie down here," the girl ordered, pushing Grazia onto a coarse woolen blanket pulled tight and tucked neatly under a thin mattress. "I'll be back with a cup of water in a —" Wisp's last words disappeared in the din of chattering, excited voices and the chiming, tinkling, and pealing of bells. Grazia let herself drift into semi-slumber, lulled by the tapestry of sound and activity, only to be awakened by Wisp thrusting a cup in her hand.

"Drink that," the girl said, and after Grazia finished, Wisp put a pebble-sized something in Grazia's hand. "Fair Vale rock," she explained. "One of Master Grayling's investors passed it out after a visit. It's sweet, and if you eat it, your aches and pains just disappear. Matron says we mustn't eat too much of it, but matron also says no food in the dorm, so . . ."

Grazia sensed the girl's shrug. With some trepidation she put the piece of Fair Vale rock in her mouth. It melted bit by bit, sweet and tangy, as she turned it over with her tongue. As she swallowed the liquor, well-being flowed down to her fingers and toes, and her heart lightened.

"That's better. You look more yourself now, miss."

"Grazia. Please call me Grazia."

"I don't know, miss. It seems cheeky . . ."

"No, not cheeky. Please. It'll make me feel like I have a sister."

Was the influence of the Fair Vale rock responsible for this admission? Grazia's yearning for parents and siblings was something she usually kept buried deep within herself.

"Wisp! You coming?" An impatient voice, one of the other manufactory girls.

"Are *you* coming, mi . . . Grazia?" Wisps asked in turn. Hesitant, expectant.

"Yes. Yes, I'll come." Grazia grabbed her valise — she could sew while the others danced.

In the four years Grazia had worked at Atelier Aurora, she had never once been to the midsummer festival — the atelier was always too busy with work for the Midsummer Ball. Nor had the prayerful sisters at the foundlings' home ever seen fit to bring their charges to it, so Grazia had never smelled the midsummer's delicacies that vendors sold — flash-fried fingerlings on skewers and deep-fried "baker's kisses," dusted with sugar, paper cones filled with fresh strawberries, and daylily fritters. Grazia bought two baker's kisses and offered one to Wisp, but the girl refused. "It's bad luck to dance on a full stomach," she explained. "Nancy! Hira! Wait up! You settle yourself right here, Grazia — you'll see our dance as well with your ears as anyone ever did with their eyes!"

Laughing, Grazia sat where Wisp told her to. High-spirited voices surrounded her, and in the background, a sound like the whoosh of a bellows, with occasional staccato snaps — the midsummer bonfire, its fragrant smoke wreathing in and out among the other scents. Grazia popped one of the baker's kisses into her mouth and savored its sweet, crispy crust and fluffy interior. Then she opened her valise, pulled the gown onto her lap, and started sewing with swift, neat stitches.

Stamping and clapping told her Wisp's dance was about to begin. It was patterned and rhythmical, like drumming. Then, rhythmic as the stamping, came the rush of wind in leaves and the sound of chimes and bells, growing deeper and louder when the stamping was faster, quieter and lighter when the stamping was slow. Grazia's heart swelled. The girls had taken her failed fabric and made something wonderful from it.

"Miss Goodchild!" The warm and friendly tones of Junio! "I never thought to run into you here—no, don't get up; I can see you're working, but let me sit beside you? What excitement, eh? The manufactory girls—their kerchiefs—they're made from the first cloth you commissioned, aren't they. Marvelous. And to think: soon the world will see—or should I say, hear—something even more marvelous."

He nudged her arm gently, not enough to interrupt her busy needle, and Grazia couldn't keep a grin from her face. She set the sewing aside. "Here," she said, practically shouting to be heard over the whoops and cheers of the crowd and the medley of other noises, "I have a treat for you—a baker's kiss."

"A baker's kiss?" he asked, emphasizing the word *baker's*, and maybe it was the influence of the Fair Vale rock again, but Grazia laughed.

"Just so," she said, holding it out. He lifted it lightly from her fingers.

"Mmm, delicious," he declared, and Grazia wondered if she'd ever felt so happy. She returned to her sewing, each dip of the needle in time with the crowd's clapping.

Amidst the clamor, something not quite audible but powerful caught Grazia's attention, and a tingling ran from the crown of her head to the tips of her fingers. The gown in her lap seemed to awaken, as if it were listening. She jumped to her feet.

"What is it?" asked Junio.

"It's Master Grayling. The fairy weaver."

Junio drew a sharp breath. "That's no weaver; that's—"

But Master Grayling—for it was surely him; Grazia could not mistake the master weaver's voice—interrupted.

"What have we here? The disgraced seamstress's assistant, reduced to sewing in the public square, my precious fabric resting on her dirty skirts. Why don't I just collect the talent in your fingers now, and then you can turn your full attention to your lover here?"

"I don't care who you are—you beg the young lady's forgiveness for that outrageous insult right now!" cried Junio, his voice shaking a little.

"Or what? You'll challenge me to a duel? You realize I can turn you into a cockroach or a fly. Or—you're an oboist, aren't you. So maybe a piping frog or—"

"Stop!" said Grazia. She wasn't sure if it was anger, desperation, or terror that fueled her agitation. "It doesn't matter how my skirts look or where I'm sewing! The dress will be finished by tomorrow, and I'll bring it to Princess Marguerite, as I promised. And it will be everything that I said it would be! So if you please, Master Grayling, leave me in peace until then!"

"Everything?" Master Grayling repeated, sounding skeptical.

"I'll prove it to you, right now," Grazia said, draping the half-finished gown around her neck. "Junio, will you join me?" She held out her arm, then crooked it on her waist, and Junio interlaced his with hers.

"I thought you didn't dance," he whispered, his breath warm in her ear.

"This isn't that kind of dancing," she whispered back. The manufactory girls were still dancing. Grazia began moving in small steps to the rhythm of their stamping. Together she and Junio went first forward, then round and round.

"But there's no melody for the gown to harmonize with," Junio murmured. "How can this work?"

"There's the sound of the bells, and there's a rhythm," Grazia replied. "I hope—I believe . . ." *that the gown can create a melody to go along with them.*

She didn't dare speak her hope aloud, and it didn't happen exactly as she imagined, but sure enough, from the gown came the trills and skirls of the fairy pipes—not a melody, but a waterfall of sound, enhancing the ringing of the bells and fading when the bells were at their fullest. And dotting throughout, quick notes on the violin and the occasional plaintive whine of the oboe. The crowd cheered and people asked, "Where is it coming from?

Where are the players?" But Grazia and Junio spun to a halt, and the music faded.

"Do you believe now, sir?" Grazia asked, directing her words toward the place where she felt the greatest tingle of magic.

"I do," the weaver said. "You must finish it, and you must bring it to Princess Marguerite, as you propose. But not looking like you've slept by the roadside. Here."

The scent of magic was overpowering for a moment, and Grazia shuddered.

"Better," Master Grayling said approvingly. "I've cleaned up your skirts for you. Very well. Good evening to you."

"A-and to you, Your Highness," stuttered Junio, and then, "It's so unnerving how fairies just appear and disappear like that."

Grazia nodded, dazed by their reprieve. When she found her voice, she asked, "Why did you call him 'Your Highness'? He's just the weaving master."

"No, Miss Goodchild; I don't know how, but you're mistaken. That was the Willow Prince from the Fair Vale, who's been calling now and then on Golden House."

"But—you heard what he said! It was Master Grayling!" Fairy princes and princesses were known for their indescribable beauty, whereas Master Grayling's gnomish form was invoked in nursery rhymes and schoolyard taunts—no one could mistake him for a fairy prince.

"I can't say why he would impersonate the weaver, but I tell you, it was the prince," insisted Junio.

Grazia shivered. Fairies could change their own and others' forms, but surely a fairy weaver would not dare to take the guise of a prince. So then . . . could it be that the Willow Prince chose to disguise himself as a master weaver? *Princes are not more admired than I,* Master Grayling had said to her that day, when Grazia had first proposed their collaboration, and he had boasted of his accomplishments. Maybe it was true, then: maybe a prince could choose to disguise himself as a weaver.

After a moment Junio continued, hesitantly, "What he said

about disgrace . . . This morning I went to Atelier Aurora to seek permission to call on you. The mistress said there was no one by the name of Grazia Goodchild in her employ and would tell me nothing about what had become of you."

"Yes . . . It's a mess," Grazia said. The memory made her ache inside. And yet, perhaps the situation could be mended. "But I may have a plan to fix it."

"You won't be sleeping by the roadside tonight?"

"I won't be sleeping at all tonight! I'll be finishing this gown!"

"Miss Goodchild, I'm serious."

Grazia dipped her head, feeling shy. "I will stay with the manufactory girls tonight."

There was a longer silence before Junio spoke again. "There is nothing forbidding instructors at the conservatory from marrying. My quarters are just two rooms, but—I hope one day I can persuade you to take my name and be my wife!"

Grazia tilted her head, smiling. "I will be happy to free myself of 'Goodchild'; it was the name given to all of us at the foundlings' home and never felt my own, whereas you, Mr. Fenwood, I would like very much to be my own."

✦✦✦

Grazia had been to the Midsummer Ball before. Mistress Meran and her assistants always attended, sitting in a tiny room adjoining the ballroom, in case one of Atelier Aurora's clients suffered a tear or other misfortune that required immediate repair. But this year was different. This year Grazia sat in the orchestra's antechamber, where Junio and the other musicians warmed up.

At the appointed time, the room emptied of everyone but Grazia as the musicians took their places in the ballroom. Grazia went to stand by the doorway, just out of sight.

The musicians played a stately march as the royalty and nobility processed in.

Princess Allegra would be entering now, in her gown with the requested scintillations and small bells. "Lovely — and unremarkable," Mistress Meran had sighed, the day they finished it, "but it fits her like a glove, and it's what she asked for." Grazia felt a pang, thinking of the mistress.

Princess Marguerite would be following her sister — wearing, on Grazia's request, the gown Marigold had altered. The princess had agreed that it would be better to change into Grazia's gown directly before introducing the ecstasie, so as to keep its magical properties a surprise. *And this way, Marigold can enjoy the fruits of her labor,* Grazia thought, though she doubted the other girl would forgive her, even so.

A quarter of the way through the evening, the music stilled. The conductor of the chamber orchestra cleared his throat.

"Your Highnesses, ladies, gentlemen. I am honored to announce that we will be joined now by Master Speedwell, a piper from the Fair Vale, for the premier of 'Midsummer Ecstasie,' a piece to accompany the dance that Her Highness the Princess Marguerite will now present, along with her partner — "

He paused as gasps and murmurs rippled through the crowd.

" — His Highness, the Willow Prince, of the Fair Vale."

The ballroom was so quiet that Grazia could hear the swish of Princess Marguerite's skirts — the skirts of the gown of harmonies — as the princess walked to the center of the ballroom. And now light footfalls, as the Willow Prince joined her.

The conductor struck the rostrum. The uncanny drone of the fairy pipes filled the air, and the music swelled.

And now Princess Marguerite and the Willow Prince must be dancing, their feet flying across the floor as the ecstasie demanded, for other music was filling the room, a counterpoint to what the orchestra played, harmonies that lifted high and plunged low, soft and then loud, always responsive to the mood of the orchestra and the movements of the prince and princess.

Just as on that day in the conservatory, Grazia felt the pull of the dance, but she gripped the doorframe and kept herself still. In time the music drew to a close, and Princess Marguerite was speaking, breathless, joyful.

"That is the ecstasie! In dancing it together, the Willow Prince and I celebrate the friendship between our peoples. Just consider what marvels human-fairy amity makes possible! The musical composition you just heard, for which Master Speedwell joined our orchestra, is one, and this, my gown of harmonies, is another. There is fairy magic in the fibers, human labor in their spinning, and human effort and craftsmanship too in the tutelage of the fabric in the ways of music, and in the stitchery of the gown itself. That work was performed by a seamstress of both skill and imagination—Grazia Goodchild. Miss Goodchild, will you join me?"

What? Heart in her mouth, Grazia walked out into the great room, where she was surrounded by deafening applause. She faltered—where was the princess? A hand caught her arm—Junio's. He escorted her to the princess.

"The words you asked me to speak—I think maybe it would be better if they came from you," the princess murmured. Grazia nodded, swallowing, and took a step forward. She took a deep breath and spoke to be heard in the far corners of the ballroom.

"Thank you, Your Highness, for your favor. Without you and Mast—the Willow Prince, there could not have been a gown of harmonies."

If the orchestra was behind her, then the little room where Mistress Meran and the other seamstresses sat must be over to the right. Grazia turned in that direction.

"But nor could the gown have been made without the training and guidance I received from Mistress Meran of Atelier Aurora. Any skill I have, I owe to her. And finally, I must thank my colleague, Marigold Dailey, whose work you were wearing earlier this evening. This gown is a copy of that one." And then she curtseyed deeply. Once again a roar of applause rose up again from the perimeter of the ballroom. Gently, Junio guided Grazia back to the antechamber.

"Now we play 'Midsummer Ecstasie' again and see how well

the ladies and gentlemen have learned it," he said to her, humor in his voice. He returned to his place with the chamber orchestra, and the melody filled the room again. Alone in the antechamber, Grazia gave in to the music and let herself spin round and round in its embrace.

Near the end of the evening, Mistress Meran came to Grazia.

"What you said this evening—it was very gracious of you. Not many people would have done so, after a dismissal," she said.

"I'm sorry I disobeyed you," Grazia replied softly.

"No, Grazia, you would be foolish to be sorry—the dress is marvelous. You cannot be sorry for that."

"But—not telling you. I'm sorry I broke your trust."

"Thank you . . . It pains me to admit it, but had you confided in me, I might not have . . . it's possible I wouldn't have been able to imagine what an accomplishment the dress could be."

The mistress, sounding hesitant! This was uncharted territory.

"It was what you said about learning from Princess Allegra's criticism," Grazia confided. "I wanted a dress that would enhance the music instead of fighting it."

"And you succeeded in creating one. And you seem to have acquired something special along the way."

"Mistress?"

"I mean the young man who came calling for you after you . . . after I . . . The musician."

"Oh! Mr. Fenwood." Grazia felt herself blushing.

"I would give my blessing, if I were in a position to give it."

Grazia was unsure how to respond, and the silence lengthened uncomfortably until Mistress Meran broke it in a swift rush of words.

"You have promise not merely as a seamstress, but as a designer. Will you come back to the atelier, not as an assistant, but as my partner in training? You have every right to refuse the offer, of course, after how I treated you, but if—"

"Yes!" interrupted Grazia, warmth and relief flooding her.

But she didn't have a chance to say more, and nor did Mistress

Meran, for at that moment the chamber players came back into the antechamber, all conversing noisily. Junio wrapped an arm around Grazia's waist.

"Friends, just one quick tune more!" he cried. "So I can dance with my sweetheart."

And this time, Grazia didn't refuse.

The Dress

Lynne April Brown

Time is running out, the queen thought as she moved slowly up the long stairs to the dress room. She used the antique iron key that she had inherited from her mother-in-law and moved inside, shutting the stubborn, creaking door behind her. This was where generations of royal brides stored the dresses each had worn on her wedding day, wrapped in tissue paper and sweet-scented herbs in long wooden boxes.

She moved to the end of the dusty room and looked, as she had once been instructed, to the bottom shelf on the left-hand side, to the shabby old box that held the falling-in-love dress, the one dress that all the queens, each in her turn, had worn. She drew it off the shelf and lay it on the long table that was the one piece of furniture in the room. She lifted the heavy lid and folded back the tissue, scattering the still-fragrant herbs, staring at the contents in astonishment.

The dress she had worn to the ball had been the height of fashion on that magical night long ago, when a poor kitchen-girl and a prince had lost their hearts to each other. Now, all of these years later, it looked completely different from the one she remembered wearing. Until she had opened the box and seen for herself, she hadn't believed the tale that the old queen had told, that magic resided in the box, to keep the dress at the height of current fashion, to be ready when needed to prevent an ancient curse from coming true.

The queen had learned over the years why fairy tales ended with the wedding, because happily ever after was a judgment that only came from looking back at the end of a life. It had been difficult to watch her son grow as she had been warned that all the men in his family had grown, cursed to care for little except power and their own pleasure, indifferent to those they were going to be ruling. Indifferent, indeed, to everyone but the women they each married.

As the prince's coming-of-age approached, she had seen that the curse was close to coming true in him, as it had threatened to come true in all the other princes who had become kings in their turn. Her fears for him and for the kingdom he was born to rule had driven her up the stairs to this room, hoping against hope that her mother-in-law's tale of the dress was as true as her tale of the curse.

She put a hand down into the box to caress the soft fabric of the dress, grateful for the gentle solution devised by the wise queens of old to wean their sons away from power-hungry dreams of war and conquest. She knew that her boy wouldn't look any farther than the pretty girl in the magical dress, any more than his father and grandfather had, but marrying that compassionate girl, one who would forever after understand the suffering of the poor because she had once been poor herself, would change his cursed fate and allow the small kingdom another generation of fruitful peace.

It's time, she thought as she carefully smoothed the tissue and replaced the lid, picking up the box to take with her back downstairs. *Not only time to plan a grand ball, but time for a queen to disguise herself as a fairy godmother and go looking for another girl of humble beginnings. Just as all the other queens have done, once upon a time.*

A Waltz for May

P.G. Nagle

꧁꧂

We therefore found a large portion of the families once more at
their homes in the Island City, and others are returning almost
daily, so that the city no longer presents the deserted appearance
that has made it so desolate during the past summer.

—Mr. Willard Richardson
Galveston News

E mma ambled along the Strand with her aunt, dutifully
dressed for the promenade in her zouave jacket ensemble.
Aunt May, fluttering as ever, wore a pale yellow dress embroidered with morning glories and a lace shawl with long fringe,
and carried a Chinese parasol to protect her complexion from the
fierce coastal sun. Beside her aunt's petite prettiness, Emma felt
large and awkward, more like the soldier after whom her attire

was fancifully designed, or like the ranch hand she had been at home since the war began.

Daisy followed a few steps behind them with a small wicker basket for marketing. Emma addressed one or two remarks to the slave, which Daisy answered in brief, discouraging syllables.

Since Emma had arrived to visit her aunt, she had noticed that May did not speak to Daisy except when giving her instructions. Emma soon gave up the attempt to be friendly, as it appeared neither Daisy nor her aunt welcomed it.

It still seemed strange to her, to live in a household with slaves. Poppa's ranch near San Antonio was run by the family. Momma, who was May's sister, managed the household herself and never gave any sign of wanting things to be different.

May's slaves had come to her from her late husband, and she took them entirely for granted. Emma found this uncomfortable, but it was the way things were, and she, being May's guest and lavished with May's generosity, was in no position to question them. Instead, she listened to May chatter as she let her gaze wander between the buildings, glimpses of the nearby wharves, and the other people out walking in downtown Galveston. Conscious of Daisy's presence behind them, she resolved to be kind to the maid, if she could not actually be friendly.

Their dawdling pace enabled Emma to take in her surroundings in detail. She noted, for example, a small, boxy cupola atop the Hendley Building, which at three stories of stout brick was the tallest building in town. The view from the cupola must take in the entire city, she thought. How she longed to go up and see, but when she suggested it, Aunt May declined.

"It looks like the merest shack, dear. I doubt it would be comfortable."

"We needn't stay long," Emma said, coaxing. "Don't you want to see the whole island at once?"

"No, I cannot say that I do. You are seeing the best parts of it from right here on the ground. Oh, good afternoon, Mrs. Dinwiddie! What a pleasure to see you. May I introduce my niece,

Miss Russell?"

Civilities duly exchanged with Mrs. Dinwiddie, who reminded Emma ever so slightly of a stuffed pigeon, they passed on. Emma paused to look into a shop window filled with souvenirs made out of seashells.

"May we walk out to the gulf this afternoon?" she asked. "I do so love to look at the ocean."

"That would be delightful, but not today, I am afraid," Aunt May said, idly twirling her parasol. "I have arranged for Mr. Strythe to come at two and give you a music lesson. You met him the other day, remember? Our neighbor to the east?"

"Yes," Emma said without enthusiasm as they walked on. "I still do not see why I must take music lessons. I can't sing a note. Even the pastor has asked me not to join the choir."

"I promised dear Eva that you would acquire a little polish, love, and since the Female Academy has *closed*," said May, a note of annoyance entering her voice, "and the Miss Cobbs have sent all their students *home*, I must fall back upon private tutors. Do not worry, my dear. Mr. Strythe is highly accomplished."

"I don't doubt it," Emma said, watching two young girls pass down the far side of the street with their mother.

Their clothes were plain, but clean and neat. The taller of the girls carried a basket from which peeped a spotted kitten.

"Do not smile at inferior persons, Emma dear. You may give them a civil nod if you wish."

Surprised, Emma looked at her aunt. "How do you know they are inferior? Perhaps they are only poor."

"It is nearly always the same thing," said Aunt May.

Emma stopped, incredulous. Aunt May continued a few steps before noting her absence.

"What is it, dear?" she said, turning round and tilting her head at a pretty angle.

"I think I will write to my mother this afternoon," Emma said slowly. "It is time I thought of returning home."

"Nonsense," May protested. "Why, we have only just settled

in!"

"My help is needed on the ranch."

"But I need you here! Your mother understands that. I cannot let you go before Albert returns."

Albert Lawford, May's perennial beau, had gone back up to Houston on business after supervising the transfer of May's household to her new home in Galveston. Emma reluctantly admitted to herself that it would be better for her aunt if she remained until Mr. Lawford was back. For years, May's letters to Momma had been full of references to him, and upon meeting him Emma had realized how very much he had been a steadying presence in May's life ever since her husband's death.

Still, Emma was not inclined to accept May's world, and May's attitudes, as her own. "You are moved in now," she said stubbornly. "And you will soon have plenty of company, if I may judge by all the people to whom you have introduced me this morning."

"Yes, but — oh, dear!" Aunt May handed her parasol to Daisy, who held it so as to shade her while she reached out both hands to Emma. "I was keeping it a surprise, but — well, Emma, I am planning a party in your honor. On September 6th, when the moon is full. You must stay until then!"

Emma glanced at Daisy, standing like a statue with the parasol held over her mistress, and let go of May's hands. She resumed walking, clasping her hands inside the wide sleeves of her jacket. She was annoyed, but she was also acutely aware of the generosity Aunt May had shown her. Why, the very clothes she wore were a gift from May. Her mother would urge her to stay, she knew.

"I wish you would add a feather or two to that hat, dear," May said lightly, catching up to her, twirling her parasol once more. "It makes your face look so severe! A flower, or perhaps some grapes — "

"I don't want my hat to look like my marketing basket," Emma said gruffly.

She lengthened her stride, her instinct to escape overriding the knowledge that her diminutive aunt would be forced almost to run to keep up. She frowned at the ground before her feet, in consequence of which she did not see two gentlemen approaching until she had nearly collided with one of them.

"Oh, I beg your pardon!" she said to the tall man before her.

He reached out a hand to steady her, and the corners of his eyes crinkled in a smile. He was some few years older than Aunt May, she thought, though still handsome, with large, dark eyes and a long, straight nose.

"We did not see you coming, I fear," he said kindly. "You see, we have just stepped out of doors."

"That's kind of you, but I fear it was my fault," Emma said. "I was not minding where I walked."

"You must forgive my niece, General," Aunt May said, catching up to them. "She has a *great* deal of energy!"

"Mrs. Asterly!" cried the gentleman, breaking into a smile. "How delightful of you to visit Galveston, and how brave of you to come in these trying times."

"Fiddle," May declared. "I don't believe the Yankee blockade will amount to a thing. Daisy, my fan please." She paused to cool herself, then added, "Furthermore, I am not visiting, I am now a resident."

For a second the gentleman looked concerned, then his smile broadened and he bowed over May's hand. "You multiply my delight, dear lady," he said.

"Thank you," May said, favoring him with a coy look from beneath her hat brim. "Will you allow me to present you to my niece, Miss Russell? Emma, this is General Sidney Sherman."

"General Sherman? Oh!" Emma hastened to curtsy as the general bowed. She glanced up at him as she rose. "I have ridden in a train drawn by your locomotive."

"Have you indeed?" he said, smiling again. "I hope it served you well. Please allow me to introduce my son, Lieutenant Sidney Sherman."

The younger gentleman, who had been hanging back, now

stepped forward and bowed to Aunt May, then took the hand Emma offered with a shy smile. He was very like his father, though his features were finer and his eyes did not slope quite as much at the outside corners. He wore the grey uniform trimmed in red that Emma knew designated artillery service.

"How do you do?" she said, returning his smile. "My brother is in the artillery also."

"Is he?" asked the younger Sherman in a quiet, firm voice. "Is his hair a bit lighter than yours? For if so, I think I met him last week. He came round looking over all our defenses."

"Such as they are," put in General Sherman.

"Yes, that must have been him," Emma said. "He is very concerned for our safety."

"Rightly so, I fear," said the lieutenant.

"Pooh," said Aunt May. "General Sherman, I have just been telling my niece she is to have a party next month. You and your son will attend it, I hope?"

The two men exchanged a glance. "We are at your bidding, ma'am," said the general, placing a hand over his heart and bowing from the waist. "But why only a party? Surely such a lovely young lady deserves no less than a ball."

"Silly man," said Aunt May, furling her fan and playfully rapping him with it. "My house does not have a ballroom, nor parlors big enough for dancing."

"Then you must have it at my hotel," said General Sherman. "I will lend you the ballroom for the evening."

"General! Oh, no, you must be joking," said Aunt May, her face lit with pleasure as she shook her head. "That is far too generous."

"Not at all," he said. "I am afraid there is little use for the place otherwise. Galveston has been so dull this summer. But a ball would be just the thing to liven us up." He looked at Emma, eyes twinkling. "You do not mind, do you Miss Russell?"

Emma, who had only danced at husking bees and the like, had been feeling increasing alarm throughout the discussion. She could not bring herself to hurt General Sherman's feelings, though, and she was conscious of having behaved badly toward her aunt.

Thus she mustered a smile, dropped a tiny curtsy, and said, "It sounds delightful."

Aunt May rewarded her with a kiss on the cheek, which she had to stand on tiptoe to deliver. Nothing would do but that General Sherman must join them for luncheon to assist Aunt May with plans for the ball. The general cheerfully abandoned his intended business for this pursuit, and Emma found herself escorted by Lieutenant Sherman while Aunt May, bubbling with schemes, leaned on the general's arm ahead of them.

Emma glanced back at Daisy, who followed patiently, her face unreadable. She began to find the maid's silent omnipresence unnerving.

"I hope it will not be a great inconvenience," Emma ventured to say to her escort.

The younger Sherman smiled. "Father likes this sort of thing, and he's right, the summer has been very — dismal."

"Do you think the danger is real? Ought we to be planning parties?"

A slight crease marred his brow. "If you are to remain on the island, I don't suppose it matters much whether there are parties or not. And, yes, the danger is real."

Emma accepted this with a nod. "I see," she said.

"Do not be afraid," he added. "We will have warning, if the Federals come. We should be able to get you to the mainland before anything unpleasant happens."

⚬⚬⚬

"Now, what of the music, Mrs. Asterly?" said General Sherman. "Does your friend Strythe wish to organize it, or shall I try for the military band?"

Emma glanced up from the vase of flowers she was attempting

to sketch. The general, whose title she had learned was largely one of courtesy, had come for luncheon and was now ensconced on the parlor sofa with Aunt May, busy with plans for the ball.

Emma welcomed his visits, as he never failed to cheer her aunt. He pandered to May more shamelessly even than Mr. Lawford, and she glowed with pleasure at each pretty compliment or little gift he bestowed on her. Emma was all the more grateful since learning that the general did not presently reside on the island but was living with his family at San Jacinto, and only came down to visit his son, who was on duty in Galveston, or to attend to matters requiring his attention at the Island City Hotel.

"Mr. Strythe does not think he can assemble enough creditable musicians for an orchestra," May said, drawing her shawl about herself.

"Then the band it must be," said the general. "I will speak to Sergeant Harris."

"Do you mean the band that plays concerts on the square?" Emma asked.

"The very same," said the general.

"They are quite good," Emma said, pausing to examine her drawing at arm's length.

She was not happy with the results. Her honeysuckles looked more like a collection of frayed toothpicks, and the clematis blossoms just looked like flat blobs. Stealing a glance at Aunt May, who was looking over a list of dance music with the general, she turned the page of her sketchbook and started over.

"That breeze is making me chill," May complained.

"Shall I close the window?" Emma offered, setting down her pencil.

"Daisy can do that, dear. Do not interrupt your work."

"I don't mind," Emma said, getting up so that Daisy need not be summoned. She stepped over to the window and shut it, though to her the breeze seemed rather warm.

"You are certain we will have enough ice, General?" May asked. "I inquired after having a sculpture made, and was informed that the ice house is empty."

"Yes, it was all taken away last spring, during the evacuation," said the general. "Do not worry, I have ice brought down on the train every week for the hotel, and I will order an extra shipment for the ball."

"Good," May said. "Emma, ring the bell while you are up. I could do with some more tea."

Emma did so, then knelt beside her aunt and took her hand, concerned. "You are not getting feverish, are you?"

"No, no, dear. Go back to your sketch," she told Emma. "I am better now."

Emma returned to her chair, but was no sooner there than she heard a knock upon the front door. She happily set aside her drawing and waited while Rupert, a giant of a negro who was May's butler, answered the summons. In a moment he brought two visitors to the parlor.

"Lieutenant Sherman and Mr. Vale to see you, ma'am," Rupert said in his deep, quiet voice.

"How delightful! Thank you, Rupert," said Aunt May, putting down her fan. "Come in, gentlemen, come in!"

"Good afternoon, Mrs. Asterly," said the younger Sherman. "I hope you don't mind my bringing a friend. He wanted to meet Miss Russell."

His friend, a young man with large hands and good features, dressed in civilian clothes, cast a glance Emma's way. She gave him a polite smile.

"Not at all," May replied. "How do you do, Mr. Vale? Are you in the military as well?"

"No, ma'am," he said, bending over the hand she offered. "My father works for Mr. Hendley, and I keep accounts in his office."

"Oh!" Emma cried. "Can you take us up to the cupola on top of his building?"

"Certainly, if that is your wish," said Mr. Vale, smiling. "I spend a fair amount of time up there myself."

"Keeping accounts?" asked May with a laugh.

"Keeping watch for enemy ships," he returned.

"Really?" May picked up her fan and waved it.

"He is one of the JOLOs," said Lieutenant Sherman.

"That doesn't explain a thing to them, son," said his father. "They have only been here a few weeks."

"Do explain it, Mr. Vale," said Aunt May. "Please be seated," she added, waving them to chairs.

"Thank you," he said, taking a place between Emma and the sofa. "The JOLOs have been keeping watch over the bay since the war began," he said. "We take shifts in the cupola on top of Mr. Hendley's building."

"And can you see the whole island from there?" Emma asked.

"Nearly. The western end is not easy to see, but there is not much there. We have a good view of the gulf," he added, glancing at Aunt May.

"Oh, I would love to see it!" Emma said.

"You would be welcome. We have had ladies to visit several times." He looked at Emma with a wavering smile. "They have been very helpful in maintaining our line of supply."

"Line of supply?" Emma said. "Goodness, how long are your shifts?"

"Don't let him hornswoggle you," Lieutenant Sherman said. "When he says 'supply' he means pies and cakes."

"And lemonade," said Vale, breaking into a grin. "That's vitally necessary."

Emma narrowed her eyes. "I see. So the JOLOs require a bribe."

"For you, Miss Russell, no," said Mr. Vale with belated gallantry.

"What does JOLO mean, anyway?" demanded Aunt May.

"Jolly Order of Look Outs," said Vale and Lieutenant Sherman in chorus, and Emma laughed.

"Some of the fellows are a bit—well, salty," said Mr. Vale. "Most are mariners from Mr. Hendley's shipping business. Let me know when you wish to visit, and I will make sure I am there."

"I am not sure this is an appropriate venture for a young lady," said Aunt May.

"Oh, there is no harm in it, dear Mrs. Asterly," said General Sherman. "Sidney will go along to take care of her if you are concerned."

Emma saw a look of exasperation flit across the lieutenant's face, then he glanced at her and gave an apologetic smile, saying, "I would have to arrange it when I am off duty."

"I don't mind," Emma said.

She liked the lieutenant; he was kind, rather quiet, but when he spoke he showed good sense, and he never put himself forward. He never exerted himself to captivate her, or to draw her attention to himself, as most other young men of her acquaintance tried to do. As a result, she felt safe in his company, something she had not felt with a man outside her family since Stephen.

With a shock, Emma realized she had not thought of her fiancé in some time. A wave of guilt washed through her. She had not believed she would ever forget him, and yet how easily she had been drawn away!

He had been killed only six months ago; she had known about it only since May. Yet she had all but forgotten him, distracted by new clothes and plans for a stupid ball. She did not even like dancing!

All her grief returned in a rush, coupled with a feeling that she had been faithless. She knew she had not, but her emotions were not subject to rational thinking, and she could not help feeling oppressed.

"Emmaline, dear, are you daydreaming?" said Aunt May. "Mr. Vale has asked you a question."

Emma looked up from her sketchbook, at which she must have been staring. "I beg your pardon, I—I was distracted." Suddenly she felt unable to be still, and stood up. "I really must prepare for my music lesson."

She picked up her pencil and sketchbook with clumsy fingers, glanced at Lieutenant Sherman and tried to assuage his evident concern with a smile. "Thank you for visiting," she said to him, and turned to his friend. "It was a pleasure to meet you, Mr. Vale."

"Emma—"

"Good afternoon, General," she added, and received an understanding smile from him as she made a hasty curtsy.

She hurried from the parlor before Aunt May could demand an explanation. Her heart was so full of emotion it seemed to burn. She ran up the stairs to her room, cast herself on the bed, and only then allowed herself the luxury of tears.

ഛ൭ ഉ൱

The day of the ball arrived all too soon for Emma, who between hasty dancing lessons and last-minute errands for her aunt was beginning to feel overwhelmed. Her spirits remained low, though she tried to conceal this from Aunt May.

She had begun to dream of Stephen again, sad dreams she couldn't remember well upon waking. She had written to Momma expressing her hope of coming home soon after the ball, but had as yet received no reply.

After dinner she yielded to May's insistence and went to her room to lie down. Sleep would not come; instead she lay on the chaise longue, thinking about the approaching evening, the new friends she would see, and how much more she would have enjoyed it if Stephen were there. Galveston was a charming city, but it did not assuage her loneliness.

Lately she had taken to escaping for long walks to the beach, looking out over the gulf. She took a friend along when she could, Daisy or Rupert when no friend would come.

A quiet knock on the door preceded Daisy's entrance. Emma sat up on the chaise longue where she had been resting.

"I am here to dress your hair, Miss," Daisy said.

"Oh. All right."

Emma rose, pulling her wrapper around her, and moved to

the dressing table. She sat gazing at herself in the mirror while Daisy brushed out her hair. It had grown nearly to her shoulders now, and lay in soft, dark waves. When she had first cut it, it had curled wildly around her face, exactly like her brother Matt's.

She remembered Momma's distress upon finding her in her bedroom, Jamie's letter in her lap and shocks of hair scattered on the floor around her feet. The bitterness she had felt then was gone now; only numbness remained.

She did not even have a picture of Stephen. She was beginning to forget what he looked like. It was nearly a year since she had last seen him.

He had proposed to her on the eve of the brigade's departure for New Mexico, and had not had time to have a picture made for her. She had gone to a portraitist for the watch-fob miniature of herself, and mailed it to Stephen for Christmas.

Looking in the mirror, she saw herself older, less vital, with hollow eyes and a mouth that lay in a sad, flat line. The face was pretty, she supposed, and the neck about which the maid's dark hands moved was long, if more tanned than May liked. Emma glanced up at Daisy's face, ghost-like in the mirror, and wondered if she also bore the weight of past sadness.

"Daisy?" she said.

The maid's eyes met hers in the silvered glass, and her hands hesitated. Emma licked her lips.

"Do you like Mrs. Asterly?" she asked.

Daisy looked away, finished twisting a lock of Emma's hair into a pretty curl and secured it with a comb tipped with sapphires, May's gift to Emma on the occasion of the ball. Pausing briefly, eyes still downcast, she said in a low voice, "She don't beat me, she give me good clothes and enough to eat, and she don't have a husband or a son to come trouble me."

Sharp dark eyes met Emma's briefly in the mirror, a glance that told more than the maid's words had done—of poverty, hardship, and most of all, fear. Daisy picked up the brush and resumed arranging Emma's hair. Emma watched her, stunned into the realization that her own woes were perhaps not as terrible as she had thought.

⚜

"This is Dr. Hurlburt, my dear," said Aunt May. "He is one of Galveston's most prominent physicians. Doctor, this is my niece, Miss Russell."

Emma curtsied for perhaps the hundredth time, and offered her hand. "How do you do?"

Dr. Hurlburt bowed. "I have anticipated this meeting with great pleasure, Miss Russell. It is an honor to make your acquaintance."

Emma smiled and thanked him, then turned toward the next guest as the doctor moved into the ballroom.

The Island City Hotel, while neither the largest nor best-known hotel in Galveston, was nevertheless the most festive on this evening. The ballroom was filled with candlelight, flowers, and the murmur of happy voices.

Emma, in her blue evening gown, stood beside her aunt at the doorway greeting the guests as they arrived. While there were not as many as May would have liked, the island being somewhat thin of company, there were enough to fill the ballroom with colorful gowns, elegant evening dress, and dashing uniforms.

The military band, resplendent in their heavily-braided jackets, played popular tunes from a platform at the far end of the ballroom. A long table down the side was spread with lavish comestibles, the centerpiece being a huge block of ice which had been carved into the shape of an urn, filled with dozens of fresh oysters and slices of lemons.

Mr. Lawford, Aunt May's perennial beau, was present, having returned to Galveston a few days previously. He had brought Emma a gift—a pretty little fan of embroidered blue silk on ivory sticks—which now dangled from a ribbon on her wrist. He stood a little way apart, chatting with General Sherman, who had coaxed his wife and two of their daughters to come down to Galveston for the occasion. Mrs. Menard, their eldest daughter, had declined to come but had sent Emma a charming basket of flowers and a polite letter expressing her hope that they might meet in calmer times.

Colonel Cook had also declined the invitation, but most of the privileged class who remained in the city were in attendance, and May was already preening herself on the ball's success, chattering happily with each arriving guest, laughing and fluttering her fan as she stood beneath a glittering chandelier. Emma smiled, shook hands, tried to commit to memory the names of new people her aunt introduced, and secretly wished for the evening to be over.

At last, with a loud flourish, the band struck up the first dance of the evening, a grand march for which Lieutenant Sherman had solicited the favor of Emma's company. She saw him approaching through the crowded room, and turned to her aunt.

"May I go now?" she said, smiling her sweetest smile.

"Yes, of course, dear," May said, touching her cheek with a hand encased in a silk crocheted mitten. "How pretty you look! I will wait a little longer for the latecomers. Go and enjoy yourself!"

Lieutenant Sherman presented himself with a bow, offered Emma his arm, and led her onto the floor. She was a little nervous of her steps yet, though she had taken lessons for three weeks and had been pronounced competent even for the waltz by both Mrs. Schwartz and Mr. Strythe, the latter of whom had given generously of his time as an accompanist.

Dancing in a ballroom full of elegant Galvestonans was different than dancing around the parlor with Mrs. Schwartz, but Emma trusted she would manage. Fortunately, the Grand March was an easy dance, being little more than a promenade with a few variations.

"You look enchanting this evening," said her partner. "I think I neglected to mention that to you earlier."

She glanced up at him and smiled. "Thank you. You look very well yourself." She paused, minding her steps as they changed direction, then said, "Is that a new uniform?" She nodded toward his crisp grey jacket, its sleeves ornamented with loops of gold braid.

"Dress uniform," he said. "I haven't had much occasion to wear it."

"Well, it is very smart," Emma told him, and won a smile in response. "I am glad you could join us this evening," she added.

"My father would never have tolerated my absence," he said, his eyes laughing.

"He has been so very generous," Emma said. "I cannot begin to thank him."

"Your adorning his ballroom is thanks enough," said Lieutenant Sherman. "He is enjoying himself immensely. Your aunt has spared no expense."

"No," Emma agreed. "I think she is having more fun than I am. Oh, that is not what I meant!" She felt herself coloring, even as her partner laughed. "I meant, she is having *even* more fun."

"Don't hide your true feelings from a friend, Miss Russell," he said, guiding her distracted steps through a movement of the dance. He lowered his voice and leaned close to her ear. "I suspect you, like I, would enjoy a quiet evening at home more than this sort of affair."

Emma threw him a laughing look. "I *do* beg your pardon," she said.

He smiled. "No need."

Emma smiled back. She was grateful for the lieutenant's presence. He seemed to understand her better than most.

The dance ended, and the ballroom filled with applause and chatter. Lieutenant Sherman returned Emma to Mrs. Asterly's side and offered to fetch them both some champagne punch.

"Yes, thank you, dear boy," May said. "Although I would prefer coffee." She pulled her shawl around her, smiling at Emma. "You looked delightful dancing, love."

"I hope to see *you* dancing before the evening is over," Emma said.

"Oh, you shall! I must have one waltz, though in general I no longer dance." She glanced over her shoulder at Mr. Lawford as she spoke, and he hastened to join them. His waistcoat of silver brocade set off the silver threads in his dark hair. He was still handsome, and Emma wondered for perhaps the hundredth time why he had not asked her widowed aunt to marry him.

"You looked beautiful on the floor, Miss Russell," he said. "I hope you have saved a dance for this ancient."

"She must dance with all the young gentlemen first," May declared.

"Then I shall have to be content to watch," said Mr. Lawford with a feigned sigh.

"Don't be silly," Emma told him. "Of course I will dance with you!"

Lieutenant Sherman returned with the punch and coffee, and Emma had time to enjoy only a few sips before Mr. Vale appeared to claim her for a reel. Emma took to the floor in a whirl of music with a succession of Galveston's best and brightest young men. She doggedly saved a schottische for Mr. Lawford, who rewarded her by guiding her through the swift dance with a practiced skill that left her breathless.

"What an excellent dancer you are," she said, curtsying to him as the music concluded. "I felt as if we were dancing on clouds!"

"I have had many years to learn," he replied, his eyes glinting at her. "Let me restore you to May. I see that she is trying to catch your attention."

Aunt May, who had moved away from the door and was now holding court from a sofa near the refreshment table, was indeed waving at her in apparent excitement. When Emma came near she saw a gentleman sitting beside her, resplendent in a grey uniform covered with gold braid, a plumed hat under his arm. His hair and mustache were sandy-colored, and he looked vaguely familiar.

"See who has come to visit you, Emma dear?" May said, as the officer rose and bowed.

Emma frowned, uncertain. "Mr. — Owens?"

He smiled, white teeth flashing beneath the mustache. "That's right, I knew you'd remember. I served with your brother."

"It is *Major* Owens, my dear," said her aunt.

"Oh, yes." Emma gave him a friendly smile. "How good of you to come."

"I must apologize for attending uninvited," he said with a courtly bow to Aunt May. "When I heard there was to be a ball in Miss Russell's honor, I simply couldn't keep away."

"He came all the way from headquarters at Houston," May said, smiling with pleasure.

Emma could think of nothing to say, so she smiled also. The musicians gave the signal for the next dance, and she glanced toward the floor, looking for her partner.

"May I have the honor?" Major Owens said, setting his hat on the sofa and offering Emma his arm.

"Go ahead, dear, I'll explain to Mr. Vale," said Aunt May.

Thus Emma found herself escorted to the floor by Major Owens, quite possibly the handsomest man in the room, with the strains of a waltz commencing. She felt nervous, being uncertain of the steps and a bit shy of her unexpected partner, but he proved himself as capable of guiding her as Mr. Lawford had been, if perhaps not quite so gentle.

She was expected to make conversation, she knew, so once she was comfortable with the rhythm of the dance, she glanced up at him and said, "Have you seen my brother recently?"

The major's smile widened. "Yes, we had dinner together when he passed through town."

"Oh."

This should have reassured her, but somehow it did not. There was a tightness to the smile, a guarded look in his eye, that she did not like.

"You look exquisite, Miss Russell," he said after a moment. "Town life agrees with you. I might not have known you, you are so changed since I saw you in San Antonio."

Emma, thinking it unkind of him to refer to her rustic life at home, but not knowing what else to reply, said, "Thank you."

"I am glad to see you are recovered from your disappointment. All your friends will agree, I am sure."

She swallowed, staring at the major's shoulder, reminded of Stephen and suddenly wishing herself elsewhere. Another couple danced rather too near them, and her partner drew her out of their way by pulling her closer. She became aware of his scent, an exotic blend of spices that stung at her throat.

"A lovely young thing like yourself should not be alone," he murmured into her ear.

"I am not alone," she said. "My aunt is very kind to me."

Emma glanced toward the sofa where May sat watching, beaming with pleasure, and felt a sharp longing to be with her. The ball was May's party, after all. Presenting Emma to Galveston society was only an excuse. It was May who craved the music and celebration. And there, behind the sofa, stood Mr. Lawford, quietly watching over May as he always did.

"Ah, yes. But, family is not the same," Owens said, his hand tightening on Emma's waist. "I don't suppose I have to tell you that I find you mighty attractive."

"I don't suppose you would have to tell that to anyone in the room," Emma said, leaning away from him.

He smiled. "I like a gal with a bit of spunk."

No, she did not care for the quality of his smile, which did not match the challenge in his eyes. Nor did she like the tone of his voice. If her brother were here, he would surely take issue with the Major's behavior.

Jamie was not here, but Emma could take care of herself. This glittering world of social expectations was not her world — might never be her world — and she was not afraid to break the lacy, crystalline rules. They were, after all, merely an illusion. Emma drew a breath, tasting freedom.

"Tell me, Miss Russell —"

"Please forgive me," Emma said, disengaging herself with a

mendacious smile. "My aunt needs me."

Emma strode across the dance floor, abandoning the mincing steps taught her by the dance teacher for her natural gait, relief flowing through her. She reached Aunt May, who looked up at her with questioning eyes. Emma picked up the major's hat and handed it to the servant who was manning the punch bowl, then sat beside her aunt.

"Aunt May, I must thank you for a delightful evening," she said, ignoring May's glance toward the dance floor, where Emma had left Major Owens. If he knew what was good for him, he would make himself scarce.

"Of course, my darling, but—"

"Just one thing is needed to crown the occasion." Emma cast a glance up at Mr. Lawford, who looked amused.

"And what is that?" he asked.

"To see you and May dancing together. Won't you ask her?"

"I have asked her repeatedly," he said quietly, his eyes softening as he looked to May. Emma sensed he might be referring to more than the dance.

"Then, May," Emma said, clasping her aunt's hands, "please make my evening complete. Please tell him, 'yes'."

The smile that bloomed on May's face reminded her of Momma. "Dear child," May said, kissing her cheek. "How could I deny you a thing?"

Mr. Lawford came around to the front of the sofa, bowing low and holding out his hand. "May I have the honor, Mrs. Asterly?"

May placed her hand in his, smiling up at him like a debutante. Emma hid a kindly laugh behind her fan, and watched with delight as Mr. Lawford led May onto the floor.

A glimpse of gold braid on grey made Emma look sharply to her side. She relaxed as she saw Lieutenant Sherman drawing near.

"Is all well, Miss Russell?" he inquired.

"Yes. Please join me," she said, patting the sofa beside her.

"With pleasure."

And that, she thought, should serve to warn off Major Owens, if he happened still to be lurking. He might outrank the Lieutenant, but it was General Sherman's ballroom.

Lieutenant Sherman had the good sense to remain silent as Emma watched her aunt waltzing with Mr. Lawford, looking giddy with happiness. It was this, Emma realized with a smile, that both she and her aunt had truly wanted all along.

Sherbet on Silver

Brenda W. Clough

St. Christopher's Day, 1867

"*H*ave you ever noticed, Marian," my husband Theo mused, "what balls resemble?"

The steps of the polka at the ball at London's Travelers' Club parted us, but when I twirled back into his arms again I replied, "Oh, you dreadful creature." What a salacious analogy!

"The physical exertion."

I had to gasp for breath—it is perilous to giggle while dancing! "The surge of animal spirits."

He sputtered with laughter. "The way one must pair off."

"But what of the rule that it is improper for a wife to dance too often with her husband?"

"And under the gaze of so many eyes, too." His own hazel eyes twinkled naughtily behind the spectacles. "Consider what that rule implies. Why, one may dance with a partner one does not even know."

I swirled my full crinolined skirts past as he neatly stepped back out of the way. "You are corrupt beyond measure." Some middle-aged couples dine every Sunday with the grandparents, or devote themselves to the family business. Theo and I entertain ourselves by playing little games. This was one of our favorites: the Green Eye.

The prospect was the more alluring because I was wearing a most striking ball gown. My satin skirts were as full as possible in shades of vivid fuchsia, with a bodice in the deepest green cut into five long points, to be the calyx. I was a full-blown rose! With a green silk-lace shawl and long white satin gloves, the ensemble was so dazzling that my uncomely face was entirely overlooked, and I was much in demand. And the steel-spring crinoline supported the weight of my derringer in a specially-tailored inner pocket.

Another twirl, and when I stepped back into his arm, he made the first move. "Who was that you were dancing with?"

"You mean Colonel Anchester? We danced the five-step waltz." If he began the play, it was my role to supply him with cause. "A fascinating man—he has just come back from a year in Ethiopia."

"No, before him. That young foreigner." We spun around so that I could see who he meant, a tall, slender young man, with a redundancy of soft black curls tumbled over his broad white forehead. He was leaning moodily near the windows, watching the dancers.

The colonel was undeniably stout. I hastened to substitute a better object for faux jealousy. "Iancu Posmantir? He looks no more than seventeen, does he not? But astonishingly well-spoken for his years, and an enthusiastic reader. Goethe is his favorite author, and we spoke at length of *The Sorrows of Young Werther*. The Carpathian ambassador over there is his uncle."

The music tweedled to a halt, and we stopped as well. When he had caught his breath, Theo said, "When he relinquished you to Colonel Anchester, Mr. Posmantir immediately sought me out to praise you, and begged for permission to call on us at home."

"Why, hail me as a belle! And what did you reply?"

This could not be the Green Eye, which calls for male sternness and scolding. Theo's portentous approval gave me my cue. "Is he not a pleasant youngster? The bookish ones are not common. If he wants to worship at your feet, he is too young for it to do him much harm. An ardent young man is safer dangling after a fascinating older lady."

This was a new game. I met his gaze and replied in the same daring spirit. "Oh, you creature. Shall it be as it is here, in this ballroom? He could watch us . . . dance."

"Or perhaps even — if we become very good friends — "

I laughed at him from behind my fan. "Positively intimate?"

Between his side whiskers and under the mustache, his smile was wicked. "Intimate, I like that, yes. He could tread a measure with you."

"While you play the wallflower and watch. And — why I hardly dare voice this, it is so bold — perhaps he could be induced to read your publications."

Theo is a publisher, and this sally made him choke with laughter. "Dear me, and I had hoped to hide my perfidy." Never have we toyed with the dangerous concept of free love, not a new notion but always scandalous! Since our games were always between us two, it would be essential never to tell this theoretical third party —

I started as a warm voice with a foreign lilt spoke. "So you agree, Mr. Camlet? You invite me into your home, I may visit you and Mrs. Camlet?" It was Mr. Posmantir himself!

How had he overheard us from across the room? We had been speaking in an undertone. "You shall not wish to journey all the way out to our home in Hampstead," I said.

"Yes, but I need no horsecars. My heart shall lend me wings!" He seized my hand. "I do not ask you, my dear Mrs. Camlet, to allow me to address you by your first name. It is too soon for that intimacy, I know. But tell it me, so that I may write it in my journal and contemplate the reddest rose in England in my lonely room, by the light of the moon."

Deliberately I replied with humor. "You keep a journal? Why, so do I. How many other female names are written in yours? Mr. Camlet, would you care to hazard a guess? I do not care to be the last entry in a long list!"

Theo laughed. "My advice to you, Mr. Posmantir, is to light a lamp. Reading by the light of the moon will strain your eyes."

Young Mr. Posmantir did not let go of my hand. "Only one other name is recorded, Mrs. Camlet! My sainted Gretchen—I would have crossed the world over to pluck a blade of grass that she wanted."

"But she has passed away?" Theo said with sympathy. "Tragic."

"She and her husband," Mr. Posmantir admitted.

I pulled my hand free. "She had a husband? Oh, Mr. Posmantir, you are too daring. You must turn your fiery heart towards a female who may return your affections."

"How can I change? My love is eternal, even if my adored one weds another. Mr. Camlet, I shall be your friend. Say it: allow me to call at your home. Mrs. Camlet, vouchsafe me the tender syllables of your name—"

What a romantic young fellow, and so determined to improve our acquaintance—this must be how Theo had acquired the notion for the new game! Young men of this temperament ought not to read Goethe. But as Theo opened his mouth, another spoke. "Iancu, you impose upon the good nature of these hospitable English persons. Madame, will you do me the honor of giving me this dance?"

A tall, cadaverously-thin man bowed before me, gloved hand on his breast—the Carpathian ambassador. I curtsied in return. "Your Eminence, a pleasure."

As Theo had observed, only at balls is it allowable to accept a dance from a stranger. His Eminence Gheorghe Strigoi was known to me only by sight. He had the same broad forehead as his nephew, white as paper, but his dark hair was sleeked back. The orchestra began a slow waltz, and I allowed him to lead me to the floor.

One expects diplomats to be conversable, but he said nothing as we made a complete circuit of the room. "Your nephew is a charming young man," I ventured at last.

Mr. Strigoi stared somberly down at me. His face was so thinly fleshed I almost fancied I could see the shape of his teeth behind his cheeks. "He has no excuse for his folly. I brought him with me to London in hopes of weaning him from it."

"He indicated he was unlucky in love," I said.

Mr. Strigoi almost growled. "He ran tame in that woman's house for years. Her husband should have horsewhipped him." When I blinked at this harshness, he went on, "Do not invite Iancu into your home, Madame. Favor him with no especial consideration. Do not be alone with him after dark."

His uncle keeps the young man on a short leash! "I will certainly consider your kind advice," I replied.

But as we twirled around, young Mr. Posmantir confronted us. "Uncle, may I cut in?"

We stopped, and the ambassador scowled over my head at his nephew. "Better you should pursue the virtues of self-mastery and prudence."

"I am driven by my heart, sir, always."

We were by this time impeding the other dancers, and I said, "I know not the custom in Carpathia, your Eminence, but in England dance-floor poaching is permissible."

Mr. Strigoi pressed his thin lips together but stepped away, and his nephew took my hand. "I love to dance with you," he sighed when we swirled away. "I wish, do not you? That this dance would last forever. That the musicians were tireless, that the sun would never rise, and that you were deathless."

I laughed at him. "But what of you, left behind lamenting and mortal? Anyone would think this was your first ball, sir."

"I have led a secluded life, I admit. I have few friends, but many books. I have promised Mr. Camlet that I will read all of the ones he publishes."

"Come, that is promising," I said. I knew it!

Although the windows stood open, the July night was warm. Every lamp was lit so that the ballroom was like an oven, and ladies must wear white satin elbow-length gloves—nothing is hotter. "What is the English word?" he said. "You glow with the heat, Mrs. Camlet. Should we pause, and perhaps cool ourselves? The club's Library is said to be full of curiosities."

"Gladly, sir. It is fearfully warm." A touch on my damp face would ruin my gloves. As soon as we halted, I deployed my fan, and in the hall Mr. Posmantir secured me a cup of punch from a passing waiter. I drank thirstily. "But are you not parched also, Mr. Posmantir?"

He held the tall door for me. "No, I am not thirsty."

I swept through with a swish of satin skirts into the club library, a vast and dim, high-ceilinged space. Laden bookcases lined the walls up to the cornice, which was adorned with a Greek frieze, and the center of the room was arrayed with glass cabinets containing curiosities and artifacts from the travels of the club members. The glow of the gaslights from the street outside glinted yellow through the tall windows. Mr. Posmantir guided me to a shadowy corner and took my free hand. "Mrs. Camlet, how I yearn to know your name!"

We are warned from girlhood to be wary of the man who advances in intimacy too quickly. But to a pretty boy half my age I could say, "Well . . . my Christian name is Marian. I am Marian Halcombe Camlet. But I must forbid you to use it except in private. In company we must be more formal."

"And you shall call me Iancu. Marian—how beautiful. As beautiful as you yourself."

"Now that is nonsense," I said robustly. "If I am a beauty, the word has no meaning."

"Marian . . ." Suddenly his arms were around me. My empty punch cup was a poor shield and fell to the carpet. "My red rose."

"Iancu, you presume!"

I might as well have not spoken. He kissed me full on the mouth and said again, "Marian."

And suddenly I was frozen, as if turned to stone. I have been hypnotized before, my will fettered by a clever villain. This was not like that. It was eerie. I was myself, fully aware and alert. But my limbs were immobile. Even my tongue, my eyelids, were stilled. He stroked my cheek, my bare neck. I expected his hand would wander lower. The breath slowed in my lungs. What if I fainted?

But Iancu's fingers gripped my throat, gentle and yet strong as steel. "Do not be afraid, my adored one," he breathed into my ear. "It doesn't hurt, even the first time. It will do you no harm, and soon you will learn to look forward to it. You are a flower, unplucked, but with me you will blossom into bliss. A sip, only, at first. To make you mine, for all time." More kisses, hungry ones, that traveled from my ear downwards.

But oh! What a relief to see, behind my captor, the slice of light as the door from the hall opened! A tall male figure was briefly silhouetted and then vanished as he shut the door behind himself. "Iancu! What are you at?"

Iancu was obliged to remove his lips from my neck. "I'm in love, uncle."

"You're insane. Here, in a public place?"

"I don't intend to feast," the younger man said. "Only sip."

"Bah! Your effete modern ways—this is not how it is done!" With a swift stride he was beside me, and the light in his eye was entirely feral. "Cannot you grasp that these creatures are food? How can you make friends with them?"

"You're entirely Gothic, uncle," Iancu replied. "In days of old, we had to be hunters. But now we can . . . domesticate. Keep them tame. Dine when convenient, as gentlemen do, instead of pursuing our prey like barbarians."

"Of all the half-witted—and now she knows too much. Do you think she will keep your secret as Gretchen and Marko did? Peasants can be intimidated into silence, but this English woman is of high kindred. She has to die!"

A fresh voice broke in. "Are you speaking of my wife?" Their quarrel must have lessened Inacu's mystical grip on me somewhat, because my heart gave a great joyful leap. It was Theo!

Swiftly my husband crossed the dim chamber to my side. But my lips would not move to warn him, and my unnatural immobility made him hesitate for a fatal instant. Behind him, far the taller, loomed Mr. Strigoi. Silently the ambassador raised both his skeletal white hands, and clapped them onto Theo's shoulders. Instantly Theo was caught in the mystic snare just as I was. Behind the round steel spectacles his gaze grew fixed, and he was struck into stillness.

Mr. Strigoi peered into Theo's face. "Who is this, Iancu?"

"Mr. Camlet, a most well-read man. Uncle, he is a friend. And if my beloved loves him, then I also may have no ill intent towards him."

Mr. Strigoi made a guttural sound of disgust. "Worse and worse. Well, let us be swift. When we are done, we may carry the bodies out the French doors. It could be that husband and wife slipped out for a breath of air into the Carlton Gardens. London brims with footpads and criminals. It will be assumed that a thief slew them."

"And drank their blood? Uncle, how can you accuse me of taking rash risks? A double exsanguination is completely unnecessary. My sway over their weaker minds is quite complete, I tell you."

Weaker minds, indeed! Inacu had turned away from me to quarrel with his uncle. And I felt it, the slipping of his attention; whatever arcane power he was using to immobilize me was fraying. My limbs were suddenly my own again. I slipped my hand into the opening cunningly seamed into the billows of my flower-petal skirts, and pulled out the single-shot derringer. Mr. Strigoi's formal white shirt front was an excellent target, but two yards away, and I fired. My shot took him square in the chest, and he staggered back.

And—that was all! The sound of the shot echoed up into the high ceiling, and the reek of gunpowder made me blink. But Mr.

Strigoi simply brushed at the freshly-scorched hole in his starched shirt front. His cold black eyes seemed to pierce me through. As he turned his full attention upon me, I cowered against one of the glass display cabinets. "A lead bullet."

"You see how useful their ignorance is?" Iancu demanded. "The lore that is handed down to every child at home is unknown here."

"You are wrong, sir," Theo shook off his paralysis. "I have read John Polidori's novel and I know of Varney the Vampire. We are Protestants and so have no relics. But our Christian faith is still a weapon against you." And he began to recite—what? I have never heard it:

"'Although the light of nature, and the works of creation and providence do so far manifest the goodness, wisdom, and power of God, as to leave men unexcusable; yet are they not sufficient to give that knowledge of God, and of his will, which is necessary unto salvation . . .'"

Iancu stared. "What on earth is that?"

"Worthless nonsense." Mr. Strigoi loomed over my poor husband.

Theo broke off. "It's the Westminster Confession of Faith, one of the foundations of the Noncomformist church!"

"Heresy." Mr Strigoi's teeth seemed inhumanly long and sharp "And therefore useless." His white hands gripped Theo by the throat.

But I too had read *The Vampyre*, and now I understood what we were fighting. I snatched up my useless derringer and smashed in the glass of the display case beside me. Inside were Colonel Anchester's Ethiopian souvenirs. I snatched up a great golden cross from the ancient Oriental Christian church in Addis Ababa, and held it up in both hands. "The Cross of Our Savior— look upon it and know your master!"

"My poor young rosebud," Iancu said fondly. "It is not the artifact that has the power, it is the belief. Do you Protestants believe?"

"I—" Certainly I did not hold by the papistical beliefs of the Romish church. How true was my faith?

But even in my feeble hand, the ancient cross had some power, and Mr. Strigoi's attention was drawn off from his prey. With a convulsive effort, Theo wrenched out of his grip, leaving only the high starched white collar of male evening attire gripped in Mr. Strigoi's long white fingers. He half-fell, scrambling across to me.

"Quickly, my love!" We both gripped the cross. He began to recite the ancient words. I knew them too, since we say them every Sunday:

"I believe in one God the Father Almighty,
Maker of heaven and earth,
And of all things visible and invisible:
And in one Lord Jesus Christ, the only-begotten Son of
God . . ."

"But you're heretics!" Iancu cried.

Whether Protestants are heretics or not, I am certain that Theo's faith turned the issue. As we spoke the Nicene Creed together we advanced, a step for every line. And Mr. Strigoi recoiled before us. The broken display case blocked his retreat, but he seemed unable to move to either side as we advanced step by step. Suddenly he fell to his knees in his turn. We stepped closer, and he collapsed to the carpet just as we got to "the resurrection of the dead." The words were too appropriate, and I stopped with a little gasp. "We have killed him."

"Not so, my dear. Am I right, Mr. Posmantir?"

"He was put into his coffin at least nine hundred years, yes," Iancu confirmed. "And it is he, and those few others of his generation, who have kept us ignorant and trapped in the mountains. It's impossible to advance, when the old do not allow the younger to rule. You have freed us, my dearest Marian."

I plucked up my courage. "And it was I who shot him, Theo." I pulled the great cross from Theo's grip and set it onto Mr.

Strigoi's white shirt front. He did not stir. I spoke slowly, thinking. "He came into the library alone, and had a—yes, an apoplectic fit, falling upon this case and shattering its glass. When Mr. Camlet and I came in we recognized him and instantly went to fetch you, Iancu, his closest kin."

The young vampire gaped at this, but Theo was used to my practical nature. "Would you fetch the Club Secretary, my dear? I shall keep watch here." As I swept through the door, I could hear my dearest man saying, "And let me make a literary surmise, sir. Were you the model for young Werther?"

Iancu exclaimed with pleasure. "How perceptive you are, Mr. Camlet! Truly our souls speak to each other! Yes, it is my claim to literary glory. Johann von Goethe modeled the hero of his *Sorrows* after me."

The rest is soon told. As soon as I informed the club secretary, our responsibilities were ended; all the club officers crowded into the library to help. Theo and I retreated to the central hallway and collapsed onto the nearest settee. Theo seized the last ice from a passing waiter's tray. "And bring me a stiff brandy," he commanded. Only after he passed me the ice did he sag a little.

"Oh, my dearest!" For want of better stimulant I thrust a spoonful of the ice into his mouth—it was frozen hard, but the implement was made for sherbets, really a silver fork with three chubby tines. "You were so marvelously resolute."

"I have not your derringer, Marian. Nor your *sang-froid*."

"Oh, don't use that term, I beg you."

But at this moment Iancu came out of the library and dropped into the chair beside me. "As a compatriot and kinsman," he said, "it shall be my responsibility to return with my uncle's coffin to our country."

"You do not seem unduly oppressed by your bereavement, Mr. Posmantir," Theo remarked. "Perhaps you hope for a reversal of fortune, once you return to your native earth."

"Quite so, sir." Mr. Posmantir smiled—so engagingly, but now I noticed the sharp canine teeth. "Unless some annoying mortal appears with a wooden stake, Uncle's inconvenience may well be temporary." He would have taken my hand again, but I clung steadfastly to the sherbet cup and fork, which made him pout. "May I hope, Mrs. Camlet, that when all these melancholy affairs are settled, you will welcome me back to England?"

"You may not, Mr. Posmantir," I said firmly. "You are a sweet boy, but I do not wish to pursue the acquaintance."

Theo agreed. "Something about being a domesticated food source is repellent to the English sensibility."

Iancu lowered his voice. "You cannot deny me—Marian."

He said the syllables of my name slowly, with what I recognized now as vampiric power. But Iancu could no longer take me unawares. With one swift motion I reversed the ice cream fork in my hand and stabbed it with all my strength into his thigh. The black superfine woolen of his formal trousers was something of an impediment, but I am very strong for a woman, and I forced the fat tines down hard. Iancu gave a gasping wail of shock, and I was startled to see threads of whitish smoke rising from where the three silver tines pierced his flesh.

"My dear, your shawl." Theo took up my green silk-lace shawl and reached it across so that the eerie vapors were veiled from casual view.

I did not relent. I leaned my full weight on the fork, digging for the bone. "You think I am prey, Iancu," I said softly. "You are wrong. I too am a huntress, a falcon, and I have struck my talons into bigger prey than you." Only then did I pull the fork out of his leg. Blood mixed with fume frothed up it, but Theo dropped the shawl onto the three punctures, and Mr. Posmantir instinctively clapped his hand down over it.

How fortunate that my wide skirts are of a color that does not show bloodstains! I let the gory fork fall before it could drip onto my costly white satin gloves and kicked it clattering under the settee just as the waiter appeared with the snifter. Theo took it, adding, "Could I trouble you for another spoon? The lady has carelessly dropped her first one." He has no shame! When the waiter turned away, Theo added quietly, "Go back to Carpathia, Mr. Posmantir. She is a bad enemy. Do not return to England."

Iancu's handsome face was mottled with shock. "She—powers below, you hurt me! I bleed!" He staggered to his feet. "Marian, my rose, can it be you do not love me?"

"A reasonable inference," I said.

From the rear premises the Club secretary appeared, and Theo said, "Mr. Posmantir is overcome with grief."

The secretary hastened to give Iancu his arm. "No wonder, sir. We propose to load the mortal remains into a carriage at the back door. Are you certain you would not rather wait for a morgue wagon?"

"No, no," Iancu gasped. "My heart is shattered, riven with grief. I must take him home. Immediately."

"A terrible tragedy," the secretary said with sympathy, guiding him down the hall. "So sudden."

"I shall never recover," Iancu said with a sob. "My life shall be a desert, a wilderness overgrown with thorns—"

Theo sipped his brandy, and I bent to pick up my shawl as they vanished. I surveyed the hall. None of the other revelers had noticed our conflict. It was almost three in the morning, and in the ballroom the Last Waltz was just striking up.

I considered the peril we had just passed. "Theo, do you think the Church of England is feared by the undead?"

"Not the way the Romish church is, unfortunately. Britain is sadly vulnerable at the moment—entirely ignorant, without even the taste for garlic in our cuisine. Perhaps I should secure the rights to *Varney the Vampire,* and reissue the books in hard covers. They were originally penny dreadfuls, but they clearly need a wider distribution, so that people may become familiar with the dangers."

The high-ceilinged hall was cool now, so late, and I leaned gratefully against the warmth of his arm. "And we must be more discreet, dearest. This all began because Iancu overheard us, I can't think how."

"I can see that the first copy of *Varney* must come home with me," he replied. "Vampires are gifted with preternaturally sharp hearing. But, poor innocent, he didn't know our playful habits."

The waiter returned with a fresh utensil, and I addressed my cup again. "Our games are endlessly diverting." One of the never-failing pleasures of the married state is communicating without speech. Very slowly I lifted the last of the sherbet to my lips as I slid my gaze sideways to meet his.

There are oh! the most suggestive ways to lick a spoon. Under the mustache, Theo's lips quirked as he clung to his composure. Really, we are so well-matched, it is fortunate we married each other.

Gilt and Glamour

Layla Lawlor

*Y*ou wouldn't think it would be hard to find a horse in a ball-room. At least, I wouldn't have thought so until half an hour ago. Say what you will about Gilded Age robber barons, I sure won't argue, but they really knew how to throw a New Year's Eve ball.

"Are you sure he's here?" I asked my partner under the cover of the music. The band had struck up some kind of fast-paced dance I didn't know the name of. Masked and costumed men and women paired off, the women in long skirts and puffed sleeves, the men in tails and top hats. A smiling woman wearing a mask shaped like a sequined bird's beak held out her hand to me. I shook my head and she moved on. The look on her face made me think she'd forgotten about me even as she turned away.

Muirin looked up from the middle of a display of flowers. She had quietly moved aside some orchids and peonies to clear a space on an ornamental molding. With deft flicks of her hand, she scattered a light dusting of pale sand on the painted plaster, one of the focuses she used for her magic. The glamour she wore made her appear as a statuesque blonde costumed as Marie Antoinette, instead of her usual five-foot self.

"The pooka is nearby," she said. "But something is confounding my magic. I can't seem to get a fix on him."

I scanned the crowd again. "Any hints you can give me? I've never seen one before."

Muirin swept the sand back into its canister and secreted it in what I saw as a dress, but knew was actually a jacket and jeans. "He will most likely appear to be human. But he will always betray himself somehow. Look for horse ears or a tail."

I looked out across rows of couples holding hands as they merged and then broke apart into individual dancing pairs. The dance floor was a bright riot of trailing peacock feathers, swirling skirts, swinging coattails. I couldn't help thinking all those costumes made a great place to hide weapons. One big bruiser dressed as a pirate had a rapier at his hip that looked all too real, even with that over-decorated scabbard and a filigreed hilt I wouldn't have wanted to try to handle in an actual fight. I counted no fewer than three different horses, two men and one woman.

"I can think of a lot of places where that would stand out more," I remarked.

I had the impression she was smiling, though I couldn't get a good look at her face. That was how Muirin's glamours worked. She didn't use them to make herself beautiful, as some of her kind did; she made herself unmemorable. My eyes slid off her face before I could get a good fix on it.

But it hadn't escaped my notice that she usually made herself *tall*. She might not be vain in the typical fairy way, but she invariably made herself appear a few inches taller than her usual self. Sometimes a lot taller. At the moment, she was almost on eye level with me, and I'm not a short guy.

I had the tact not to mention it.

She'd also covered me with a glamour of my own. I hadn't asked her what my costume was, having a feeling I didn't want to know. While I could see Muirin's guise, I couldn't see the glamour on myself, except in a slippery soap-bubble kind of way, flickering around the edges of my vision. When I looked down at myself, I saw a plaid shirt and paint-stained jeans. And the sword, of course, the wide leather belt and ancient, stained scabbard.

I would scandalize the entire ballroom if they could see me as I really was, as *we* really were—a pair of freelance supernatural troubleshooters, wandering briefly through their glittering world.

Or maybe they wouldn't care at all.

For we were not in the real New York in the fading years of the 19th century. We were in its shadow.

All things cast a shadow, cities no less than anything else. Shadow New York is an idea of a place. It exists under, or maybe adjacent to, the real New York. Every place and person from the New York, from all eras of history, exists here in some distorted form.

This party had happened over a hundred years ago, in the real New York, and had been enough of an event to cast a shadow here that had lingered all these decades. Or perhaps this was more than one party, blurred together until it was more like an idea of a party than a real one.

It looked real enough, a dazzling kaleidoscope of color and motion. Not everyone was in costume—the older people especially—but the ones who had dressed up had really gone all out. One young lady was dressed as a tree, her branches spreading out several feet beyond and above her body. I pitied her dance partner, who kept having to duck to keep from being swept off his feet along with anyone in her immediate vicinity. Someone else was wearing what appeared to be an actual taxidermied cat, and one woman had managed to get her skirts to light up, flickering like a firefly as she swung in and out of the rows of dancers. If the dancers weren't enough to brighten the ballroom, flowers were everywhere, even small palm trees in pots, turning the room into an indoor garden.

The crowd was almost certainly a who's who of New York high society at the close of the 19th century. Not that I could tell by looking. Would you recognize Andrew Carnegie if you saw him at a cocktail party? Especially when many of them were in costume. The only person I recognized was Boss Tweed, and him only because of vague recollections of political cartoons in my old American History textbook. He noticed me looking at him and winked at me from across the room.

I looked away to avoid getting drawn into what was bound to be an awkward conversation and reached for a glass of champagne from a passing waiter, but my fingers passed through it. Oh well. You never could really tell what was solid and what wasn't in this place. The waiter faded to invisibility from one moment to the next, a stray whisper of an echo from the other city wandering briefly through our reality.

"Pay attention," Muirin whispered at me, still focused on the spell she was trying to weave between her cupped hands.

"I'm looking, I'm looking."

By now I'd been watching the dance long enough that I was pretty sure I could do it. It didn't look too complicated. People joined hands in chains, skipped around in time to the music, let go to twirl their partners, and joined in different combinations.

"Wanna dance?" I asked, holding out a hand to Muirin.

She gave me a look. "We're here to work."

"Doesn't mean we can't have fun."

She shrugged and looked down at her handful of sand again. "I would prefer not to linger overlong."

"Why?"

The music went quiet just then, the musicians adjusting their instruments and flipping sheets of printed music, a babble of voices filling the silence. Muirin didn't answer until a cheerful chorus of violins led into another piece and the revelers swung into another dance.

"There were quite a few of my kind here in this time," she said, so quietly I had to lean close to hear her. "Tuatha Dé Danann. Some of them came over with the waves of Irish immigrants in the 1800s. Others were drawn to the glitter and energy and life of this land." She might have smiled again. "My people enjoy a good party."

I could read between the lines: it wasn't just that she might run into someone she knew, it was also that this place reminded her of the world she'd left behind. "Any chance some of them are here tonight?"

"It's possible."

"And if we happen to run into them . . ."

"I will need to make a rapid and discreet retreat."

"Oh come on," I said. "They can exile you, but they can't stop you from being anywhere they are."

She gave me a look; for an instant I glimpsed her behind the glamour, the real Muirin, her pale eyes more weary than amused. "Do you want to argue the point with them?"

"Fair enough." I gave up and let my hand drop. "Tell you what. You keep doing the magic thing. I'll go mingle and see if I spot anyone pooka-like."

Muirin gave a brief nod, more of a tilt of her head.

I made my way across the ballroom, glancing at faces, wondering if I'd know a pooka if I saw one. This particular pooka was a persistent pain in the ass who'd been bothering vacationing New Yorkers and tourists along the Long Island shore for years — back in the real world, not here. It liked to show up as a black horse, browsing on rosebushes and lawns, and flirting outrageously with anyone who noticed it . . . until it managed to get someone on its back. Then it raced off to the ocean, taking its terrified rider on the ride of a lifetime and finally leaping into the surf and abandoning them to swim back to shore.

So far, it hadn't drowned anyone. It wasn't a kelpie. But it *could*. Pookas did. They might be helpful or cruel according to their whim. Most of the fairy folk were like that. I tried not to fool myself into assuming that Muirin thought the way I did.

I glanced back to see a drunk gentleman, his waistcoat straining over his stomach, attempting to engage her in conversation while she conspicuously gave him a cold shoulder and an occasional glare. God help him if he tried to put a hand where it shouldn't be. Just last week I'd seen her eviscerate a grindylow with the razor-sharp glass knives she was never without.

Of course, it wasn't like he was alive, as such. It was always hard to tell how *there* people were in Shadow New York. Some of them were no more than ghosts, wavering and translucent, endlessly going through the steps of a dance their real-world antecedents had danced a hundred years ago. But others stepped out of my way or made polite greetings. And I nearly jumped out of my skin when a woman laid a hand on my arm.

She had chestnut hair pulled up in a crown of braids, with strands of pearls woven into it. They matched the white bodice on her plum-colored gown and the white feathers framing her purple mask. "May I have this dance, sir?"

The band had segued into a lively waltz, a dance I actually knew. And why not? I was a bricklayer's son from Binghamton and a freelance monster hunter. I didn't get a lot of chances to waltz with beautiful ladies who might be Astors or Rockefellers for all I knew.

So I put my hand on her shoulder, my other hand at her narrow, corseted waist, and swung her into motion. She smiled, moving with me in a way that was almost, but not quite, leading.

I didn't know much about turn-of-the-previous-century women's fashion, only that I liked the way her gathered purple skirts swished around her feet and swung against my legs as we waltzed. Her shoes clattered lightly on the polished wooden floor.

"Don't suppose you've seen a guy who looks like a horse lately," I said as we swirled around the ballroom.

She laughed, not a giggle but a deep, throaty chuckle. I had thought her young at first, but now revised my estimate upward. She had the gravitas of maturity.

"Dressed as one?" she asked. "Or looks like one? Because I've seen both."

"As long as you don't think *I* look like one."

Another of those rich, deep laughs. There was a light spray of freckles on her cheeks under the mask. The shadows of its eyeholes made it impossible to tell the color of her eyes.

"What did this man who looks like a horse do to offend you?"

"I didn't say he offended me. Maybe I owe him money and I want to pay it back."

"Oh really? Is there a finder's fee?"

"A kiss at midnight," I said, on a whim.

"Oho! You go straight for the kill, don't you?"

A chill went up my spine. There was more truth to this than she knew, as the sword reminded me with its familiar weight at my hip, moving with me as I moved. "I prefer to think of it as 'nothing ventured, nothing gained,'" I told her.

"And how does that principle usually work out for you?"

"I guess I'll know by the end of the evening, won't I?"

The edge of her mouth curved under the feathered edge of the mask.

There was little point in flirting with a Shadow ghost—they were mere echoes of real people—but she was more fully realized than most, if a ghost was indeed what she was. There were real people here in the shadow city, I'd been told, those who accidentally found a Door and couldn't find their way back, or didn't want to.

And she *felt* real, her fingers warm in mine, her slim waist solid against my hand.

"You're a fine dancer," I said. "Do you have a name?"

She glanced down at her skirts, in their many purple shades, belling out across the dance floor. "You can call me Violet."

"Hmm, well, you can call me Bill." I looked around for Muirin and found that she'd extricated herself from her gentleman paramour and found a chair to sit on, where she could spread out more of her magical paraphernalia on her knees.

"I've always liked the name Bill," she told me as I spun her past the other couples. "Simple. Plain. A bit stodgy, but refreshingly devoid of unnecessary fluff."

"I can't figure out if I'm being complimented or insulted."

Another Mona Lisa smile under the edge of the mask. "What are you going to do to this man who looks like a horse if you find him?"

The dance came to a sudden end just then, saving me from answering. I whirled Violet to a stop and gave her a quick bow. She curtsied in return.

A clear ringing sound carried through the ballroom, as of a fork tapped on a glass. I glanced around to see that one of the hosts had climbed up onto a chair to command the room's attention. "The turn of the year approaches!" he declared, sweeping a hand toward a grandfather clock standing in pride of place, surrounded by a bower of tropical flowers.

"Oh, this part is my favorite," Violet whispered into the sudden hush.

The minute hand of the clock ticked forward, and the first deep tone of its chimes rolled through the ballroom. The entire crowd shouted out, "One!"

Violet leaned close, until her feathered mask brushed my face, her lips almost touching my skin. "Happy New Year, and good luck in your hunt," she whispered, her voice nearly lost in the chorus of "Two!" as the clock struck again. In a single swift motion, her light touch withdrew from my arm; she stepped away in a rapid flurry of skirts.

And there it was, under the edge of her skirt: a flash of black hooves with white socks and a black-and-white tail.

Well, hell.

I made a grab for her. She flashed a teasing smile and was gone into the chanting crowd. At least her dress was bright enough that it was easy to catch glimpses as she surfed through the distracted crowd, running lightly for the stairs.

"Muirin!" I started to shout across the ballroom, only to have my partner duck out of the crowd at my elbow as I broke into a run after that elusive flicker of purple. I shoved people out of the way, leaving a ripple of angry exclamations behind me. "Can a pooka be female?"

"Five!" the crowd shouted gleefully, paying us no mind.

"I suppose so. I've never met one . . ."

"Great. Now you tell me."

"It would explain why my spell was coming up blank," she said. "I was focused on the wrong template."

The countdown crescendoed behind us as we pounded up the wide, sweeping staircase after the fleetly running pooka. She was incredibly fast, even encumbered with those massive skirts—but, of course, she *was* a horse.

"Eleven . . . twelve!"

As the ballroom burst into cheers and cries of "Happy New Year!" we slammed through a set of double doors at the top of the staircase into an opulent hallway. I caught a teetering cherub I'd almost knocked off its stand and set it back upright. There was no sign of the pooka anywhere.

"Can pookas teleport?" I asked, resting my hand on the hilt of the sword. "Turn invisible?"

"Invisible to humans, yes, but not to me. She's probably headed for a Door," Muirin said. "That's what I'd do. If she gets through it, she'll vanish into the maze of the city. We'll never find her."

"How many Doors are near here?"

"Besides the one we came through, there's one I know of in the master bedroom. There may be others."

Great. And the doorway we'd used to step from our world into the Gilded Age was all the way out in the mansion's gardens; on this side, it took the form of the door on a stone mausoleum. "I'll check the bedroom, you take the garden."

She nodded and pointed down the hall. "Two lefts, up a flight of stairs. It's the door to the closet. I've never used it, so I don't know where it goes. You'll know you have the right one by the brass handle shaped like a lion's head."

On a *closet*? "Meet you back in the real city if this doesn't pan out."

She nodded and dashed off. I was unsurprised to see that she didn't head for the stairs back to the ballroom; she was taking a shortcut. Probably going to jump out a window into the garden.

I'd seen her do a lot more than jump twenty feet and land unhurt.

I followed her directions to a room that only qualified as "bedroom" because it had a bed in it. My entire house back in Binghamton, minus the woodshop, could have fit in here. It had conversational furniture groupings, chandeliers, and a small garden of tropical plants in the enormous bay window.

The bed was occupied, but they took no notice of me, being otherwise engaged. They were translucent as smoke, mere ghosts whose faint cries and gasps went on in a loop that never ended. I guess there are worse ways to spend eternity. I didn't look at them, trying to give them privacy they wouldn't care about anyway.

There were several closets, but only one with lion-head knobs on the doors. It slid open, not on rows of hanging furs and silk gowns, but on noise and frenetic activity.

Shadow New York is a place of ideas. Similar places are always close together, no matter how widely separated in geography or time, and so I walked out of the Gilded Age mansion at midnight on New Year's into Times Square, stepping out of a Starbucks just as the ball dropped and the crowd went wild.

I felt a tingle on my skin as the glamour dropped. The Door had severed my connection to Muirin and therefore her ability to hold magic on me. Fortunately a big guy in a plaid shirt stood out a lot less in Times Square than at a masked ball among the late-1800s New York society set.

Especially here. It was a diverse crowd around me, and not just in the usual New York way. I saw people in Civil War uniforms, people dressed in shells and furs, people on horseback. Regardless of what time anyone seems to think it is, Shadow New York is stuck permanently in early evening, but no one seemed to notice or care that the sky was bright overhead. I guessed from the modern look of the screens on the buildings that it was relatively close to the present day, perhaps just a few years ago.

If the pooka wanted to vanish, she couldn't have picked a better place. I'd never find her in this crowd.

And yet, there she was, waiting for me.

At least that's why I assumed the big black and white horse was standing on the sidewalk, head up and ears pricked, watching me. She was a Vanner horse, mostly black with splashes of white as if someone had thrown paint on her. Her long, flowing mane was half white, half black. She had three white socks and a white nose.

I laid my hand on the hilt of the sword. Normal humans wouldn't have been able to see it, glamour or no. It has its own magic that way. But she laid back her ears and stamped her hoof.

"Okay," I said, taking my hand off the sword. "No swords. You want to talk?"

Violet clattered a few steps closer. I now recognized the hollow sound of her hooves that I'd taken for shoes in the ballroom.

"Hard to have a conversation like this," I said.

"You'd be surprised."

It was the same rich, mellow voice as in the ballroom. Eerie to hear it coming out of a horse's mouth, but not the weirdest thing I've ever seen.

"You want me to go for a ride?" I asked.

"Of course. What else?"

"You could drown me."

She snorted. That sound was all horse. "And you could chain me. Care to try?"

She bowed gracefully, bending to one knee to invite me aboard. There was no supplication in it, nothing of surrender. Her head was up, her ears pointed forward, and there was challenge in her glittering black eyes.

I'd heard of pookas being harnessed and tamed by putting on a special bridle. Too bad I didn't have one of those. Anyway, I didn't really want to harness her—and I didn't want to kill her. She hadn't hurt anyone yet.

Yet.

I got on her back and she straightened; I caught a fistful of her flowing mane to stop myself from sliding indecorously off her glossy hide. I had ridden a few times, but never without a saddle. It was a lot less comfortable without the ability to lift myself in stirrups, but it was also a strangely intimate experience. I could feel her skin ripple when she tossed her head, and the rise and fall of her flanks as she breathed.

"All settled up there?" she asked, flicking an ear back while the other pointed forward.

"I guess s—"

The rest of that sentence was lost as she surged into a gallop.

It was a good thing I had a grip on her mane. I seized hold with the other hand. I couldn't see; her mane was at least two feet long, lashing my face like being whipped with tree branches. Squinting my watering eyes and twisting my head to the side, I glimpsed people flinging themselves out of our way in panic. I yanked on her mane. "Slow down!" I yelled. "You're going to kill someone."

She just snorted and turned to the side. Suddenly we were out of the crowd and galloping down a long, strangely empty boulevard. Above us the sky was the color of sunset; the street lights were just coming on.

Shadow New York is infinitely large, but it's also unpredictable once you get outside its neighborhoods. I've never explored enough to know if it just keeps going out into the distance, or if it fades into nothingness when you get far enough from whatever place or event left enough of an impression on the substrate of the world to stick around.

We were still in Manhattan, but we were the only people there. There weren't even any cars, just a broad empty street going on and on. Violet stretched out, running with speed and grace no mortal horse could match.

Now that she was no longer jinking through the crowd, I was able to relax a little, though not much. Drowning was still on the table as an option, and we were headed south, toward Battery Park and the East River. No matter which way she went, she'd hit water eventually anyway. A normal horse would probably have tired and slowed before it got there, but Violet wasn't even breathing hard.

"If you're planning to kill me, you should know I don't go down easy." I didn't reach for the sword; I didn't want to take even one hand off her mane, let alone give her an excuse to buck me off. At this speed, I might not survive.

"I haven't decided yet."

"You dropped an eighty-year-old woman in Long Island Sound two months ago. She was in the hospital for weeks."

"Ah, but what a story I gave her to tell her grandchildren."

"Yeah, that time she was abducted by a horse who scared the wits out of her and almost drowned her."

"It's your people's fault for being so fragile. I can't be bothered to try to remember it."

Fairies don't feel empathy. You can't force it into them. I'd learned that the hard way.

She ran as fast as a car drives, and with no traffic to slow her down, we were already through Midtown and into lower Manhattan, where the regular grid of uptown streets turns into a lot of smaller grids hooked together at odd angles. The light was that of a winter evening, the air sharp and cold. I wondered if the world would run out before my luck did.

"I don't suppose I could talk you into staying here, in the shadow city."

She snorted a laugh. "It's fun to visit, but no fun to stay. What is the point of tricking mortals who are no more than ghosts?"

"Some of them aren't."

"Nice try," she said.

"Let me put it this way," I said. "Sooner or later, whether you mean to or not, you're going to kill someone. Before you do that, hopefully, and certainly afterwards, I'm going to stop you. I'd rather just have you stay here, or go home, go back to Ireland, where they know what stray black horses are all about."

The pounding of her hooves slowed, not because she was

tired — there wasn't a speck of sweat or foam on the glossy hide — but because we were approaching Battery Park. She clattered to a halt on the waterfront promenade. It was almost full dark. I could see the dark water lapping at the concrete edge of the promenade, but not what lay beyond it, if anything did. Behind us, a sunset glow framed the buildings in entirely the wrong direction for sunset. It made it seem as if the city was on fire.

"Violet," I said. "One of these days you're going to kill someone, and you're going to die. Go home."

"Should I stay or should I go?" she sang in her husky voice. The brogue was there now. I couldn't recall when it had begun creeping into her accent. "I think I'm going to . . . swim."

Her muscles bunched under me. I struggled to get off and found that I couldn't. I might as well have been glued to her back. Just like a kelpie.

"Damn it, Violet. I'm not here by myself. Killing me won't fix anything, it'll just mean that my partner will kill *you*. Violet — "

She leaped, a powerful, impossible bound that cleared the railing by several feet and left my stomach behind on the promenade. I had the presence of mind to get a breath, and then we hit the water with the force of a bomb, and went down, and down.

It was cold in these depths, cold and utterly black. I drew the sword. It gleamed with a chill blue fire that lit the pooka's glossy hide and her swirling mane.

One stroke. I could have done it easily. But I hesitated, and then she twisted out from beneath me, graceful as an eel in the water.

I floundered, thrashing helplessly. I was free of her back, but no better off. It was dark as a pit, with nothing for the sword's light to reflect, and I couldn't tell which way was up. I didn't dare let go of the sword, but I couldn't swim with it in my hand, and wasn't sure if I could resheathe it with nothing to brace against, nothing but cold black water all around me. Was I even still in the city, or lost in subterranean limbo? My lungs ached for air —

A great warm bulk rose beneath me. The pooka's broad back

pushed me to the surface like a dolphin supporting its calf. My head broke the surface; I gasped and sobbed for air, then managed to jam the sword back into its sheath with the other hand holding onto the pooka's streaming mane.

"Do you still think I'm a killer?" Violet asked.

I coughed and gulped a few more greedy breaths before I managed to say, "I never thought you were a killer. I just think you're going to kill someone because you don't care if you do or not. It's all a game for you, but it isn't for us."

"Humans are so strange," the pooka mused, pushing me toward shore. "So caught up in their petty, narrow little lives."

"Our lives are all we have." My voice broke on a cough. "Do you blame us for hanging onto them?"

"You should try being something else for a while. A bumblebee, maybe, or a cloud. Does wonders to clear the mind."

"We can't do that."

"Oh," she said. "That's right, I forget. Well, you should try it anyway."

She braced me from below while I hauled myself, with difficulty, up the concrete breakwater. I wondered how she was going to manage, but when I looked around after getting all my limbs under me, there she was on the promenade, shaking her coat and whipping her mane around like a wet dog. I couldn't help laughing, though it set me coughing again.

"I find you amusing, too." Violet nudged at me with her nose, too hard to be affectionate, more like poking at a dead thing to see if it would move. "There is a Door out of this place nearby."

"What's out there?" I asked, waving my arm at the water and the utter blackness where lightless water met lightless sky.

"I don't know. I've never swum far enough to find out."

I got to my feet by holding onto her mane. I didn't *want* to have to kill her, damn it. She didn't mean any harm. She just needed to be among people who had two thousand years of folklore teaching them better than to accept rides from strange black horses.

Or maybe . . . people who wouldn't *mind* accepting rides from mysterious black horses even if they knew what they were. That might work.

"There are worse places you could be, I guess," I said as we walked toward where she claimed there was a Door, with me using a hand on her flank for support. By this point I was mostly shamming weakness, in case I had to fight. "No wonder you're not—" And I shut my mouth.

"What's that?" she asked, flicking an ear back.

"Nothing."

"You're trying to use trickery on me."

"No, it's just that the thought occurred to me that the reason why you're here is because you can't cut it in the old country anymore. It's too hard. They're wise to all your tricks. You had to go out West where you could find people who were naive enough to fall for you."

Violet huffed out a low snort. "This is a transparent ploy."

"There's no way you could get anyone in Ireland to fall for the old 'I'm a stray horse, please ride me' trick anymore."

"Shows what you know," the pooka said loftily. "I've tricked *many* people."

"Yeah right. I mean, hell, I *dare* you to find a single person willing to ride you on a Dublin university campus. You want to talk a tough audience? Urban college kids. Especially in a country where they grew up hearing stories about you."

"You are trying to trick me."

"It's just that I don't think you can do it."

Muirin was going to have my hide. One of the first things she'd taught me was *Don't make bargains with fairies*. Trying to trick a trickster was probably even worse . . . especially since I was attempting to inflict the pooka on the college-age population of Dublin. I had a feeling, though, that the one at a disadvantage in that situation would be Violet, and if anyone could cope with taking an unexpected ride into the middle of the bay, it was a bunch of college kids.

"Listen, you've been alive for how many hundreds of years?" I said. "You must be pretty jaded by now. They say you can't teach an old dog new tricks, and I expect it applies to horses, too—"

"Absurd!"

I shrugged and slipped off her shoulder when she stamped to a halt in front of the door of a closed office building. The sky was brighter here; although we had been proceeding at an angle to the north-south streets rather than back uptown, we had walked out of the twilight back into the soft sunset tones of mid-evening.

"I'll believe it when I see it," I told her.

The horse abruptly melted into the woman in purple, no longer wearing her mask. Her hair was damp with bits of leaves and mud tangled in it. I found myself wondering where her clothes went when she was the horse. She planted her hands on her hips and scowled at me.

"I'll have you know, I find your trickery ludicrously plain."

"It doesn't matter if it's obvious, if it works. And let me tell you, I have a pretty good idea you're standing there right now thinking, what if he's right? What if I don't have what it takes to cut it in Ireland anymore? I've been getting soft, messing around with these humans who not only don't know pookas, but don't even know *horses*, or how a normal one is supposed to behave—"

"Very well." Her eyes flashed—black eyes with hints of red and gold. "Do you care to place a wager?"

Well, this was exactly the kind of thing Muirin had warned me about. But I *had* her. All I had to do was get her to swear to it. Fairies couldn't lie to humans. "Sure. I bet you can't find a thousand college kids in Dublin—"

"One," she snapped.

"Hell no, there are too many ways you could work around that. Let's say . . . five hundred. That should be a good sample." And take her a good long time.

"Five."

"Come on," I scoffed. "Four hundred, and you can't come back until you do."

"Ten. What do I get if *I* win? Your immortal soul?"

My heart tripped over. Fear, I knew, would cost me in this game. "Not mine to give away. Two hundred, and they have to know who you are *before* they get on your back."

"Twenty, for your whole, entire name, and five years of your life."

"What kind of fool do you take me for? Two hundred, and you haven't answered the other part yet. They have to know who you are. And," I added, "all of them must live, or they don't count."

Her black eyes narrowed. "*Someone* has taught you how to bargain."

"Does that mean you agree to my terms?"

She tilted her head and regarded me for a long moment. At last she said, "I will accept it, if you will accept one hundred as your number and give me an hour."

"An . . . hour?"

"That's right," she said with a smile.

"An hour of my time?"

"Just an hour."

"An hour in general?"

"An hour," she agreed.

This seemed highly suspect, but as far as things she could have asked me for, it wasn't too bad. At least, I couldn't think of too many ways it could come back and bite me later. "And if I give you that, you'll promise to stay in Ireland until you can find a hundred college students willing to ride you, knowing full well what you are?"

"I do so promise," she said, and plucked a chestnut hair with a quick twist of her fingers.

I took a breath and plucked a hair from my own scalp. Hesitated. I'd just thought of another way she could screw me over. "An hour of actual time, not distorted fairy-time. An hour in the real world *and* an hour wherever I happen to be."

"I do so agree."

"And so do I." I held up the hair, pinched between my fingers, and she held up hers. I'd seen this done before, but it still made me jump when both hairs went up in a tiny puff of flame.

The pooka came forward with a clop of hooves, moved as if she was going for a kiss, but brushed my arm with the back of her hand instead. "This has been fun," she said. "Come visit me in Ireland, if you like. Though I expect I'll be back before you know it. May I have a head start, going through this Door?"

"Sure," I said. "If I give you an hour head start, does that count as my hour?"

She chuckled. "You mortals are so funny." And then she was gone through the Door in a flurry of purple skirts.

✧◌❋◌❋◌✧

It took me a few Doors and a few wrong turns to get back to the place where we'd started out. The other side of the Door Muirin and I had taken to the 1890s belonged to a garden shed behind a Southampton mansion. I looked around carefully before stepping through, since I didn't have Muirin's don't-notice-me field this time to keep me from being spotted and arrested for trespassing. It was night on this side, and no one was around.

All the mansions backed onto the beach. It was dim but not dark here, the lights of the houses along the shore producing a reflected half-light that caught on the water's glitter. I walked down to the ocean's edge and spotted Muirin a little way along. She'd dropped the glamour of the tall blonde in a Marie Antoinette dress and simply gone for I'm-not-here. I wouldn't have been able to see her at all without the sword. As it was, I only had a vague impression of her until she straightened up and let the glamour fall away, revealing her as she really was, short and stocky, wearing a SUNY sweatshirt despite the humid night, with a permanent ball-cap crease in her short brown hair.

"You're wet," she observed.

"We were after a water horse. It goes with the territory."

"Is she gone?"

"She's gone." More or less.

Muirin didn't ask for details or apologize for not backing me up. I knew she couldn't track me through the Doors. I hadn't expected it.

Instead we walked along the beach, the sand tugging at our shoes, back toward where we'd parked the car. It was going to be a long drive home, and I was getting hungry. At least it wasn't a bad time to drive through the sleeping city, avoiding most of the traffic.

After the flat, lightless dark of the Shadow New York waterfront, I couldn't help noticing how much light there was in the sky, in the water, even in the pale beach itself. A million stars glittered overhead.

"Muirin, did you ever go far enough in Shadow New York to know what happens if you just keep walking away from a neighborhood? Where do you end up?"

"In the between space, I assume." She picked up a pebble, tossed it and caught it. "It's possible to take shortcuts through it. I know some can. I haven't the knack, though."

"Dangerous?" I asked.

"For a human? Very."

Ah well.

But it made me think about how much older than me she was, and how very alone. Cast out by her people, exiled to spend her life among short-lived humans. I was used to her, but sometimes, as now, I ran into a reminder that she was something far older and far less human than I often liked to think.

But she was still Muirin.

"You never got your New Year's Eve dance," I said.

Muirin gave a small snort. "It's August. Anyway, I don't care much about the human calendar."

"Come on. Dance with me. Or don't you know how?"

"Of course I know how."

"So." I held my hand out and waited.

With a very put-upon expression, she placed her hand in mine.

It took us a moment to get the rhythm of it, stepping through the sand without music to guide us. As we began to get a feel for it, I realized that I *could* hear music, an echo of a waltz, very distant.

"Are you doing that?" I asked her.

"Of course I am."

So we waltzed on the beach to music only we could hear. She was solid and small in my arms, not like Violet at all. The stars were our witnesses, the sand our dance floor, as I whirled her beside the endless sea.

⸸⸸⸸

It was two weeks later when Muirin slapped a newspaper down on the kitchen table beside my toast and coffee, and said flatly, "I don't suppose you have anything to do with this."

The newspaper was the *Irish Independent*—she subscribed to a number of papers from the old country, out of (I assumed) some combination of nostalgia and wanting to keep up with the mortal spin on various supernatural goings-on. This one was folded open to an inside page with a black-and-white photo featuring a lawn with blurry buildings in the background and a sign up on poles that read RIDE A PÚCA! Under the sign, a black and white Vanner horse posed grandly. I had never seen a horse smirk before.

"Oh," I said.

"Oh," Muirin repeated. "Oh, indeed."

"She's in Ireland, out of our hair. That's where we wanted her, isn't it?"

"Did you make a deal with her? What were the terms?"

"She has to find a hundred students willing to ride her knowing what she is."

"Well," Muirin said, gathering up the paper, "from the look of it, she ought to be done by Tuesday."

"So we'll deal with her when she comes back, if we have to." I reached for my coffee cup.

Muirin placed a hand over it, small and square with bitten-off nails. "And what did you promise *her* in return?"

I hesitated, but I might as well get it over with. "An hour."

I was fully expecting her usual "Bill, you idiot" look along with the discovery that I'd slipped into a well-established fairy trap and bargained my life away or some such thing, but instead she merely looked puzzled. "An hour of what?"

"That's what I asked. I take it that's not a standard medium of exchange."

"Not in my experience. You *did* remember to ensure —"

" —that it would be an hour in the real world as well as wherever I was? Yes."

"Is that exactly what you said? The real world?"

"Ye . . . es."

"All worlds are equally real, Bill."

"Okay, fine," I said, nettled. "If I disappear to the Irish other-world for three hundred years next Tuesday, you can say 'I told you so' when I get back."

"Oh, that's not the only thing she could do. She could take the hour you need to defuse a ticking time bomb, for example —"

"You can stop explaining anytime. I've made a terrible mistake, I will never bargain with a member of the fairy realm without consulting you, et cetera."

She pressed her lips together, but a smile quirked the corners as she took a piece of my toast.

I pulled the paper toward myself and took another look at the smug horse. It really wasn't such a bad thought that she might be back. Compared to some of the things Muirin and I had tangled with, Violet — or whatever her real name was — had been refreshingly fun to deal with. Challenging, with a whole lot less slavering and fangs than the kind of thing I was used to. It was kind of nice to deal with a supernatural threat with my wits instead of my sword.

And I never had gotten that midnight kiss.

Lily and Crown

Sherwood Smith

A Last Invitation

Later it was said that Colend danced its way to independence, but never by those who were there.

The one inarguable fact is that the night three kingdoms changed began, and ended, at a masquerade ball. Though court archivists have a propensity to tidy away anything they consider awkward or inconvenient, you can usually find the truth if you know where, and how, to look.

I know where, and how, to look.

Let me begin not with captains or kings, but with a sharp argument between two people with aspirations to become stewards.

They had both been asked by Herald-Scribe Third Secretary Martande Lirendi to help put together a masquerade ball for the guild chiefs, the provincial counts, and any of their landholders who had come to the tri-annual assembly. It was to be held in the great guild hall built on the northern bank of the conjunction of two rivers, in the quaint trade town of Alsais, central to the loose collection of counties and towns sometimes referred to as Kei Fael.

"There is never," stated Chief Cook Perin, who reigned over the kitchen at the largest inn in town, "too much decoration. Not in a vast barrack of a building like this." He threw his hands wide. "Stone! Nothing but stone! Everywhere you look! The third secretary asked for flowers, and flowers he shall have."

First Designer Halas of the silk painters' guild looked around her, hands rising to either side of her tumbled coronet of gray-streaked ruddy hair as if to hold her skull together. Everywhere cornucopia spilled cascades of flowers, and as the sun began its westward descent, ochre rays slanted in on masses of blossoms set on every possible surface. Above and around garlands looped along balustrades, pillars, and cornices. The clash of color and floral perfumes overwhelmed the senses, languorous reds next to sweet, simpering pinks, spicy yellows jostling cool-scented violet, tart orange bravely clashing with heady crimson and mauve.

To an eye trained for fifty years to the subtleties and symbols of color, it was worse than horrible, it was a disaster.

Halas let out her breath, laboring conscientiously to shed her anger. "There is never too much food for such a gathering, and the chief cook should be justly praised for everything I've glimpsed in the kitchens. Where I dare not offer my uninformed opinion." The meaning here caused Perin to flush and cross his arms.

Hers were already crossed. "Liberality in refreshments is praiseworthy. Food will get eaten. But this . . . this profligacy . . . and the lilies are just now bringing in! The lilies are the most important, so the third secretary said."

'You put them in the middle!" Perin wound his hand in a circle. "Flowers aren't like cakes and pastries. There's always room for more."

Halas let out a second, longer breath, which hissed with her effort to control her outrage. Then she said, with the merest tremble in her voice, "The third secretary requested me to be in charge of the decorations."

Perin knew that, but he had been working secretly on his

grand design in hopes of a steward position when It would happen. (No one quite dared to spell out what It was, but everyone knew *something* was going to happen. Expectation scintillated in the air.)

"I took steps to aid you," he said. "See? All these flowers here are reflected in icing on pastries and tarts. Including lilies!"

A pause ensued as onlookers watched intently — entertained or outraged, depending upon their partisanship — and Halas tried to find words.

Before she could speak, the foremost town florist hailed from the great doors at the far end. "Ho! Lilies are here! Best get them to water soon. In this heat, they'll wilt fast."

Halas turned to Perin. "You *cannot* crush lilies into the center of these . . . these riots!"

Riots? The line of servants carrying trays of cleverly carved vegetables bunched up at the far door. Everyone halted in the midst of what ought to have been the last stages of preparation, to watch the duel.

As Steward Perin scowled, lips working, a whisper rustled along the perimeter in the wake of a newcomer.

Here was Herald-Scribe Third Secretary Lirendi himself.

He entered with his characteristic quick step, his dove gray herald-scribe robe swinging at hem and sleeves.

"Third Secretary," both Halas and Perin exclaimed at the same time — for once in agreement, however inadvertent.

Third Secretary Lirendi looked around with an appreciative air, the thin black mustache above his dashing, pointed beard emphasizing his smile, his many long, glossy braids swinging about a fine set of shoulders as he turned this way and that. "A marvel," he exclaimed, his light voice somehow carrying throughout the vast chamber. "And look at the artistry here!" He paused to admire the closest tray of vegetables, bedewed with moisture to keep them crisp. "So perfect, I can scarcely keep my hands away."

"Try one, try one," the chief cook said, his silent workers, still holding their trays, exchanging glances — they had been threatened with terrible things if anyone stole as much as a single carrot with its clever curls to resemble golden lilies in bloom.

"Oh, I shall," Lirendi promised, clasping his hands. "Once the guests have had a chance to see what marvels you've wrought."

He whirled, robe billowing and falling against the straight lines of his body as he held his hands out as if to embrace the room. "You are all so gifted."

Then he turned, indicating the door with a well-made hand, elegant (some said) if you ignored the calluses across the palm. "And *there* are the lilies. They're perfect!"

The florist flushed, then spoke in a much milder tone. "They better get into water."

"A fine suggestion." The third secretary now opened his hand toward the linen-covered tables lined before the cold hearth, which had been mostly obscured by masses of flowers. "Chief Cook Perin, I congratulate you. New delights will be appearing, besides these vegetables?"

Perin was very aware that his own schedule had ground to a halt while he argued with Halas. Figuring the stewardship might be still possible if he retreated to his stronghold, where he knew nothing could be deemed amiss, he gestured grandly toward the kitchen. "You shall see at once!"

"I'll join you in a moment."

Perin was about to protest that they could go together, but reflected that he could use that 'moment' to make certain his own domain was at its best. He marched out, jowls jiggling.

The third secretary turned to Halas, his light brown eyes warm and appreciative. "This room, I find, has excellent bones, so to speak."

"Austere, but it is quite the finest building in town." Halas nodded, as they both looked up at the late afternoon light slanting in rays of gold through the trefoil clerestory windows, as if in benediction.

"I quite agree. Perhaps these delightful shades of red would be the very thing to greet arrivals at the carriage yard? And all these sunny oranges . . ." He touched the daisies clustered among red roses. "Might they brighten the stonework along the birch walk, should guests stroll out to take the air?"

Halas agreed even more fervently. Motioning to her workers, with a few terse words, she had them separating colors and textures, baskets of clashing hues going out in three directions while clever fingers worked the remainder into far more artistic bouquets.

The overpowering whelm began to diminish, replaced by clusters of pale blue starliss and the silver-white late lilies, framed in aromatic twists of blue cedar.

When Perin returned to fetch the laggard third secretary, it was to see Lirendi himself carefully setting a sprig of golden kingsfold in a centerpiece of coraleth the hue of a summer sky.

Before Perin could speak, the third secretary smiled his way. "Let's see what you have in store for us. I'm looking forward to your ginger-nut tarts, quite the best I've ever tasted, especially with that lemon-flavored, oh, what do you call it, a drizzle so artfully placed on the top . . ."

His gentle flow of words carried them back in the direction of the kitchens, past the alcove where musicians sat with kerchiefs tied around their necks to protect their clothes as they stuffed themselves in preparation for a night's unending labor. On entering the kitchen, Perin inspected the trays of spiced rice, artfully carved vegetables and crisp fruits, and sniffed the fresh-water fish simmering in wine and truffles.

Then the chief baker stepped up to inspect tiny cakes coming out of the bakehouse, to be set out to cool before decoration.

"These are the last of them." The chief baker spoke past Perin to the third secretary, who had stopped in the doorway, so as not to get in the way of scurrying kitchen help. The chief baker mopped his brow. "We've figured half a dozen for each count and family, the guild chiefs and their families, and the four trade envoys."

"Ah, yes. Trade envoys. Will there be enough for the Chwahir trade chief and whoever he brings?" Lirendi asked.

Everyone stopped working, and the faces turned toward him ranged from astonishment to horror.

The herald-scribe stood there in the doorway, hands behind his back, his light brown gaze pellucid.

"Chwahir?" Perin repeated, in the tone of one picking a many-legged spim from what had been a perfect glaze.

"Yes. I sent that polite young Messenger Yedoc back to her trade chief with an invitation. After all, every trade envoy in town is coming. Honor requires me to . . . no, I really should use the excellent word in your Kifelian, *melende* improves so much on the ritual-bound Sartoran notion of honor. It's that gentle emphasis on civilized manners. Or, as one of our local poets here said not two days ago, the life—" He opened his hands. "—of art. Should the Chwahir not be invited to enjoy our arts, especially if they come to trade?"

That left the staring group nothing to say.

The third secretary did not appear to notice their congealing expressions. "Thanks to your foresight, yes, there really seems to be enough here for an army."

Was there irony in that last word? But Perin saw none in the scribe's attentive face, or heard it in the next rush of softly spoken words: "I'll get out of your way, as I see you are very busy with the last preparations, and I have somewhere to be." He glanced around, his gaze resting briefly on the newly-hired delivery man standing in the doorway, and flicked his neat beard as he said airily, "It would be so rude to keep a barber waiting when everybody wants his attention." A flash of his hand as he examined his nails. "I really ought to get these freshly painted as well."

Lirendi put his hands together and bowed his head, then walked out the door opposite the watching delivery man.

At once a clamor of voices broke out.

"Chwahir? Why would he invite *them*?"

"Traders, tchah! Nothing more, or less, than brigands."

"They won't come. The idea of Chwahir at a masquerade is like, is like putting a robe on a horse!"

"Or asking a snake to partner you in the two-step!"

"Gardener sent these tubs of ferns," the delivery man cut in, his accent heavy.

"Take those to the front entrance," the baker said impatiently. "Can't you see this is a kitchen?"

The delivery man vanished, forgotten in an instant as righteous indignation against the marauding Chwahir spiced the last efforts of preparation.

Invitation Accepted

On the other side of the river, inside a Chwahir military tent, stood two people with a third kneeling, all three black-haired and pale. Nanijo, or Warlord, Vessler Rajin glared at the kneeling runner before him and exclaimed, "A what?"

"Masquerade," the runner, whose name was Yedoc, said in the flat, humble voice that runners learned early to use around ambitious and tetchy warlords.

"What is a masquerade?"

Yedoc hesitated, sensing a trap. Runners who knew too much didn't last any longer than runners who corrected their commanders. Her head dipped lower, her thin, bowed shoulders tensed.

"I'm told they wear masks." That was her twi-cousin, scout captain Danlo Sonscarna, coming to her rescue. But then the warlord side-eyed him, gaze narrowed.

Yedoc held her breath. Danlo and Nanijo Rajin had trained together, but since they'd come over the pass, tension had sharpened between them. However, a scout captain was supposed to seek information. Yedoc watched the warlord in an agony of dread as he considered what might underlie his scout captain's words.

Curiosity won. "Masks?"

"They take on the semblance of others. Like disguises," Danlo said in a flatly neutral tone, expression detached. No insubordination here!

"Disguises!" The warlord's thin brows shot upward, and he uttered a laugh. "Like us! *Traders.*" He spat the word in the direction of the striped trader's robe lying over a camp chair, and Danlo didn't move a muscle at the oblique attack. "It's a ruse, then? But why would I be asked to it, if everyone is in disguise? Surely they are not making trade deals anymore today?"

"The assembly is finished for another three years. I believe this event is a celebration, warlord," Danlo said, still utterly impassive. He paused and glanced outside the tent, where his chief spy, wearing the garb of one of the many short-term delivery hires, made a sign. Danlo nodded an acknowledgment and said, "We have a report that all the trade guild leaders will be there."

"Celebration," the warlord repeated. "Of what?"

Here it was safe for Yedoc to speak, as she had been the principal runner in carrying the warlord's messages about trade to the Sartoran envoy, Third Secretary Lirendi.

She said to the ground, "The purpose has not been stated. But all the territorial leaders are invited as well as the trade chiefs, and I was informed by the third secretary that they were all expected to be there."

"Really!" Rajin's amazement stretched the sword scars on his hard, bony face. "All their 'lords'," he left off the 'war' prefix to show his scorn, "gathered in one place?"

"So I was told, warlord."

"*I* couldn't have planned it better. Of course I'll go. I can assess their defense myself." Scorn sharpened the word *defense*. "Convenient of this third-assistant scribe, or whatever he calls himself, to aid me so well. You'll go with me to interpret." He snapped his fingers at Yedoc, still kneeling at his feet.

Since that kind-voiced Third Secretary Lirendi had extended the invitation to her also, she had been worrying about how to ask permission without being annihilated. She'd just decided it was better to keep mum (and alive) when the warlord added that rider, before issuing a new stream of orders.

She bowed low, hands pressed to knees, hiding a tide of relief, amazement, joy, and always, always, worry, as she waited to be dismissed; she didn't see the covert glance of guilt-driven concern Danlo shot her way.

It was he, believing that Rajin really did seek a trade alliance, who had recommended transferring Yedoc from Princess Leig's service, as she knew the language of Kei Fael. What he had thought would be a splendid opportunity was inescapably proving to be the worst decision of his life.

Anticipation

At the guild hall's kitchen wing, assistants garnished honey-nut rice cups, hastily put together after the astonishing announcement about inviting the Chwahir. Heat-exacerbated affront relieved itself through that congenial state wherein everyone is in total agreement in slandering someone else. They were still venting about those Nightland-accursed, moon-faced barbarians when a newcomer appeared in the doorway.

Perin and the baker both recognized the short, snub-nosed Herald-Scribe Third Guide Winza Gaszin. She walked in carefully, wearing a very fine thigh-length doublet stiff with linen quilting, and sewn over with rings small enough to turn an arrow. It had been embroidered with highly stylized acanthus and holly, the shoulder spaulders decorated with smaller versions of the same pattern. The color was dominantly brilliant jonquil, her trim waist sashed with crimson silk. She had thrust a dagger through the sash.

Over the doublet she wore a gold-embroidered crimson baldric. A blood-red stone glinted on the sword hanging from it. At her side, depending from the sash, swung a round fan on a silken cord, bright yellow on one side, dark blue on the other. Not one of the kitchen crew recognized a military signal fan.

Below that, her loose riding trousers were stuffed into blackweave boots, the folded tops worked with golden leaves studded with ruby flowers. She carried a voluminous cloak of bright red, matching her hair.

"You look splendid," the baker's assistant said with honest admiration. "But aren't you warm in that?"

"Very. But it's the only fine thing I have. The crown prince —" Winza corrected herself quickly, "that is, his majesty, the new king, gifted us with these doublets for our journey. He chose the colors himself." She gave them a slightly inquisitive, lopsided smile, but it didn't occur to anyone there to wonder why a king did anything, much less give extremely expensive formal wear for a routine duty that recurred every three years.

Winza twirled around, careful to keep her sword in its baldric from knocking the tables. "I don't dare eat, or do anything, really, lest I slop something over myself. May I wait with you? It seems I'm a bit early."

"Of course," Perin said readily, hoping that they might hear some insider gossip.

Winza was well-liked by everyone. Though in rank she was second only to Martande Lirendi, she was always willing to carry a message to the third secretary, even from a stable hand. On her arrival, she had made amusing errors in the Kei Faelian dialect of Sartoran, but accepted corrections with the same happy smile she gave them now. Her heavy Sartoran accent, everyone had decided, was charming.

"We're just finishing." Perin sighed, then — lest she think they hadn't planned well — he added, "Not having thought those Chwahir would be included."

"Utter waste, if you ask me," the baker's assistant put in (though no one had asked her), as she tossed halved nuts in spice before sprinkling them on the rice treats.

The chief baker said doubtfully, "I never thought anyone would say it was *melende* to invite Chwahir, who everyone knows just want to steal from us, whatever they're pretending."

"Right!" Perin mopped his crimson face. "They have no honest reason to be here. Chwahir!" The word, expelled on an outgoing breath, came out sounding like a curse.

"I'm told the ones here want trade," Minza said as she climbed carefully onto a high stool in the corner. And, seeing the doubtful looks cast her way, "The truth is, Chwahir linens are world famous, especially their canvas. Sartor has to get theirs by ship clear around the eastern end of the continent. It would be so simple for the guilds here to trade right over the mountain."

The baker shook her head. "They weren't *trading* six years ago! And the Altans say they're still running raids off their southwestern border, there in the north."

"Well, those raiders were driven off, were they not? Who's to say they're in any way related to these seeking trade?" Minza asked reasonably.

The fading light in the door darkened. They turned to discover a tall, thin, pale-faced Chwahir dressed, like all the Chwahir, in unrelieved black linsey-woolsey.

"Greetings, Messenger Yedoc," Minza said.

Yedoc observed her troubled expression, and suspected that Minza was wondering how much she had heard. No one likes to be caught in an awkward position. Though so far Third-Guide Minza, she of the wonderful red hair, had always been polite and kind, Yedoc knew how quickly an assumed moral superiority can spark hostility.

To spare them all, she looked around vaguely, and put her hand up to her eyes as if she couldn't see into the gloom. "Be here Scribe Lirendi?" she asked.

They had become accustomed to how the few Chwahir who could speak a civilized tongue seemed utterly unacquainted with simple verb tenses.

Perin advanced toward the door, jowls wiggling, as if he intended to defend the kitchen against attack by the thin, unarmed Chwahir. "*Third Secretary* Herald-Scribe Lirendi," he corrected incorrectly, though his voice was not unkind now that he recognized the mild Chwahir messenger.

"I be sorry," Yedoc said, hands flat on her knees as she bowed. "I be give a message for he."

Winza had seen how the anxious, run-ragged Chwahir looked at the third secretary. She said in her most friendly voice, "You should find him at the Scribes' Guild House, over there across from the carriage yard."

"I be sorry," Yedoc said, a phrase she seemed to preface every sentence with. The silent kitchen crew had seen her around, always quiet, always stepping out of others' way. But she humbly accepted all the snubs and snides. "Forgive me for trouble you," she added in the slightly singsong Chwahir accent, her big gray eyes earnest in her round, pale Chwahir face, "but first I look there."

"Ah-yi!" Winza snapped her fingers. "I forgot! He and the rest of the fellows all went off to get their beards barbered. The masquerade will be starting in . . . no more than an hour, surely. If you go out through the hall entrance, you take the path to the riverside, cross the bridge, and not a hundred paces to the right, you'll see the sign." Minza made a motion as if clacking scissors, and indicated the inner hall.

Yedoc bowed again, and obediently followed Minza's finger to the inner door. A few steps took her past the antechamber where the musicians ate, their caps carefully lined up on a side-table, each sporting the golden feather rosette that meant they had once won the highest prize at the fiercely competitive Sartoran Music Festival. She knew all about that festival, though her people never took their music outside their borders.

The musicians were talking as they tuned their instruments, their accents the broad, slightly nasal intonation very different from the liquid vowel of Kei Fael's dialect of Sartoran.

The corridor opened into the grand hall, and Yedoc stopped involuntarily, staring in heart-squeezing wonder at the garlands of green frosted with lilies and deep blue flowers, reminding her of the summer sky.

Snow-white linen almost as fine as the linens at home prepared foods that sent out enticing aromas.

Yedoc resolutely turned away from these tables that she dared not touch, though her stomach wrung with hunger. She and the other three runners had been kept moving since dawn.

She headed for the doors standing open to the path beyond. As she crossed the vast chamber, which was noticeably cooler than anywhere else, she spotted a young woman seated on a cloth-covered bench, sketching. Yedoc drifted past and glanced down. The artist was busy sketching all the details of the room, muttering under her breath as she added shading and detail.

A passing servant, his empty tray tucked under his arm, poked his nose over her shoulder and said with a laugh, "Aren't you a little early for that? Bell hasn't even rung!"

Without looking up, the artist said, "Background is always easier to get the details when it's fresh. Before the people obscure everything."

This meant the sketch would be a painting. Yedoc backed away, looking around as the details assembled in her mind: the artist, obviously hired to record an important event, the renowned musicians from far away.

Third guide was as confusing as *third secretary*. The distinctions of these titles from far-off Sartor made no sense to Yedoc. They did not translate into Chwahir military hierarchy.

The third secretary, in his invitation, had said that he'd put together the masquerade to celebrate the end of the tri-annual assembly of regional guild leaders, the counts, and the Sartoran envoy (himself), but it seemed to her that the planning went back much farther than a few weeks. That was puzzling, but it was not her puzzle.

She spotted the scissors sign, grateful that the red-haired "third guide" had given her proper directions. Unlike many others, who had entertained themselves by sending Yedoc to remote parts of the town. But, she'd told herself, she learned where things lay that much faster.

She hurried to the bridge, then stepped aside to let a group of finely dressed people stroll pass. Two of then glanced her way, and, as always, she saw upper lips crimp with disgust.

She rushed across the bridge toward the shop. Through the windows, she heard that voice she thought of as molten silver. She knew that both Chwahir and Kei Faelians alike would unite in scorning her if they knew how her heart beat hard against her ribs when she heard the herald-scribe speak, and when she saw his long hair, as blue-black as any Chwahir, held with fine pins, or his light brown eyes—another color found among the Chwahir, though less common than the usual gray or black. It was only his warm brown skin that marked him as a southerner. That, and of course, speech, manner, and clothes.

He could never be a Chwahir, and yet somehow that added to the enchantment that shimmered around him. Knowing that the locals would despise the intensity of feelings they'd feel she had no right to, she was grateful that they largely snubbed and ignored her.

But *he* never did.

She smoothed her face, a skill honed by self-preservation.

"Messenger Yedoc," the third secretary said as she entered the barber shop.

Finely dressed people filled the shop; the flash of decorative metals prompted the fancy that up north in Chwahirsland, such a gathering would be a pre-war strategy session, but here in the warm and wonderful south, it was merely a gathering at a barber's.

They had fallen into as complete a silence as if she had intruded on an actual strategy session. Intensely aware of those unwavering stares, she enunciated carefully, "I be sorry, I interrupt to say that Warlord Nanijo Rajin attend, and I bring he at the proper time, when that be."

"Did I not say? Forgive me. The bell will be ringing very soon," the third secretary said, with his kindly tone and smile. "Bring him at any time convenient to you both. I hope you'll enjoy the masquerade!"

Yedoc bowed, laughing inwardly at the idea of her own convenience ever being considered, or "bringing" a warlord anywhere. They went where they willed, and everyone else came to them.

As she left, she heard the silver voice drawing attention away from her as he said, "That reminds me. The bell! Really, where did they get it? So sour a clang! What this town needs is a proper carillon, don't you think?"

The Host Alone

The sun sank in a ruddy welter below a line of dramatic clouds, blue-purple edged with fire. As it vanished, taking the warm color with it, leaving dark gray, the bell began tolling.

Third Guide Minza Gaszin had stationed herself near the open door to the kitchen, the most-used entrance and exit for the army of people who had set up the masquerade, many of whom were staying, as the third secretary had extended his invitation to all those who prepared the event as well as the exalted counts and guild chiefs. Those who had managed to put together masquerade costumes went to don them, and the rest trooped home, preferring a quiet evening with feet up to a hot, crowded hall, especially with a storm coming on.

Minza kept to her station, watching progress inside and outside. Her own people turned up periodically to report, then vanished without notice. The echoes of the tolling bell died away as her brother Ianzi drifted up, almost invisible in his enveloping cloak of forest green, until the golden light spilling from the doorway brought the color to life.

"All in place." He cast a glance upward at the emerging stars in the east, deceptively peaceful: the west was dark. "I have a feeling we'll be glad of these." He shook back his cloak. The faint shimmer of magic over it testified to the strength of the rain-repelling spell.

He might have stayed longer, but a couple of chattering servants approached. He backed up two steps and slipped into the shadows.

He'd said what she'd waited to hear. It was time for her to do a last perimeter check, for her own peace of mind. She glided along the north wall of the guild hall, the only light glowing in the clerestory windows above.

When she reached the back of the building abutting the wild garden shaded by aromatic trees, she spied a familiar silhouette half-obscured by a blue cedar. Marvelous, the human eye, she thought as she picked up her pace: no more than the outline of a shoulder, and the turn of his head, but she knew that shadowy figure for Martande Lirendi.

She took care to let him hear her footfall. He didn't move, which meant he recognized the sound of her walk. Ears, another marvel.

When she was three paces away, he turned.

Her breath caught. In the diffuse light from above, he looked like an ancient painting of a fabled hero. Truly these doublets did more for the masculine form than for the short, round female form such as hers. She closed the distance between them, admiring his cuirass with its stylized Venn knots worked around a single white lily, so stylized the lily could equally represent a dagger. Her thoughts splintered: on the surface was the heat of attraction that from long habit she subdued, but beneath that the distinct, and troubling, admiration for what was, after all, the garmenture of war.

The golden light from the tall windows high overhead threw hard shadow under the ridge of his cheekbone, and gathered with eerie lucence deep within the lattices of what was whispered to be the most valuable diamond in the Sartoran monarchs' royal vault, affixed at his shoulder as a clasp for his cloak. It smoldered with its disturbing inner fire, and she reflected that few could wear that thing without being entirely overpowered. But in this light, even his absurd feathered mask did nothing to hide how his eyes looked like molten gold. He had inherited those from his great-grandmother, whose golden coloring had been famed in countless portraits written, sung, and painted. Below the mask his thin mustache and neat beard added a severity to the bones of his face that, even with the mask obscuring his high, intelligent brow, rendered him curiously ageless.

He was not aware of any of that: his thoughts had turned entirely inward, until he heard her footfalls.

She closed the distance between them, and as the light fell full on her face he saw her astonishment as she stared at the diamond.

He uttered a soft sound that was almost a laugh, except for its lack of humor. "It might fall and become someone else's burden."

She knew him well, and understood that for *it* he meant *I*, and the burden the task ahead.

Her throat dried. As for the jewel, what if a triumphant Chwahir carried that thing back to his capital as a trophy, and Princess Ilneas found out?

He saw the distraught tightening of her features. "It won't launch a war, whatever happens to it. Eniad is too smart to let Ilneas use it as a pretext."

Martande, Minza reflected, was one of the few people who could call the king simply by his name—who thought of him that way. Even as lowly herald-scribe apprentice and crown prince, they had been Martande and Eniad.

As the diamond glittered with his indrawn breath, she remembered beautiful, complicated Princess Ilneas standing on Chandos Way as she handed it to him, her impassioned tone too low for anyone to hear the exact words, though the entire company, plus the Court of Star Chamber, had been watching.

Minza said, "She gave it to you out of love."

His expression tightened, his head turning away. "No. As an anchor." He touched the diamond, then dropped his hand and faced her again. "She'll replace us both fast enough."

Minza slowly shook her head. Replacing that diamond—if it was a diamond, for she had never seen one with actual light in its depths that compelled your gaze, and then seemed to hook your mind—would be impossible.

So too would be replacing him. But she would never say anything that could be misconstrued. Long-held tradition decreed that herald-scribes under orders were not to distract themselves with dalliance. And they were under orders. So they were friends, but she acknowledged that their friendship was more precious to her than . . . well, than diamonds.

Her gaze strayed to that coruscation on his shoulder, and she remembered that Martande had been locked in a long conversation with the king the morning before they left. And, unlike other previous conversations, Martande had not told her what had been said. Approaching it obliquely, "Won't Pr—King Eniad object to its being given away like that?"

Martande shrugged, and the fire within the diamond leaped, ruddy crimson to gold. "If anything, I suspect he'd wave at the vault and tell us to help ourselves to more."

She tried to laugh, but it sounded strangled. She knew she'd been deflected from whatever the king had said, as always in the kindest way possible. So she went along with the new subject. "He did joke once about his ancestors being the worst sort of hoarders."

Martande reached out and rested his fingertips lightly on her shoulders, so lightly she didn't feel them through the flared spaulders on her doublet, but she was aware of his touch even so. She locked her knees lest she make any movement, however slight, that would cause him to withdraw.

"Sorry, Minza," he said, low-voiced, and she wondered what he saw in her face, there in the almost-darkness. "You know my moods. I was standing here reflecting on the fact that the next step commits us irrevocably. Until now we could always turn back."

She let out her breath. "And?"

"And what would you do?" he said, and there was the light tone back, and the quick, reckless grin she loved so much. "Call it, Minza. I'll go either way."

"Martande, is there really any turning back?" She saw the truth in a subtle tensing around his eyes, then stated clearly, "I wouldn't even if there was."

"Are you certain?" he murmured, so close she could feel his breath on her forehead. "You know me better than anyone. These past weeks. Months. I've been running headlong, but a moment ago I was alone here for the first time in . . . It doesn't matter. It's just that I find I can't see past myself."

"I can," she said steadily. "It's right. I saw it happen, how the counts you've come to trust, trust you back. Same with the guilds. Even without this other trouble. And as for that, ah-yi! We're all in place." She tipped her head back, seeing the movement of shadows in the upper windows, which she knew gave onto the back of the guild hall's gallery. "The musicians are about to begin."

"Then let us not disappoint them." He tugged at his mask, an absurdity made mostly of layered feathers. "This thing is crooked. Will you retie it for me?"

"Bend down. These boots won't let me stand on my toes."

He uttered a voiceless laugh and obediently stooped. He had pulled his braided hair up high, catching it with two silver flying crane ornaments, to match his nail polish. She tied the ribbons securely below the braid, and stepped back.

He shook out a voluminous robe of sky blue, embroidered with flying cranes in palest peach, and pulled it on over his doublet as they began to walk the riverside path. The light inside slanted down from the long row of windows, light, dark, light, dark.

She reminded herself firmly what experience had taught her during and after postings all over Sartor since early childhood: most friendships were ephemeral, dependent on proximity and context.

So she braced her spine and faced the path ahead, while he, locked inside his skull with a thousand whispering voices, felt the shifting of her attention like stepping from sunlight to darkness.

If I survive, he promised himself.

The Guests Assemble

Voices bright with anticipation and laughter rose on the warm, humid air as a slow breeze began whispering through the treetops. A few steps farther, and here were the first arrivals, brilliant in crimson and violet and the intense green of early spring, bedazzled by saffron highlights, sequins and feathers.

Butterfly-wing sleeves here, tight trousers over the confident curve of well-molded thighs there, and everywhere the insouciance of masks complemented the face paint of the more daring. A young fellow more dashing than most had crowned his elaborate mask with a kind of lantern, which bobbed along with his swinging stride, as though a separate entity.

When Minza and Martande reached the open doors, she slipped inside, leaving him standing alone, light pouring all around him, to welcome his guests.

The Grand Promenade and Sarabande

"Dancing cranes," the Count of Nashan muttered to his consort as they walked into the fabulously decorated hall. They had been coming to the place ever since they were young heirs, but it had never been decorated like this.

Ever since the Sartoran envoy had ridden into the town at the head of a column of herald-scribes—the men wearing those dapper beards, on some intriguingly sinister—the count had been feeling distinctly behindhand in fashion.

"It can't be helped," his consort soothed as she expertly priced the costumes around them, though she knew, and she knew he knew, that some would cast side-eyes their way as soon as the masks came off. Nashan, the western-most reach of Kei Fael, vaunted its reputation perhaps a little too readily for being closest to Sartor and thereby being the first to know the newest fashions.

The party from Eth Endra (lying to Nashan's southeast) certainly thought so. "I wonder if that pompous twit Nashan will hide his face," the Count of Eth Endra murmured to her current favorite as they followed behind someone costumed in silvery

layered scales. A mer person? A dragon? The snickering suggested youth. "Magic can do many things, but it cannot grow a
respectable beard in days."

She cast a quick look of approval at her favorite, who, tall and
fair (and also beardless) had opted to dress as a famous female
poet, thus evading the fashion question. A breeze scoured in the
side door and set his veils and draperies a-flutter. She quickly
twitched them into place, glad she had opted for sturdiness: she
was going as Sartor's famous Prince Tivonais in a purple velvet
dueling suit, copied from an ancient painting.

"Do you really think there will be trouble at a masquerade
ball?" she whispered, having made certain that nothing showed of
the gambeson her favorite wore beneath his pretty robes.

"No notion. Which, I suppose, is why I'm a guard captain and
Lirendi's a herald-scribe third secretary."

She blew out her breath, which sent the curling feather against
her left cheek dancing. "I wonder if Alarcansa will come."

He laughed softly. "If he does, it will be a first."

"I suspect," she said as the musicians struck up the familiar
prelude to the Sartoran Promenade, "there will be many firsts this
night. Oh, look." Both glanced at the newcomers. "There's Altan,
and those tiresome twins of his."

The consort was thinking that the Count of Altan's daughter
might someday be all right, if she could get away from her snob of
a twin brother, as he bowed to the old Count.

The Count of Altan bowed back, then turned away, not certain
who that tall female was. He hated masquerades—hated not
knowing who he was talking to. But they were popular, so he
endured, confining his objection to wearing the same costume
since his grandfather had handed it off, along with Altan county,
to him when he turned twenty-five. It was a loose, gaudy garment
called a battle tunic, made of the finest linen likely to outlast ten
generations, thick with embroidery of dragons chasing fire along
the hem and broad sleeves, with what he'd been told were Venn
runes down one side. No one in the family could read them, of

course; it was rare for Venn, who traded at every port, to penetrate so far inland.

But the battle tunic, a battered helm with fresh plumes, and his old sword served more than one purpose besides masquerades. As for everyone recognizing it, who cared?

Well, his two children did.

Fliss sighed and ignored her hopeless father's mumbling about idiotic mask wearing; Hende's lips tightened as he raked his gaze over his father in that outmoded old garb. He twitched at his magnificent midnight-blue cape studded with diamonds, as if to draw all attention to his finery as protection of the family reputation. At least his sister looked all right.

Fliss preened, sure that few looked as fine as she in layers of moth-gauze, pale yellow silk roses in a slant from shoulder to hip, and the filmy trousers fixed at her ankles with more roses, above golden dancing slippers.

Since no one seemed to be admiring her, or her brother, as people spread into the vast hall and began forming into a circle, she glanced back at the tall figure in the silken robe with the dancing cranes. "I wonder if the rumors are true about Third-Secretary Lirendi making some new pronouncement from the king?" she asked.

As much as one could read around their masks, the count looked surprised and her brother irritated. Hende had always made a point of ignoring the third secretary on his previous visits. "Everyone says he's personal friend to the new king," she said defensively as Hende's mouth twisted in scorn. "Even related. Their great-grandmothers were half-sisters, I believe."

The count thought both his children had been oblivious to the indefatigable work the third secretary had done, and how he had successfully managed to bring together a group known for its frictions and factions. "He certainly seems to know everyone," the count added peaceably, as all three Altans watched the third secretary greeting a large, noisy party that could only be the numerous Ranflars.

"His great-grandmother was not a Landis," Hende said. "Merely a Dei. They were nothing before King Connar became besotted with Alian Dei. They're still nothing. And he's not even one of the Deis. Some even more mediocre family."

"The envoy's name," the count said, "is Lirendi."

"Utterly undistinguished," Hende stated.

Ignoring her brother, Fliss turned to the count. "Gelis Ranflar told me that Third-Secretary Lirendi was with the Count of Alarcansa six years ago, when that Chwahir army tried to take the—"

"If you start in about mines again, I will faint from the heat and boredom," Hende drawled. "That fashion for beards. Everyone says the Sartoran court was forced to grow them because Prince Fish Face grew one to hide his lack of chin." With that he walked off, leaving them, and the subject, behind.

The count watched him go, heart-wrung. He loved both his children, but he'd begun to wonder if he would have to find an heir somewhere else, until Fliss, at least, had suddenly begun showing an interest not in fashions and duels, which was all Hende paid attention to, but in regional affairs, ever since they'd come to the assembly.

Fliss was not going to tell him that her interest had been sparked by her interest in the third secretary, but the longer she'd listened, the more she found aspects of the recent past raising questions about events that hitherto had all just been *there*. Like the fact that the seldom-seen, martial Count of Alarcansa was half-Chwahir, and that his mother had once fought against her own countrymen in a war far nastier than the one six years ago. In that early one, the Count, only fifteen at the time, had managed to kill the warlord who'd stabbed his father, getting that sword scar down his face in the process, and leaving him not just the title but the task of guarding the eastern pass. He'd been four years younger than she was now.

No wonder everyone seemed to defer to him!

She looked around at chatting, flirting pairs coalescing into the huge circle for the Promenade, as the musicians expertly repeated the prelude half a step higher. She wondered if the Count of Alarcansa would actually attend, when everyone knew he never went to parties. And would she recognize him if he did?

Ten steps away, Gelis, the Count of Ranflar's granddaughter, thought happily that a ball was a lifetime in itself. Everything previous is forgotten, and each touch of gazes or hands, each exchange, anguish and happiness, are years squeezed into a night that . . . oh, if it would never end!

Everything was fascinating! Even the older people. Usually so boring. It was strange, how expressive elders were when you couldn't see their faces. Like when the whisper went around that that tall man dressed as a Venn warship captain was the Count of Alarcansa. Gelis bounced on tiptoe, staring at him in his horned helm, his step faintly chinging with steel beneath his fabulous battle tunic of white with a tree worked in green, crowned with stars of real gold.

She was not the only one staring. Runnels of light flashed along silk, and jewels trembled and glittered as heads turned, dragon-fly quick, to watch his progress through the room.

Gelis's view was blocked by a person dressed as one of the fabled tree people from the coast of the Sartoran Sea, from nose to feet covered in hundreds of floating curls of brown and green gauze. A fabulous headdress with branches reached over their head, revealing only a pair of laughing eyes.

"Join me for the Promenade?" a voice whispered.

The elders' impenetrable politics sank below the enticement of someone interested in *her*. Did she know this mystery partner?

She took the proffered warm hand to join the circle. Her joy wavered when greenish lightning flashed all along the northside windows, overpowering the candlelight as an ominous growl rumbled through the stone, thinning the music to a frantic insect-whine.

Everyone paused for a breathless moment, until the thunder began dying away in fretful grumbles, and the music and candlelight regained prominence, restoring the celebrative mood.

It was then that the Chwahir commander, swathed in an ill-fitting striped trader's robe, stepped into the doorway, mentally dismissing the man in the silk covered with cranes. In his view, anyone ordered to be greeter at a door must be the lowest of the servants. His dismissive gaze snagged on the gaudy gem this underling wore at one shoulder. In an orderly society, servants did not dress to draw attention.

"Be welcome," Martande Lirendi said to the warlord's back. "Enjoy the evening!"

Yedoc, two paces behind the warlord, instantly recognized that voice of silver, but she dared no response. Since being transferred from Princess Leig to Nanijo Rajin, she had endured petty cruelties at any sign of what he called presumption, which made her rebel with inward celebration at every small setback or weakness, even if imagined: she knew he was here to surveille the enemy, but she would let him discover Herald-Scribe Third Secretary Martande Lirendi on his own.

Or not.

She would sneak all the enjoyment she could until then.

As she entered the crowded hall, she saw the guests falter at the sight of her, for Rajin had told her that as a servant she was not entitled to disguise. She knew better than to point out that as the only person wearing unrelieved black and with a bare face, she would not be invisible.

Nor was he, in spite of the striped robe he wore carelessly over his battle gear, as he had refused to consider the idea of a mask.

Martande had spoken to the elderly Count of Ranflar a few moments before, "If the Chwahir, ah, trader appears, may I request your expertise in making him welcome? The world knows you are the most beloved host in Kei Fael—no one has your gift of setting people at ease."

Every word was sincere as well as true, but what she remained unconscious of was her calm air of gentle civility, the very opposite of militant threat.

And so her short, white-haired figure in mauve and green

advanced on the warlord, her mask not hiding gray hair or the soft flesh under a sagging chin. Yedoc held her breath as Rajin's expression tightened, lest he utter something annihilating, for she knew he respected no older persons who had not fought their bloody way to admiralty or war commander.

The woman in mauve and green stopped and spoke.

Rajin flicked an impatient glance at Yedoc. "What did she say?"

"She invites you to join her in dancing the Promenade, Nanijo Rajin."

"What is that?"

"A circle dance . . . she says it is a slow, easy pattern. It is about to begin, and she will show you."

His gaze ranged the room. Yedoc knew he was looking for the dais, or throne, or some sign of the most important chair — where a warlord would sit and command the room.

Yedoc's innards cramped during the protracted silence as the older woman waited patiently. Then the warlord's frown lifted. She sensed that he'd seen the advantage of a slow-moving circle, which would mask his true purpose while enabling him to scan the crowd more easily.

"Wait at the side," he ordered in Chwahir. "If any of these idiots pull you into this circle, get what information you can."

She bowed, and he turned back to the woman and enunciated some of his few words of Kei Faelian, "You be lead? I learn."

He walked off, the woman speaking slowly and carefully, her voice drowned by cascades of brassy, shimmering fanfares that signaled the start of the Promenade.

Yedoc's breath caught. Her eyes stung. Giddy, she listened, entranced as the people in the vast circle began to step, dip, turn, and sway in time to melodic music that had nothing to do with the polysemous transcendence of the Chwahir Great Hum. But that was all right. The world was better for music in all forms.

A rumble in her middle reminded her she had yet to eat that long, tiring day, so she drifted behind the servants watching the great circle, unnoticed by all except Martande Lirendi, who—because a masquerade annulled the obligations of rank—had chosen one of his own people to dance with, so that he could keep all his attention on the room as a whole.

Though Rajin had overlooked him, the rest of the guests knew who had welcomed them. From the other side of the circle Luor Iventh watched him beneath lowered lids as she partnered the second son of Gyrn's third prince, who was in Alsais to oversee orders for his new winery.

The beautiful Luor danced in a silence that made it abundantly clear that she was already tired of this son of a prince who had little prospect of the sort of rank she craved. Her moth-gauze gown, and the veil that revealed more than it concealed, was supposed to represent a Morvende cave dweller famed for her conquest of a king of Sartor, but she had designed the ruinously expensive costume to frame her own dark hair and flawless bronze skin, not even remotely resembling the white-haired, pale-skinned cave dwellers.

This princeling knew she was on the hunt. He decided after he ventured a few comments, to be ignored as her restless gaze swept the room, that he may as well entertain himself by discovering her prey. "The wagers are up to a hundred, or more, whether or not Alarcansa will condescend to attend," he observed as they started for the second time around the circle.

Luor, who suspected that the tall man wearing the Venn tree was Alarcansa, lifted a shoulder, her blue gaze indifferent. "What's Lirendi's family, do you know?"

Was *he* her target? Lirendi had been trailing along in the envoy's train for the past twelve years, the princeling was thinking. "Lirendis," he drawled, "have been in service to the royal Landis family for generations. Stewards, scribes. Cooks, for anything I know."

Luor listened to the words, but she was too disengaged to bother with the spite in his tone. On inheriting, each count had traveled to Sartor's capital, at great expense and trouble, to make their bow to the old king, thus confirming their status. She had met the then-crown prince, but the only golden-eyed person among the courtiers surrounding the royal throne-tree had been an old woman from the decorative Dei family.

She shut out the disparaging remarks by the princeling whose name she was already forgetting as she observed how very well Lirendi moved. He had become the center, not in any obvious way (it escaped Rajin, for example, who was still watching for the command behavior customary to the Chwahir), but Luor had grown up aware of the subtleties of preference and deference. There were always some who expected to become the principal person in a room, even demanded it, and then there were those, like Lirendi, who moved as serenely as the sun overhead, as all the flowers turned to face it.

Thus, by the end of the second circle, she was intrigued by an odd pattern: the most voluminously masked and cloaked guests made certain to keep him in view. These had to be his herald-scribe captains.

Power, she thought complacently as they commenced the third and last circle, was the most effective adornment, even more than diamonds. Though by morning, with his glossy black braids undone and spread upon her pillow, she would see to it that he'd beg her to take that ridiculous gem throwing back scintillations from the chandeliers overhead.

The Promenade ended, and she walked away to begin her campaign as—on the opposite side of the room—Rajin tried to map the dizzying flow of a big circle breaking into countless smaller ones, no one standing still, leaving him no closer to any clues to who was in command here.

Overhead, the musicians glided straight into a sarabande, so traditional it was known over three continents. Aigrettes and feathers twinkled and bobbed, ribbons fluttered and fringed sashes danced and swung as people found new partners; Rajin's old woman was replaced by an even older woman, whose quick gesture shooing away what sounded like chattering youngsters beneath those masks seemed to indicate someone of prominence.

At last. He snapped his fingers, but the duty runner wasn't to heel. Before he could look around for her, the newcomer said, "I speak some Chwahir. Let us discuss trade. Unless you wish to dance?"

He knew nothing about trade, and cared less, but that ostensibly was his guise. The dancing so far had been as simple as promised, and he did need to keep canvasing the room until he found these supposed lords. He would look a fool capturing a parcel of cooks as the lords and their warriors closed in on his camp from somewhere else. "Dance," he said. "Trade later."

The old woman drew him into a square there at the end of the room, among youngsters busy preening themselves and admiring one another as they pranced and twirled. Rajin, drawing on years of iron discipline, forced himself to follow the basic steps as he peered determinedly past servants skimming with firefly grace between the guests, their dove-gray, diaphanous sleeves fluttering behind as they wielded the lacquered trays that clever Designer Halas had produced from ancient storage. On those trays long, iridescent blown-glass goblets rested, full of blue wine from the southern reaches.

As Rajin was led with his square down the room in one direction, Martande Lirendi slipped from conversation to conversation in the other, his goal the tall, somber Chwahir messenger Yedoc, who stood alone half-hidden behind one of the ferns obscuring the fireplace, behind the refreshment tables. Lightning flared through the windows far above as he stepped up to Yedoc, and bowed.

People did not bow to runners. She slanted a glance to see if the warlord had noticed. She could be beaten for presumption. But he was at the other end of the room.

"Messenger Yedoc," Martande said, and was sorry to see her wide rain-gray eyes lift defensively to his, then shutter as she turned her head slightly, her thin shoulders tensing as she took a step back. "Would you like to dance?"

Though she had not dared to touch a drop of the blue wine, she was giddy with euphoria from the delectable flavors in the food, and the beguiling music whose stories were too elusive to grasp. She was about to disclaim when she remembered her orders. "Yes," she said faintly, sorry and happy at once. "But I know not how."

"I can show you the basic steps right here. They're simple enough, once you catch on. Then it's only a matter of touching palm to palm with the person to your right as you exchange positions, and begin anew."

He demonstrated, his fluttering silk swinging at his legs, revealing and concealing the gleams of blue and silver beneath. She stumbled after him, her mind reeling with one terrible realization after another. Was it possible that he—and that man with the tree on what looked very like a battle tunic—were wearing fighting garb under those fluttering silk robes? Costumes, she tried to tell herself. After all, they masked themselves as fabled heroes.

He said, "Do you want to join the others? Or are you still confused?"

"Confused," she repeated. "I—I be better here," she added breathlessly, her emotions in the ferocious turmoil of wind-whipped sparks flying upward from a fire.

Lightning flared, and the storm broke overhead.

At the other end of the hall, Rajin ignored it with the habit of one raised in a harsh environment. He watched shock stir among the guests, his eye caught by a short one swathed in red who neither recoiled nor tensed. No clue to age or sex, until he saw a small hand emerge palm down in command and reassurance. No boy, that—the knuckles and wrist were too refined, and no boy would move with the trained assurance of a warrior, everyone else giving way. She lifted her chin and shot a glance across the chamber.

Curious—maybe he'd finally found one of the counts—Rajin followed the direction of that glance, toward the tall, broad-shouldered man in the hero costume with the Venn knots and the tree, standing alone at the wall near a trio of servants holding trays.

Rajin had assumed at first that because this tree man stood near the servants he must be another one, but Rajin was now was close enough to see the man's face below the mask, specifically the Chwahir dueling scar, much like his own.

He ignored his partner's inane questions and turned sharply as the dynamics in the chamber took on an entirely new perspective.

While her commander sustained perspective realignment, Yedoc stood before Martande, her gaze reaching beyond him into the worst dilemma of her life.

She had discovered on her return from the barber shop that two strike companies had been ordered out, and further, the warlord had never intended to trade. It had just been a ruse. She hadn't seen Danlo, and had to assume that he'd been ordered to prepare for an attack, instead of the trade negotiation he'd continued to expect.

An attack *tonight*.

People would die. On both sides, and even if she became a traitor and warned this Sartoran standing before her—even if he chose to believe her—he could not stop it any more than she could.

She didn't perceive Martande's compassionate gaze on the moisture in her eyes, sequinned in the candlelight. How very tenuous, this moment! Used to being ignored, she had no idea how much of her inner thoughts he guessed. He also knew that the wrong question would send her in headlong flight. She was loyal, but to whom? Or better, perhaps, to what?

So he offered an indirect question. "May I ask what a twi is? Did I hear the term right?"

Her reverie broke, but her stricken expression did not lessen. "Yes. It be our—ah, our child-time group."

"A class?"

"Much more. When we be five, our elders put? Be put? Yes. Be put us in a twi of eight before we go to training. We be everything to each other, until such time we be, beed, adults, get our first orders, send off . . ." With every word, she felt true meaning slipping away, for how to explain a trust so strong that your twi's family could become yours, the dearer if you had none yourself? Like Danlo, cousin to one of her twi-mates, who watched over her as well as anyone who had blood-brothers and sisters . . .

On the other side of the room, the warlord turned in a slow circle, obliquely observed by Martande Lirendi as he listened to Yedoc's halting explanation. The warlord's posture radiated tension. Something had happened, which meant he was about to lose Yedoc. So, when she came to the end of a sentence, he took a risk. "Yedoc, what troubles you?"

Her pale skin actually blanched, then flooded with color. She turned away, but not before he saw a tear bounce off her collarbone, then she stiffened, mouth a white line.

"I be summon," she said, hoping that he might somehow understand. This was as close to a warning as loyalty permitted: a summons could only mean military purpose in Chwahirsland.

And there was Rajin, coming their way, looking as furious as he felt for being duped by this mask idiocy.

She was already moving before he snapped his fingers. She darted between the guests, falling in behind her warlord, leaving Martande standing alone on the guild hall dais where a throne would sit.

The Roundelay of Masks

"The ones in the big silk cloaks," Rajin said in Chwahir. "The warriors, which means they must be guarding the counts. No need to identify them. They all have to be there."

And he spoke an order, sending her running into the wild night.

Back in the guild hall, Third Secretary Lirendi stepped quietly to the Count of Renflar's side.

"What did he say?" he asked her.

The elderly woman's face was still hidden behind her mask, but her voice carried all her regret. "If he's a trader, then I'm a hoptoad. He didn't even pretend, just kept watching everybody."

Minza reached them. Martande said to her, "Pass the word."

She nicked her chin down and exited through the side door, noticed by few.

But one of those few was the Count of Alarcansa, to whose tone-deaf ears music was just noise. He made his way around the perimeter of the room and joined them as the Count of Ranflar looked from one to the other, aware of their sudden tension. "Is it war?" she whispered.

The Count of Alarcansa knew what war was. The corners of his mouth deepened sardonically, but before he speak, Martande said smoothly, "We won't let it get that far." Then he bowed to the older woman. "Honor Ranflar, may I entrust the evening to you?" His gaze rested on a pair of youngsters dancing to a sprightly roundelay, stamping and twirling to the frisky beat as circles merged and parted. "Let them all enjoy themselves. A disturbance contributes nothing. We'll return shortly. Alarcansa?"

The count smiled grimly and fell in step beside him. A few paces away, the captain of the Eth Endra guard kissed the velvet-clad Prince of Tivonais, took his sword from her gaudy baldric, and followed after, his veils flapping with his long strides.

The Count of Altan found his daughter, bent to kiss the top of her head, and murmured, "If I do not come back, I want you to take Altan."

Fliss was fast putting together the clues. "I'll come with you," she said, and at his raised hand, palm out, she forced a laugh. "Why else have you made us study the sword all our lives?"

"If we don't return, you will have to lead the resistance," he said unanswerably, and went away, still looking for his son. But Hende and a few select companions had vanished into a side room for a private party away from the crush of undesirables, Hende still complaining that he never would have come if he'd been warned that he might have to dance with the lackey who'd sewed his clothes.

Martande crossed the room, then paused a step before the side door. Here he carefully removed the robe of dancing cranes, and laid it and its mask under a table of cakes. Then, with a host of silk-covered figures joining him, he vanished into the night.

Tambourtan of Drums

Just describable, confusing in hollows and salients, silent figures drifted with intent past the ghost pale birch grove in the weakened light of the new moon briefly appearing between ragged thunderheads to ride the rooftops.

Then it was gone. Lightning flared, striking raindrops to silver and bleaching the brave colors of cape and doublet to shades of gray. Dark swallowed every vestige of light as thunder smote the air.

Though it was not cold, Yedoc shivered, wet to the skin, as she splashed and blundered along half-remembered paths toward the designated meet-point, where the captains awaited orders.

Back in the hall, the more observant noticed a stir at the side door, as Eth Endra and Altan vanished through the door along with Eth Endra's Captain of the Guard in his flutter of veils, leaving the Count of Ranflar alone, her demeanor forlorn.

The Count of Nashan elbowed his way through the dancers, drawing more attention with every step, and confronted the older woman. "Where are they going?" His choler reddened his ears. "A secret meeting? What kind of underhanded deal is going on, without the rest of us?"

The Count of Ranflar snapped, "Keep your voice down, Honor Nashan."

"I will not keep my voice down," he retorted. "Until you tell me what's going on. I will complain to the envoy at once. Here, where's the Third Secretary? These damn masks—"

"He's gone," she said, and as the widening circle of curious, whispering guests looked ready to scatter, she raised her voice, which quavered thinly as she said, "The truth is, I am very much afraid that the Chwahir are about to attack."

An outcry rang through the circle. The musicians, becoming aware of the stir below, faltered and stopped, peering over the guard rail in confusion.

The Count raised her hand, and when the noise died to whispers, she said, "The Chwahir, it seems, do not understand what a 'count' *does*."

A short burst of noise, punctuated by some nervous laughter, was broken by a grizzled scribe guild chief. "Counts *count*," he said, earning an outburst of laughter far stronger than the hoary old joke deserved.

But laughter released tension. It felt good. If others could laugh, then surely things were not so dire, and so his following somewhat self-important remarks about how scribes worked for their counts in counting *everything*, from road traffic to taxes on sales of goods to overgrazed fields earned more attention than perhaps they deserved.

The Count of Ranflar waited patiently until he paused to draw breath, and once more raised her hand. "I believe we can say that, because counts count everything, armies don't go unnoticed, even if they might wish to."

At that point a stir at the side door drew attention. Of course some of the more curious and adventuresome young people had poked their heads out, to discover herald-scribes, armed with steel, surrounding the building.

"Go back inside," one shouted against the roaring rain. "The Chwahir won't get anywhere near."

The Count of Isqua stepped up beside his mother-in-law. He tipped his head back and gazed up at the gallery. "Musicians! Give us a lively one! I can't do anything but wait, so I might as well dance. Who will dance with me?"

The musicians, perhaps relieved or inspired (alone of all there, they left no records of the event) struck up a rousing tambourtan, playing with irresistible brilliance, and soon the room became a revolving constellation of swinging silks, glittering jewels, and flushed faces beneath the wild masks. Shoulders shook counterpoint to hips as dancers twirled faster and leaped higher, stamped harder, laughing for every reason and no reason — because it was possible to laugh, though hearts drummed in counterpoint with stomping heels.

The Dance of Death

There is little purpose in describing the details of the sortie that many of those inside the guild hall, in their ignorance of such things, later described as a war. There are plentiful records left by nearly all those who survived.

Ianzi Gaszin had had orders to deploy scouts to observe the Chwahir since the time the warlord and his company neared Alsais, but to hang back unseen in case they turned out to be the traders that the messenger claimed them to be — in all good faith, Lirendi had insisted.

Familiar with the tangle of gardens and haphazard houses, Minza's and Martande's two companies flanked the Chwahir when it became apparent they were deploying for attack, and so, when Yedoc, rain washing the tears from her face, conveyed the orders to strike, the Chwahir rode straight into a wall of steel.

It might have lasted longer had not Yedoc, in hopeless misery, sought her twi-cousin. She hardly knew why, for she had no weapon, in fact, would likely have been struck down in the chaos. Her only thought was that, though she could not save the situation, she could at least try to protect her twi-cousin, and if she died in the doing, she was resigned to it.

She ran blindly into the stinging rain toward the clashes of steel and the screams, then blundered into the Third Runner. Yedoc asked her where Danlo could be found. The Third Runner's astonished face, bleached of color by lightning, struck terror into Yedoc, as the runner shouted against the thunder, "Did you not know? He was confined at camp, against execution at dawn!"

Yedoc whirled and ran.

A burst of hail lacerated her face and hands but she ignored it, arriving sobbing for breath in the camp at the same time as the First Runner dashed in from the opposite direction. He shouted over and over, "The warlord is dead! The warlord is dead!"

So were his two captains, the Second Runner reported moments later.

Which left Danlo the senior officer, surrounded by three of four runners.

As he wasn't bound by anything but a sense of honor, he stepped out of the isolation tent to gaze into the faces waiting for orders. Then he ran for his horse. "Let's save who we can. Yedoc, fetch the gong, and come."

Though she wore neither armor nor weapon, Yedoc sprang inside to grab one of the brass gongs that the Chwahir used for sounding mass tactical shifts.

They rode for the river as lightning revealed the scene in brief, shocking shards. Though what Yedoc saw was a chaos of horror, Danlo recognized the signs of a rout that, if he did not interfere, would swiftly become a slaughter.

He kneed his horse up next to Yedoc's, took the gong from her, and with his much more powerful strike, beat three fast double-tones.

Retreat! Retreat! Retreat!

The brassy clangor reverberated between dying rumbles of thunder. The summer storm, as such storms often do, was already moving off, leaving a world of drips and little streams.

Chwahir faltered, swords lowering.

As soon as he saw the enemy waver, Ianzi Gaszin — commanding the right flank alongside the river — flashed his signal fan and his equerry blew a long, hooting wail on his horn. That was soon echoed by Martande Lirendi's equerry west of the town hall.

Both sides disengaged, moving at first with wary caution, then more swiftly, and as the herald-scribes reformed into their defensive line, wing riders with arrows nocked, the Chwahir limped back in the direction of their camp; the gong and horn echoed around the river bend, north of the guild hall, as Martande Lirendi signaled Minza to halt the guild hall defense.

Danlo and Yedoc rode in silence to camp in the slackening rain, until they reached the perimeter guards.

Starlight opened overhead, and the moon briefly slid from behind one cloud to the one chasing after; they recognized by its place in the sky that the time was nearly midnight.

They dismounted and stood side by side, too overwhelmed for speech. Beyond the musical plink-plunk-splash, they heard nothing but the sounds of their own people approaching. The shouts, screams, and clashes of fighting had ended.

Then Danlo turned to Yedoc. "I told Rajin they were ready for us." He shook his head, lightning reflecting off his somber profile. "But Rajin didn't believe me. He couldn't. He had to win, or he could never go home. His brother's knives were waiting."

Yedoc wisely kept to herself how very little she cared. "And so he condemned you?"

Danlo tipped his head back to look up at the breaking clouds, and sighed. "You have to understand that I spent all that time you were gone trying to talk him out of it, once he gave us to know he never intended to negotiate any trade alliance. For the sake of our past, he said I could fight to the death, rather than kneel to the executioner's blade . . ." He shrugged. "It's irrelevant now."

"Do we surrender?" Yedoc asked, shivering inside her sodden clothes.

"If we must," Danlo said, and walked with her to the command tent, where he brought out a cloak and set it around her shoulders. "But until today, didn't the Kei Faels believe we were here to trade? Since it seems I must conduct the surrender myself, why not try?" Danlo said. "What more do we have to lose?"

Danlo turned to First Runner. "Get the medics and search for wounded. You go with him," he said to the second. "Find someone to round up the horses," he said to the guards who had, until a short time ago, stood perimeter watch.

Then he turned to Yedoc, whose rain-washed face was painful with expectation. "You know their language far better than I," he said, reluctantly, even guiltily, for he suspected something of her secret heart. "I hate to make you face them again, but I don't see another way."

"For peace," she said, "I will gladly go anywhere."

The Lily-King's Rigadaun

As the bell clanged the midnight hour, Martande Lirendi turned to his own captains and those of the counts who had sent forces to join him. "We're definitely getting rid of that bell," he said with forced lightness.

The more observant among them reflected on that "we." Everyone else was too euphoric at their victory, talking over one another in those loud, sharp voices you only hear after extreme danger, when the heart is still racing, but no longer from fear.

They entered the guild hall again, to light and music and the wide-eyed looks of the dancers as the defenders strode in triumph, no longer hiding behind the silks and masks they had shed outside in their rush to defense. The guests ripped off their own masks so that they could better see the rich glint of gilt, the twilight blues and summer greens and daffodil yellows and stately violets of the defenders' splendid armored doublets, the cool glint of metal in sword hilts and sheathed knives.

The only one who masked his emotions was Martande Lirendi. As soon as he walked from darkness into the light of the guild hall, his gaze raked the room—at the same time Minza Gaszin entered from the kitchen corridor, her own eyes searching.

Their gazes met, and for a heartbeat both saw more than they had expected to reveal in the other. That was just, it was right, finally it was right: they were alive, and he promised himself that everything was going to change.

He opened his hand in their private signal, and she flashed

hand signs, reporting the few dead and the larger number of wounded, ending with the two-finger twirl that meant her brother was overseeing the retreat of the enemy.

It was done, except for cleaning up the blood, but the departing rain obliged them in that.

Martande Lirendi had worked carefully on what to do and say — assuming he survived the attack he'd anticipated. But he had reckoned without the wild exhilaration of shared danger.

As everyone else exclaimed in celebration, the Count of Alarcansa strode out into the middle of the guild hall. He held up his hand for silence. Being a tall, commanding figure, he got it.

"The Chwahir warlord Vessler Rajin attempted an act of treachery. We defeated him, but we could not have done so last year, or even last spring."

Firm nods and puzzled looks met this statement, but no one argued.

"I've been coming to these assemblies every three years since I turned sixteen," he went on, his voice hoarse from shouting orders on the field. "I listen to you complaining about where your taxes are going. How long it will be before you get an answer from Sartor. Having to travel to court. Sartor does nothing for us beyond what we have right here."

A noise of agreement met this, and he waved his hand again.

"I've spent my life defending the eastern pass, and coming to the aid of the Altans when the middle pass is threatened. We say the western pass belongs to others, but the truth, as we experienced today, is that every single time the Chwahir come over seeking to take our land, they turn east, toward us."

Another pause, attended by nods and shifted looks, as no one so far had been willing to take on the hard work of defending the western pass.

"Martande Lirendi commanded today, he commanded the reinforcements six years ago, and during the Alarcansa Attack when I was a boy, I first met him holding a bridge so my mother could lead a charge. He's a year younger than I am."

That caused a noise of surprise and exchanged looks.

"I say," he raised his voice, "we invite Martande Lirendi to remain here permanently."

A much larger shout of approval met that, but again, Alarcansa raised his hand.

"I say," he shouted, "we make him our king!"

The crystals overhead trembled in the volley of sound.

Not everyone was pleased. The Count of Nashan gasped. "There *was* collusion! The entire . . ."

"Defense," murmured his consort, which took the wind out of his indignation, though even her sympathy did nothing to lessen his resentment. This cooled to a lifelong grudge passed down to his successors, but that history does not belong here.

Everyone else went wild with relief, joy, and that heady sense that today, this moment, would be forever remembered. Various people began to orate to their neighbors, but most scarcely got past a sentence or two of agreement with Alarcansa, well sugared with praise, before being interrupted by another speaker who pretty much repeated the same words.

Martande Lirendi stood surrounded by noise and praise, in that moment curiously isolated, for no one yet dared to approach him, not even Minza, who stood uncertainly, watching the artist she'd seen earlier, now frantically sketching.

Oblivious to them all, Martande's mind leaped from the past— Eniad saying, *If you wish to settle there, I'll make you a prince* —to the word *king*, and what it meant.

He had spent too much time as boys rolling around in the dirt with Eniad Landis, and attending him when he was puking drunk as teens, to believe in the inherent glory of rank, notwithstanding the ancient glory of the Landis name.

Social hierarchy was nothing more than an agreed-upon fiction, but nothing *less*, because that agreement happened, for whatever reason, between the governed as well as the governor. Everyone grew up hearing the story of Mendaen the Assassin, who had become a steward, slit the throats of the royal family while they slept, then rang the bells and proclaimed himself king, just to be cut down by furious servants wielding kitchen implements, after which they hauled an old recluse Landis princess out of her bed on the other side of the city and clapped the crown on her head; the nobles, on waking the next morning in their silken beds and discovering the abrupt change of monarch, had deemed it wise to concur.

So why not call himself a king? The essential differences between a king and a prince were twofold: a prince collected taxes and passed most of them on, whereas a king kept them; a prince implemented the king's will and passed state trouble on, whereas a king had no one to pass responsibility to, lest he lose his crown.

At least three quarters of Kei Fael's assembly arguments had been dissatisfaction with what their taxes brought back to the hinterlands of Sartor, always at least a year late. He was too experienced, having served as herald-scribe in the Court of Star Chamber between field assignments, to believe that the counts wouldn't rapidly fill that three quarters with other demands if he did become king.

But he knew he could deal with them.

A step at his side, and Minza broke his reverie, question in her puckered brow. He looked around, realized that the talk had been dying, and everyone expected something from him.

They wanted a king, did they? Then they would want a court. Time to spread what largesse he had, which right now was entirely confined to that shared agreement, for he had spent all the material largesse that he'd brought.

"I will serve as your king," he said, and watched as the entire room fell to a hush, "only with the aid of your talents and ideas and willingness to serve this new kingdom! The counts will become duchas, which means you will first replace—in an orderly, peaceable way—the Sartoran tax guild with your own counts."

A cheer went up at that! No more Sartoran tax collectors!

Even better, titles! A duchas was once step down from prince!

"I even have a name to propose," he said, "for I've come to

love this land. In Old Sartoran, *Coh-al*, country, and *end*, the prefix for loved: modernized a little, it becomes *Colend*, the Beloved Country."

A brief buzz of comment rose, and he heard doubt, question, and perplexity, but approval was strongest. This was enough change, perhaps. "The rest," he said, "can wait. We are all here, with excellent musicians, food, and something to celebrate, so let us dance!"

He reached for the nearest hand, which turned out to belong to the Count of Isqua, and looked expectantly at the gallery

After a hasty whisper, the musicians struck up what would become The Lily-King's Rigadaun, and the young people — entranced by seeing one another without masks — were the first to form around the new king and begin dancing, which pulled more in as the floor cleared.

Sarabande, Roundelay, and the Stamp of Bandatta

That dance ended, and another began.

Before Martande could fetch the drink he had been craving for the last hour, he was intercepted by a sinuous figure in white moth-gauze woven in the shape of stylized poppies and the leaves of lotus. With the assurance of one who is never denied what she wants, Luor linked her arm through his, and guided him into the last circle forming for the elegant sarabande.

She had begun the evening idly thinking he would be worth a night, but kingship implied queenship.

"You are one of the Deis," Luor said after they had bowed and turned. She favored him with her practiced smile as her gaze drifted admiringly from his hair to his boots. "You have Valisan Dei's golden eyes. I've never seen anyone as beautiful since, old as she was. Until I met you."

"Thank you, though I feel obliged to point out that my family name is Lirendi." He dipped his head, almost a bow, but instead of returning the personal compliment she complacently expected — the first steps toward intimacy — he deflected airily in the manner that his court would come to know quite well. "Valisan Dei was one of eight great-grandparents. Nine, actually. Connar Narath was the best of the lot, though he wasn't blood-related."

"Narath? I never met anyone of that family when I attended Star Chamber," she observed as they dipped and swayed.

"You wouldn't meet a scribe family in Star Chamber. He and my great-grandfather met in an ink shop, as both were illustrators."

For a night of fun, she wouldn't have let him get past the mention of Star Chamber, but with a crown there within reach, she kept her smile in place. "While I am thoroughly in favor of our ruling ourselves, I can't help but ask, will there be trouble from Fish Face?"

"From whom?" he asked as they did hands across, and stepped around in a circle, eyes on eyes.

"Prince Fish Face. Now the king. Surely you know that. Everyone in the first circle says it."

"Ah, but I find him beautiful," Martande said.

Luor slanted a glance of derision, assuming shared mockery, to smack into a wall of sincere conviction.

"Beautiful," she repeated, the exclamation half question. "I've seen him, when my mother presented me at court. He cannot have changed so materially in ten years."

He lifted a shoulder as they dipped, turned, and met palm to palm again, toes pointed, shoulders back. "We know the word beautiful," he said in that tone of calm sincerity, "but I expect we all define it differently. For me, that which delights my heart is beautiful, and King Eniad, in all his painstaking doubt and generosity of spirit, is beautiful."

And he kept talking about King Eniad's attributes until the beguiling melody began drawing to a close.

He bowed as the music ended, no sign of his thoughts evident in face or voice, but he was far more experienced at the court mask than she. Part of kingship, he had learned watching the crown prince grow up, was finding common ground with people like Luor Iventh. "Thank you," he said. "But if I don't get something to drink in the next few moments, I'm likely to expire of thirst, establishing the world's shortest reign."

The calm detachment in his mild voice kindled an intensity that was not quite erotic; for the first time, the spark was not his body, attractive though it was. It was his mind she found both elusive and alluring. Men, so far in her thirty-three years, had been there for the taking and discarding, her trophy sketches capturing handsome faces, the only part of them worth remembering. She—so subtle and complicated—had not the vocabulary, or the experience, to recognize the dawn of respect.

She was not one to give up easily, and as the musicians started a lively roundelay, this time with the addition of singers well-lubricated with blue wine, she kept to his side. But a stir at the doorway caused him to glance that way, quick as something with antennae.

There, framed in the open doors, stood two Chwahir, flanked by four of Ianzi Gaszin's biggest riders. As more of the young people joined the singing and dancing, many of their elders gathered in angry knots, hostility evident in their glares at the two Chwahir.

"Everyone dance," Martande said to the closest group. "My invitation still stands, and our guests are unarmed."

Alarcansa had started toward the Chwahir, hand on the hilt of his sword. Martande mistook his intent at first, catching up in a few fast steps. He perceived a strong resemblance between the tall, hard-boned count and the young Chwahir standing beside Messenger Yedoc, mostly in the high forehead and around the brows. But as Minza stepped up to Martande's right hand, Alarcansa lifted his chin in approval, changed direction, and walked away without speaking to anyone.

Yedoc stood rigid, too terrified to take her gaze away from Martande Lirendi, who had been so kind hitherto. Danlo, far more

used to the subtleties of eye and hand signaling intent, had watched the tall man who reminded him of his second cousin, and wondered if indeed this was the descendant of his fabled great-aunt.

Then Yedoc said in an under-voice, "Here is the third
secretary," and Danlo gazed, startled, at the eye-commanding
brilliance of that diamond. It took an effort to look away, and he
blinked at the blue armor with the elegant white lily. Or dagger.
Or lily.

This man was a *scribe?*

Danlo spoke his carefully planned words. "We be come to
surrender. If demand you the life it will be I." And then in
Chwahir to Yedoc in an undertone, "Did I say it right?"

Martande smiled at Yedoc, willing that deathly expression
from her face.

She whispered "Yes," in Chwahir — Martande understood that
much — and then said to Martande, "Be some want trade, and
not —" And she stopped there, unwilling to face scorn and
disbelief.

Martande took in her anxious stance, and the stolidity of the
young man, who bore himself as if he expected execution. To
Yedoc, he said in his mildest voice, "Tell him I know he cannot
speak for all the Chwahir." A diplomatic way of acknowledging a
kingdom that had sustained several violent changes of monarch in
a generation, for of course none of them could know that Danlo
would within ten years become Chwahirsland's king, uniting all
the factions for the first time in years. "What we want is peace, but
there are also those among us who might sit down to discuss trade
benefits for both sides of the mountains."

His reward was in the shuttering of her eyelids, and the glisten
of moisture below. That only lasted a heartbeat, then she
translated far too swiftly for him to follow, and watched the
corresponding easing of the man's expression.

Martande decided it was time for a non-subtle hint, as these
two were clearly unacquainted with diplomatic ritual, "Who
might I have the honor of speaking with?"

Yedoc stumbled over Danlo's rank, as he was now acting commander, causing Martande to reflect with inner humor that titles had been hopping about pretty freely that evening. He then gave in to impulse, and searched around for the Count of Alarcansa. As expected, he stood a distance away, but he was watching. "Alarcansa. You speak Chwahir, I know. Let's establish a semblance of a treaty with the interim commander here, to be reworked at leisure. Minza, will you take Messenger Yedoc to get something to drink?" He added under his breath, "In fact, would you send one of Perin's people for a jug of water? I think we could all use something besides wine. I certainly could."

Minza delivered the message to a young fellow who bounded out to the well, then drew Yedoc away. Seeing that nothing interesting was going on but talk, the rest of the guests danced with the abandon of a long summer's night after enduring a storm of emotions.

Minza walked Yedoc the length of the guild hall, Minza's round signal-fan swinging gently at her left knee.

Yedoc appreciated the lack of triumph, even if it was only the mask of good manners. Her countrymen had died that night. Not as many as could have, but to each family of the dead, that one would be the only death that mattered.

And yet she felt she had to speak first. "My—ah, Captain Danlo Sonscarna first try, talk Nanijo Rajin to come to you for trade, and try warn him," Yedoc said. "But the warlord say, scribes never offer a worthy battle."

"Herald-scribes," Minza corrected gently, her gaze still lowered. "The heralds keep the peace in Sartor, as well as announce the king's will."

"But scribes be not warriors?"

Minza stopped to face Yedoc, her eyes wide enough to reflect the candles overhead, some of which were beginning to gutter. Below the gallery, the singers had gathered into three groups singing a lively round, as a few hardy dancers kept at it on the floor, stamping and clapping in counterpoint.

"What is a warrior, really?" Minza said finally. "We talk about it, oh, so much. I believe we all have a warrior in us, when necessary. The ideal is to make a life so that the warrior is never necessary."

Danlo had said something similar on their walk over. *We Chwahir fight for rank, and talk about strength to survive, but what if we had enough of everything? I'd be happy to never pick up a sword again, except in play. I can't be the only one. The only way to get there that I see is more trade.* Perhaps now he might be heard. A little of Yedoc's sick sense dissipated at that thought. Yes, news of Rajin's defeat would make a difference to Princess Leig, back in Narad.

Some of the bleakness lifted from her heart, and Yedoc said, "I not know."

Minza said with sympathy, "I think the third sec—the new, ah, king—he never told you that we were ready for whatever might come so as not to put you in an impossible position. Your Commander Rajin was not one to listen to ideas countering his, I gather."

"It be so." Yedoc bowed her head. There was so much she had mistaken, and she could not bear to talk about that single, precious conversation there behind the tables, as the third secretary showed her how to dance.

But this much she could say. "So he know the attack be to come."

"Yes," Minza said softly.

"And yet, his title be Third Secretary. Be so humble a title a . . . a war ruse of yours?"

Minza chuckled. "Oh, not at all. Sartoran titles originated out of the idea of service. But humans appear to be much the same everywhere, and so you often find that the more protestation of service, the more prestige the speaker expects. A letter signed 'your humble servant to command' is a formality so severe that it is very akin to a threat."

"And so, Third Secretary mean what?"

"Threes are very important in Sartor, and three is higher than one, you understand. You cannot get higher than three without being lofted to the next level, which would be a different title."

"It be the opposite for us," Yedoc said. "I be Fourth Runner, the least. It be this word 'secretary,' and your title, 'guide,' I think we not understand."

"Reflect upon the root of the word *secretary*, which is *secret*. Heralds not only are responsible for disseminating royal law, but also we must protect and enforce it. A secretary is more important than a guide such as myself. We guides are mere sword swingers in the worst case—we carry out orders, but never issue them. A secretary can issue orders, to further the monarch's will. Though I believe that's about to change."

"Change?"

Minza glanced back, saw that the three were already done, and stood in a row watching a pair of dancers showing off their skills, tapping and stamping to a bandatta in the middle of the floor, as the singers belted out a ballad in wicked triplets.

She smiled at Yedoc. "That is best addressed directly to Martande. Go talk to him!" And when she saw color flare in those thin cheeks, she said softly, "And if talk should lead to something more tender, well, you both have earned some comfort under peaceful stars."

"I cannot."

"Why not? I have eyes. I can see what you—"

Yedoc made a little gesture of warding, her eyes tightly closed, her mouth a thin line. "Even if it be possible. It be not right," she whispered. "I see what be, with the two of you."

Minza stood on tiptoe and kissed Yedoc on the cheek, a gesture of kindness Yedoc had not experienced since leaving her twi.

"You're the only one who's seen that," Minza said, smiling crookedly. "And there is nothing yet. It was not right, as you say, perhaps for some of the same reasons. That time might be right soon, but until then, he is warm and generous, and life is short. Love in all its permutations is precious!"

Yedoc turned and nicked her head down, arms held out in a circle, hands folded one over the other in that curious Chwahir way. "I honor you," she said, "for your words. Your generous heart. But I . . ." She looked down the length of the ballroom, to where the new king stood beneath the brilliants in the chandelier, which lit his hair to gold.

Danlo turned then, and met her gaze, and his relieved smile drew one from her. A few long steps and she joined him; after a short exchange of formal good wishes between the four, the Chwahir stepped out into the moonlight night, their black hair and clothes swallowing them instantly, hiding the way Danlo's fingers closed warmly around hers.

"I believe," said the Count of Ranflar, coming up to join those remaining, "that half their terrible reputation is that insistence on wearing black. The color of Norsunder, the evil beyond time. Do they do that deliberately?"

Minza laughed. "I'm told the black is because their sheep are black. And you have to admit it is easier to hide grime."

Martande turned to her. "I suspect that this will be the last dance. And sadly, I've only managed to have one. Will you help me make that two?"

Minza held out her hands.

The Morning-Star Valsa

Neither spoke until they reached the center of the room. The musicians had begun the old, slow twirl-step in triple beat. Exhilarated, tired guests were picking up masks and bits of shed costume preparatory to leaving. The singers scattered, many youths protesting weakly as they were herded firmly away.

Luor cast one long look at Martande and Minza, then slanted a smile of invitation to the heir to a baras from Locan Jara, her princeling having prudently decamped at the first announcement of trouble.

Presently Minza said slowly, "I'm beginning to wonder if you told me everything King Eniad said to you the day we departed."

Martande was silent, step-two-three, step-two-three, spin and whirl. Then he murmured, "He said farewell."

At first she thought that a deflection, then the meaning sank in: not *farewell and see you before winter*, but *farewell* as in *fare well*. Though she did not falter in her step—she discovered that he was holding her too close for that—she tightened her own grip on his shoulder and hand before she tipped her head back to gaze into his face as the truth struck her: the king had not only ordered Martande to announce the royal decree making Kei Fael into a principality, he had also appointed the possible first prince.

Which meant . . . "He doesn't want us back?"

"It's me he doesn't want back," Martande said apologetically. And, because she was one of the very few within his tight circle of trust, "Because of Ilneas. He knows very well what she wants."

"You," Minza stated. "The entire kingdom knows that."

"More specifically, she would like to use me to make a play for the throne. For all the wrong reasons."

Minza sighed out a curse. "I knew she was trouble, but—"

"Make that troubled. And she can't see that the two of us sitting decoratively in the throne-tree at Star Chamber, her brother's blood still drying while everyone bows low, will not fix whatever is wrong within her."

Minza sighed again, keeping to herself her private opinion of the beautiful, willful princess. Whom she would never have to see again!

Leaving a much larger question. "Are you really going to make yourself a king?"

"You heard them. If they wake up tomorrow—today—and still feel the same, why not?"

Minza remembered the counts' families all expressing delight in the notion of becoming duchas. Oh yes, they'd still feel the same. "What do you think King Eniad will say?"

"Since he wanted me to get the assembly to accept me as Prince of Kei Fael, I can't see him troubling over a change of title, as nothing will materially change. We and the guilds will see to it that trade will proceed unhindered, even if we dicker a bit with definitions of taxes and tariffs."

Minza accepted that, but her mood was still unsettled. Something was missing. Something important.

They stepped and turned. In the movement, she spied the artist slowly bundling her drawing chalks together, her gaze gone distant. You didn't hire artists unless you expected an event to be worth the labor of paint.

They danced in silence, he watching her knit brow, as around them more people departed. Some first glanced their way, noting the tall man in blue and silver and the short woman in yellow and red gripped in one another's arms, moving as one, and decided that any questions or comments could wait.

At last she raised troubled eyes, and broached the question that had troubled her the most. "And so I must ask, who laid a trap for whom?"

"Trap?" he repeated, then added with a reflective air, "Odd, that. How 'trap' means strategy in the context of violence, but smacks of trickery in the context of social exchange. So distasteful."

"As distasteful," she retorted, "as violence. I know you didn't want the Chwahir to attack, but you expected it. We both did. However, did you foresee how subsequent events fell out?"

He breathed softly, almost a sigh, and looked up and away, through the windows, astonished to discover that they had begun to lighten to the deep blue of impending dawn, the same blue he had chosen as his own.

Blue and silver, not Sartor's violet and gold. Lily, representing the life of art.

He shut that stream away with some effort, and peered down into her waiting face. The trust between them was more important to him than anything else in life, and somehow he had nearly lost it. He had to figure out how.

He spoke carefully. "If the word *trap* implies military strategy, I'll grant the warlord and myself an equal share. You know I expected an attack. And, yes, I dangled this night," he tipped his chin toward the rest of the vast hall full of wilting flowers, "as bait. I chose the ground, but I did not choose violence. I would have done my best to beguile Rajin into talking trade if he'd come here with any willingness to listen."

"No, he chose the violence," she said, "but did you count on its effect?" She saw surprise in the quick pucker of his brows, and breathed easier. "The artist, who will no doubt make a splendid royal painting? The musicians with their rosettes meaning they were Music Festival champions, and . . . what happened in this room, right here, and why it happened that way. We all expected you to make some sort of announcement tonight, but you waited until after the Chwahir defeat."

"It didn't seem right to announce it before, when we might lose the town in a bloody battle," he retorted mildly. Then he checked, and said, "Ah-h-h. I think I see now. The musicians and the artist were sent by Eniad, and while I did save the musicians for tonight, it was to assure us a ball to remember. The artist . . . I thought she was for Eniad's benefit."

Minza laughed, dizzy with relief, not just at her incorrect assumptions, but because they were talking so freely. "Of course. Eniad wants a record of your pronouncement, but what she got instead is a possible chance at art that will be truly memorable. What do you think it will be, a tapestry? Mural?"

"I expect it will depend on what we, or the king, or both will pay," he said. "Who can blame her for ambition?"

"Not I," Minza said, and then, because she could share every-thing, began to feel her way into the misgivings she had never thought to air. "Though you didn't foresee it, perhaps you ought to have, or both us should have. Is it human nature everywhere?"

"Go on," he said.

"It was the way Alarcansa hailed you as a king not for all you've done these past weeks in assembly, because he could have done that yesterday, or even at the commencement of the masquerade. But he did it after you won a bloody conflict. And I found myself as moved as everyone else. As strongly as we humans deplore violence, we are drawn to it, we remember it, we memorialize it. I hate that in us. I hate it in myself."

His smile vanished. "I know. I thought of that as well. But that reinforces the idea I've been exploring these weeks, to fashion a way for us to mask those impulses with all the arts of civilization. Creating channels — canals — for discharging our less admirable emotions safely, the way this town tames the two rivers with the four canals. Let us by all means fashion more canals."

"A meaning for melende," she said.

"And one of our tools will be fans." He glanced down at the signal fan swinging from its cord at her waist. "My great-grandmother's weapon of choice."

She uttered a soft laugh, then shook her head. "Melende as a weapon — the wording troubles me."

"Where wills conflict, anything can become a weapon." He turned slightly, and she was distracted by the way that the candles overhead, still burning bravely, ignited a ruddy-golden glitter in his diamond clasp. "Anything."

She thought of Princess Ilneas, who would be infuriated that in spite of all her power and wealth, she couldn't hold, or lure, Martande Lirendi against his will.

"But at least melende is a weapon one can walk away from." He saw her acceptance in the easing of the tension in her brow, and his tone lightened. "Will you help me?"

"As?" she asked, stepped back so that could look up into his face.

"As what you will," he said, with quiet intensity. "You'd be perfect as duchas in that area up in the northwest, which is going to require constant vigilance. How does Duchas of Gaszin sound? You'd be the best choice for duchas, but then so would your brother. He might be happier there, for what's needed is a military stronghold until the Chwahir turn their interests in expansion elsewhere. He can learn about mines. As for you, I'm afraid that my choice would be to yoke you to a kingdom, at my side. Share and share alike. You know how good we are now. I think, I believe, we could be even better. Together."

Though she couldn't keep her face from firing up to the color of her hair at his low tone, she chuckled under her breath. As far as she was concerned, she had seen the personal question answered in his anxious gaze the moment he had entered the hall again, surrounded by his celebrative captains. They had looked for approbation, but he had sought *her*, as she'd sought him, to see if they had each survived.

The question before her now was merely political. "Yes," she said. "We'd be very good together," she promised, and felt a corresponding tightening in all the muscles in his body. She smiled into his shoulder, then gazed beyond him, her mind leaping from promise to possibilities. "This town is beautiful, but it will never be defensible."

"This land will never be defensible, in the usual sense," he said quickly. "But just as canals can tame the rivers and add a measure of beauty, so Alsais can become a work of art that would be beautiful from every angle, and confuse a would-be conqueror."

"Melende not as a weapon, but as a defense?" she said.

"And everyone walks away." He smiled hopefully. "What do you think? The structure here is good, just needs expansion, taking advantage of the light. First Designer Halas of the silk guild would give us exactly what we need, and Perin can run it. My only stipulation will be that wagon-yard. It would make a fine rose garden, four trefoils."

"A labyrinth," she breathed.

"In disguise." He flashed a grin of self-mockery. "Not completely like those in Sartor. But that structure is buried deep within us — and anyone who comes with evil intent will be a-mazed."

"'So he shall use beauty to disarm the world,'" she quoted in the herald's hieratic accent, then whispered, "Otiose."

His laugh was soundless as his arms tightened around her.

She reached up and at last, at last, she kissed him.

And though by then the musicians had packed up and trooped

off to their well-earned rest, and the sleepy morning crew were trudging in to begin the monumental task of cleaning up, the two danced alone, around and around under the guttering candles, to music only they could hear.

About the Authors

Marie Brennan is a former anthropologist and folklorist who shamelessly pillages her academic fields for material. She most recently misapplied her professors' hard work to the Hugo Award-nominated Victorian adventure series The Memoirs of Lady Trent; the first book of that series, *A Natural History of Dragons*, was a finalist for the World Fantasy Award and won the Prix Imaginales for Best Translated Novel. Her collaborative novel *Born to the Blade*, written with Michael R. Underwood, Malka Older, and Cassandra Khaw, was recently published by Serial Box. She is also the author of the Doppelganger duology of *Warrior* and *Witch*, the urban fantasies *Lies and Prophecy* and *Chains and Memory*, the Onyx Court historical fantasy series, the Varekai novellas, and more than fifty short stories. For more information, visit www.swantower.com

Lynne April Brown has wanted to be a writer since the far-distant age of twelve but, up until now, could only prove that she was a savings-and-loan teller or a proofreader in various aerospace publications groups. She is careful to keep cats so that the neighbors won't think she is talking to herself when two or more of her characters are arguing with each other and using her voice to do it.

Brenda W. Clough has been publishing novels since 1984, the best known probably being *How Like a God*, which came out from Tor

Books. Her novel, *Revise the World,* is available in electronic format at Book View Café. A version of it was a finalist for both the Hugo and Nebula awards. In addition to her seven novels, she has written many short stories, nonfiction, and innumerable book reviews. Her latest book, about the further adventures of Marian Halcombe, is *A Most Dangerous Woman,* just out from Serial Box. Her complete bibliography is up on her web page, brendaclough.net

Marissa Doyle originally intended to be an archaeologist but somehow got distracted, so instead she excavates tales of magic and history from the matrix of her imagination. Or something like that. She's responsible for the young adult Leland Sisters historical fantasy series as well as other works of fantasy for both adult and YA readers. She lives in New England with her family, her research library, and a bossy pet rabbit. "Just Another Quiet Evening at Almack's" is set in the world of a forthcoming series, The Ladies of Almack's; for updates please visit Marissa's website, www.marissadoyle.com

Francesca Forrest is the author of *Pen Pal* (2013), a hard-to-classify novel from the margins, and *The Inconvenient God* (Annorlunda Books, 2018), as well as short stories that have appeared in *Not One of Us*, *Strange Horizons*, and other online and print venues. She's currently working on a post-apocalypse novel that focuses on the hope rather than the horror. She lives in western Massachusetts.

Charlotte Gumanaam is the *nom de plume* of a reader, dreamer, and writer who first discovered fan fiction in middle school, and who has danced in many worlds since then.

Layla Lawlor grew up in rural Alaska and now lives on 11 acres of former mining tailings on the highway north of Fairbanks, where winters dip to 50 below zero and summers yield 24 hours of daylight. She has an art degree and half an archaeology degree, as well as a lifelong interest in history and the premodern world. Between the two of them, she and her husband possess a useful array of apocalypse survival skills including gardening, spinning, blacksmithing, gunsmithing, soapmaking, and collecting wild plant foods. You can read more about these characters and Shadow New York in the urban fantasy novel *Wayward Myths* and its forthcoming sequel, *Echo City*. More of Layla's fiction and comics can be found at www.laylalawlor.com

P.G. Nagle is the author of the Far Western Civil War series of novels, of which *Galveston* is the third. A native and lifelong resident of New Mexico, she has a special love of the outdoors, particularly New Mexico's wilds, where many of her stories are born. Her shorter work has appeared in national magazines and anthologies. She is a founding member of Book View Café Publishing Cooperative.

While **Gillian Polack**'s novels range from kinda-sorta urban fantasy in *The Wizardry of Jewish Women* (a Ditmar finalist) to kinda-sorta time travel but probably alternate history in *Langue[dot]doc 1305*, she is a Medieval historian (Ph.D. and all) and was a folk dancer for many years. This story was not kinda-sorta at all, then, but practically wrote itself the moment Sherwood said "dance."

Writer and editor **Irene Radford**, aka **P.R. Frost**, aka **C.F. Bentley**, has been writing stories ever since she figured out what a pencil was for. A member of an endangered species, a native Oregonian who lives in Oregon, she and her husband make their home in Welches, Oregon, where deer, bears, coyotes, hawks, owls, and woodpeckers feed regularly on their back deck. You can find her steampunk collection at bookviewcafe.com/bookstore/book/steampunk-voyages.

Deborah J. Ross is an award-nominated writer and editor of fantasy and science fiction, with over a dozen novels and five dozen short stories in print. Recent books include *Thunderlord* and *The Children of Kings* (with Marion Zimmer Bradley); *Collaborators* (as Deborah Wheeler), and *The Seven-Petaled Shield* epic fantasy trilogy. Her short fiction has appeared in *F&SF* and *Asimov's*. Her work has earned numerous award nominations, including the Lambda Literary Award and Gaylactic Spectrum Award. She's currently on the Board of Directors of Book View Café. When she's not writing, she knits for charity, plays classical piano, and practices yoga.

Sherwood Smith studied in Europe before earning a masters in history. She worked as a governess, a bartender, an electrical supply verifier, and wore various hats in the film industry before turning to teaching for 20 years. To date she's published over forty books, nominated for several awards, including the Nebula, the Mythopoeic Fantasy Award.

Sara Stamey returned to hometown Bellingham, WA, after treasure hunting and teaching scuba in the Caribbean; backpacking Greece, South America, and New Zealand; operating a nuclear reactor; and owning a farm in Chile. She just retired from teaching creative writing at Western Washington University. Her near-future Greek islands thriller *The Ariadne Connection* won the Cygnus Speculative Fiction Award and the Chanticleer Global Thriller Grand Prize; her Caribbean suspense novel *Islands* won the Hollywood Book Festival Genre Award. Her website is www.sarastamey.com

ABOUT BOOK VIEW CAFÉ

Book View Café Publishing Cooperative is an author-owned cooperative of over fifty professional writers, publishing in a variety of genres such as fantasy, romance, mystery, and science fiction.

BVC authors include *New York Times* and *USA Today* bestsellers; Nebula, Hugo, and Philip K. Dick Award winners; World Fantasy Award, Campbell Award, and RITA Award nominees; and winners and nominees of many other publishing awards.

Since its debut in 2008, BVC has gained a reputation for producing high-quality e-books, and is now bringing that same quality to its print editions.